WORLD PACIFIC

ALSO BY PETER MANN

The Torqued Man

WORLD PACIFIC

A NOVEL

PETER MANN

HARPER

An Imprint of HarperCollins*Publishers*

HarperCollins books may be purchased for educational, business, or sales promotional use. For information, please email the Special Markets Department at SPsales@harpercollins.com.

hc.com

FIRST EDITION

Library of Congress Cataloging-in-Publication Data
Names: Mann, Peter, 1981– author.
Title: World pacific : a novel / Peter Mann.
Description: First edition. | New York, NY : Harper, 2025.
Identifiers: LCCN 2025001401 | ISBN 9780063375345 (hardcover) | ISBN 9780063375352 (trade paperback) | ISBN 9780063375383 (ebook)
Subjects: LCGFT: Spy fiction. | Detective and mystery fiction. | Novels.
Classification: LCC PS3613.A5497 W67 2025 | DDC 813/.6—dc23/eng/20250228
LC record available at https://lccn.loc.gov/2025001401

25 26 27 28 29 LBC 5 4 3 2 1

To my sister, Melissa—my original sidekick

Life itself is always a shipwreck . . .

—José Ortega y Gasset

Beach your vessel hard by the Ocean's churning shore and make your own way down to the moldering House of Death. . . . Once there, go forward, hero.

—Homer, *Odyssey*

So many career intelligence officers went around looking terribly mysterious—long black boots and sinister smiles. Nobody ever issued me with a false beard. And invisible ink? I can't even read my own writing when it's supposed to be visible. My disguise was my own reputation as a bit of an idiot.

—Noël Coward

Contents

Part I

FLOT/AM

San Francisco Chronicle, October 13, 1939:

HALIFAX DEAD, COURT DECLARES

Author-Adventurer Drowned on Chinese Junk in Typhoon in Pacific, Jury Holds

KANSAS CITY, MO., OCT. 13 (AP)—

Richard Halifax, author-adventurer, last heard from in May after a typhoon hit the Chinese junk *Soup Dumpling*, was declared legally dead today. After two search-and-rescue missions, a jury concluded he died on May 28 near the international date line while attempting to sail from Hong Kong to San Francisco. He is survived by his parents, Franklin and Regina Halifax, and was predeceased by a brother, Wesley.

Richard Halifax made a name for himself as a world traveler for the stay-at-home crowd. He was the swashbuckler of the *Ladies' Home Journal*, Don Quixote of the dining hall, Lord Byron of all dreamy-eyed schoolboys. Neither a poet nor an explorer himself, he brightened the annals of adventure by following in the footsteps of the greats, adding a fresh coat of charm and, as many critics observed, a good deal of manufactured drama and drollery. Wherever he went, Halifax always found himself "in a tight spot," usually of his own making, which he met with Midwestern cheerfulness and the breeziest of styles.

Halifax was born on February 11, 1900, in Kansas City, Missouri, where he attended the Country Day School. After studies at Princeton, he stowed away on a steamer to Rotterdam and tramped his way across Europe and Asia. This became the subject of his first book, in 1925, *Romance by Rucksack*, and the beginning of his career on the lecture circuit. More trips and books soon followed. *The Glorious Wanderer* (1927) retraced the odyssey of Homer's eponymous hero. *The Magic Carpet* (1928) chronicled his journey across the deserts of Africa, the Near East, and America in an open-cockpit airplane. *The Glittering Kingdom* (1929) found the writer trekking through the ruins of Indochina and Siam, while that same year *Steppe Lively!* recounted a train journey across the Soviet Union.

In 1930, in the first of a series of trips titled "Paths of the Conquerors," Halifax walked Cortés's route from Veracruz to the ancient Aztec capital of Tenochtitlán. There he met the Mexican painter Diego Rivera, who joined him on the next leg, by car, to the Panama Canal, where, after securing permission from the U.S. naval authorities, Halifax swam the channel.

Halifax was always in search of a good swim and even better stunt, stripping down in picturesque ports and diving in while the press watched from ashore. During one such feat, while he was attempting to mimic Byron's splash across the Hellespont, several papers reported him drowned. Three days later, the author-adventurer surfaced in a Turkish fishing boat, where he was photographed grinning at news of his own demise.

The anecdote was indicative of Halifax's charmed life in that period. During the worst years after the Wall Street crash, he lived the high life in San Francisco, emitting a steady stream of exotic hijinks for those who could only dream of travel—let alone climb Mount Fuji in the dead of winter, ride an elephant across the Alps, or be feted by a seven-foot-tall Arabian king at Mecca, just before trying to sneak inside the gates. His 1934 *Codex of Wonders*, a compendium of world marvels for young readers, was a *New York Times* bestseller for nearly two years and spawned the Dicky Halifax Junior Adventurers Club, a newsletter subscription service that put the author in direct communication with his legion of pint-sized admirers.

But by 1937 hard times caught up with Halifax. A novel home on the cliffs of Laguna Beach drained his wealth, a stint in Hollywood led to a box-office flop, followed by rumors of missing funds intended for the doomed Spanish republic. Halifax went to the Orient, splitting his time between Bangkok and Shanghai. But rather than chronicle heroic swims or elephant rides, his dispatches told of Japanese atrocities and air raids.

In 1938, Halifax announced he was preparing for his greatest adventure yet: an ocean crossing from Hong Kong to San Francisco on his custom-built junk, the *Soup Dumpling*. She was to have been exhibited last summer at the World's Fair on Treasure Island as part of its "Pageant of the World Pacific." To raise funds for the voyage, Halifax, ever the entrepreneur, sold a package of Junior Adventurers Club subscriptions that, for the price of five dollars, would send his young readers letters written aboard ship and mailed from ports of call en route.

On May 27 this year, the *SS President Coolidge* received a radio transmission from the *Soup Dumpling*, its position some five hundred miles west of Midway Island. In what would prove to be the author-adventurer's final words, Halifax reported that a typhoon had struck the ship: "Gales . . . squalls . . . bunks soaked, lee rail underwater . . . having whale of a time . . . wish you were here instead of me."

1

HILDEGARD RAUCH

How could you? I don't understand. Of course the world is a disaster, your own life a ruin, and the future without hope. But to Werther yourself right out of existence? What a horrible cliché. You always wanted to free yourself from Father's shadow, but now look where you are. No doubt tomorrow's papers will report that *Son of Germany's Greatest Living Writer in Exile Was Not Up to the Task*.

I'm so angry, I could pull those tubes right out of your throat. That would give the newshounds a better headline: *Daughter of Germany's Greatest Living Writer in Exile Murders Twin*. Sounds like a story out of the High Priest's own corpus: early middle period, when incest and sex-murder were all the rage. Sickly, fine-boned brother arrives in fleshpot metropolis, reunites with his likeness in feminine form (though let's be honest, I'm far manlier than you could ever hope to be), whereupon they bathe in blue waters, sun themselves on the cliffs, and, after he cries on her shoulder about the last mean boy who broke his heart, the two fall quite naturally into the embrace they first knew in the amnion. Brother, tormented by guilt, swallows his suitcase full of chemicals, which doesn't quite do the trick, until hysterical sister comes to finish the job. I call it "The Geminicide"—doesn't that have a nice ring to it? The Viennese would have eaten it right up.

Of course, that's a story for a world that no longer exists. And the real one of today is so much drabber: Penniless brother and hopeless drug addict, having destroyed the last shred of patience among family and friends in Los Angeles, flees to San Francisco and calls upon sister, whom he's neglected for the better part of three years but who surely must pity him enough to throw him some bread. When she refuses—only because she knows every cent will go straight into his veins—he says he's only one unmet fix away from offing himself. She calls his bluff, tells him the meat cleaver is in the top drawer on the right, that he's welcome to borrow it but could he please wash it before bringing it back? The next morning she gets a call from the manager of the St. Francis Hotel, saying Mr. Heinrich Rauch was found in his room unconscious and rushed to Mount Zion in an ambulance.

Of all the stories we could have lived together, Eiko, why this one? With me stuck in a hospital room, seeing your sallow form laid out, listening to the precarious beep of your pulse. We should be at Treasure Island right now, looking at my painting in the new exhibition, winning prizes at the shooting gallery (me for accuracy, you for consolation), and licking ice cream cones like real Americans.

You always say it's harder for the sons of great fathers than it is for the daughters. But that's only because nobody expects, let alone recognizes, anything of merit from the daughters. So how exactly is that less of a predicament? I suppose you've tried to win that argument here with this ridiculous act of desperation. "See, Ildi, it really was too hard for me!" To that I say, in my best American accent, *horseshit*. You didn't have to become a writer. You didn't have to become a drug fiend. And you surely didn't have to become such an exasperating prima donna who, blinding yourself to everyone who loves you, swallowed those pills. Don't you realize that if you end the story this way, you don't get to tell any others? Please wake up so I can scream at you.

I went to get your things from the St. Francis today. Glad being broke didn't stop you from springing for the suite for the last six weeks. Pretty high-tone for one of the self-proclaimed "Lumpenproletariat of Literature." When Monsieur Gaurin presented me with your bill, I thought I was going to have to make a run for it. Thank God he's the last of San Francisco's old-world hoteliers and didn't expect payment upon departure. You'll be glad to know I've forwarded the bill on to the High Priest.

Wish I could be there to see his eyes pop when he sees the tally. Though I doubt Mother will even mention it—wouldn't want it to interfere with his work, especially now that Father thinks the fate of

Europe hangs on his prose. He was out for his constitutional when I called to break the news of your trip to the underworld. I told Mother, who insists it must have been an accident, that you're stable and that you will eventually wake up; we just don't know when. That's what the doctors have said, more or less. They have also said that you may remain in "a chronic vegetative state of indeterminate length" and suffer "permanently impaired brain function." These I did not share.

And, yes, I found your note. Witty and impeccably typed, even as you board Charon's ferry. I grant you, the world is not a pleasant place to lay over right now. That little black spider, hatched in our own rotten garden, will soon ensnare all of Europe, if not the world. But this is what makes me so furious with you, why I stand before your action uncomprehending and seemingly without pity. While others are interned or shot or run down by tanks, you, one of the lucky ones, take your precious gift of life up to the twelfth-floor suite and, surrounded by the splendor of the Pacific, try to cash it in. Why?

You've always said you feel called to death, whereas I am called to life, but I don't think you understand death in its brutal simplicity. You seem to regard it as some kind of realm or state of being, when it is simply a negation. The fall of a blade, the flip of a switch, the crushing of all into dust. That is death and nothing more. And you have not yet earned it. I must say, it's easier to argue with you in your unconscious state. You can't disagree with me or call me an aloof aesthete or a manly giantess. Though I wish you would, because the silence of your acid tongue makes me fear you are not there at all.

But there's something else—something I don't understand. And I need, above all, to understand you. You said in your note that, despite how it looks, it wasn't Hitler or his war, it wasn't the loss of your homeland and years of exile, it wasn't your literary failures or the towering shadow cast by Father and his public contempt for your work, it wasn't even your crippling dependence on drugs and booze that made things unbearable. It was the pain of lost love. Love!

Yet not three days ago you were telling me about that Croatian tennis player, laughing at how boring he was and that the only thing you'd miss about him was how marvelously he filled out those white shorts. Surely it wasn't the souring of this little fling that made you want to throw yourself overboard, and in any event I believe his name was Marko. How, then, am I to understand the parting declaration of your note? *I just can't bear to live in a World without Dick.*

Assuming you were talking about a man and not an appendage—your appallingly German habit of capitalizing nouns in English has complicated things—I have only one question for you: Who the hell is Dick?

2

To: The Dicky Halifax Junior Adventurers Club
From: Dicky Halifax
Aboard the Wreckage of the *Soup Dumpling*
Adrift in the Pacific

Summer 1939

Ahoy, my dearest boys!

Sorry I haven't fired up the mimeograph machine these last few weeks—she got a bit waterlogged—but boy howdy, have I got a tale for you.

Your old pal Dicky sure ended up in the weeds this time. For a second there, I thought it was *so long, world, and sayonara, Dick.* But what do I always say? If the brain stem's still glued to the spinal cord, it's not lights out yet. No sirree, when you find yourself in a tight spot, you gotta make like Ulysses and use your noggin. We hardly know all the goodies it's teeming with till Dame Fortune has boxed our ears and sat on our chest—and let me assure you, boys, she's a big girl, the Dame. Besides, that's the whole point of adventure. If we wanted to take it easy, we could have stayed in Kansas City and gone for a ride on the Brush Creek gondola with all the other weak sisters.

But not me, boys. While the rest of the adult world was punching the clock, I was astride the prow of the *Soup Dumpling*, sun on my bare chest, beaming like a priapic god as we cut the waves along the Chinese main. The firecrackers from our glorious send-off out of Hong Kong were still ringing in my ears, and my grin was so wide the salt spray made my gums bleed.

This was the moment I'd spent my whole life dreaming of and the last two years busting my hump to make happen. All the keen scores and lucky breaks, the failed business pitches, pulled endorsements, and pillows soaked with tears—it had all been worth it. Even when that stuffed suit from Buick said his company couldn't afford to be associated with anything called a "junk," even when those pussyfoot investors from the San Francisco Chinese Benevolent Society jumped ship because they were worried about "my assessment of the Japanese threat," and even when that sour English spy in Bangkok said he'd chase me down and kill me if it turned out I was grifting him. All those moments had led me here, and now the rest was pure adventure.

I was recalling these travails from my perch when a shriek rang out that nearly sent me overboard. It sounded like the roar of a breached sea dragon, but when I turned I saw our surly captain, Pengelly, his ulna burst through his skin, and my man Roderick brandishing a kitchen knife.

Despite how things looked, it was an accident. Pengelly had slipped on Roderick's martini puddle after sneaking into the galley to make one of his sickening Cornish pies. Roderick warned him at knifepoint to stay out of his kitchen, and Pengelly, being the uncharitable, suspicious sort, accused Roderick of planting the puddle there as a trap. The arm could not be reset and, seeing as we were only two days from port, Pengelly demanded we turn back. In short, a real *porty pooper*. He vowed to sue me the moment we reached the harbor, which still bore faint traces of smoke and confetti from our big send-off.

Demoralizing as it was to abort our maiden voyage before we'd even gotten the tip in, it was for the best. I'd grown tired of the Cornishman's glower, and just the thought of enduring ten thousand miles of his disapproving looks was too much. Of course, I didn't wish for the man to suffer a life-altering, artery-rupturing arm break. But the Fates are mysterious ladies, boys, and some say they follow a cosmic justice.

Plus, truth be told, the little drop-in motor that Pengelly had insisted on was never going to get us to Formosa, let alone across open ocean. And our resident Harvard crybaby, George Winslow III, having acquired a walloping dose of the clap just before we left harbor, had spent every minute at sea dunking his hair snake in talcum powder, howling like a banshee.

So we hightailed it back to Hong Kong, where we sent George and

Pengelly off to hospital and parked the *Soup Dumpling* in Ming Fat's shipyard. Don't be fooled by the funny name, boys—Ming Fat was thin as a bed rail and cunning as a jackal. He'd taken his sweet time building the junk to my specifications on the first go-round, always second-guessing me. I told the man I wanted a traditional Chinese junk, made just like the one Zheng He sailed when he kissed the coast of Peru, but with a few modern appurtenances. Well, hang me if ole Fat didn't use my own words as a license to suck Dicky dry of every last dime in his pocket. He proceeded to build my junk by the slow-boat-from-China method, with wooden mallets and pegs and a whole lotta *penge*! I'd still be sitting in the Hong Kong boatyard if I hadn't butted in and introduced the crew to the wonders of iron screws and a drill.

I practically had to fishhook Ming Fat by his thick custard bun of a cheek to accommodate the new inboard diesel shaft engine I'd wanted all along. This required a reconfiguration of the entire hull—eliminating the captain's quarters (why not? We'd already eliminated the captain!), reducing the kitchen space (Roderick could make a martini in a steamer trunk), and finding a new housing unit for the mimeograph machine. It was his opposition to the mimeograph machine that really put Pengelly on my sore side. "Not up for discussion, you Cornish pustule!" I told him. As you know, boys, I would sooner find myself at the bottom of the ocean than be separated from you, my dues-paying Junior Adventurers.

So, while the shipwrights refitted the *Soup Dumpling* for the twentieth century, your man Dick found himself, once again, back in port. Back in our hotel room in the Peninsula, with the same singed curtains and charred ceiling from an earlier mishap, or, as was more often the case, down at the docks, opposite a high-smelling soy-sauce factory and the Gentleman's Beauty Parlor, chewing the Fat and dancing his shipyard shuffle (you know the tune: wait, wait, scream—pay, pay, pay).

I was, it must be admitted, eager to set sail. The whole of San Francisco was lining the Treasure Island Gayway in anticipation of our arrival, and with every minute stuck in Hong Kong, my costs, along with the chances of run-ins with angry creditors and unwitting investors, ticked upward. But was I going to just twiddle my thumbs and bitch? No sir!

Roderick and I were in the Pedder Building, monkeying around without our pants while a Red Gang tailor measured us for another pair of suits—seafoam gabardine with rose silk lining—when in loped four young sandy-haired Davids fresh from Michelangelo's mold. "Are you Richard Halifax?" asked the lead boy, aiming a well-tanned finger right at my heart.

"That depends . . ." I said. See, boys, certain pranks had been played by your man Dick over the years as he rimmed the oyster of the world, and I wasn't sure if this young man was one of those humorless weak sisters, like that English pimple back in Bangkok, who'd lost their laughing muscles.

"It is, it is!" said one of his mates. He whipped out a folded page from his shirt pocket. "See?"

There was my mug, grinning atop Chichén Itzá beside my pudgy, paint-spattered amigo Diego. "Huzzah!" they cried. "That means we're not too late!"

"Too late for what?" I asked.

"We're your biggest fans, Mr. Halifax! And we've come all the way from New Hampshire to join your crew."

"My crew?"

"See, we're on the Dartmouth sailing team, and when Stephens here told us you were assembling a crew to sail across the Pacific, we ditched our final exams and caught the first steamer to Yokohama, then a trawler to Hong Kong. We were afraid we'd missed you, but then we saw a giant painted boat up on blocks in the shipyard and we just knew it was the *Soup Dumpling* . . ."

The boy had talked himself right out of breath. They must have sprinted all the way from the harbor.

I looked at Roderick and saw he was giving them the certified Roderick once-over. "Any of you collegians ever sailed on the open sea?" I asked.

"Sure, loads of times," said the one called Stephens. "Chet and I sailed last summer all the way to Prince Edward Island."

"And Dwight and I sailed out to the Vineyard from Falmouth over Easter break," said another.

"Sounds like you're all salts to a man."

I checked in with Roderick, who still had his brow screwed up in appraisal. "Do they cook?" he asked.

I knew their fates now hung in the balance. The boys looked sheepishly at their scuffed loafers. There were some feeble mutterings about making peanut butter sandwiches and Ritz cracker hors d'oeuvres. One said he'd once assembled a Jell-O mold under his mother's guidance. But, no, truth be told, none of them could cook a blessed thing.

Roderick's scowl resolved into his usual mien of empty-headed placidity. "Just tell them to stay out of my kitchen."

They had passed the test. And the timing couldn't have been better, as the doctors had informed us that neither Pengelly nor George Winslow III would be fit to sail in the next month.

"Well, I hope you packed your whites, boys," I said, turning to the sailing team. "'Cause you're all hired!"

It was a plum trade, as far as I was concerned: four of Dartmouth's finest for one disapproving Cornishman and a debauched Harvard scion with a drippy urethra. Of course, I also requested that the boys each wire their parents for the mandatory thousand-dollar expedition fee, which would help offset the cost of our repairs. The ten thousand sterling from my mark in Siam had kept the dream of the *Soup Dumpling* alive at a crucial moment in the initial building phase, and I even found a way to tack on a little cumshaw at the end. But now I had a new hole to plug. George Winslow III, whose only apparent skills were playing the accordion and blowing through his inheritance in a comprehensive tour of Chinese brothels, had nevertheless been a valuable member of the crew. Why? Because his mother, the widow Martha Winslow, née Beerenbeck, had money coming out her ears. She'd pinned a seven-thousand-dollar check to Georgy boy's cap provided I let him come along. But now that he'd poked his ding-dong in too many wrong holes (the doctors were saying they'd never seen so ferocious a chancre), the voyage of the *Soup Dumpling* was going to be free of both his tango serenades and Mommy's money. So I snatched up those darling Dartmouth boys and told myself I'd make up the difference once we reached Treasure Island and set out our shingle at the fair.

Even with all the harrowing turns of events at sea that followed, I still think we were better off for it. Just wish those lads had been better swimmers.

A week later, we peeled out of Kowloon Bay and were soon cutting waves. By God, boys, it was glorious—wind in our faces, roar of diesel in our ears. It looked like we were on track to reach Formosa by teatime.

We had skipped the fanfare on our second departure from Hong Kong, since it's bad luck to shoot the firecrackers and spill the rice wine twice for the same voyage. But this time the painted eyes of our junk remained above the water, which, according to the custom, was an auspicious sign. Ming Fat had come through (kicking and screaming and robbing me blind, of course).

Our *Soup Dumpling* was a wonder to behold. A three-masted sixty-footer made of golden teak, ablaze with carmine foresail, white lightning mainsail, and a scarlet mizzen. She rode high and proud in the water, thanks to the towering poop I'd installed in order to accommodate the pair of painted fire-breathing peacocks designed by yours truly. A gorgeous big-aft girl she was, boys. Pretty as your mother.

My crowning triumph, if you'll allow me to boast, was the set of glass skylights I fought tooth and nail for so I could have good working light during the days below deck. Ming Fat said a storm would smash the glass to bits and that the skylight cuts rendered the saloon structurally unstable, but on this matter I would brook no dissent. Because it was by this light, boys, that I would write my letters to you.

I'd had Fat repaint the eyes on the stern six feet higher than before, both to account for the added weight of the diesel engine and extra crew and to keep morale high. Everyone but Nacho Fu, our half-caste cabin boy from Macao, threw their hats in the air when we saw those greasepaint peepers peering out auspiciously above the surf. I don't know if that's because Nacho had no hat to throw or because he was a bit of a hard case, which he was. He'd spent most of his time onshore slumped against a piling with his nose in a book, and the only time he uttered a peep was to say, in his churlish fashion, that there wasn't enough ballast in the keel, that the rigging was poorly secured, that the diesel engine wasn't properly mounted to the ribs, etc., etc. A bit of a drip, to be honest. But at least he was no power-mad Cornishman. And, unlike the latter, he didn't insist on making pasties in Roderick's kitchen.

All in all we were a merry band, drunk with the adventure now finally underway. No matter what happened to us, we knew we had succeeded in catapulting ourselves out of the mundane and into a wild life of action. And that, my boys, is no mean feat.

That first week, as our little *Soup Dumpling* bounced along the salty broth of the South China Sea, I had to make my first tough decision as skipper. Pengelly had demanded we hug the Chinese mainland and shoot the gap north of Formosa. Reason being the trade winds would be blowing like Aeolus at his birthday party, and unfortunately he'd be aiming at candles in the colossal sheet cake of Australia. Which meant we'd be fighting gales the whole time and would likely end up as some headhunter's dinner in New Guinea rather than enjoying our prime-rib welcome in SF. And though I certainly wanted to keep all my own ribs intact, that particular calculation was made with our former little nance of an engine, not the manly diesel that belched and hummed like a Slovakian lumberjack. With our new motor, the southern route around Formosa now seemed both viable and quicker, and would help make up for lost time.

On top of that, the Japs were making awful trouble along the Cantonese coast. In fact, just before our first maiden voyage, a wayward Japanese bomb had blown out part of the train station in Hong Kong. War was right at the colony's doorstep, which made for a fine evening light show from our hotel balcony but not such good sailing weather. As we waited for our repairs, we heard report after report of attacks on Chinese fishing junks in the area—junks that looked an awful lot like ours, except some of them were outfitted with cannon. We couldn't spare the weight for mounting cannons ourselves, but thanks to Roderick and the magnetic properties he seemed to possess with regard to firearms, we managed to get ahold of a clutch of shotguns and a fine pair of Thompsons. I'd also unearthed a proper buccaneer's cutlass at an antiques shop, which, with a little carnauba wax, I was able to polish to a shine. Roderick, not one to be outdone, came home with an evil-looking bludgeon that he called a Siamese ax. He said it was made for cracking open betel nuts and could be thrown as well as hefted. Fearsome as he looked with his ancient nut-crusher, I still doubted we'd be able to fend off a Jap gunship. And my right of safe passage from the maritime office in Yokohama would work only if we were given a chance to present it before being blown out of the water.

Were the Japanese navy the sole threat, I would have been willing to take the risk. But pirates were also prowling the Formosa Strait, preying on the chaos of war and the absence of the Chinese coast guard. And they recognized no rights of safe passage. Don't believe the legends, boys. There is no honor among waterborne thieves. Armed robbery at the pain of rape and murder is as unpleasant at sea as it is on land. And since I'd already been bled dry by Ming Fat at the shipyard, I decided I'd had enough thievery for one trip. At least on the receiving end.

So the decision was easy. Well, almost. Because the one thing we couldn't do via this new route was drop off my first batch of ten thousand letters to you, my loyal Junior Adventurers, as planned. By skirting Formosa and missing the Philippines, I'd have to wait till Midway Island, some two thousand miles away, before I could find a mailman. But I knew you'd understand, boys. So we stowed our extra five hundred pounds of mimeographed dispatches and headed south, out into open ocean.

The distant lights of Kōshun were the last signs of civilization we saw for weeks. The sea stretched all around us into an unbroken horizon, our eternity punctuated by the rhythms of the sun and the duties of sailing life. The Dartmouth team showed they knew their way around the mast, though none of us, except young Nacho Fu, had ever manned a junk. It took some getting used to, working the battened sails, and that long rudder was a doozy, but the collegians were quick studies. And, unlike Roderick, who'd gone to fat, they were all trim and tan to a man. I've said it before, boys, and I'll say it again: Don't become a fatty. Nothing ruins a dashing pose or a picturesque scene like a gut spilling out over a waistband or a bare chest with droopy teats. One of the many virtues of the active life is that it keeps a man strong and firm and makes him a pleasing image for all who dwell in his company.

And we were dwelling in close quarters at that. Roderick and I slept in a bunked cabin; Dwight, Floyd, Stephens, and Chet piled into the other; and our cabin boy, Nacho, hung his hammock in the larder with the dry goods, water casks, and firearms. You'd think men in such confined conditions would become irritable, as we had been under Pengelly's brief captaincy, but those first two weeks in the Philippine Sea were marked by a sublime tranquility. Other than some friendly porpoises and flying fish, we never saw another soul. The SS *President Coolidge* was cruising the sea east of Luzon, and we radioed greetings while we were in proximate waters, but no mast disturbed our solitude. A cool breeze mellowed the sun's harshness and filled our mainsail as we lazed on deck and fed on the bounty of Roderick's kitchen.

Roderick, as you boys know, is a man of Sancho Panzanian disposition. No highfalutin ideals of chivalry for him—just a hot meal thrice daily, with supplementary elevenses and afternoon tea, followed by a few pulls of the wine bag and nine hours of repose in a soft bed. He differs only in that he lacks the Spanish squire's garrulity; in fact, he's as laconic as an old Indian chief. But he takes equal pleasure in the sating of others' appetites as he does his own. Which is why, when it was just the two of us, I called him Mother.

All in all, we were a happy family: Roderick wearing the matron's apron in the galley, me playing the paternal role of skipper, with our four bright beaming college boys and young Nacho Fu as their kid foster-brother and mascot. They were kind to him too, in their collegial Dartmouth way. They rubbed his head for good luck so often that he developed a premature bald spot. They put shaving cream in his hand while he slept, tickling his nose with a gull feather until he slapped himself and was thrown from his hammock with a face full of cream. Perhaps their crowning hijinks came in the form of stealing his pants and making him climb, naked as a jaybird, up the yardarm to retrieve them. It was a lark. Why, I felt as carefree as if I were back in Old Nassau, cutting class and playing pinochle with Scott Fitzy, before the booze, fame, and crazy ladies wrecked him.

That's how I should like to remember us, boys—laughing beneath clear skies, our bellies full of Roderick's chili, watching little Nacho scamper up the ropes with his shrimp and grits bobbing in the breeze.

Then, all at once, everything changed. A deep gloom invaded the sky. Wrath-woven clouds blotted out the sun, and the wind began to howl. We shivered as we furled the sails and battened the hatches. It was as if Poseidon had just learned we'd blinded his one-eyed son. Waves as big as city buildings rose and fell beneath us. Our sea legs toppled like bowling pins, and we began to retch. I radioed the *Coolidge* that we were in for a drubbing and to come join the fun. I don't know if it was received, but it was the last message the *Soup Dumpling* ever sent.

When the storm cracked open overhead, we were curled up like pill bugs on deck, lashed to the forecastle and clutching our life vests. We all took our feckless turn at the helm, thinking each shift would be our last. Trying to steer against vengeful sea gods is a lesson in humility, boys, and I recommend you try it, though take care to keep your teeth. For that tiller wants nothing more than to smash every molar you've got. It reminded me of a dentist I once visited in Texas, who was of the opinion that extraction is the best course of action: "Can't rot 'em if you don't got 'em." Unfortunately, young Stephens learned that the hard way. He'd have been on the milkshake-and-porridge diet when he returned to Dartmouth in the fall. But, as you've likely gathered, that won't be happening.

I tell you, boys, every minute at that helm was a lesson in the futile heroism of man. We all went in sissies and came out Sisyphus. It was the essence of adventure. And it was only just beginning. Will tell you the rest very soon, but for now . . . nature calls!

Yours,
Dicky

P.S. I imagine there will be some lag in these letters making it across the Pacific, but I have faith you'll get them eventually.

3

HILDEGARD RAUCH

You've been lying there stone-like for weeks, yet your chaos continues to engulf me. Clearly you skipped the whole "put your affairs in order" part of this time-honored exit plan.

Each day I receive your forwarded correspondence from the St. Francis: a deluge of creditors, writers, and donors no doubt demanding their money back if the journal is, as rumored, going under. And I suppose it is, since Hank Rauch, sole editor of *The Reckoning*—something of a necessity after you alienated everyone you'd ever collaborated with—is still asleep.

I must say I resent this assault on my mailbox. You know I made a point of having nothing to do with your journal, that I wished you well with it but needed a clean break from that world. And yet, when I called to have the St. Francis reroute the mail to your journal's PO box in Los Angeles, I was told it was full and that my apartment had been designated as *The Reckoning*'s satellite office. How kind of you to consult me.

It's not that I despise Weimar on the Pacific. I understand it is a lifeboat for so many amid the current shipwreck. And I certainly don't begrudge our fellow refugees for trying to keep some semblance of cohesion with their shattered lives. Our parents still dine with the Franks every Friday, just as they did in Vienna, and the High Priest still creaks across the tennis court once a week with Herr Schoenberg. Yet something in me resists it, needs to flee from it. I do not want to preserve my old life, like some hothouse flower of the tropics transplanted to a greenhouse simulacrum. I know I would wither.

I suppose the reason is glaringly obvious. Because presiding over this refugee kingdom in Los Angeles is the High Priest himself. And though I certainly do not hate our father, I cannot say exactly that I "love" him. Again, that baffling word. You both love and hate Father with all your being. But the High Priest is too aloof to arouse such passions in me—or perhaps, as you say, it is I who am too aloof. I regard him with a cool admiration, as one does a heavy object—the distant planet of the patriarch—whose mass exerts a dangerous gravitational pull. I have seen the danger of that force when one does not fully surrender to it. A self may be led to believe it is charting its own path, creating its own destiny, when really it is only circling the celestial body of the father.

I knew that if I was going to thrive here on the far side of the earth, I had to set out on my own. Beyond the pull of Father and his world, including you and your journal, as well as the bootlicking, backbiting cliques of writers and artists who have been orbiting him since forever. That is why I took the job last year at Mills. The idea of a small women's college in Oakland seemed a world apart from the High Priest's realm in the south, and I believe it has been good for me.

I am trying to live artfully. By that, I don't mean like a reckless, pretentious shit but rather with diligence and care. Even the routine of my long morning commute has become a source of heightened significance, because I imbue it with the sanctity of a ritual. It begins with parting the curtains to let the sun pour into my southern bay windows and warm the apartment. Even on overcast days, the flat is suffused with a crispness utterly alien to the coal-smudged aperture above Central Europe. Once dressed and armed with my trinity of book, sketchbook, and pen, on my way out I touch a photograph tucked into the corner of the mirror. Yes, you little shit, it's one of us—at the beach in Rügen, with me, nearly twice your size, atop your sloped shoulders. I had already begun sprouting breasts and hair, while you still looked like a choirboy. "Beauty and the Beast," you dubbed it.

Upon exiting my building on Hyde and Vallejo—the English mixed with Spanish never fails to delight me—I soak in the morning light until I hear the approaching ring of the cable car. Ignoring the men who insist on offering their seat so as to stare down at me, I always stand on the running board and bathe my face in the wind. At Market, I resume my journey on foot, past the clubs and cinemas, past Omar Khayyam's, fragrant with Turkish coffee and spiced meat and the lemony scent of sumac. I make a point of paying attention to everything that crosses my field of vision, even if only for a second—the mauve high heels striking brick, the freckled nose of the shoeshine boy, the quickly averted gaze of a man in the bakeshop window, even the shitting back end of a horse. I do not look away, only take in and take note. I try to make myself into what Baudelaire called *a kaleidoscope gifted with consciousness.*

When I reach the Ferry Building, I take my breakfast at a counter run by a Slovene couple. They are kind, and unlike many of the proprietors at other restaurants and luncheonettes in this city who can't bear to see a woman dining alone, they let me eat in peace. This morning with my eggs I read a short chapter from Poe's *Arthur Gordon Pym*, which is shaping up to be a very silly book. I can finally read English with more joy than effort, which allowed me to cast a skeptical eye as Pym and Dirk Peters, having survived shipwreck and cannibalism, reached the temperate center of the South Pole, home of the black-toothed natives. You'll laugh, but it made me think of white-toothed Richard Halifax, vanished at sea and recently declared dead. In fact, now that I think of it, that was likely why I was drawn to the book in the shop a couple of weeks ago, right after you tried to punch your ticket to oblivion.

When we met him in Ethiopia, Halifax was on one of his mad dashes around the globe and had decided to drop in at Addis Ababa to dine with Haile Selassie. He'd said that while he didn't think he could help the emperor defeat the Italians, he could probably get him on the cover of *Time* magazine. And to our great surprise, he did. You and I had laughed at him, mostly because he kept lapsing into hideous German to try to impress us. But . . . well, I never told you this, but as buffoonish as he was, with his boyish American swagger, I found him rather charming. Certainly enough to spend a night with. And while I didn't often go for men at the time, especially a grinning American man-child, there was something beneath the dimples and icy blue eyes that seemed wounded and vulnerable, and I wanted to see it. So, after sharing a nightcap in the lobby bar of the Itegue Taitu, I brought him back to my room.

I never told you because I knew you would have hounded me about it to no end, and because nothing actually happened. After some kissing and a few tentative caresses, Halifax said something about a parasite he'd contracted that had, as he put it, wreaked havoc on his internal mechanisms. He offered to give me a "licky-loo" instead (hand to God, his words) but, since all erotic thoughts had evaporated the moment he uttered that phrase, I declined. So we just shared another bottle of wine and, lying side by side on the unsullied bed, we talked. He was actually quite sweet. He told me about his brother, Wesley. Two years younger than him but practically his twin, he had died from diphtheria when Richard was eighteen. He told me he was jealous of how close you and I were (even though that trip was right when we began to fray). He said that he wished for nothing more than to go on an adventure with his brother and that some irrational part of his brain still thought that if he traveled far enough, he just might one day find Wesley, "living like a sheik in some mud palace in Timbuktu." The next morning the Italians bombed Addis Ababa, and all the foreign correspondents fled.

I am sad that he is dead. I know many people dismissed him as an egotistical fool and his voyages as reckless stunts, but to undertake something so fantastic, to carry a dream into reality, regardless of how silly it sounds, takes real courage. The courage to pursue your own vision, to summon something deep within yourself, to reach for something beyond. No matter how quixotic, there is a kind of truth and ecstasy in that way of living. And those who rebel against the grinding inertia of reality will always elicit my sympathy. I suppose that's why I hung on to the chrome cigarette lighter he left in my hotel room that night. A little flame of adventure to light me on my path.

On the ferry I sat, like I always do, on a bench in the aft, watching the city recede in the distance. The smell of coffee from the MK and Hills Bros. plants mingled with the sea brine, and Coit Tower stood like the lone pillar of a ruined temple. It is my favorite part of the journey. To leave or arrive somewhere by water feels elemental. And I imagined I was an ancient ancestor setting off on a long sea voyage and not, as was actually the case, someone on her way to teach American girls how to draw.

Over the din of traffic on the Bay Bridge, I could make out the distant peal of a brass band on Treasure Island, awakening the fair to another day of pleasure. I still haven't gone to see my painting in the fall exhibition. I suppose I'm waiting for you to come with me, as we had planned. So I will continue to wait, until you wake up. Though I fear if you don't hurry, there may not be a world waiting for you.

At Jack London Square, I caught the Pullman south to Fairfax, then walked the last mile to campus, past the casitas with yucca and lavender, and along the low stone wall of the Jewish cemetery. It's funny—I never thought of myself as a Jew until my fellow citizens wanted to murder me. It was to no avail that Mother's family converted a generation ago in order to appease an older, gentler strain of hate. Of course, that taint, along with Father's "mongrel South American blood," would have been overlooked had the High Priest given his pen to the regime. He certainly took his sweet time deciding, despite our objections, hoping to wait things out from his mountaintop. Thank God it finally became clear to him that the flood was not receding and would soon engulf him and anyone else who had a shred of decency. After that first thunderbolt of opprobrium, suddenly Theodor Rauch was a "defiler of the race" and the leading voice of the anti-Nazi opposition and you, Mother, and I were Jews. And now, true to form, we are wandering Jews, our home in Europe having ceased to exist.

The other day I saw my faculty bio, describing me as an *Austrian painter*, and I nearly demanded a correction. But then I thought, what would I request instead? How could I explain to the department secretary that, yes, while it was true that our mother was thoroughly Viennese—which in her case meant Catholic, Jewish, German, Czech, Italian, and, at the same time, not any one of those things—our father, a Bremen German with a Basque Argentine mother, made any authentic identification with the fledgling, now extinct, nation of Austria impossible. Besides, by the time it came into existence after the war, through abortive revolutions and prolonged street fights, you and I were at a boarding school in the Bavarian forest, learning about the veil of Maya and the thrill of sexual touch. No wonder Berlin became our home after such a schooling, where the only identities I would have then claimed were as a child of pleasure and citizen of the world. It is only now, after all our particular portals to a cosmopolitan European identity have been slammed shut, that I realize how much we took for granted.

Two hours after leaving my door in Russian Hill, I finally arrived at the art department. With still over an hour until class began, I went to the shared studio to work on my woodcut. I divide my artistic life here neatly in two, with five miles of bay water marking the boundaries. Campus is for the workshop activities of printmaking and teaching; my home studio is for the private odyssey of painting. I settled into my space in the corner, beside the tall windows that open onto a courtyard thick with fuchsia and wild fennel, and was sharpening my gouges when I noticed a man walking across the patio. I observed him from behind the glass as he walked by, until, suddenly, he sensed my gaze behind the reflection and averted his face.

This action filled me with an uncanny sense, as though I were reexperiencing it.

"You look like you've just remembered that you forgot something," said Walter, who had just come into the studio and seen the puzzled look on my face. "Either that or you're constipated."

His joke made me smile and broke the spell of déjà vu. "I *am* constipated—in my brain. That's how far the shit's backed up."

Walter Seidler, whom I'm sure I've mentioned, is a fellow refugee, from Budapest by way of Berlin. Aside from you, currently out of the running, he is the only acquaintance here with whom I can speak in the pungent manner that, more than German, is our native tongue. I suppose that makes him my best friend here, because normal conversation—unbarbed, unfunny, unvulgar, even with smart, well-meaning people—feels like I'm slowly drowning. I suppose I have you to blame for this, since we spent our formative years locked in a game of perpetual banter and teasing, designed to elicit laughter or, better, shock. As a result, I adhere to the following rules of engagement: Seriousness is for solitude. Company requires wit.

25

Walter and I joked more while he made tea on the hotplate by the sink. I told him about our friend Mercedes who, that first autumn of the war in Spain, had been suffering a terrible cold and asked one of the press corps in the lobby of the Hotel Florida if she could borrow a handkerchief. Arthur Koestler, never missing an opportunity to play the gallant and thereby increase his odds of getting under a woman's skirt, hurried to extract his own from his pocket. Meanwhile, Mercedes, not realizing that *estar constipado* is a false cognate in English, explained, "I'm very constipated and just need to blow it out." Koestler arched his brow and, with handkerchief held out to her, said, "In that case, my dear, I think it's best you just keep it."

Walter laughed, then, turning solemn for a moment, said that he had heard Koestler was trapped in France, the Third Republic having rounded up all enemy aliens.

"Yes, so I heard."

"But don't worry about that mean old Hungarian bastard—if he can survive Franco's prison, a French detention camp will be a garden party."

"Speaking of mean Hungarians," I said, "how is your Moholy-Nagy exhibition coming along?"

Walter is an art historian with a particular mania for the graphic arts. "I'll have you know László is a consummate gentleman," he said. "He just happens to be languishing in Chicago doing the layout for mail-order catalogs. You'd be surly too if you went from running the Bauhaus to advertising special socks for foot fungus."

I've never met Moholy-Nagy, but, thanks to Walter, I now own one of his paintings. *A 19*, it's called—ostensibly one of the many color studies that poured out of the Bauhaus in the twenties, with the constructivist penchant for dynamic lines and semi-opaque circles. Axes and lenses, layers of reality assembling and disassembling before the eye. At first I thought it was too cold, too clinical. But the longer I look at it, the more it resonates with me. Two realities—the black and the red—mapped onto each other, slightly askew, producing a third, shadow reality. The lens, or is it a moon, holds everything aloft. If it weren't for the moon and its luminous self-containment, the colliding axes would drag everything in the composition into ruin. I like to imagine myself dwelling somewhere in the interstices, deep in the center.

"And Sleeping Beauty?" asked Walter.

"He sleeps still. Just as well, I suppose—he's not missing anything. In fact, this coma might be the only way to keep him sober and alive."

"Well, he should sleep for a year, then; maybe he will wake up to a nicer world."

"What did Schopenhauer say about optimism? A doctrine not only false but pernicious?"

"I'd be pessimistic too if people thought I was more boring than Hegel. In the meantime, I think you should come to one of our parties. So does Nadia. She thinks you need more friends."

"Yes, I would like that," I said, while inwardly I groaned. "It's just that sometimes Berkeley seems so far."

"So sleep in our spare room. Nadia would love it. She longs to adopt a younger woman as her kid sister."

Walter's wife, Nadia, several years his senior, was a Litvak from Warsaw. She had come to America before the last war but then spent several years in Berlin, where she had been Walter's Russian teacher. And while Berkeley really *is* annoyingly far from San Francisco, the real reason I resisted visiting the Seidlers was her. For one, she's a militant anarchist, and I always feel in her company like I'm being either recruited or denounced. Or possibly seduced. I feel no sexual charge from Walter, much as I like him, but Nadia is a different story. And while I'm no stranger to dalliances with women, even older women (though it's been quite a while since I've dallied with anyone), the problem with Nadia, in addition to being the wife of my friend and colleague, is that—well, there's just no nice way of putting it—she's scary.

"We're having people over this Saturday, for Halloween," said Walter. "A proper American Halloween party—costumes and all. You'll come, right?"

I couldn't refuse another of his invitations. I was already on the verge of being rude. "Alright, sure. What should I come as?"

"Whatever you want, so long as you don't come as a witch—Nadia's already claimed it." That she had.

By the time Walter left, it was nearly time for my class. I made a few obligatory cuts, clearing away some ground on the key plate, just enough to feel that some minuscule progress had been made, then spent the next three hours in front of twenty freshmen, pretending I knew what I was doing.

Most of the students are competent but untalented. As evidenced by the sea of young beauties in my classroom, Nature is generous with her temporary gifts. But with gifts that can fuel an entire life of purpose she is exceedingly stingy. I'm still not sure if I myself possess such a talent, but at this stage in my life I'm ready to give myself to it entirely, to be sustained by it alone in the absence of all other sources of meaning. I do not want a husband, I do not want to be a mother, and, frankly, I don't particularly want to be a teacher either. The mantle of presumed authority—"This, girls, is how one draws"—I find ridiculous and off-putting. Though it's good to have something rooting me to the external world, and I find it easy enough to be supportive or, when something isn't working, gently critical. But I keep my mask on tight, wear my pleasant exterior, and cork the sailors' bar of obscenities that would otherwise pour from my mouth.

Once class was over, I repeated my travails in reverse—walk, train, ferry, walk, cable car. It was just as I was boarding the latter, as the sun dropped behind Twin Peaks and dusk fell on the city, that I noticed him.

The man with the twisted face, the one from outside the studio on campus. There he was again, averting his eyes. And this time I remembered where I had first seen him—this morning, on Market Street, in front of the bakery. The same stranger, three times in one day: in the morning downtown, two hours later across the bay at Mills, and now right there at the corner waiting to board. There are half a million people in this city, and a fraction of them cross the bay in the morning and return in the evening. And while I believe most patterns of meaning are built from the meaningless collision of chance, this one yielded only one plausible conclusion: I was being followed.

Unnerved, I got off the cable car three blocks before my apartment, walked fast up Larkin past the French launderette, ducked into a crowded bar for a few minutes, then circled back to my building from the north. No one was there. But I felt so frazzled that I didn't remember walking up the three flights of steps. Instead, I seemed to have floated right up to my door and inside, where there on the mat, come through the door slot, was a new pile of mail. It was as if the uncanniness had followed me inside, for at the top of the pile was an envelope bearing my name—different from all the others, yet startlingly familiar.

The shaky writing on the envelope, just like the message inside, could have come from only one hand. The hand of someone still comatose. You.

4

To: The Dicky Halifax Junior Adventurers Club
From: Dicky Halifax
Aboard the Wreckage of the *Soup Dumpling*
Dreaming of Ice Cream Floats

Summer 1939

Dear boys,

Last I wrote you, Stephens was cracking his wisdom teeth on that
wild truncheon of a Chinaman's tiller. Now, I had told Ming Fat I
wanted a proper navigational wheel, but of course he plugged his
ears with my money and muttered something about tradition and
me being a stupid foreign devil. Those were the last thoughts I had—
recollections of a bad business deal—when our destiny materialized in
the form of a wave. "Wave" is perhaps the wrong word, since this was a
black wall of sea, looming up starboard like a skyscraper and plunging
us into a seething pit. If you've ever wondered, boys, what it would feel
like to get sucked into Satan's anus, then put yourself in the swirling
vortex of a typhoon.

Everything went twisted and black. It felt like we were being rolled
into a thousand wet carpets. I tried to yell out for Roderick but got only
a belly full of seawater. I thought of my parents, pushing me and my
baby brother, Wesley, on a blue tricycle, all of us smiling and squinting
in the afternoon light, the faint smell of Daddy's pipe tobacco and
Mother's rosewater toilette floating in the spring air. I thought of dear
Wesley, his corpse as white as ivory, dressed in the Brooks Brothers
suit he'd never gotten a chance to wear except at his wake. And then
I thought of that nutty German scribbler, Hank Rauch, trying to kiss

me on the cliffs of Laguna Beach. Why did I think of that? Who knows? The drowning brain works in mysterious ways.

Little did I know that my Woe-Is-Dicky-Death-Dream was premature and that weeks later I'd be cranking up the ole mimeograph machine, so to speak, and telling you all about it. And what a tale it turned out to be! Let that be a lesson to you, Junior Adventurers: There's no story without the suffering, and there's no fun in suffering unless you turn it into a story. It's like that delicious *tehal* the hammam attendants fed me in Marrakech after a long night in the hash dens: a giant camel spleen stuffed with chopped offal and spiced with harissa and lemon. Without that pungent filling of pain and fear, you've just got a flabby, tasteless spleen. And without the cohesive splenic form of story, you've just got a dreary pile of ground-up toe meat and snout.

My skull was starting to cave in on itself as the ship plummeted to the depths, my temples like the collapsing walls of an old barn, my lungs like an accordion in an ice bath, when I felt something pull my leg and drag it furiously toward the surface. All of a sudden, I broke through the watery veil and shot into the light.

I must have gotten tangled in the strings of Roderick's kitchen apron, which was wrapped around him and the bedpost of our wooden bunk. No doubt when he saw the wall of death rise up before us, he slunk away below deck to cower in his cabin like a first-class weak sister. But it was a lucky thing he did, because the bunk came unmoored from its housing and, mad with buoyancy, shot through the hatch like a cannonball, carrying us with it.

Above water, the storm was still raging. The rain lashed our faces, the sea utterly electric with lightning. But by God we were alive. Vomiting up salt water never felt so good. I looked around for our shipmates but saw no one. I cried out for the Dartmouth sailing team—"Dwight! Floyd! Stephens! Chet!"—but heard only the wrath of the gods in response. Then I thought I spotted little Nacho Fu bobbing over a wave not a hundred feet leeward of our bunk bed, clinging to a water cask like a drowned rat. So I shook Roderick out of his panic-paralysis, and the two of us began kicking furiously against the current. "Hang in there, Nachito!" I yelled. "The lifeboat's a-coming!"

31

But our efforts were in vain. We had escaped the lethal suck of the vortex and now the current was pushing us away. As Nacho swirled and then vanished into the void of the *Soup Dumpling*, Roderick and I followed our hyperbolic destiny.

It's important to admit when you're wrong, boys. Only weaklings and imbeciles can't own up to their mistakes. And, boy howdy, had I made some boners. In hindsight, I suppose Ming Fat had been right when he'd cautioned me against carrying too big an engine, to say nothing of the mimeograph machine. That miserable drip Pengelly also had a fair point when he warned against the volatile open sea and fierce headwinds of the southern route. Even Nacho may have been onto something about the faulty rigging. But admitting mistakes is one thing and admitting defeat quite another. The latter you must never do. Never give up, boys. Never give in to doubt or despair or the crushing pessimism of the weepy Werthers who'll whisper in your ear that it's better never to have been born and second best to die soon. No, my happy, resilient boys! Under no circumstances whatsoever should you become a Negative Nancy.

The only answer is to pop those pimples of despair and get on with the living. So we got to work refashioning our upended bunk bed into a catamaran. Thankfully, Roderick still had his Siamese ax tucked into his belt—he'd been using it to slice lemon twists for our martinis right up till the end. We chopped out the mattress boards from each bunk and lay them across the frame for our deck, holding them fast with torn strips of kitchen apron. She was no *Soup Dumpling* in terms of appearance, but at least this junk would float.

We lacked only two things: food and water. Of this, Roderick made a regular point of reminding me. Three times a day and at his usual call to snack, he would begin sighing audibly and smacking his parched lips. Truly, boys, there is no worse sound than a mouth devoid of saliva trying to wet itself. These affronts to the ear of man were followed by low groans, then dog-like whimpers, then full-blown sobbing, at which point Roderick would lick his own tears for sustenance.

On the third day, the clouds vanished, and added to our growing hunger and thirst came the blistering agony of the sun. Roderick's tear ducts had long since gone dry, as had our bladders. The first two rounds of urine had been a potable exchange—though it made me nostalgic for the many swordfights we'd had with the Dartmouth lads in simpler times, before they and their clear abundant streams were claimed by the deep. Now only a scalding uric dribble could be squeezed from our bodies, and it burned our lips to the touch.

As the harsh rays of Helios roasted our flesh for several consecutive days, Roderick began flirting dangerously with the temptation to drink seawater.

"Don't do it, Mother," I warned. "You'll only die of thirst all the sooner."

"Just one little sip, Dick. Just so I can feel something fill my stomach."

"Eat your peeling skin, then." Our flesh was burnt to a purple crisp and bubbling with pus.

"Can I dunk it in seawater, Dick?"

"Fine, but just once."

I eyed him warily as he tore a blackened flake from his shoulder and dipped it greedily in the ocean, using his cupped hand to get a furtive mouthful.

I was becoming worried about Roderick. He and I had been through thick and thin together, since we first were bunkmates at Boy Scout camp. Roderick was a taciturn youngster, ignored by others and disdainful of company. His parents had sent him to scout camp praying he would make friends and get a dose of manliness, just as mine had sent me in hopes that the fresh air of the Ozarks would do my sickly constitution good and keep me from another bedridden winter.

I'd arrived late to camp—my mother had suffered one of her spells in the car and we were forced to go back for her medicine—so the only free bunk was the one above Roderick. Determined to stay out of my sickbed that coming year, I had decided I would throw myself into whatever situation I was faced with and make the best of it. Not just make do but thrive. I wanted to be fit like Wesley, who at ten was already a baseball star and who had elected not to go to camp so that he could stay home and lead the Brookside Possum Trotters to another

Honus Wagner Junior League pennant. So when I saw the scowling face of Roderick peer up at me from over his volume of Carlyle, I told him I, too, had read that cantankerous old Scot, and while he had some fine things to say about heroes, he was not nearly so good as my book about Davy Crockett. An hour later, the two of us were sucking down peach floats outside the Iconium General Store and planning our first adventure: to canoe the Osage River past Osceola all the way to the Sac. Or, rather, I was planning it, and Roderick was rehearsing for the role of grumbling, cowardly sidekick.

He'd played the part to a tee in many an adventure since. Always worrying, always hungry, always stuffing his face while disparaging the quality of food made by anyone other than him, always, as it were, out of his element. Where, you ask, was Roderick's element? You'd think it would be dithering in the kitchen or lying on his living room divan back in Kansas City, but in fact Roderick loathed the idea of being left at home. When I abandoned him to fly around the world on the dual-cockpit plane, only after the pilot refused to accommodate my request to add a third seat, the poor man had nearly died of despair. Paradoxically, where Roderick felt most at home was by my side on an adventure and emitting a steady torrent of half-verbalized complaint. That, along with his domestic bent and penchant for catastrophic thinking, was how he'd come by the cognomen "Mother."

Yes, the old boy had pulled a Hegel and made himself at home in his estrangement. And, in a way, it was through Roderick that I myself had become brave and cheerful. He always thought of the worst outcome and slunk away at any sign of danger so that I could run and meet it with a smile.

But now we were in one doozy of a pickle.

With no food or water, no land or ship in sight, Roderick and I were sailing swiftly toward the river Styx. I broke out the ole Halifax Cost-Benefit Calculator and did some computations. We had now been shipwrecked just over a week, drifting in the open ocean in a southwesterly direction. Between us and the next landmass must have been a thousand miles. Our organs were desiccated from thirst, our skin burnt beyond recognition, our eyes swollen shut, and our hair completely white. Assuming the state of Roderick's face was a fair indication of my own, we were no longer men but demons. Four-limbed ulcers on a floating bed in hell.

Now, if I were to die before him, Roderick would be alone on the open seas, like a dog who's lost his master. The blow to him would be crushing, a death in life before the death at sea that surely awaited him. So really two deaths. Whereas if Roderick died first, I would be heartbroken, without a doubt devastated, and—at least metaphorically—gutted. But I would probably survive. In fact, if one of us died first, then, in accordance with the age-old law of the seas, the other would be within one's rights to live off the sustenance of his expired companion. A terrible thought, boys, yet that is why we have laws: to keep a grip on our humanity, even in extremis. But I felt certain that Roderick, though preoccupied with food, would not dare eat yours truly. He could barely swallow his own skin crusts. And if he could not bring himself to gnaw the bones of dear old Dick, then he would inevitably perish from hunger.

I checked my calculations and the results, it appeared, were incontrovertible. If we both waited for death to take us, as it surely would in the next day or so, then two men would die. If somehow only I died and Roderick lived, then, as explained above, we would be condemning him to die twice and me once. Thus three deaths—even worse. But if only Roderick died, then your man Dick, albeit feeling bereft and forlorn, would live on (and so, too, would our Junior Adventurers Club and, with it, our rich correspondence). Horrid as Roderick's passing would be, we would have in sum only one death to grieve and all of us could mourn together. The choices then were: three deaths, two deaths, or one. And I don't have to tell you, Junior Adventurers, even the most math-deficient among you, how the reckoning of those numbers works out. If you can save a life, boys, then you must.

"Mother," I said, "let me see that Siamese ax."

"What for?" moaned Roderick, who was sucking a briny thumb and hiding his eyes beneath a scrap of apron.

"I see a fish here near the surface. I think I can get him."

"Let me see!" He pulled the fabric from his face and lurched toward me.

"No, no! Stay very still. We don't want to scare him away. You just give me that ax and stay exactly as you are."

Roderick withdrew the bludgeon from his belt and handed it to me. "I don't think I can last a minute more, Dick. I feel death creeping in."

"It's okay, Roderick. It's okay. Dinner's coming."

"You're always so optimistic, Dick. Do you really think you can catch it?"

"It's going to be tough, but I do."

"Aw, catch us a fish, Dick," said Roderick, lying back down and placing the apron over his scorched eyelids. "Do you remember when we caught those catfish on the Osage?"

"I sure do, Mother. You were afraid they were going to give us worms."

"They were terrible, but you said that was all part of the fun. And then we got ice cream sodas afterward. God, those were good."

"That's it, old boy. Think of those peach floats. The sweet tang of carbonated stone fruit, the creamy delight of that melting vanilla scoop." My voice quavered as I cast a shadow over Roderick's head.

"I sure wish we could have one of them floats now."

"I know, pal. Me too. Me too."

"Life sure is goofy, isn't it, Dick? Say, there's something I should tell you about the N—"

And those, my dear bright boys, were the last words my loyal sidekick spoke before he embarked on his adventure to the great beyond.

I'm afraid that's all the ink I can squeeze out for now. But will write more very soon!

Yours,
Dicky

5

HILDEGARD RAUCH

It was only a short walk from the streetcar line in Berkeley to the Seidlers' house, but it was uphill, and my genie slippers were unforgiving on the graveled drive. I arrived limping, with rocks in my shoes and regret in my heart.

I was in no mood for a party. Playing on a constant loop in my mind were the contents of your belated letter, which had arrived at my door weeks after you wrote it. Scribbled in a barely legible hand on the St. Francis's stationery, like a frantic companion piece to your suicide note:

> *Ildi,*
>
> *Why don't you answer the Telephone? You know I don't believe in Ghosts, but I've just spoken with a Dead Man. It's Dick—him, but not him. I'm scared. If anything happens to me, something you must see to. In the High Priest's Library, behind the Zweig Biographies. Everything you find there—burn it.*
> *~Eiko*

Were you out of your mind on drugs? When did you write this? Before or after you typed your suicide note? If only I had been home to answer the phone, perhaps I could have stopped you and prevented all this madness.

Instead, the only thing I could figure out about this baffling, urgent request was the time lag in my receiving it. And that's because you stupidly addressed it to unit 201 instead of 301. Was it a sign of your delirious state or of how estranged we've become?

Once I realized the error, I rushed downstairs and knocked on 201. And now a portly coffee salesman named Dennis in the flat below is dead set on having me over to listen to his records. All I learned for my efforts was that the letter had arrived sometime in the last two weeks while he was away on business, and only yesterday, upon returning, had he delivered it to me. I'm adding this abortive encounter—and I fear it is the first in a long string of future ones with neighborly Dennis—to your bill of emotional debts.

The next morning I rang Mother and Father, but no one answered. I called the Franks, and Frau Frank informed me that they were in San Diego until Sunday—the High Priest was giving a lecture at the Athenaeum. And, no, she did not have a key to the house. "Do I look like your parents' charwoman?" she shrieked. So I was left cooling my heels until they returned, wondering what the hell was in Father's library and why it needed to be burned, and why you thought you were in danger.

Then, of course, there was the same question as from your suicide note, just as perplexing: Who was this Dick? At least I could now be sure it was a person. Or perhaps, as you said, a ghost or doppelgänger. You seemed to have dropped me into a Hoffmann story. Pretty soon I was going to lose my mind and start smashing violins or learn you've fallen in love with an automaton. Addled as I was, the one thing I knew for certain was that a man was following me. I had seen him again and he was no figment.

I imagined him hiding in the bushes watching me as I emptied my slippers on the front porch of the Seidlers' bungalow, wondering if it was too late to turn around and go home.

"That's why genies fly through the air—to avoid getting pebbles in their shoes."

It was not the imagined creep in the bushes but Walter. Blood dripping from his fangs, cape spread like the wings of a bat. He had discovered me outside his door.

"That's also why people pave their driveways," I said.

"I was beginning to think you weren't going to make it."

"That makes two of us."

"Well, I'm glad you beat the odds."

I had called that morning to get out of it, explaining that I was sorry I would not be able to come to the party because I had to go to Los Angeles at the last minute to see my parents. But Walter said what a perfect coincidence—he, too, was going there, to consult on the new Fisher Museum at USC, which meant I could stay over and the three of us would drive down together the next morning. Stumped for further objections and thoroughly routed, I had no choice but to accept.

"Now, please, come in, my dear," said Walter, switching to a Transylvanian drawl, "and let me drink you—I mean, let me fix you a drink."

The party was in full swing. It was a quaint affair by our old standards but better than I expected for Berkeley. Benny Goodman on the gramophone and a few dozen scholars, radicals, and artists donning masks and dancing off the fetters of civilization.

I was wise to come late. People were long past the agonizing small talk at the sober start of a party and past the collective hand-wringing and useless arguments about how to stop the world from burning. At this point in the evening, their worries had all been drowned in alcohol and set ablaze with carnival spirit.

Walter brought me a martini, and with the first sip, like liquid steel, I felt that perhaps he had been right and a night of drunken dissolution was just what I needed. To escape, for just a few hours, your breathing tubes and your crazy note and my mysterious stalker. I downed the rest of my drink in one gulp.

"Easy, sister. That's not water."

"The next one better not be either," I said, handing Walter my empty glass. He bowed like an obedient butler and went off to make me a fresh one.

I scanned the party for familiar faces. Some were strangers, presumably from the birth-control clinic Nadia worked at or from her various anarchist circles of reading group, vegetable cooperative, and furniture syndicate. But even with the people I knew, the costumes added a layer of disguise and required some decoding. Least among them was the buxom Pocahontas—jitterbugging with the clown Pierrot—whose fringed cleavage immediately identified her as Rosie Adams, the secretary of the Mills College art department. Pierrot, on closer examination, turned out to be Charlie Ingersoll, a Renaissance-painting expert who'd tried to seduce me the first week I arrived on campus and whose horse-faced wife was in the corner, making daggers at Rosie's glorious orbs. The Little Tramp Chaplin-waltzing with a geisha was the master woodcut artist Chiura Obata, who had graciously welcomed me into his studio to watch him pull proofs. Pancho Villa, bandoliered, sombreroed, and sipping punch beneath a mustache that would have made Nietzsche weep with jealousy, was the spritely sculptor Beniamino Bufano. And, though it took me a while to identify them, I was delighted to discover that the Egyptian mummy on the sofa was the anthropologist Alfred Kroeber, beside his pharoah wife, Theodora. You'll recall me gushing about the Kroebers. They're the couple I named when you asked me, if I could select new parents for us, whom I would choose. And a far cry more sincere than your answer—albeit a good one—of Margaret Dumont and Groucho Marx.

I was just beginning to make my way toward them when Walter returned with my drink, in the company of a ghastly witch.

"At last she comes, the countess of *Kultur*, Hildegard Rauch."

"She's a genie, *Schatz*," said Walter, "not a countess."

"Hello, Nadia," I said. "You look . . . bewitching."

"I thought genies are supposed to be little things, like fairies or nymphs. Those long beautiful legs would fit in no lamp I've ever seen."

There it was, that same double-edged tone. At once mocking and flirtatious.

"I am terribly sorry to hear about your brother," she said, putting a long-nailed hand on my arm. "I do hope he wakes up soon."

"Thank you."

"Now, please, we mustn't mope about anymore. Come ruin our rug and dance."

What happened between martini number two and the couch I awoke on the next morning had vanished in a gin-permeated mist. I could see only fragments here and there on an otherwise effaced composition. Dancing—with Nadia and Walter, then with Beniamino, then with who knows? I remember that I tore off my sweaty veil and genie's vest and then—had I? Yes, I had—dunked my head in the ice bowl.

I don't think I ever managed to speak with the Kroebers, which is a shame because I wanted to know if they'd seen my painting at the fair—inspired by Dr. Kroeber's lecture. I had attended his public talk last spring, "On the Meaning of Culture in an Age of Destruction," and was so taken with his roving, compassionate intellect and by his own self-description as "a humanistically tinged natural historian" that I felt compelled to paint him. Dr. Kroeber said the world could learn from the remarkable Yahi Indian man Ishi and his native culture what he had learned from him, which was, as he put it, "how to find a footpath through the lava fields"—creating patterns of harmonious life in the midst of catastrophe. This is what painting means for me, some kind of a bridge between past and future, and it seemed only right that he should have the work he inspired. But I had to first know if he liked it, because nothing is worse than receiving a work of art one dislikes. It's quite possible the Kroebers had expressed their enthusiasm too, but I had no recollection of speaking to them. All I could muster was a hazy memory of looking into Dr. Kroeber's mummified face on the deck when someone handed me a dope-laced cigarette. Had I smoked it? Naturally. Which is why, along with however many martinis had gone down the hatch, my memory had become so unstitched.

It's hard to believe I used to enjoy that scattered feeling of hash on the heels of a spree, the way it chopped up the linear perception of time and tossed it in the air like confetti. That is how I remember Berlin—intoxicated fragments strewn on the floor of my brain. You and I would perform our cabaret act at the Stork's Nest, sober save for a couple of brandies to loosen us up and a Benzedrine to keep us sharp. Then afterward Rautenberg stood us all drinks—I don't recall ever being paid in any other currency. When my energy had peaked and I felt like I was heading for a crash, that's when I'd smoke hashish and sink into a languid, blissful netherworld, only to come to hours later to find little shreds of memory.

But then you began your eternal quest for more—upping the dosage, more booze, more pills, more powder. The party never stopped for you, such that our act grew worse by the night. You forgot your lines. You showed up late or with a black eye after a lovers' spat or a mugging, or, as it sometimes happened, both. And then you discovered morphine and decided to make that your sole muse for a while, until settling back into a more catholic regimen. Meanwhile, Rautenberg canceled our act, and all our plans for conquering the world together were put on hold. I didn't realize that it would be not just a hiatus on our creative collaboration but the end of it.

Witnessing your descent certainly dampened my zest for the chemical life. Though even in my party days, I knew that I was plodding along a path that I would not stray from. Drink and drugs, like men and women, would be my occasional companions on this road, something by which to refresh or amuse or briefly erase myself, but the journey I was on was mine and mine alone.

I know what you would say. You would accuse me of the same cold self-absorption as that of the High Priest, for whom the world is either the unleavened raw material of his art or merely the noise outside his library door. And that his newfound political voice as the defender of humanism—freedom, democracy, *Bildung*—is just an aesthetic posture, a work of artifice and thinly transfigured ego, just like his novels. And then you would call me an aesthete, indicting my paintings as rearguard works of Expressionism—an irresponsible escape into subjective emotion and the world of dreams.

But just look where ideological commitments have gotten us. Need I remind you that until recently, I, too, used to join you in shouting myself hoarse about the evils of fascism? If our trips to Ethiopia and Spain taught me anything, it's that most of the world doesn't really care, and the ones who do often have ulterior motives. Now even Stalin, supposedly the stalwart of the Popular Front and the vanguard of human liberation, has become Hitler's dinner companion, dining out on a Poland-for-two. If you ask me—and I find it indicative of your increasing dogmatism that you refused to talk about it—the Nazi–Soviet alliance reveals the fundamental likeness that was there all along: two tyrants at last aligned, feeding on lies and blood.

Personally, I've taken it as the cue for my stage exit from politics. My time is better spent trying to find sponsors and visas for the real people in danger, which I do in the face of truly dispiriting results.

Otherwise, I prefer to be painting. But I will not compromise my art by turning it into a broadsheet. Art should not shout; it should resonate. So if an entire civilization is going to sleepwalk off the cliff, as it seems certain to, then I will use my final moments before being carried off to remain awake, bearing witness to my bewilderment.

I dimly recalled engaging in some form of this dispute with Nadia last night. Only, at the point in the argument where you and I would go round in circles, treading over the same ground until we got bored or angry or made each other laugh, Nadia and I dissolved our argument in the haze of another marijuana cigarette.

But what else had I told her, I wondered, as I came to on the Seidlers' couch. I winced at a thought of babbling about your incomprehensible letter and hoped it was not a real memory. My head was pounding, and the sour taste of refluxed gin and tobacco rose in my throat. Along with it came another thought, through some pathway the booze must have unblocked. Staggeringly, I'd never pondered it until then: *If anything happens to me, something you must see to.* Were those the words of a man on the brink of suicide? Was *if anything happens to me* your euphemism for suicide? Yet you claim to hate euphemisms. So who or what were you scared of?

It was all an absurd mess, just as my decision to come to the party last night now struck me. I should be in Los Angeles already, finding whatever it was I was supposed to find on Father's shelf. It had been kind of Walter to offer to drive me, but at that moment I just wanted to get on a train and go.

Hoping to make my getaway before anyone came downstairs, I went to the closet to collect my overnight bag. I had just laid hands on my valise, with my head in the coats and my ass sticking up in the air, when I heard Nadia thud down the steps.

"Praise be," she said. "The dead have risen!"

6

To: The Dicky Halifax Junior Adventurers Club
From: Dicky Halifax
Aboard the *Tonan Maru*
Plowing the High Seas for Whale Meat

Summer 1939

Dear boys,

I know my last letter must have shaken you to the core and sent some of you running for your mother's skirts. Roderick was my loyal batman and oldest friend. Could I really be so heartless as to club him over the head and cut him up for steaks?

I'm ashamed to say I got as far as raising the ax, but I couldn't do it. There I was, blade overhead, Roderick lying lamb-gentle and still, my whole body trembling. Call it moral restraint, weakness of will, or, better, just plain friendship, but I could not bring that evil ax down on Roderick's noggin. I was stuck. And sometime during my paralysis—I can't say how long it lasted, seconds? minutes? days?—Roderick slipped his mortal coil. It was only when a gust of wind blew the rag from his face and roused me from my trance that I saw my friend was dead.

So, no, I wasn't heartless, boys. I was wrecked. Roderick had been my sidekick ever since summer camp. We'd seen the world together and laughed and cried into his perfect dry martinis more times than I care to admit. He had an amazing gift for knowing how to squeeze milk from a stone and keep our adventures afloat. If it weren't for him, I'd be dead broke, lying in the gutter somewhere. Or, worse, I'd have given up on the life of adventure altogether and become a dead-eyed academic, stuck in a department meeting arguing over the merits of some weak sister's dissertation or some wheedling egomaniac's bid for tenure.

The thing is, boys, and it's hard to communicate this in a letter to you Junior Adventurers, but the fact of the matter is it takes only a few unlucky breaks for a man to feel backed into a corner. The will to survive is a beast that, when circumstances demand, tears the coat and trousers of our humanity to shreds. In other words, boys, I loved Roderick like I loved my own brother. But I was damn hungry.

And if there's one thing I've learned about the *corpus humanum*, it's that when the cooperative spirit of the body breaks down and the organs become locked in a *bellum omnium contra omnes*, the gut will always devour the heart. And if you don't think I chewed my own heart to pieces while I feasted on the plump beefsteak of Roderick's ticker, then you don't know all the pain that lurks beneath the hard-won optimism of your pal Dick.

You also can't imagine how addled the sun-poisoned brain of a starving man becomes. Long before I dug into Roderick like ole Ugolino chowing down on his own sons, my gut had already gnawed off large hunks of Halifax Gray Matter. I could barely remember my own name, and when I tried to rattle off the list of U.S. presidents, I kept getting stuck at Buster Keaton. That's when I knew I was cruising into the realm of *non compos mentis* (though, strangely, my school Latin seemed to have returned with a vigor). How else could I account for the fact that never once in my delirium did I notice that the submerged portions of our bed-raft were coated in barnacles that, when plucked and cracked with the ax, were nourishing and delicious? Sadly, it was only after I'd drunk several pints of Roderick's blood that I came to this realization. Bitter wisdom indeed.

The more I ate of Roderick, the more my wits returned, fitfully, like a flickering fire, along with a rising horror at my deed. In fact, I was so busy stuffing my face with Mother's rib meat and crying tearless heaves that I didn't notice the Japanese whaler appear on the horizon. It must have approached for several miles before I heard its horn.

The low reedy bellow made me recall the sweet serenade of the *duduk* at an Armenian wedding I once attended. It was deep in the Caucasus, where these mountain folk and their ancient ways remained undisturbed by the bloodbaths of the recent past—no marauding Turks, no collectivizing apparatchiks, just a nervous groom, a raven-haired bride dressed in all her dowry finest, and a hundred swarthy relatives drowning in Georgian sweet wine. How beautiful life is, I thought, as I raised my glass to toast the happy couple. That's when my reverie broke and I came to, hoisting Roderick's humerus and looking at the squinting faces of the crew lined up along the gunwale of the *Tonan Maru*.

The *Tonan Maru* was a whaler, but to conjure the right image of it, boys, you must dismiss from your mind all associations of Nantucket and New Bedford and the glory days of the *Pequod*. No sir, this whaling ship, with its tangle of steel towers and looming smokestacks, looked like a modern factory. Not a scrap of sail or splinter of wood to be found. Instead, a floating tryworks bobbed five stories over the salvaged bunk of the *Soup Dumpling*, belching black fumes. I watched, stupefied, as a boat slipped down a ramp in the stern and four Nipponese whalemen paddled out to meet me.

I was, of course, profoundly relieved to be rescued. And it's a good thing the Jap whaler showed up when it did, because the sharks had begun to circle, and it wouldn't have been long before both Roderick and I would have become meat for another gut. But upon seeing the crew's stricken faces, I felt self-conscious and deeply embarrassed to be receiving guests into such an untidy home. It had been only two days since I'd begun my grisly banquet, but I had made quite a mess of the old boy. I looked like I had just pigged out on Kansas City barbecue and forgotten my napkin.

Warily, and with much shouting among them, the sailors took me aboard their dinghy and returned to the mother ship. I was hosed off on the try deck, which was stained pink with the blood of a thousand whales and now that of my dearest friend as it ran from my beard and arms and collected in puddles astern. All the while the crew fixed me with looks of aghast curiosity.

One of them brought me water and a ball of rice stuffed with pickled radish, which I ate, though to be honest I was feeling pretty stuffed. As I choked down that water and rice ball, safely aboard ship and surrounded by my fellow man, I thought, So I will live, and the story will continue. Then I became very woozy and the pink deck came spinning up to catch me.

I awoke in a dark, airless cabin. The brig, I suppose it was. There was a gamey, fetid smell about the place, no doubt from all the disarticulated whale carcass in the ship's hold. I hollered for one of the crew to come let me out, as I felt a powerful urge to urinate. It was the first time I'd had to drain the hair snake in more than a week, and the familiar sensation felt like an old friend back from a long stay in the hospital. I banged on the door and summoned the few Japanese phrases I could recall from my trip up Mount Fuji. *"Toire onegaishimasu! Herupu arigato!"*

I went on like this for some time, until suddenly a voice came from the corner. "Don't waste your breath, Dick. This *is* the toilet."

"Who's there?" I asked, frightened, for I had believed I was alone and didn't see anything in the corner but darkness.

"Don't you recognize your own best friend, Dick? Why, you've still got bits of me stuck between your teeth."

"Roderick?"

"Unless you've eaten anyone else."

"But it can't be. You're . . ." I felt my grip on sanity starting to slip.

"Oh, keep yourself together, Dick. You really think you're only now in danger of losing your mind?"

"But I'm talking to a figment!"

"That's the least of your troubles, pal."

"What do you mean?"

"I mean, these Japs are going to make whale meat out of you."

"That doesn't even make sense, Roderick. Besides, you're the one who's blubbery."

"Lucky for you, Dick. Had I hewed to your bulimic ideal, I would have hardly provided enough nourishment to sustain you."

"Roderick, truly, I'm sorry. I feel rotten about it. I should never have teased you for becoming a fatty. And the sound of that ax biting into your flesh will haunt me for the rest of my days."

"But you would do it again, wouldn't you?"

"What? No!"

"So you wish you were dead now, the two of us drowned in our sea bed and gobbled up by sharks?"

"Well, no, I suppose not."

"Then have the courage of conviction to stand by your actions. I died to save you, Dick. So that you could eat me and live."

"I didn't even know that was possible, Roderick. I thought death and erections were the two things beyond the powers of sheer will."

"That's what makes me the sidekick and you the hero."

"You mean you wouldn't have eaten me?"

"You know I wouldn't."

"So does that make you a better person than me?"

"Aw, stuff. It just makes us different."

"But, still, Roderick, I almost murdered you. You don't realize how close I came."

"Oh, Dick. You really think I believed you were going to catch a fish with that ax?"

"You mean you knew?"

"I may have let myself get a little thick around the middle, but I'm not stupid."

"So you were going to let me kill you?"

"I would have, Dick. But it was easier for both of us if I just let go. I'm better off dead and you're better off alive."

"You really think so, Mother?"

"You know what they say: Mother knows best."

I thought on this for a while. Was Roderick absolving me of guilt?

"But, Roderick, I'm still concerned about the metaphysics of this conversation."

"You needn't worry, Dick. I am in you now. My flesh is your flesh. My spirit is entwined with your own."

"If I didn't know better, Roderick, I'd say you were a Papist."

The figment spat in contempt, which confirmed my test of authenticity. Roderick had a lifelong antipathy to Catholics—I never could determine why—along with Freemasons, Jews, Jehovah's Witnesses, bohunks . . . Well, come to think of it, just about everyone.

"Laugh while you can, Dick. Things are going to get worse before they get better. My death was only the initiation."

"What? What do you mean? How do you know?"

As you may have heard me say over the years, boys, Roderick was a keen reader of situations. With his catastrophist's eye, he could gauge the risks attendant upon any enterprise and spot disaster hiding in plain sight. Now, as for making judgments on how best to manage those risks and devise an optimal course of action, he was worthless, for Roderick saw only the worst-case scenario. But he could present you with a whole briefcase of bad possible outcomes that would have eluded your less imaginative captain of industry. For instance, he could look at a factory floor or a set of blueprints and in a trice tell you how one might unwittingly start a gas fire and blow the whole operation sky high. Or how a gap in the security protocol exposed one to risks of theft. This skill had served him well in his career as a risk assessor in munitions factories and is what made him such a high-level inspector in his recent tenure at the Norden plant.

So when Roderick said the crew of the *Tonan Maru* had ill designs on me and I was in for the business, I took notice. Granted, he had made several such dark predictions about my voyage plans for the *Soup Dumpling*, which I had taken in stride and largely ignored. But I made it a habit to hear the man out before neglecting his counsel, just as he made it a habit to wax catastrophic before deferring to my authority. Ah, boys, if you come by a sidekick as good as Roderick, think damn hard before you eat him.

"What do you mean your death was only the initiation, Roderick?"

"It was a gift to harden you to the ordeal to come."

"Yes, but what ordeal?"

"That's for you to find out, Dick," he said in a fading echo.

I sensed that his figment was dissipating. "Wait, Roderick, don't go! There's one last thing. You died before you could finish your final thought. You said: 'There's something I should tell you about the N—' The N-what? The next life? The nautical charts you'd been studying when the storm hit? Come on, man, out with it!"

But Roderick's shade spake no more. I moved to embrace him, or, more precisely, the core of darkness where his voice emanated from, but while my arms, predictably, caught only air, my feet stumbled over an inert mass.

I heard a low groan and saw a figure emerge from the shadows.

"Roderick?" I asked. "Have you reclaimed corporeal form?"

But instead of Roderick, I saw the contours of a much sullied bucket and the beleaguered face of our little cabin boy, Nacho Fu.

Well, I guess that will have to do for now, boys. The whalers have 'pooned them a big one, and they need old Dick to help harvest the sperm!

Yours in adventure,
Dicky

To: The Dicky Halifax Junior Adventurers Club
From: Dicky Halifax
Aboard the *Tonan Maru*
Tutoring a New Sidekick

Summer 1939

Dear boys,

While Roderick, or rather his figment, had been very forgiving of all that had passed between us, our cabin boy, Nacho Fu, seemed to bear your man Dick a grudge. And despite his skinny boy-limbs and much wasted state, that little half-caste fought like a rabid wolverine.

Upon seeing me in the hold of the *Tonan Maru*, Nacho launched himself at my chest. I had braced myself for a lonely boy's grateful hug, but the little hellion chomped down on my ear before I could throw him off.

"Nacho, you runty demon," I shouted. "What's gotten into you? Don't you recognize me? It's me, Dick—your beloved captain!"

He stared at me. I suppose I looked different, given my shock-white hair and my skin burnt to a scabrous crust. Even my own voice, I noticed, sounded strange and growly. I supposed the acid from my several draughts of urine, followed by a very long period of thirst, had corroded my vocal cords.

"Captain Dicky?" he said.

"That's right, son!"

He came at me again, fangs bared and madder than ever, but this time I gave him the ole Princeton haymaker and laid him out flat.

I pinned his arms behind his back and sat astride him like he was a hobbyhorse.

"You evil man!" he shouted. "You left me to drown!"

"Not so, Nacho," I protested. "You've got it all wrong. We tried to rescue you."

It occurred to me that if we had in fact rescued him, my beloved sidekick would still be alive and the two of us would have made quick work of our ill-tempered cabin boy. Though, compared to the juicy rib eye of Roderick, Nacho would have made for pretty slim pickings.

"I hate you, Captain Dicky."

"You're just hungry and tired, Nacho. I won't take it personally." I asked him if he had seen any of the Dartmouth lads. He shook his head. "Well, I suppose they died a sailor's death. Poor boys."

Nacho chortled derisively. "I'm glad they're dead."

"Now, now, Nacho," I said. "You shouldn't speak ill of the dead."

"How is that speaking ill? They are dead. And I am happy. Isn't it good to make people happy?"

Clearly, the Portuguese part of him had a flair for Jesuit casuistry. "Well, it's still very rude."

I gleaned that Nacho didn't take kindly to the pranks the collegians had subjected him to. What can I say, boys? Some folks simply aren't born with a funny bone. My advice to you is grow one! And if that fails, become a priest.

Once Nacho calmed down, I let him out of the Halifax Half Nelson and asked how he'd fared since we'd parted and how he found himself aboard the *Tonan Maru*. He wasn't much of a yarn spinner, but I got it out of him in sulky spurts. Apparently, Nacho had floated on that water cask for three days, perched up there like a monkey riding a baseball, before the Japs came across him. He was in bad shape, having been driven to the brink of sanity by the tantalizing predicament of sitting atop a hogshead of fresh drinking water yet being unable to get at it for so much as a sip. He'd scratched at it till his fingernails tore out, then sucked his little bloody stumps in consolation. That was how the harpoon boat found him. From a distance, they must've thought the cask with Nacho's ruined hands laid over it was a wounded humpback and been shocked and disappointed to discover otherwise.

They hauled Nacho back to the ship, gave him the rice-ball-and-water treatment, and threw him in the brig. But as he revived, some of the whalers began paying him furtive visits, and not kindly ones. Nacho didn't want to say—and it's not fit for young boys like you to hear—but let's just say old Dicky knows how to read the signs, and it was some foul funny business indeed. The kind that priests and prisoners get up to, as well as lonesome sailors and even some Hollywood actors. But Nacho wasn't eatin' what they were servin', or rather he was and he'd had his fill. That is to say, he must've got sick of having his holes plugged, 'cause the next harpooner that came for him left two inches shorter than he'd arrived, with Nacho spitting out the business tip of a Japanese sausage.

This did nothing to enamor Nacho to his saviors and captors. Instead, they beat him senseless, cut his rice-ball portions by half, and locked him in the brig to rot. He'd been languishing there for a week by the time I arrived. All things considered, then, I had to cut Nacho some slack for his prickly demeanor and my less-than-warm reception.

"Don't you worry, Nacho," I told him, while he shivered in the corner in a lifeless heap. "I won't let anybody lay a hand on you."

I knew there had to be an inkling of humanity in those Jap whalers' pickled hearts, or else they would have just tossed Nacho overboard, drowned him like any wharf rat. Instead, they were still sharing their rice with him. But I soon learned that, while the man-boy handling had stopped, the crew of the *Tonan Maru* had further designs on us. The day after my arrival, they put us to work swabbing the deck and greasing the gears in the boiler room. Never mind that Nacho and I barely had strength to stand. The first mate kicked our rumps and slapped our ears if we showed the slightest signs of flagging. The beatings were not heavy, but they were constant and without mercy. Our only respite was when a whale was sighted; then we were locked in the brig and kept out of the way for the duration of the hunt. But if the harpooners were successful, then the real work began.

The *Tonan Maru* was, as I mentioned, a whale-processing factory unto itself. The great sea beast was winched onto the flensing floor and, in a matter of hours, rendered into vats of oil, spermaceti, and ambergris. Mechanized as this process was, with steel cables, drills, and a frighteningly colossal band saw, harvesting whale still took a lot of manpower. Without knowing the first thing about the craft, and receiving precious little instruction save for a hard boot in the keister, Nacho and I found ourselves neck-high in whale guts. A nauseating sight, especially as it called to mind guilty memories of Roderick. Back and forth we carted the unwanted bowels from the carcass to the ship's bow, where we dumped them into the sea and wondered when, and if, our apprenticeship would ever end.

Over the course of our servitude, Nacho and I became pals. At first it was more of a détente, in that he stopped trying to attack me and less frequently told me that he hated me and that the *Soup Dumpling* was the single stupidest expedition ever launched in the history of mankind. I gently reminded him that the annals of exploration were riddled with spectacular failures—Scott in Antarctica, Cabeza de Vaca in the American South, the Franklin expedition in search of the Northwest Passage.

"Besides, Nacho, my boy, you've got seafaring in the blood. What would your proud Lusitanian forebears say to hear you quail in the face of shipwreck?"

"I wouldn't know, Dicky," said Nacho, his voice laced with that sarcasm that, frankly, boys, I find ugly. "My mother was a Hainanese concubine bought by my 'proud Lusitanian forebear,' who dismissed her from his house when she became pregnant."

"Now, now, Nacho, you know what the immortal Ben Jonson said: *Sarcasm is the last refuge of scoundrels.*"

"That was Samuel Johnson, you moron, and it's patriotism. *Patriotism is the last refuge of scoundrels.*"

The little wharf rat was too clever by half. Remember what I always say, boys. Reading is good for putting muscles on your brain, but nobody likes a smarty-pants. And I can't help but wonder if it was Nacho's precociousness that attracted the sexual advances of his seniors. In other words, boys, don't act the show-off, or you just might get raped.

Eventually, though, a sense of camaraderie bloomed from our shared ordeal. We would lie on our respective patches of linoleum and tell each other about past adventures and future dreams. Nacho had been orphaned at a young age and, as I suspected, had been schooled by the Macanese outpost of the Society of Jesuits. They filled him with Greek, Latin, English, and French, which, in addition to his native Portuguese, Macanese, and Cantonese, had swelled his brain and stunted his character. His soul proved too squinty and irascible even for the Jesuits, so they turned him loose, and for the last five years he'd earned his crusts as a deckhand and cabin boy, bobbing around the harbors of Canton and Hong Kong and sneaking into the City Hall library to feed his book habit. Nacho knew his way around boats, though he had no great love for the sea. He said he'd rather have been a barrister or a scholar, but, given that those paths were out of reach for someone of his station, he was thinking of going into trade unionism, organizing the longshoremen, shipwrights, and merchant marines.

"Careful, Nacho. That sounds like communism. You won't win any friends following that road to perdition, except for maybe Leon Trotsky and ole Koba Joe. That is, unless you're a big fat teddy-bear charmer like my pal Diego, who can all at once paint your rich daddy, bed your sweet sister, and keep the whole family laughing about the liquidation of the bourgeoisie."

I tried to turn the little swotter's mind to more healthful pursuits like badminton, horse racing, and the high dive. "With a few pointers in form, Nacho, a svelte boy like you would cut the water like a knife." I told him that as soon as the Japs gave us a break from our labors, I'd show him how to take the Dicky Plunge. I'd developed it at Princeton in my swim-club days and showcased it around the world, from the crags of the wine-dark Aegean to the cliffs of Acapulco.

Nacho rolled his eyes, as only a teenager can. "They're not going to give us a break, Dicky. Not for your stupid diving lessons or any other reason."

"Oh, cheer up, my moody pubescent friend. Sure they will. Eventually this ship will put to port and then they'll have to let us go."

"First of all, Dicky, I'm twenty-two. And second, how can you be so naïve? They can do whatever they want with us. We're their prisoners."

With his dark fears and foreboding, the boy sounded like a regular Roderick. "They're fishermen, Nacho. As ill-bred as these Nippers are, they're not at war—that is, unless you're a whale."

"What about that man in the navy uniform who is always standing on the bridge while we work?"

"That's the ship captain, naturally."

"No, not the captain—the man wearing a line officer's cap and the shoulder boards of a lieutenant commander of the Japanese Imperial Navy."

"Nacho, what have I told you about deluging people with arcane knowledge? Not everyone has read books about Japanese naval insignia, nor cares to."

Nacho protested that he hadn't learned it in a book but rather from years of running from the Japanese navy along the coast of southern China. But I told him there was no use worrying about the import of anyone's uniform or the shape of the future. We'd just have to take things one day at a time.

The next day we sighted land. We'd been pursuing a southerly course throughout, and by my calculations we must have been somewhere north of New Guinea and east of the Philippines. Given the rising sun flapping from the harbor tower of the naval base as we approached, I guessed it was likely the Jap-controlled Marianas.

The *Tonan Maru*, we've just learned, has made its final whaling voyage, and we the last men to spill whale guts over its bow. It is now being commandeered as a vessel of the Imperial Navy, which means we're getting off here. Damned if that smarty-pants wharf rat wasn't right again.

Sure hope these letters are reaching you, boys!

Yours in adventure,
Dicky

8

HILDEGARD RAUCH

Walter was too hungover to drive, so he crawled into the back seat and slept while Nadia steered us down the California freeway, toward either Los Angeles in record time or, as seemed more likely, a grisly death. The woman took curves at hair-raising speeds and insisted on looking more at me beside her than at the road. The only time she slowed down, and ever so slightly, was to light a new cigarette from the end of her old one, which, on account of the road's bumpiness or her residual tremors from alcohol, required her to remove both hands from the wheel.

The second time she pulled this stunt, I grabbed the wheel to prevent us from careening into the guardrail. "Do you think you might slow down a bit, Nadia?"

She laughed. "Sure, if you want to give time for that tail to catch up to us."

"Tail?" I asked, confused.

"*Dein Schatten.* That shadow of yours is what the Americans call a tail."

"But . . . how did you know?"

"What can I say? My English is better than yours."

"No, I mean how did you know I have a tail?"

"Because I got a lovely view of your rear end this morning. You also mentioned it last night, and sure enough he was there after breakfast, yawning in his Packard."

It was as I'd feared. Drunk Voluble Hilde had said too much. "Is he still following us?"

"Not at the moment, unless you want me to slow down."

"No. Go ahead. But, please, Nadia, let me light your cigarettes."

"I thought you'd never ask, sweetie."

I regarded Nadia as she punched the gas. She had removed her costume, but something of the witch remained. In profile, her face was all sharp angles—brow, nose, and chin looming over the steering column. But her eyes, close together and deeply set, seemed concealed, like they were retreating even when piercing you with their gaze. From the neck down, her sharpness softened into a more matronly girth, her figure having already passed, in subdued fashion, through the brutal chrysalis from lithe nymph to turnip sack. And yet, even with thickened ankles, she exuded an unsettling sinuous air.

"How did you know the man in the Packard was the one following me?" I asked.

"Oh, please. I can smell these Hoover dicks a mile away."

"Hoover dicks?"

"Federales. American Cheka. The FBI."

"Why would the FBI be following me?"

"Any number of reasons. One, you're a foreigner. Two, you're a refugee. Three, you're a Jew. Four, you're the daughter of Theodor Rauch, the leading voice of German opposition to Hitler. Five, according to some, you're what they call a sexual deviant. And, on top of that, or rather because of all that, they naturally assume you're a communist."

"That's ridiculous. I'm no communist."

"No, as you made perfectly clear last night, you are a bourgeois little *Künstlerin*, clinging to empty ideals like humanism, thinking you are somehow above the fray. The spitting image of your dear father. Now, of course I know all that, but these Hoover dicks don't know anything beyond their own hat brims. They're used to busting up union strikes and Chinese gambling rings or catching young lovers crossing state lines."

Walter emitted a groan from the back seat, but when I looked at him, he appeared still to be asleep.

"How do you know all this, Nadia?"

"Because, silly, I'm an anarchist. Not to mention I help women from becoming involuntary breeding machines. You see, those of us who went to Spain have been marked for life. If I weren't an American citizen, they probably would have deported me by now. So your tail in the Packard might be mine. They swap them out every so often. Now, tell me, did you ever go to Spain?"

"Yes, early in the war. Eiko and I went to raise humanitarian aid."

"Aha!" said Nadia. "To the FBI that translates to, 'My brother and I went to Spain as agents of Moscow to wage worldwide revolution.'"

"That's absurd. So the FBI is following me because I oppose fascism?"

"Now you're catching on, *ketzeleh*. But, tell me, what have you been up to lately that would make them suddenly take an interest in you? Any new associations, new friends? Join any new clubs?"

I told her that I'd begun writing letters for the German Jewish Children's Aid, ever since the Wagner–Rogers Bill languished in Congress. Twenty thousand children it could have saved, but that would have required raising the quotas on Jews. Then I mentioned that since you had been in the hospital, all your mail for *The Reckoning* had been coming to my flat.

"*Ach so!* Then you are both a refugee smuggler and an associate of a notorious leftist émigré journal. Tell me, where does your brother get his funding for this journal?"

"Mostly from subscribers, I think, plus a few donors from my father's rivals, who stepped in after he pulled his funding." Of course Nadia inquired why he had pulled his endorsement, so I told her about the recent feud between you and the High Priest, the editorial you signed his name to without asking, the retraction he demanded and you refused, and the scolding letter he published in response—all the drama I've tried to keep at arm's length.

After a stop for pea soup at Andersen's, Walter went back to sleep and Nadia continued to pepper me with more questions, more "tell mes," as though I were her hypnotized patient. And while I sensed that Nadia was asking rather a lot of questions, and generally I prefer to be the one asking, I was too hungover, as well as stunned by the news that the FBI was now watching my every move, to take over the interrogation. So I simply answered her questions. I told her how I had seriously turned to painting in Berlin at the ripe old age of twenty-four, then in Paris for two years, and finally in Vienna, after I went back to pull Mother and Father out—a yearlong process of convincing and foot-dragging, helped along by a failed kidnapping attempt that finally woke them up and got them on a ship to Shanghai, then on to California. I told Nadia how you were already in Los Angeles by then, typing words and taking pills, taking pills and typing words, writing your embittered and ignored novellas, writing your film treatments and scripts that never made it to screen, corralling all your disappointment and failure into the idea of a journal that would, you hoped, blow down the walls of both philistine American culture and the oversophisticated elite culture of the émigrés to inaugurate a new era of freethinking literary socialism for all.

"Tell me," said Nadia, "does your brother have contacts in China?"

"China? I have no idea. Why do you ask?"

"You mentioned that your parents came east through Shanghai. I happen to know some Poles and Russians there. They're surrounded by Japanese soldiers and looking to make connections with their fellow refugees who've ended up in sunnier climes. They'd love to come to California, but of course America only lets in a thousand immigrants from the East each year, even if they're white as snow with noses like Eleanor of Aquitaine."

I gave honest answers to Nadia's questions all the way to the Santa Monica Mountains, when she asked why I was going to visit Mother and Father. "Walter said it was urgent—is everything okay?"

I told her that Mother had fallen and sprained her ankle—the first lie that came into my head—but that she was fine, I was just looking after them for a couple of days.

"What a sweet little bourgeois daughter you are, Hildchen. Now, tell me, when do you go back to San Francisco? Perhaps we can give you a lift."

"Very kind of you," I said, "but I'm not yet sure when I'll return." I had decided eight hours of Nadia's interview was enough.

9

To: The Dicky Halifax Junior Adventurers Club
From: Dicky Halifax
Captive in Saipan
Fighting for His Life

Summer 1939

Dear boys,

This is where the story starts to get hairy. Of all the close scrapes
I've had, all the times I blundered into a hornets' nest or was caught
taking pictures of military installations on Gibraltar or got dragged
to a pretty lady's bed only to find I was flaccid as a gym sock, this
one took the cake. Surviving the wreckage of the *Soup Dumpling*
and swabbing out whale carcass had been a Sunday picnic compared
to the pickle your Dicky found himself in with the Jap navy. They
might be small, but make no mistake: Those boys are some tough
customers.

Now, before I explain what happened to me and Nacho, let me say
this: I've visited Japan before—once to climb Mount Fuji in winter,
and just recently to Yokohama to secure a right of safe passage for
the *Soup Dumpling*. On both occasions I was treated with the utmost
respect, though on this last visit I was forced to cede my place in
line at the maritime office to a shipload of Hitler Youth, who had
just arrived for what appeared to be an urgent student-exchange
program. In any event, Japanese hospitality is legendary—bows,
smiles, declarations of lifelong indebtedness simply for having come
to one's shop to slurp noodles or buy an ice ax. Never have I felt so

well attended to, almost revered. Granted, there had been a large betting pool about whether I would freeze or fall to my death on the slopes of Fuji-san. But at least when they were dealing with me face-to-face—or, as it were, face-to-navel—they were paragons of graciousness.

I guess that graciousness doesn't export well, because the Jap soldiers here are even meaner than those crusty salts on the *Tonan Maru*. We were led off the ship with slaps, received on the pier and loaded onto a lorry with punches, and welcomed into our internment camp with slaps, punches, and kicks.

The camp was just a patch of mud and weeds fenced in by split bamboo. A tarp suspended over filthy thatched mats served as the barracks, which were unfortunately only ten yards from an evil-smelling, overflowing trench that was clearly the latrine.

"Makes you just about pine for our bucket in the whaler brig, doesn't it, Nacho?"

Nacho didn't respond. I couldn't tell if he was just in a foul mood or in shock. Or maybe one of those Jap welcome fists had caught him on the chin.

No other prisoners were in the camp when we arrived, just two guards with goofy hats, short clubs, and sabers. I caught the eye of the one closer to me and, though I wagered my English wouldn't land, I pleaded my case as best I could.

"Look here, chief, I'm afraid there's been a mistake. My name is Richard Halifax. The author-adventurer? Halifax? Famous writer? I'm something of a household name. I, rather we," I said, pointing at Nacho, "sail on ship, the *Soup Dumpling*. Start Hong Kong, go all way to America. United States of America, my home. We go on ship, but big storm come. Lightning, thunder, monsoon, typhoon, tsunami, yes, yes, big tsunami come and wreck ship. That's why we in ocean when *Tonan Maru* find us. You understand?"

The guard, who appeared to be taking some of this in as I spoke, stepped forward and bashed me in the face with his club. *"Damare!"* Not sure exactly what that means, but I've come to learn it is what one says after hitting someone in the face.

Figuring I'd better not try my luck with the other guard, I sat down beside Nacho and watched the blood pour from my nose.

At sundown, the other prisoners returned to camp. As I would soon learn, they were out mining phosphate for a twelve-hour stretch, which explained why they looked nearly as bad as we did. They were all Orientals, mostly Japanese, but I heard a couple of other languages being muttered as the men dragged themselves back to the barracks and began boiling water for their dinner of discarded rice.

"Nacho, wake up, lad. Do my ears deceive me or are those boys in the corner speaking Cantonese?"

Nacho listened for a moment. "It's Hokkien. They're from Formosa."

"Close enough, my friend! Let's go talk to them."

I was confident we could get a game of telephone going. Surely some of those boys spoke Japanese too, which meant if Nacho told them our story they could inform the authorities of our wrongful imprisonment.

But when Nacho narrated this to the Formosans, who relayed it to the rest of the prisoners, the reaction was general laughter. Everyone here, it turned out, was wrongfully imprisoned. Some for illegally fishing in the waters of the South Seas Mandate of Japan, some for deserting from their military post and hiding out in the geisha parlors in town, and some for trying to duck out of their contracted labor in the sugarcane fields of the South Seas Development Company.

"No offense, gentlemen," I said, "but mild as those transgressions sound, they do seem vaguely like violations of the law. I, on the other hand, am guilty of nothing other than trying to sail a traditional Chinese junk across the Pacific and bring joy to millions of boy readers."

Nacho didn't bother translating for me. But he did manage to get a rusty tin cup of watery rice husks for us to share. Over our meal, one of the Formosans informed Nacho of our location. Turns out we were in a penal camp attached to a naval garrison on the island of Saipan, a hundred miles north of Guam and at the far-flung frontier of Japan's southern empire.

"Aha!" I said, pumping my fist in victory.

"What could possibly excite you about that news?" asked Nacho.

"I guessed we were in the Marianas. Looks like the ole Halifax Compass is still tickin'."

"Compasses don't tick, Dicky."

"And nigglers don't survive long in prison camps!" I said a bit testily. You wouldn't believe how short a man's temper is when he's fed only rice, boys. In fact, I had been having recurring fantasies of gnawing on a great big joint of beef, only to realize with horror what I was remembering.

In moments like these, I missed Roderick. And not just eating him, but his company too. I couldn't help but think that he would have been a more helpful companion in suffering than my surly little half-caste. Not only could Roderick endure my adventures and what some critics have called my "irrepressible effervescence." He also possessed many talents: gastronomy, risk assessment, arms procurement, a passionate interest in his Germanic heritage, and, most of all, a criminal mastermind's flair for theft. Ever since he stole those ice cream floats from the drugstore counter, I'd been feeding off his sticky fingers. Case in point, I'd never have been able to sell those antiques to the Chinese if it weren't for him, or appear like a bona fide arms dealer to that sour Englishman in Bangkok. It was a crying shame I'd missed the chance to capitalize on Roderick's pièce de résistance—a little souvenir he took with him from the Norden plant. Yessir, your Dick could have been a rich man if he'd played things differently. But you mustn't dwell on the past, boys, or wallow in the could-have-been.

I apologized to Nacho for snapping at him, said it was just the hunger talking. I told him not to worry and that we were going to get through this ordeal in one piece. "After all," I said, "we're in this together."

Then the garrison commandant and his officers entered the campground, followed by guards carrying cane chairs and a foldable dais, which they erected near the mud pit. The commandant and his officers took their seats and gestured toward us.

"Hallelujah!" I shouted. "See, Nacho, these men will hear our case. Bring that Formosan, and have him translate for the head honcho."

But as I moved toward the dais, I received another club blow. The guard pushed me toward the giant mud puddle and shouted something nasty.

"What's he saying?" I asked. Nacho conferred with the Formosan, then said, "He's saying it's time for you to fight."

"Fight? Fight who?"

But Nacho couldn't answer, because the guard was raining blows on his back as he pressed him toward me in the pit.

"*Tatakae!*" he shouted, which is one of a handful of words I've come to learn very well.

Oh, boys, my sweet, frail boys. I don't think I have it in me to say what happened next. There are some things a man should never be forced to do. Or even forced to tell. For, try as I might, I fear my style is not up to the task. I thought I could breeze right into it, like I always do, but my pen's gone dry and the mimeograph machine is jammed.

I hope you won't think me a weak sister, boys, but a little piece of Dicky lies buried in that mud pit. Call it what you will: heart, soul, that tiny gland where our humanity dwells. Whatever it is, I can still feel its raw, wounded stump.

Do you ever feel that way, boys? I sure hope not.

Still yours,
Dicky

10

HILDEGÅRD RÅUCH

It was just after seven o'clock when we reached the Palisades and Nadia and Walter dropped me at the end of the palm drive of the High Priest's monastery, so I knew I hadn't yet missed dinner.

As you well know, nothing—not war, revolution, or exile—could alter the daily schedule of the Rauch household. I've always imagined Father's routine as a perfectly tailored exoskeleton, accreted from the two abortive identities of his youth: apprentice in a Bremen shipping firm, followed by his Italian sojourn as a decadent poet. Presumably some synthesis of these polarities had occurred. He had come home, washed the sticky absinthe and D'Annunzian *belleza* from his soul, and consecrated himself to literature in Protestant fashion—forgoing incense and ermine robes for a respectable marriage, a soul-assuaging bank account, and devotion to a calling that exalted one thing above all else: productivity. By the time we came along, Father had established the daily ritual that ensured the holy word count and remained inviolable for over thirty years:

7:30 a.m.: reveille; morning ablutions and stretches at the window.

8:00 a.m.: breakfast; silent but for necessary communication.

9:00 a.m.: work begins in his library; silent hours through the house.

12:30 p.m.: lunch, social; postprandial cigar and catnap on the divan.

2:00 p.m.: afternoon walk of at least five and no more than eight kilometers.

3:30 p.m.: reading hours in the library or on the terrace, answering correspondence; weekly tennis.

6:00 p.m.: social hour, enlivened with brandy or beer; High Priest available to receive guests or amusements from his children.

7:30 p.m.: dinner, often with guests.

9:00 p.m.: postprandial cigars in the living room, with records and light reading.

10:30 p.m.: all guests must leave or go to their rooms. Quiet hours. Reading in bed.

11:30 p.m.: lights out.

Only three and half hours of the day spent actively groveling before the Muse, yet everything, even the smoking of cigars on the divan and the spinning of the gramophone, is part of a coordinated effort to lure and permanently entrap her.

I remember the first time I learned there was something unusual, even remarkable, about this way of meting out the day. Our cousins came for a week one summer when we were about ten, and they couldn't understand why we had to remain stone silent in the house from breakfast until lunch. That's when I realized our father was different. But different was not necessarily bad. For he was not severe or scary the way other fathers could be. He never laid a hand on us; I could hardly recall him raising his voice. Those roles fell to Mother, though she wasn't really cut out for them either. In fact, the only thing either of them was strict about was his schedule. The silences and mealtimes had to be observed. And that was all that was demanded of us. We were quite free to run wild on our own or play whatever outlandish games came into our heads.

To me, Father was a benevolent, albeit distant presence, like a god who looked kindly on his creation but didn't have much time for it. Remember how we used to cast him in unwitting roles that capitalized on this aloofness? When we were landsknechts marauding the forest, he was the Swedish king Gustavus Adolphus, too cowardly to fight us on the battlefield, holed up inside writing dispatches to his mercenary armies or smoking on the divan. I once dared you to launch a harquebus attack on the Swede king's fortress (i.e., his library), and you, reckless idiot that you were (and still are), actually did it. I felt bad afterward, especially because you were sent off to bed without dinner, but I was also proud of you. You always faced the High Priest head on, whether in rebellion or emulation. You needed Father's attention—his respect, his love, his disapproval—in a way that I never did. No matter the cost to yourself, you refused to let him remain undisturbed in his solitude. That was why you, the son of Germany's Greatest Living Writer, chose to become a writer. Which was quite brave but also rather stupid.

I rang the bell and Mother opened the door.

"Ildi . . . ?"

I could see the surprise on her face curdle into fear. "Don't worry, Mother. It's not about Eiko. I just came down for the weekend and dropped by to say hello."

"Oh, thank God." She squeezed my arm and pulled me inside.

"Nothing's changed, you know. He's still in a coma. In the hospital." I felt guilty about leaving you for even the weekend, yet nearly three weeks had passed with death hovering over you and still they had not visited. The High Priest was beyond hope, but Mother I could blame. I am aware this is a double standard. Is it because Father is a genius, someone who suffers from some kind of prized congenital defect that makes him unlike others, whereas Mother, more reliably human, is simply his aider and abettor?

"I know perfectly well where they keep people in a coma," said Mother in her grumbling Viennese, having sensed my accusatory tone. "But your father's been giving lectures—six in the last two weeks—and of course he needs to work when he's home."

"You could always come on your own," I said, then instantly regretted it. The mild satisfaction of seeing Mother act motherly—and not like the clerical arm of the High Priest—would be vastly overshadowed by having to play host to her. As you know, I have an allergy to houseguests, even the company of close friends and family, for anything longer than a single evening and overnight stay. By breakfast, every guest is an interloper and thief of my time.

Fortunately, she thought it an equally bad idea. *"Bist Du deppert?* What would your father do? He'd starve!"

"You fired the cook?"

"Don't be fresh, Hildegard. You know what I mean. Your father says nothing is to be gained from watching Eiko sleep. Still, it's good he has you there with him. In any event, I'm certain he will wake up soon. Now, come. It's nearly time for dinner. Your father will be delighted to see you, and so will the Viertels—that is, until we tell them they'll be getting smaller portions."

"The Viertels are here?"

"Yes, and unlike you, they actually phoned to say they were coming."

"But what about their Sunday salon?"

"Some sordid drama with the kitchen counters being redone—best not to mention it. Oh, and they've brought that snot-nosed Englishman Philip."

"Philip Ravenswood?"

"He's living above their garage. And yet he acts like he's Oscar Wilde gracing us all with his wit."

I know you and Philip Ravenswood have fallen out of late, but he is, I'm happy to report, still exceedingly handsome and very much snot-nosed.

I was glad he and the Viertels were there. Not only would it make Mother and Father wear their human masks, but I wondered if Salka or Berthold knew anything about you and your mysterious Dick. Or if they didn't, maybe the snot-nosed Englishman did.

We dined on the terrace, lit by lanterns and surrounded by the small orchard of fig, avocado, and lemon trees that would inevitably one day be lost in a landslide. But for now it sloped only gently toward the sea, a silver band visible above the foliage. The air was sweet with bougainvillea and rosemary, and the warm evening breeze that blew ripples across the reflecting pool was only a faint harbinger of the winter devil winds to come. I know you scoff at Father's classicizing posture, and

I agree that his attempt to call the house *Knossos*, in keeping with his search for a new Ur-foundation of humanist Europe, is a bridge too far. Thankfully he hasn't inscribed the name anywhere on the premises or taken to calling himself King Minos. Yet. But you have to admit that the house is gorgeous. Clean white walls, red tile roofs, tiered terraces, an interior patio, and exposed beams of thick blond oak. The sole concession to modernism, floor-to-ceiling glass along the back wall, brings the sunsets right into the living room. It is, in effect, the idyllic Mediterranean refuge all artists of northern Europe have dreamed of since the Renaissance.

It's funny—the High Priest has always oriented himself to the south and the east, away from his native northwest corner of Germany, only to have traveled so far east that he's arrived in the far West. He decamped to Vienna, married a Jewess with Slavic and Friulian roots, and took inspiration in his work from Italy, the eastern Mediterranean, and the Orient, source of the Dionysian currents running beneath Apollonian Europe. In the public feud with his brother before the last war, he denounced the hollow civilization of France and England, and yet over the course of the last twenty years, in his unceasing defense of culture, humanity, and the anarchic power of art and irony, he has become the sentinel of Apollo, the guardian of light and reason against the forces of barbarism. It seems fitting, then, that when those forces of barbarism came from the West in the form of Nazi book bans, death threats, and kidnapping plots, Father chose to flee Europe for America by way of the East. Paris and London had been forever tainted by his brother, as had Marseilles, where he shot himself. So Theodor Rauch traveled south and east, from Trieste to Shanghai, then Shanghai to San Francisco. It is also in keeping with Father's inordinate luck and unshakable patricianism that he sailed in fine style, with his library and paintings in cargo, on the very luxury liners that two years later would be crammed with his fellow exiles from Austria, desperate to arrive in ports now besieged and hammered by Japanese bombs.

When my thoughts returned to the dinner conversation, Berthold was telling an old story from his film *The Man from Yesterday*, the one about a soldier presumed dead who, years later, appears to his wife while she's on her honeymoon with a new husband. I had missed the setup and caught only Berthold telling the punch line, gesticulating with a crust of bread in hand and a stained shirtsleeve that had been raked across his plate.

I looked at Father at the head of the table, a wry smile on his face as he primly cut his veal. His immaculate white cuffs hovering above his béarnaise showed no signs of befoulment. He felt my gaze and met it with a playful arch of his brow. "That's precisely the kind of foolishness our dear little painter here has fled. Isn't that right, Ildi?"

This was what he did, to win me as his ally, his confidant. A sidekick who could laugh at Mother and her quirks—how she hummed to herself when others were present, how she seemed to care more about the upholstery of her furniture than the people sitting on it. Or to laugh at you, who was always too serious, too emotional, too much.

"Tell me," said Father, "what do people in San Francisco talk about at dinner, since they don't have movie stars and film productions to gossip about?"

"I honestly wouldn't know. I've been busy working and rarely go out."

"Oh, Hilde, that sounds dreadful," said Salka. "You really should come back here—even if you're tired of your old friends, I have at least fifty people who I'm positive would adore you."

"Hear that, Hilde? It's not just your father and I who think you belong down here."

I ignored Mother's comment. She had already told me that the High Priest's speaking engagements were such that he needed a full-time secretary and interpreter, and, with Mother's angina slowing her down, of course his top choice was me.

"Yes, but would she adore *them*?" said Philip. "Hildegard is not what the Americans call 'a people person.'"

"You behave, you little monster," said Salka in mock reproach. "Or I'll make you live *in* the garage rather than above it."

"Philip is right," I said. "I don't miss the socializing. My work feels like sufficient company."

"You are your father's daughter," said Berthold.

Another arched brow from the High Priest.

"My point exactly," said Mother. "I was just telling Ildi that her father needs someone who understands him. He can't simply hire some stranger who happens to speak German. He needs to feel her and trust her as he does his own right hand, his bone, his blood . . ."

"You mean his appendage," I said.

"Don't be coarse, Hildegard," snapped Mother.

"I for one believe appendages make the man," said Ravenswood. "And I know your brother feels the same."

Seeing that this joke fell flat, both because it was lame and because it invoked you and your absence, Ravenswood turned to me and tried to bury the failed wit with sincerity. "Do tell him to wake up for me, won't you? He and I stopped speaking last year, but I can't bear the thought of him not being here."

"When was the last time you saw him?" I asked.

"Last summer in New York. He stood me up twice, then, when he finally showed up, called me a fascist stooge and stole fifty dollars from my wallet."

"A political education that cost you only fifty dollars?" said Father. "You should be grateful. I fear to think what my son has charged me for mine."

The table gave him a polite laugh, but Mother let out a long sigh that signaled she did not want further discussion on the topic of you.

Salka, who as *salonnière* was accustomed to rescuing the mood with a non sequitur disguised as a segue, said, "Speaking of political education, I have a story for you. This one takes the cake!"

But before she could launch into it, Father suddenly spoke from the head of the table. "The painting, Ildi—is it a really a vocation?"

I registered the gravity of the question, for there were few words as hallowed for Father as *Beruf.* A vocation. A calling.

"Yes," I said. "I believe it is."

"Would you give up everything for it?"

I wondered if he thought he had given up everything—this man who, even in exile, seemed to have everything. "I don't know. I think so."

"You must. Otherwise it is not a calling."

Is this why you haven't visited your son in the hospital? I wished to ask him. But I was too cowardly. It felt too cruel. After all, he thought I was his ally.

When the evening concluded at ten-thirty, as it always did in the land of the High Priest, I proposed to Philip and the Viertels that we drive down to the beach for a walk. Salka thought it a grand idea, while Philip said he'd always wanted to get raped and murdered on the beach at night.

"You'd make a beautiful corpse, Philip," I said.

The tide was out and there wasn't a soul on the shore. We walked toward the Santa Monica Pier. After about a mile, we stopped at a driftwood log as white and smooth as bone and shared the bottle of Bordeaux I'd pilfered from the kitchen.

Berthold, who was suffering from gout, said he would wait for us on his log throne. We left our shoes and socks with him to guard, along with the wine as consolation.

"We won't be long, *Liebchen*," Salka shouted.

"Take your time—I'll compose an ode to the moon."

We continued on and Salka talked about the spate of good luck she'd had writing scripts for Garbo. Salka was so poised and talented yet remained modest, perhaps on account of her humble Galician origins—she was among those whom Mother referred to as "real Jews."

"Well, I wish *my* luck would change," said Philip. "I've been churning out drivel for a hundred dollars a week, but not even the people paying me at MGM will bother to read it. Though I suppose it still beats dreary old England. Just when you think it can't get any grayer or damper there, the clouds of war descend. No, I'll take my itinerant bliss in the California sun, thank you very much."

"What happened to the Philip Ravenswood I knew in Berlin," I asked, "who only dated working-class boys with political convictions as well defined as their muscles?"

"The follies of youth. Plus, the world's gotten too bloody serious. Or, frankly, just plum mad."

"Yes," said Salka, "did you hear? The Anti-Fascist Writers League just issued a statement supporting the Nazi–Soviet Pact *in the name of peace*. Disgusting."

"That reminds me," said Philip. "Just this week I saw a piece in *Free Masses* that someone had left in the stall at MGM: on *the social fascism of Venice Beach*. Can you imagine how much *ressentiment* one must harbor to write such sanctimonious drivel?"

"What's *Free Masses*?" I asked.

"Picture a magazine twice as popular as your brother's journal and half as smart," said Salka.

But before I could keep the conversation directed toward you, Salka and Philip assaulted me with questions about my love life. I batted them away with groans. "I have made a friend, though," I conceded. "He teaches with me at Mills. He used to live in Berlin, actually."

"Oooh, a teacher romance—sounds steamy," said Salka. "What's his name?"

"Walter. Walter Seidler."

"That name sounds familiar, but I don't think I ever knew him."

"If Salka doesn't know him, he must be a nobody," said Philip.

"Oh, do shut up, Philip," said Salka. "You know, I do remember a Walter—I know his last name started with an *S*, it may have even been Seidler. This was just before the war, in Prague. A young student radical who was trying to organize the university staff and theater workers. I heard he went off to play a role in Béla Kun's regime in Hungary and was shot by either the Romanians or one of Horthy's thugs."

"Well, my Walter *is* from Budapest originally, but he fled Hungary and became an art historian in Berlin and is very much alive," I explained, even more embarrassed, as it now sounded like I was defending his existence and claiming him for myself. "He was in Bauhaus circles. He and Moholy-Nagy are close. Knows Koestler too."

"Nope. Never heard of him," said Ravenswood. "Though he sounds like a perfect candidate for a good Hilde-humping."

"He's married," I said.

"Even better!"

I pushed Philip into the surf, and Salka joined in until we had soaked him up to his waist. He caterwauled like a drowned cat. "You wicked, feral maenads! Unhand me!"

After the giggling and shouting abated and we all fell silent to catch our breath, I seized my opportunity. "I need to talk to you about my brother. Was he involved with anyone down here called Dick? I mean romantically?"

"Your brother was romantically involved with a great many dicks."

"My mother was right, Philip—you really are an astounding wit. But I'm serious. Did he have a lover named Dick?"

I noticed Philip and Salka furtively meet each other's eyes.

"What? Do you two know something?"

"I promised him I wouldn't tell you," said Salka. "He said you wouldn't understand."

"It's important, Salka. Eiko's suicide note said something implying that he was distraught without Dick. I mean a person, Philip. Please resist the temptation."

"Suicide note?" said Salka. "Your parents said it was an accidental overdose."

"That's what they prefer to believe."

"I see. Poor Eiko. Well, I don't know if they were lovers, but I know that your brother had recently developed one of his infatuated friendships with Dick Halifax."

"Richard Halifax?" I asked, incredulous. My mind flashed to Addis Ababa, to the hotel room—the two of us smoking cigarettes together on my bed.

"I think she means Lord Halifax, the British foreign secretary," said Philip. "And, yes, he was giving him a good rogering, you can be well sure of it."

"Richard Halifax the travel writer," said Salka. "And whether he and your brother were actually lovers, Hilde, I don't know. You know how Hank could get an idea in his head."

"Yes," I said absently. I was floored. Not by the revelation that the Dick in question was Dick Halifax—though that was a surprise—but that, at least until the very end, you hadn't told me and had confided in others instead. "But why didn't he want me to know?"

"He said you wouldn't understand, that you'd never let him hear the end of it. You had met him once in a Spanish war zone and thought him a perfect ass."

"Ethiopian," I said, correcting her. "It was in Ethiopia we met him." And then I laughed, thinking that I had kept my one-night liaison with Halifax hidden from you for exactly the same reason. Perhaps I now understood why he had behaved so diffidently with me in bed. "Is that when it began between them?"

"I'm not sure. I know Halifax lived here off and on when he was dabbling in pictures," said Salka. "Berthold and I met him once at some fundraiser Malraux did for Spain. Never saw his movie, which looked like worse than drivel, but I do remember hearing about some parties he threw at his mansion in Laguna Beach. No one from circles that I know went, except a few heiresses from the Pasadena set. But they've avoided me like the plague ever since I got them to cough up money for Eisenstein's Mexico debacle."

"Perhaps he and Halifax were together in China," said Philip. "That's where Hank said he was going when we last spoke. Isn't that where Halifax set sail from?"

"Your brother was very excited about going to Shanghai," said Salka.

"Shanghai? Are you sure?"

Salka said you had told her about it with a gleam in your eye that reminded her of the Heinrich Rauch she'd known in the Berlin days. "He was effervescent, even a bit grandiose. This was not long after that terrible public row with your father. He said something about a new funding opportunity for the journal and planned to come home replenished, with a new start for both himself and *The Reckoning*."

I knew you had traveled to Hong Kong and up to Canton, ostensibly for a piece for your journal. But as far as I know, no article came of it. And you never mentioned anything about Shanghai.

"Perhaps he went there out of love," said Philip. "Braving Japanese bombs, all for a bit of hanky-panky. Speaking of which," said Philip to Salka, "when's your gal GG going to play Helen of Troy? After all, she's the original femme fatale."

"If only I had a nickel for every time some dummy tells me he's got the perfect femme fatale role for Garbo . . ."

"Then you could build a better servants' quarters above your garage."

"Yes, and fill it with real servants instead of loafers like you."

I had stopped listening. I was recalling something you said to me before your trip.

"Would you be willing to do something evil?" you had asked me, apropos of nothing. "Something you knew was wrong and found repulsive, but for the sake of a higher good?"

We were at the Cliff House, looking out over the Sutro Baths, watching the surf break against the rocks. You had graced me with your presence for a few hours the night before you set sail. "Is this going to be another one of our arguments about the Soviet Union?" I asked. "Because, if so, I'm not feeling up to it."

"No, not exactly. I suppose it's a simple means-and-ends question—a bad act for a good reason."

"Too abstract," I said. "I'll need examples."

"Okay. Agamemnon's sacrifice of Iphigenia to get his ships to Troy."

"Murder your daughter so you can go fight a war? No thanks."

"But to Agamemnon, fighting the war is worth that cost, or else why would he choose it? Avoiding a mutiny and honoring his pledge to his brother to bring his wife back from the Trojans is more important than his daughter's life. Now, perhaps you don't agree with Agamemnon's decision, but all that matters for our consideration is that he's gutted by it. It's not an easy choice for him. He knows he's doing something terrible that he feels terrible about, but he still thinks it's the right choice to make."

"So what are you asking me?"

"I'm asking how you can be sure you're making the right choice when you're about to do something terrible."

"You can't. That's the whole point of tragedy. We act out of ignorance, no matter how smart we think we are. Our actions always have unintended consequences."

"So if we can't predict the consequences, how do we choose one action over another based on our reckoning of the outcomes?"

"I suppose it's an act of hope as much as knowing. But, as I recall, it doesn't go well for Agamemnon in the end."

"No, but it wouldn't have gone well for him if he had chosen otherwise.

He either dies on that ship at the hands of his own men or he waits till he comes home ten years later as a war hero and his wife greets him with an ax in the neck."

"War hero and daughter killer," I said, "or feckless general and enemy of the gods. In effect, he chooses who he wants to be when he dies."

You thought on this for a moment. "So the question is, who do you want to be when you die?"

"Yes. I suppose that's always the question."

"Well, in your case that's easy—you'll be a toothless old hag with a hooked back and full mustache."

"And in your case?" I asked.

"For me, the question is always more pressing."

The house was dark when I returned.

Philip and the Viertels had let me out of the car on the condition that I stay through the week. They knew I wouldn't, as did I, yet I promised all the same. The back door through the garage had been left unlocked for me. But the inner sanctum I wished to enter was, of course, sealed.

I had snuck into the High Priest's library only once before, in your company, back when the library existed in our home on the edge of the Wienerwald. We sat in his chair and smoked one of his cigars, laughing hysterically as we palmed every object on his desk, taking turns doing our best impressions of him. You wanted to look for his diaries, but I forbade it and was obeyed only because the cigar had made us ill.

Ever since the day of your infamous harquebus attack, the library door had remained locked. But children are natural spies, and it had taken only a minimal effort at surveillance for us to learn where he kept the key: out of reach above the doorframe. An obstruction easily overcome with you on my shoulders. Now, too tall for too long, I could easily reach it on my own. The only problem was that in the High Priest's California house, the stucco doorway to the library was arched, without a protruding frame.

I searched other potential hiding spots. The umbrella and alpenstock stand. In the alcove that housed the telephone. There were far fewer ledges in this house than the one in Mödling. What if Father now kept the key in his jacket pocket? What if he was sleeping with it beside him on the nightstand? Would I have to knock tomorrow while he was working, under some pretense of emergency to get inside? And then what? The one thing I could not do was tell him the truth—that you had somehow broken into his library and hidden something there. But if you had gotten in, then you must have known where the key was. Which means either you had watched the High Priest take the key from its hiding place before entering his library or you had found it on your own. If you could do it, I reasoned, so could I.

These thoughts came as I paced the hall beside the large Koloman Moser painting of Lake Garda. I had never paid it much attention when it hung in our old home. I much preferred *Venus in the Grotto*, which showed a naked girl stepping through a viscous portal, into another dimension: the act of giving birth to oneself. That was the image I thought of whenever I thought of my own path as a painter. But this more subtle landscape, with its foreground of sun-dappled lake and the sweep of the green Alps, had lived at the margin of my awareness for years. Only now, looking at it in its new home, did it finally come alive for me. I recognized it as precisely the same view of the San Francisco Bay looking north to the hills across the Golden Gate. Or, rather, Moser had seen the mountains ringing Lake Garda precisely as I saw the headlands of Marin looming over the bay. He had imbued the land with his own enchanted way of seeing it, but one that pointed away from the ego and expressed something primordial, something vast and deep across the gulf of time. That was how I wanted to paint. I touched my hand to the top of the painting, as though in benediction, and felt my finger land on something metallic.

The room was larger and the view of the ocean had replaced the wooded hills and aqueduct of Mödling, but I had the uncanny feeling of being in the same library I'd known as a child—translated onto the other side of the world. The same, yet not the same. Just like me.

I thought of a conversation I'd had earlier that evening with Ravenswood. I said that in exile I often had the sensation of being my own double, another version of myself, now in America. In response, he'd espoused his pet theory that even inanimate objects were metaphysically reconstituted in the languages they are known by. "A bottle is not *eine Flasche*," he said. "A chair is not *ein Stuhl*—rather, they inhabit parallel yet distinct universes." Similarly, when you had gone from being Heinrich Rauch to Hank Rauch, you had become a different person. "Heinrich," Philip said, "has been left behind at customs."

"Does that mean Heinrich Rauch is not in a coma?" I asked.

"Metaphysically speaking, no. Though Heinrich cannot be revived until Hank returns to German-speaking lands."

"And what of the many of us who continue speaking German here in America?"

"They are like air bubbles in a glass of beer. It's only a matter of time before they rise to the surface and pop."

It's Dick—him, but not him, I suddenly recalled, thinking of your scribbled letter, that perplexing sequel to your suicide note. Had you been referring to Richard Halifax then? But that was impossible, because that was just weeks ago, and by then he had been dead for months. Even if it was true that you and he were lovers, the only Richard Halifax you could have possibly seen that night was, as you said, a ghost.

The High Priest's *Schreibtisch* was exactly as I remember it. The desk—the only piece of furniture they'd taken with them when they emigrated—occupied the center of the library like an altar, and I felt like I was seeing it with the same awestruck eyes of my ten-year-old, tomb-raiding self. The faint forest scent of the Brazilian rosewood, the finely carved edges, so pleasing to run one's fingers along, the eight clawed legs that evoked an ancient offering at the sacrificial table. Atop it was his current manuscript in a red vellum folio, a smaller appointment book of notes and doodles, a Montblanc pen set, and a smattering of totems and amulets—a Cycladic figurine, Byzantine candlesticks, scrimshawed whale tooth, Scythian blade, and a Quattrocento plumb bob—all arranged symmetrically.

Was it possible this thing before me had become a writing desk? One look at it was enough to know that Philip Ravenswood's theory was wrong. So long as it belonged to our father, this object could be known by one name only: *Schreibtisch*.

I went to the shelves. Everything was mixed together and only loosely alphabetized. Too orderly a library, Father once said, is a sign of a narrow mind. Genres and ideas recognize no borders, and it is a fool's errand to try to impose them. Galsworthy liked rubbing shoulders with Frazer's *Golden Bough*, and Goethe, unlike Faust, would not suffer to have his soul split in two.

The same went for the author of your chosen hiding place, Stefan Zweig, who had spread himself across fiction, poetry, and popular biography. The latter was arguably his chief métier, certainly the primary source of his income, but also what earned him the High Priest's derision. That and his collection of autographed memorabilia—a chit signed by Beethoven to his tailor, a wadded-up Latin assignment by a school-aged Victor Hugo, a grocer's bill made out to Denis Diderot and found on his corpse. There was perhaps something unseemly about Zweig's biographical fascination, as though he cared more about the aura of persona than the work itself. Redolent of the middle-brow dilettante and armchair Romantic. Which was perhaps why Father detested his work—because it veered dangerously close to his own.

Contrary to your and Father's opinion, I don't think Zweig is talentless, and I always thought him a friendly, cheerful man who seemed unspeakably sad. But it was his sycophantic tendency toward both his subjects and his peers that undid him. Do you remember how whenever he came to visit us in Mödling, he would gift Father with his latest book? An impressive yearly occurrence, and another thing that provoked the High Priest's contempt. The fly page would be filled with a groveling inscription that always managed to outdo the last one in hyperbole. Once Zweig left, Father would thumb through to find the most insipid sentence in the book, heave a sigh of relief, and say something to the effect of, "Ah, Zweig, God bless him—it must be liberating to write without the slightest concern for style."

Out of either pity for the man or his own vanity, the High Priest had kept all Zweig's inscribed books over the years and even shipped them to America, where they clearly remained unread (I suppose that's why you chose them for a hiding spot). I pulled them from the shelf, nearly a dozen in all, taking care to search the pages for notes, letters, or whatever it was you had instructed me to look for there. But I found nothing, other than inscription after inscription about *laying an offering at Mount Olympus, paying a visit to the Parnassian heights, a token of gratitude for the air of pure poetry you allow us all to breathe.*

I was starting to feel truly nauseated, when I turned over the flyleaf of *Joseph Fouché* and saw it.

Though what *it* was I hadn't a clue. I had expected to find something of a personal nature—a page from your diary, a confession, a will, something you deemed necessary to hide and then, later, to burn. But this . . . what I found seemed innocuous, irrelevant. Idiotic, even. But there was a connection to Richard Halifax.

To: The Dicky Halifax Junior Adventurers Club
From: Dicky Halifax
Breaking Rocks & Having His Rocks Broken on Saipan

Summer 1939

Dear boys,

Death tends to make a man philosophical. And this adventure has received enough visits from the grim reaper to turn me into a veritable Socrates. Except that old Athenian knee-bender was a weak sister who couldn't wait to bring the hemlock to his lips. Now, I'm sure you'll hear different from your schoolmasters, rattling on about him being a martyr to reason and the dawn of civilization and such, but don't be fooled, boys. Which sounds braver to you? Taking a really long nap or staying awake for another boot kick right in the kisser?

If you want a hero to emulate, look no further than Oedipus. Now there's a boy who knew how to take his licks. Killed Daddy and knocked up Mother without even knowing it. But then when he learns the terrible truth, what does he do? Does he run and hang himself like his mother-wife? No sir, he skewers his own eyeballs like he was gonna roast 'em over the campfire, then lives out the rest of his days in defiance of both death and life.

I'll admit it took me a long time to come around after I left poor Nacho there in the mud. He fought his wharf rat heart out, and seeing them carry his crumpled little body off like a pile of dirty rags, I truly wished he'd been the stronger one.

For days afterward I lay immobile in the barracks, crippled with grief and guilt. No amount of beatings could entice me to rise and go to work. I refused my fetid bowl of rice and fed only on the thought of joining Nacho and Roderick and Wesley and all my other friends in oblivion.

But then one night, after weeks of praying for death to take me and receiving nothing but the steady drip of rainwater from my thatched ceiling, a memory from boyhood dropped right into my brain. The Halifax family cat Maximillian, whom we affectionately called Maxi Halifaxi, had been run over by the milkman, and your man Dick, at the tender age of nine, found him hiding under the porch, mewling his own dirge. He was in bad shape, my poor furry sidekick, and while the state of him was shocking and his cries pierced my young heart, there was a fullness to the moment, something that made it stand still and envelop me. As I stroked his shattered ribs and whispered his name, doing my best to ease his way into the void as his howls grew faint and his breathing ebbed, I was aware that I was witness to the unfathomable essence of life. That all of its mysteries and meanings lay in the immensity of that experience and the simple crossing of a threshold.

When Maxi's breath finally ceased, he looked, despite his mangled limbs and dented skull, like a king in repose. I can't describe to you the peace I saw in those vacant, blood-filled eyes. But I knew then two things, which cannot be reconciled: There is no life beyond the body—not in the way church folk shout about. And yet whatever Maxi Halifaxi was, he was certainly more than just his corporeal form. I had experienced in his death a great paradox. While I came away from it grieving Maxi's absence, at the same time I was filled with his spirit, more certain of his existence somewhere deep inside me than I had been when he was licking my fingers or tearing the wings off pigeons.

That same regal stillness that had ennobled my poor dead cat had indeed come over young Nacho when he was lying face down in the mud. I had been so distraught over my own hand in his destruction that I had forgotten about the sublimity of death itself. I'd neglected the communion that comes from witnessing this great crossing from endless struggle to eternal peace. A transubstantiation of sorts, as had occurred with ole Maxi and, in more literal form, with Roderick. This was another paradox of life I've often wondered at: Killing is evil, yet death is a blessing. As horrible as it was, I wondered, had I perhaps given Nacho a gift?

"Oh, Nacho," I wept. "Your spirit is still with me!"

It was at that very moment, while I was lying on my miserable bed mat, that I suddenly heard the voice of my late beloved cabin boy.

"Yeah, no thanks to you, Dicky! You don't fight fair!"

Then I felt my little deceased friend's fists rain down on my chest, just like they did when he was alive.

"Oh, Nacho," I cried, my eyes clamped tight in anguish. "I will cherish your memory in my heart forever. Battered, as it is, by your ghostly legacy."

"Dicky, you dimwit! I'm alive."

I opened my eyes, and to my shock there he was. Nacho in the flesh, still bruised from the pummeling I'd given him. And surly as ever.

I leapt from my mat and tried to hug him, to make sure I wasn't dealing with another Roderick-style figment. And right as I reached for him, Nacho met me with a swift, all-too-real knee to the groin.

"Oh, Nacho," I cried, in both jubilation and a surge of nausea from the pit of my scrotum. "You really are alive!"

The next morning the two of us were up with the sun. We devoured our rancid rice, washed our faces in a puddle of effluvia, and filed out with the rest of the prisoners to the phosphate mines. By God, it felt good to be alive.

But here's a tip, boys. When you start thinking about what you'd like to be when you grow up, keep phosphate miner at the bottom of your list. I'd sooner do a thousand apprenticeships on the meanest whaleboat than work another day in the limestone pits of Saipan. The labor is straightforward enough: Carve out chunks of petrified bird shit from a blindingly white rock seven days a week from sunup to sundown and keep doing it until your spine gives out or your kidneys explode.

Even so, those first few days were a dream. With Nacho at my side again, I hardly noticed the murderous labor. I seemed to float above the guano mounds, swinging my pick like a parasol and taking beatings like compliments. I was decidedly not a murderer, and I still had a sidekick. On top of that, I could now take a little pride in the fact that I had Dempsey Rolled my opponent right into KO Land. What could be wrong with the world?

Nacho and I never spoke of the brutal wrestling match that had been foisted upon us. I suppose he was still a little sore that I whupped him so bad. But he never tired of telling me what a peach the sick ward had been. The rice there came from the soldiers' commissary and so was not nearly as rotten. The bamboo mats were plush and dry. In fact, he said, our only chance at survival here was to end up in the sick ward again. Either that or escape. "And I don't know about you, Dicky," he said, "but I didn't survive all your insanity only to be worked to death in a bird-shit mine."

If it had only been the grueling work itself, we might have stood a chance. But, as Nacho and I learned, the Japs add a little ambiance to the endeavor. The guards at the mines, who were clearly graduates of the same school as our camp guards, found it great sport to jab their rifle butts into the back of our heads. This was a not-so-subtle reminder to keep the pace up, though it didn't make a lick of difference how fast we worked.

There were three of them, and they would take turns coming over to stand at the top of the pit, looming over us. Unless it was high noon, we knew they were there, because their shadow would provide a merciful coolness, but this sweet shade was always a sign of impending pain. And no matter how much you steeled yourself for the blow, stiffening your neck, clenching your jaw, keeping your shoulders square, there was just no way to anticipate or soften it when it fell. Without fail, the thump of the rifle butt rattled the brain in its cage and knocked one's teeth together like a steel trap slamming shut. Men lost pieces of tongue; a few passed out and slammed their faces on the rocks. One little Okinawan fellow, whom they must've thumped right in the sweet spot, dropped stone dead. The three guards seemed to enjoy playing this game to pass the time, and they placed bets on who could earn a knockout. Needless to say, if any of us tried to dodge it or protect ourselves, that was considered cheating, and the three of them would come together and beat the man senseless.

This was a game we prisoners simply had to endure. And your man Dicky got his bell rung more times than I can count. In fact, the ole Halifax Calculator all but broke down after the umpteenth skull crunch.

So, too, apparently, did Nacho's own Fight-or-Flight Assessment Tool. For after receiving his latest thump and cracking his nose against the sharp wall of the pit, my young sidekick said he'd had enough.

"Haven't we all, friend? What's there to do, though, but keep our heads down and jaws locked tight?"

But Nacho, as you may have gathered, was a born fighter. Not necessarily a winning one, mind you, but the kid had sand. The Portuguese can be real donkeys, and once they get an idea in their head, there's no dragging them away from it, even if it means driving themselves right off the cliff.

"You do whatever you want," said Nacho, "but I won't let that happen again." And that's all he would say on the matter.

I had to hand it to him. He had *colhões*, far bigger than fit in his little nutsack. Let that be a lesson, boys—when you get out of the shower and catch a glimpse of yourself stepping into your pajamas, you might see a sorry bundle there between your legs. But the kind of equipment that makes a fella manly is far more figurative than your typical locker-room banter might suggest. Why, I've seen dinguses all over the world, and it's clear some get the whole linguiça, while others just get drippings from the pan. But no kitchen scale can tell you who's going to man up when it's time to lay your meat on the line. In fact, of the cowards I've known to tuck tail and run, several truly had themselves a tail to tuck—lest it slap them in the chest. Whereas the bravest fellas I can think of—my brother, Wesley, and swift-footed Achilles—had a little button mushroom and eggs that barely poked out their inguinal canal.

All this is simply to say that Nacho's resolve reminded me of my younger self, when I was starting to figure out how I wanted to be in the world. As mentioned before, though I don't like to dwell on it, I was a sickly child. The doctors had found a spot on my lungs, and even though I felt more or less fine, Mother and Father kept me cooped up in bed for nearly two years. They hardly let me even see Wesley, who had been my first true sidekick, for fear I might be contagious. So from age ten to twelve, for what felt to my boy-mind like an interminable prison sentence, it was pretty much just me, my books, and my weak-sister lungs.

I don't know if it was the heap of Seneca and Epictetus or all the explorers' tales I'd been reading, or if I just got too darn sick of being an invalid, but I started getting some heady notions about my powers of will. And, since I spent most of my days alone, I'd gotten in the habit of talking to myself, telling myself the story of what the rest of my life would look like, the kinds of adventures I'd have, and how I'd make up for lost time.

And then one day, after two years in bed, I realized that if I was going to do those things in the future, I'd have to change myself in the present. That's when the voice came.

It was a Sunday morning. I awoke to sunlight and birdsong and the smell of our cook, Miss Alice, making country sausage in the kitchen, and as incontrovertibly as if I'd said, "Bill Taft is president" *or* "Kansas City barbecue is the best," I said to myself: "Dicky, you will not be sick anymore."

Now, I bet you boys have said things to yourself before, maybe "good job!" when you hit a triple, or "you worthless pansy" when a pretty girl touches her foot against yours in English class and you ask to be excused to the bathroom. But this voice I'm talking about was not the typical auto-monologue or what we writers call our inner critic. No, this utterance was an oracle, boys, like the words that leak out of the crack at Delphi—something I had no choice but to obey.

And just like that, I began my convalescence. At first my mother wouldn't believe it, said I must be feverish. But I had made myself well and would brook no opposition—from her or Father or anyone. By the end of the week, I was running around the yard with Wesley, the two of us donning coonskin caps and Kentucky long rifles, raising holy hell against the Santa Anna of mother's rosebush. Come summer, I went away to the camp where I met Roderick and began the life of adventure.

So when I heard Nacho say, "I won't let that happen again," I recognized that voice and I knew he meant it. There would be no more beatings. Even if neither of us had the slightest idea how.

But sometimes spontaneity beats all the planning in the world.

'Cause the next day at the mines, when the sun was at ten o'clock and my sweat was sizzling on the guano, I suddenly felt the hovering presence of the guard as he bathed me in shade. I knew his cheap blow was coming soon. But rather than brace myself for it as usual, when I perceived his shadow shift its weight to the back foot, I swung my pick behind me and caught the guard right in his armpit. A second later, the other end came poking through his throat, with part of his windpipe hanging out like a bolo tie.

"Nacho," I whispered, just audible above the man's choking. I couldn't have managed any more than a whisper, shocked as I was at my own handiwork.

"Holy shit, Dicky! What did you do?"

"I thought you'd be happy. Remember? No more beatings?"

"You idiot, I meant we should escape! Now what do we do?"

So far nobody else had noticed a thing, but when I shrugged in response to Nacho's question, it dislodged the pick from the man's throat. The blood spouted out of him like a Roman fountain, and he fell headlong onto the rocks.

That's when all the others took notice, prisoners and guards alike. There was a brief lull as each party meditated on what was to come next. Nacho and I stared at each other, alive to the pregnant moment, aware that I had thrust us, perhaps by way of misunderstanding, into uncharted territory.

Then all hell broke loose.

The guards, realizing they were outnumbered ten to one, began blazing away with their rifles while my fellow prisoners, seizing their chance, scrambled up the pits in an ax-waving fury. The guards got off only a few rounds before the miners hacked them to bits. In the melee, I saw Nacho lay into one of our tormenters with a fine crack to the chest. "Atta boy, Nacho!" I shouted from my cover in the guano pit, until suddenly my fellow prisoners leapt in and hoisted me on their shoulders. That's right, boys—your man Dick had become the Spartacus of Saipan.

It was swell for a minute—that is, until the reinforcements from the neighboring quarry rolled in and broke up the party. They shot down the men holding me up and laid into the rest of us with their swords and clubs. The rebellion I'd unwittingly started was over before I knew it, and both my head and Nacho's were mashed in worse than ever.

As we were lorried off to a new holding cell in the Imperial Navy compound, spitting out teeth and coughing up blood, I couldn't help but smile. "We done good, Nacho."

"I hate you, Dicky," he replied. But I knew what he meant.

Hope you're keeping well, boys. I'll bet summer's nearly over where you are and the school bell will soon toll. Better get those adventures in while you can!

Yours as ever,
Dicky

12.

HILDEGARD RAUCH

You really are the most exasperating person. If I weren't your wombmate, I'd have long since abandoned you. You've always had a bit of a sadistic streak, which I put up with because I believe it's your warped way of showing affection. Plus, I quickly learned your idea of fun and gave as good as I got. In fact, I can now pull back your hospital gown and still see the scar around the edge of your nipple made by my adolescent teeth, a memory your chest hair refuses to forget. But this game you are playing with me now—it's not fun. Because nothing about it makes sense and I don't know how to play it.

You write me a letter—presumably the same night you decide to give up and write a suicide note?—then you send it to the wrong address, to the creep beneath me, who takes two weeks to forward me your urgent plea and who's now made it his mission to take me out on a date (I'm trying to project ice-cold bull dyke, but he seems too stupid to notice). At your belated yet urgent command, I go down to the Holy See at Santa Monica, enduring both a hangover and an eight-hour Russian harangue, followed by family dinner, thankfully in the company of Salka and Ravenswood, only to have them inform me, apparently the last to know, that you've fallen in love with Richard Halifax.

Why?

No, not why Halifax? Of course he's a buffoon and, yes, I would have teased you. But I understand your attraction—something about that wild, anarchic enthusiasm of his, like a puppy skittering across a hardwood floor, which surely comes from its opposite, some impossibly dark, forlorn place. What I mean is: Why didn't you tell me about him?

Did you think I would have disapproved? I guess I wouldn't understand if you truly loved him. I don't believe I've ever heard you use that word in earnest. Is it possible you could have experienced real love and decided to keep it from me? It makes me realize how little of each other's actual lives we've known these last years. We used to tell each other everything, good or bad, especially in matters of "love." And until now I would have sworn that we both felt the same way—that love was a series of misadventures and intoxications, which wove lasting enchantments around some people though not us. But I wouldn't have begrudged you for discovering otherwise. How little you must think of me.

If only your mad game had ended there, with the mystery of human connection and your wish to die for love of a dead man whose ghost you saw that night in your hotel room. This part was no longer such a mystery to me, as I pieced together that your attempt at oblivion was the same day a court had ruled on Halifax's disappearance and declared him officially dead. So, freshly reminded of your grief, officially bereft of hope, you took the plunge. As much as that could ever make sense to me, it made sense.

But then you have me break into the High Priest's library—and I, hopeless sap that I am, believe that whatever is hidden in the pages of poor Stefan Zweig's unloved book will finally give some clarity to the chaos you've spun around yourself and now me. And what do I find there?

A letter to a stranger. And a fucking receipt.

To be precise, a receipt for two silk suits and pocket squares from a Hong Kong tailor, and a letter from your secret sweetheart, Richard Halifax, to one Sally Bent. The latter's name sounds vaguely familiar, though I'm quite sure I don't know any prostitutes here (how dull my life has become compared to Berlin once upon a time). Allow me to read said letter to you, so you can appreciate the full crushing weight of its inanity:

Dear Sal,

Why does nothing ever go as it should? We're two weeks behind schedule, and there are at least half a dozen people I could blame—

Pengelly for undermining my authority and second-guessing
my every decision, Roderick for his endless stream of worry
and jealousy, and, of course, my private demon of a shipbuilder,
Ming Fat, who seems intent on robbing me of every last bit of my
remaining money and patience. I won't bother boring you with
the exploits of our blue-blooded clap-trap George Winslow III (I
imagine you hear enough gonorrheal sob stories). But, really, I
worry the problem is with me. Even if everything goes according to
plan, there's a part of me that thinks I'm burying myself with this
project, which is nothing more than a stupid stunt. What if I've built
a bespoke coffin for myself with this breezy, romantic adventurer act
and the Soup Dumpling expedition will just be the final nail? When
I can't sleep, Wolsey's lines from Henry VIII rattle around my brain,
taunting me: . . . I have ventured, Like little wanton boys that swim
on bladders, This many summers in a sea of glory, But far beyond my
depth . . .

I must stop glorifying myself—I'm getting sick of it and so is the
public. And yet I know only how to keep plowing fallow ground. I
dream about writing a book about someone else, something dark and
serious, with my name only on the spine rather than on the page as
the idiotic hero. Will I ever grow up? I long to give up the boy persona,
but something won't let me. It's as though I still need it, even if I no
longer want it. A dark, vaguely sinister force always stays my hand
and keeps the tiller pointed in the same direction. I was once naïve
enough to think success in Hollywood would allow me to course-
correct, and now I'm hoping our operation at the fair will give us the
financial freedom to strike out in new directions. One last hurrah in
the harem for you; for me, one more stint as the starry-eyed buffoon.
Here's hoping it's not all just another dream. . . .

Okay, please ignore mopey Richard. Sometimes the loneliness
sneaks up on me when I'm writing by lamplight and whispers
despairing thoughts. As to the question in your last letter, I say
take the loan for the whole ten grand. Even at that egregious wop
interest rate—I suppose it's redundant to say criminal—we'll make
hand-over-fist with the cruises. Hell, if you've already sold out the
first month, we'll be debt-free by July, and then, apart from general

ship maintenance and the champagne, the rest of the year will be pure profit.

Will send word once we reach Formosa. In the meantime, take care of those luscious legs!

Yours,

Dick

P.S. I'm attaching the receipt from a little sartorial expedition Roderick and I made here in Hong Kong. I'll cut a dashing figure at the helm in these new duds (can't say the same for Roderick, as he's not exactly wasp-waisted these days), so seems prudent to write off as a business expense. Please add it to our bucket.

This is what you wanted me to burn? Well, I haven't. It's not worth the butane. I keep thinking there must have been something else you wanted me to find in the library, and yet I'm certain there was nothing there. I tried decoding with a few of our childhood ciphers but got only worse gibberish than before.

Why, I keep asking myself, did you have Richard Halifax's sad letter and receipt in the first place? The obvious answer, which I was rather slow in deducing, is that Halifax gave it to you in Hong Kong with the purpose of bringing it back here and delivering it to this woman Sally Bent. You of course returned from your China trip before Halifax was due to arrive in his junk, so it seems natural that he would use you as his courier. But why, then, did you not deliver the receipt? Why instead take it back to Los Angeles and stash it away in Father's lair? Presumably, you hid it there before you left L.A. this summer and came up here and, no longer having a permanent home of your own, thought the High Priest's library the most secure location. But why did you need to hide it in the first place? Were you afraid someone might come looking for it? What value do this silly letter and suit bill hold for you—or, for that matter, anyone?

Just as I suspected, you have nothing to say for yourself. The only thing I can think of is that perhaps this was the last memento you had from Halifax—which, even if not written to you, was his last utterance.

And then, after he was gone, you saw no point in sending it to Sally Bent. Maybe it had become a sentimental keepsake, its mundaneness transfigured into something precious.

I wish you would wake up and sort this all out, because your shuttered face has been dominating my mind's eye, and I can't bring myself to put it in paint, which is how I would normally deal with such a disturbance. Some kind of irrational Dorian Gray belief that if I turn you into art, you will remain forever a still life.

Instead, I've been wrestling with another Kroeber painting. It's not right, and I fear I'm only making it worse, but what is there to do but go on? Walter is fond of quoting Valéry that works of art are never finished but abandoned. The French have such a talent for making profundities out of nonsense. Though I fear they stole that trick from the Germans.

Speaking of Walter, I've done something stupid. I didn't mean for it to happen, and I don't believe he did either. It's funny—there wasn't a hint of sexual tension in the air with him before. Not that he isn't handsome, or witty, or sad in that peculiar way that somehow beckons me; it's just that I thought of him as unavailable. And I was pretty sure he had written me off as the same. But then last night in the faculty lounge, I saw him hunched over the mimeograph machine, all back and arms and a tender little cleft where his suspenders hoisted up his trousers, and twenty minutes later we were on the couch in his office, admiring his Moholy-Nagy without our clothes on. If anyone else was in the art department, they surely heard everything.

"You're a bit of an Amazon," Walter said afterward, handing me a cigarette.

"Did I hurt you?" I asked.

"Not at all. Well," he said with a grin, "maybe a little."

I thought Nadia would have put him through far worse but kept my mouth shut. I didn't want her name to intrude on our scene quite yet.

"But it was *swell*." He liked peppering his German with Americanisms said with a dripping irony.

"Yes, well, we probably shouldn't do that again."

"If you're saying that because of Nadia, you should know that she and I don't really . . ."

"What, fuck?"

He laughed. "I'm not sure we've ever *fucked*. Of course, we've had sex, though not for quite some time. She's rather traditional for an anarchist. Actually, they all are. Puritans with dynamite. You can't be that idealistic without sublimating most of the libido."

"I'm surprised. I thought it was she, not you, trying to lure me into bed."

"I told you, Nadia wants a younger sister. A kind of platonic cata-mite, or whatever the sapphic equivalent is."

"I'm often told I resemble an Alcibiades in skirts."

"Oh, please. I've never seen you wear a skirt. Or a dress. Though I did rather lust after you in that billowing genie costume."

"I believe I was too drunk to notice. The bartender put too much gin in my martini."

"The swine. He did the same to me."

I lit another cigarette and tucked myself into the hollow of Walter's shoulder. I didn't want this liaison to end yet. I suddenly felt a deep urge to unburden myself. Only then did I realize that the sexual desire had simply been the prelude to my even more urgent need.

In one long breathless rush I told Walter everything—your suicide note, your cryptic declaration of love for Richard Halifax, your belated command to burn documents in Father's library, and now this stupid letter and receipt from Halifax, all addressed to a woman named Sally Bent, whom I had no idea how to find other than looking in the phone directory, which had yielded nothing.

Walter looked speechless.

"I know I must sound like a perfect madwoman. And I swear if I get another incomprehensible note—from either Richard Halifax or my comatose brother—I really am going to go nuts."

"The Nude Ranch," he said.

"What?"

"Sally Bent's Nude Ranch—it's an attraction at the fair. Haven't you seen those signs? *The Most Natural Attraction on the Gayway!* Or my favorite: *Come See Our Milkers!*"

"I think I would have remembered seeing a sign like that."

"Why don't you go ask her about that letter?" said Walter. "Maybe she can clarify things?"

"Maybe so. But why did Eiko want me to destroy it? I can't help but worry I'm somehow betraying him if I do anything other than burn it."

"And yet you haven't burned it."

He was right.

"If you want, I could come with you."

"Are you offering to escort me to the Nude Ranch?"

"I am."

"My, Walter," I replied. "How gallant of you."

To: The Dicky Halifax Junior Adventurers Club
From: Dicky Halifax
Hanging from His Ankles, Spilling His Beans

Summer 1939

Dear boys,

Oh, to be back breaking rocks in fresh air with the sun on my face! I'd sooner hack out ten tons of ancient bird turds than be here where I'm currently writing you. Apologies if my style falters or the type appears garbled—it's hard to compose with a full four quarts of blood crammed in your cranium. Thank God Sensei Kanemoto had his guy cut a slit across my nose to let some of the pressure out. He really is a thoughtful man.

I couldn't have written a line with the migraine I had going before, though now the blood runs out in a steady stream over my eyes, which is a nuisance. But I just have to hold out until Sensei K. returns from sharing with his colleagues all the info I gave him. And once he convinces them that I really am the illustrious writer-adventurer I purport to be and not a Dutch spy, I'm sure they'll turn me right side up, slap a Band-Aid on my snout, and send me off with a handshake and no hard feelings.

Of course, they'll have to wheel me out, because there's no way I'll be able to stand on these pudding feet. Did you know, boys, that the human foot has twenty-six bones in it? Neither did I, until Sensei Kanemoto told me just before he broke each one. It makes me realize how much I once took the foot for granted. Like me, you probably think you've got a foot with a heel, an ankle, maybe an arch and ball, and then five toes. What delusions we live under, boys! I feel all fifty-two of those broken bones now, not to mention the sixty-six joints and over two hundred muscles and ligaments—all mashed to a pulp. They feel like bowls of poi, with my own fried nerve endings attached. It's amazing the damage a stick of brazilwood can do when guided by the expert anatomical knowledge of someone like Sensei Kanemoto. He assures me that under proper care, the bones will eventually heal, though every step I take will forever bear the weight of his teaching.

Sensei has taught me so much already, far beyond the vast microcosm of the foot. Really, I owe my life to him. You see, boys, when they whisked us away after the mining incident, the authorities had every intention of bringing Nacho and me back to the penal camp the next morning, whipping out one of their ceremonial swords, and lopping off our heads. But it just so happened that news of my impromptu revolt attracted the attention of a visiting official, Dr. Haruto Kanemoto, here on business that I can only guess pertains to the medical administration of the colonies or naval operations or both. He is a very learned man, with excellent English, impeccable manners, and is clearly a person of some authority.

When he heard that the prisoner who started the trouble at the phosphate mines was a white man who claimed to be an American, he took a sudden interest and came to visit me in my cell. I was so dazed from the beating I'd taken, I didn't register that he was speaking English. He had my wounds cleaned, brought me water and fresh rice with a pickled plum and even a small piece of fish. Other than Roderick, it was the first meat I'd eaten in months, though my mouth was too broken to properly taste it. Once I had recovered enough to speak, Dr. Kanemoto began questioning me. That's when I realized he was speaking fluently in my own language and that I had at last found someone to whom I could explain my predicament. I rushed to tell him my story, though my jaw and lips were still badly swollen.

"Which part of America are you from?" he asked.

"Kana Shee-ee. Buh now I li in Cah-i-hawnia."

"And you are a writer?"

"Yesh."

"A novelist?"

I tried rolling my eyes, but the lids were still heavy with blood. "No nah-elist. Wri-er-avenshuher."

"Writer-adventurer, you say? Like Ernest Hemingway?"

I groaned an emphatic, exasperated *no*. In no way, I explained to Dr. Kanemoto, was I like that prodigious fraud from Oak Park whose name shall never cross my lips. And unlike novels, which these days are just the thinly veiled fantasies of a disordered brain, my books were chronicles of real adventures. A more or less truthful tale of one man hurling himself at the world, wringing art from the kitchen mop of life. Sure, I always make a few sartorial nips and tucks to narrow the waist and fill out the crotch, so as to cut a nice figure on the page, but the real appeal is in how the work reflects the living.

"If you ask me, sir, ambulance-driving seems like an apt profession for someone carting around that sickly prose. All sullen silences and icebergs and Say, Bill, I'm feeling tight, like it's some kind of a goddamn revelation."

"I'm not sure I caught all that," said Dr. Kanemoto, as it had come out of me in one long gurgling moan. "But just to verify: You claim to be the same writer-adventurer Richard Halifax who disappeared while sailing a boat from Hong Kong to San Francisco this past spring? Did I understand that correctly?"

"Yesh!" I said.

"Very good, then, Mr. Halifax," said Dr. Kanemoto. "I will return soon, and I look forward to hearing more of your story."

A flood of relief washed over me. At last my ordeal would be over, and I would be able to return home to you, dear boys, and tell you my hair-raising tale in proper form.

But then I remembered something. "Wai!" I yelled. "Wha abou Nasho?"

"Is that the recalcitrant Eurasian boy in the neighboring cell?" he asked. I told him it was. He seemed glad to learn this, since all his previous attempts to elicit my wayward cabin boy's name had earned him only an "Up your ass, mister!"

"Peashe don' 'urt 'im," I begged, since at that moment I still thought of Sensei Kanemoto as a bog-standard prison-camp interrogator and not the great teacher he turned out to be. "He'sh my fwend."

Dr. Kanemoto told me not to worry, that Nacho was being well tended to, and no one would have their head chopped off just yet.

That evening, I tried to communicate with my young sidekick through the cell wall. "Hang in there, Nacho," I yelled at the bloodstained concrete. "You've survived the wreck of the *Soup Dumpling*, a crew of handsy whalers, the prison-yard death match, and those infernal guano mines. What's a little jail cell by comparison?" But I got no reply. "I'm going to get us out of this fix, Nacho. I promise. That's a Halifax Guarantee." Of course, given my injuries, it was likely hard to decipher, but I hoped he'd taken heart.

When Sensei Kanemoto returned a few days later, he was with a soldier carrying a valise of ropes and instruments. He said there were many details to my story that we must go over carefully and make sure they bore scrutiny, lest someone mistake my account for fiction and accuse me of being a liar.

"I must be perfectly frank with you, Mr. Halifax. My colleagues are of the opinion that we should kill you immediately and bury you in an unmarked grave in the jungle, like any common spy. The Richard Halifax you claim to be is presumed dead. We would simply be making reality conform to what the world already believes."

He gave me a moment to let this sink in. "I, however, see potential in you, Dickee-san. May I call you Dickee-san?"

I told Dr. K. he could call me whatever kept my head attached to my neck.

"Very good, Dickee-san. And I'm glad your swelling has gone down, because, provided you can speak with clarity and allow us to collaborate, I can do just that. I'll help you excavate the truth of your story until my colleagues are satisfied and allow you to go free."

"And Nacho too?" I said. "He's my sidekick."

"Of course, Dickee-san. And Nacho too. So do we have a deal?"

"You bet, Doc."

He said that I could call him "sensei," because in Japanese "sensei" was an honorific for doctors like him but, more important, because "sensei" meant teacher. And, like a teacher, he was going to help me learn things. "Does that sound agreeable to you?"

I told him it did.

"Wonderful," he said. Then he looked at his colleague with the valise and gave a little upward nod of his head.

The next thing I knew, I was hanging upside down.

"Do you know, Dickee-san," asked Dr. Kanemoto, "how many bones there are in the human foot?"

Thus began my first lesson. I learned that the foot holds even more secrets than it does bones and ligaments. It is the key, Dr. Kanemoto explained to me, to the entire *corpus humanum*. The lymphatic system, the liver and kidneys, even the ole poop chute and trouser snake have embassies in the foot. The same goes for all the dimensions of the human personality. The foot is the foundation of who we are, the joint between man and world. You can walk a mile in another's shoes, but not in his feet. They are irrefutably our own. And yet the feet, like all things, as Dr. Kanemoto taught me, are subject to change. Not even the sturdiest pair of clodhoppers can keep the feet from soaking in the river of Heraclitean flux.

Dr. Kanemoto says that if you want to remake a man, then you need to remake him from the ground up. And that starts with the foot. Our first few sessions, I didn't quite understand what he meant. It seemed an awful lot like torture. Dr. Kanemoto would ask me questions about my life, in particular my travels in Asia, and Corporal Isaya, the wielder of the brazilwood bludgeon, would strike precise blows on my feet. I would scream and beg them to stop, then Dr. Kanemoto would calmly tell me that he needed to extract the truth of my story from every place it could possibly hide. Just as crystals of uric acid gather in the toes of gout sufferers, so little deposits of truth follow gravity down into the nooks and crannies of the foot. By hanging me upside down and loosening the deposits, the truth could trickle down through my body and come tumbling out my mouth.

"But I'm telling you the truth!" I screamed, though that was still something of a lie. I thought if I told Dr. Kanemoto the full extent of my arms dealings in China, it might complicate my return home. Remember, boys, every story has an audience, and the tale we tell must take their wishes into consideration. But no matter how much I shouted or vomited from sheer pain or protested that I had already told him everything, the indefatigable Dr. Kanemoto nudged me on toward clarity.

"What is it you want, Dickee-san?"

"To go home."

"Good. And I can help you get home. But then, once you are home, what will you want?"

"I don't understand. Just to be home. In my bed, at peace, back in my old life."

"Oh, Dickee-san, how little you must know yourself if you think you will be at peace once you are home. Didn't you tell me you undertook the voyage of the *Soup Dumpling* precisely because you were unhappy with your life at home? That its very foundation was cracked?"

In fact, my house in Laguna Beach creaked with every step, and the cantilevered kitchen listed something awful. But I didn't realize I'd already told him about that lemon.

"I mean it metaphorically, Dickee-san," said Dr. K., noticing my perplexed look. "Do you really imagine that a restless soul like you will be content to lie around doing nothing? That none of these intimate brushes with death will haunt your dreams and destroy your sleep, and you'll just carry on as before, with your beer busts and swimming parties?"

I told him I was willing to give it a shot.

But Sensei Kanemoto explained that, having undergone a horrific ordeal, I was still in a state of sustained shock about what I had endured and the kinds of desperate acts I had been forced to commit. "Just think, Dickee-san, if we were to send you back to America on the next mail ship, what would happen? Imagine going around the country on a lecture tour, looking into the eyes of your millions of young readers, and telling them how you beat a boy not much older than them within an inch of his life in the mud pits of Saipan. Or telling the Daughters of the American Revolution over a hot pancake breakfast how you axed out cutlets from the back of your dear childhood friend. The truth is, Dicky, that you would be unable to integrate the terrible experiences you have undergone, the savage deeds you have done in order to survive, and you would suffer a kind of ego estrangement and waking death that is more agonizing than any thirst or imprisonment. It would be a psychological shipwreck worse than the shipwreck itself."

He was right, of course. The thought of returning home, which had sustained me all these months, now suddenly filled me with terror. I would be a pariah. People would shrink from me. My name would be raked through the muck of every rag in the country. My publisher, already skittish about my prospects since the film flop and bestowing ever-shrinking advances, would drop me and let my books fall out of print. Speaking engagements, usually my bread and butter even amid dwindling book sales, would dry up, and my agent, Fred Feakins, too spineless to cut me loose, would just stop returning my calls. My debts from the failure of the *Soup Dumpling* would mount, and my bespoke money pit in Laguna Beach would finally swallow me whole. I'd come out on the other side of bankruptcy with nothing—not even the shoulder of my beloved sidekick to cry on, because in a moment of weakness I'd eaten him. I would become one of those wretches scrounging from the trash and spewing my lunacy on the streets, scaring mothers and children with hard proof of just how miserable a human life could become.

Yet even if I acknowledged the impossibility of returning home in my current state, I still wasn't convinced why the good doctor had to liquefy all the bones in my feet.

"As I told you, Dicky, we must reset you, just as a clock that has lost time must be wound and set anew. For a man, this requires coming to terms with every shard of truth about your life, from infancy right up to your recent tenure in the phosphate mines. Confronting one's past is, I'm afraid, a painful experience. For the mind to free itself, the feet must suffer. But I assure you it is not torture. Rather, it is a salutary suffering, aimed to make you healthy again. Think of it like visiting the dentist."

So I took a deep breath and let the doctor go to work.

You wouldn't believe what tumbled out of me. I spilled beans like the Heinz factory after an earthquake. I told the sensei about Wesley—how we used to sleep together as boys, butt naked on hot summer nights, dreaming about sailing to the North Pole or riding stallions across the

Gobi Desert. I told him how, when Wesley and I were even younger, Mother—not Roderick but my actual mother—used to dress the two of us as little girls and take us out to tea at Union Station. We'd sit at a table closest to the concourse, and Mother would delight in all the compliments we received from strangers coming off the trains about what "precious dolls" we were. I told him about how my only friend when I was in my sickly phase was a sweet girl named Sally Bent, who lived in the house behind us. She often had to miss school to care for her father, a crippled alcoholic who'd lost his leg to diabetes, and the two of us would sneak out of our windows after lunch, when my mother was on her Veronal nap and her daddy was passed out drunk, and we'd play together in the strip of woodland that separated our yards. It was like it existed out of time, that little border wood, with us a couple of fugitives stealing out in the light of day while the rest of the world was in school, at work, or in a chemically induced stupor. Sally was two years older, but she didn't treat me like a pest the way most girls did. And I didn't pull her hair or put bugs down her dress the way I usually did with the fairer sex. Instead, we talked. Not shooting the breeze or spinning yarns either. Just honest talk. Sharing memories about things we'd seen or felt, venting our frustrations about our mutual confinements and the custom-built insane asylum that is every family.

One time I told Sally about how my mother used to dress us as girls. And Sally, rather than laugh, asked me how it made me feel. And I said, well, you know, it was kind of fun. Being yourself but being somebody else at the same time. People thinking you're one thing, but you know you're something else. Or, rather, you're that thing they see, but you're also not that. It was fun fooling people, and I guess our mother enjoyed pretending she had two adorable daughters instead of two little hellions like me and Wes. But what I really liked was the feeling of duplicating my experience of the world. Like I was putting on a play for the world while the other part of me watched. And that, just by changing my clothes or the way I talked, I could act out a whole different part. Sally said that made sense to her—that was why she liked singing and dancing and acting and was going to be in show business when she grew up. Then Sally asked me if I wanted to swap clothes and wear her dress for a bit. At first I thought she was fooling, but she said, "Go on, Dick. It's just us here. You said you remember liking it. Why not give it a try?" So we swapped, the two of us stripping down like we were brothers, and she looked at my parts and I looked at hers and she said the only trouser snake she'd seen was her daddy's, when his bathrobe came awry. I told her the only time I'd seen a girl's gash was once at the country-club swimming pool, when I'd gone into the ladies' locker room by mistake and come face-to-face with a pair of haunches flanking what looked like a hairy pile of roast beef. I felt like I'd been struck by lightning and bolted right there to the tile, turned to a pillar of salt for staring into some profane mystery. Even when the ladies noticed me and started screaming, I still couldn't move, not till one of them chased me out with a towel. Sally laughed but said I shouldn't call it a "gash" (and neither should you, boys), because it was coarse. I asked her what she called it instead, and she said she called it her honeycomb. Then she handed me her dress and I gave her my pants and shirt and the two of us got dressed as the other. And damn me, boys, if we didn't enjoy ourselves. Got up like a boy and with her hair pulled back, Sally even reminded me of Wes. Same light freckles on her cheeks, same pink fleshy ears.

From then on, whenever Sally and I met in the woods, we'd swap clothes and then talk as we had before. Sometimes Sally would practice her kissing on me too, and one time after we'd swapped clothes, she said we should touch each other in our private places. She guided my hand into her trousers and past the sparse flaxen hair of her pubis into the warm humid folds of her honeycomb. At the same time, she reached under my dress and gave my little pecker the gentlest squeeze.

I also told Dr. Kanemoto about my water-skiing accident, years later, the summer after Wesley's death. It was just another carefree July day in Kansas City with a coupla beers out on Lake Tapawingo, pulling stunts off the back of my friend Russ's motorboat, until suddenly, in a moment of carelessness, I felt a little pinch and the whole lake seemed to fill with my blood. The engine blade had sliced right through the tendons that make your trouser snake stand up and salute a pretty girl dressed as a boy like Sally.

I even told him about the whole brouhaha I had going with that pouty German puck, Hank Rauch. Explaining *that* situation required opening and spilling several other cans of beans too. So out came the little business Roderick and I had developed. A business that capitalized on his skills for infiltration and thievery—along with his robust connections to the munitions industry—and mine for talking a winning game. That's when I told Sensei we had sold carbines to Chiang Kai-shek and even rattier old shooters to the communists, which I guess didn't help my case in the eyes of the Japs. Though I also told him about other deals we had done, which more or less evened the scorecard.

And then, since the whole world is one tangled web and you can't really yank on one thread without unspooling the rest of it, I told him about Roderick's pièce de résistance—getting his hands on the Norden plans.

Dr. Kanemoto narrowed his eyes tight to conceal his interest, but I could tell there were little bells ringing in that doctor brain of his.

"When you say Norden plans, Dickee-san, are you referring to the secret American technology for accurate aerial bombardment?"

"That's the one, Dr. K."

To his rapt attention, I explained how Roderick had shown up in Hong Kong with them sewn into his girdle. At first, I'd been alarmed. Running guns to China is a fairly straightforward business. All you need are a few lucky contacts along the Yangtze and in the hill country between Siam and Yunnan, plus a gift for palaver and a hundred-dollar smile. That is, provided you have a Roderick to oversee procurement and logistics. But stealing military secrets? Well, that was a new one for me, at least mostly.

"Roderick, you dingbat, what in the hell are we supposed to do with that?" I'd asked, seeing a whole mess of diagrams spread across the bed.

He said we should sell them to the highest bidder. We'd already found ways to cash in on wars in Spain, Abyssinia, and China, and more war was sure to come. A highly coveted technology like the Norden bombsight, he said, was guaranteed to make us a fortune. Lord knows the *Soup Dumpling* could have used some of that dough, the way ole Ming Fat was sucking dollars out of my pocket. And my pecuniary troubles went far beyond the ship itself. Once I sailed into

San Francisco, I'd have a whole pile of loans to work off. Not to mention the state-of-the-art financial abyss of a home I'd left behind down south. Word of advice, boys: If a fancy-pants architect tells you he has a vision for a house on the edge of a cliff in earthquake country that defies all the rules of traditional building, including the laws of gravity and soil erosion, and tells you he can build it for a certain price in a certain amount of time, run!

So when Roderick said these drawings fresh from his girdle could make my money problems go away, I was all ears. However, I was still reluctant about doing something outright treasonous, like stabbing Lady Liberty in the back.

That's when Roderick and I landed on the idea of not selling them to anyone. Instead, we could simply threaten to sell them and then sell them back to the Norden suits for a tidy sum. Money in our pocket and the plans back where they belonged—a double victory. We had pulled this kind of fake-a-roo on overeager gun shoppers before, like that sour English fellow in Siam.

But I've gotten ahead of myself. I was telling you about Hank Rauch. Hank was, like me, a writer, though, like most writers, considerably more of a sissy. He had that impish European intellectual thing down pat. He was one of those poets who fed on the darkness, was shameless about his perversions, and looked at the world through sunken eyes. But he was a born hell-raiser too. Never far from a bottle, a needle, or vial of pills, Hank could keep the party going through breakfast the next day. Wailing on the piano and singing old German ditties or the latest Duke Ellington tune, with that crazed look in his eyes that told you he just might get up at any second and either dance the jitterbug or fling himself off a bridge. I liked the guy well enough, in spite of himself. His twin sister was probably the better man—funny, direct, nothing coquettish about her, though she did once try to climb Mount Halifax. But until someone opens up a new horizon in urology, boys, that summit will remain unconquered.

I never much talked about it before Sensei Kanemoto opened me up, and still won't dwell on anything too lewd for your young ears, but permit me a quick word of advice. Never take anything for granted, boys—especially the mysterious workings of the *corpus cavernosum*, which will transform the droopingest of shriveled appendages into a blood-filled lead pipe. Every tumescence is a miracle. And as you boys are entering a period of life where random sproutings become such a regular occurrence as to be considered a nuisance, just remember there are people on this earth who would give ten botched surgeries and too many sad contraptions of rubber bands and Popsicle sticks to have what you have. So be grateful, boys, and remember: Whenever engaging in any activity riskier than a brisk walk, wear a jockstrap.

Now, where was I? Oh, right, Hank Rauch. I'd met Hank and his sister, Hilde, briefly in Addis Ababa, but I actually got to know him out in Hollywood the following year, 1937. Hank had originally come out in '35, left briefly to clench his fist in Spain (we'd just missed each other there, with the Rauches in Madrid and Roderick and me in Barcelona), and he returned to the Hollywood grind right as your man Dicky began to hit a rough patch. He'd been hired as one of the six script doctors on my film *Ulysses, Junior* and since the other five had already butchered the thing beyond recognition, I didn't blame Hank for the parts he lopped off. If anything, he tried to sew some of my mutilated parts back on. He was the only one of those vultures who told me he thought I had star quality—said I was twice as handsome as Clark Gable, with normal-sized ears and my own teeth to boot. Well, I knew Hank was alright after that. And while Roderick never took to him, I'd invite him down to Laguna Beach to come for a swim or toss the old pigskin around the living room and laugh about our problems.

Ulysses, Junior proved to be a flop, and nobody in town showed any interest in seeing my mug on another reel of celluloid. I lost my writing credit on it, too, and vowed from then on to stick to books. Like I said, a little rough patch, but Hank, it seemed, was always in a rough patch. In fact, he'd grown up in one, thorny with the accolades of his illustrious father. That old blowhard Theodor Rauch was considered the greatest German writer since Goethe, and Hank just about couldn't stand it. He said his father had been too cowardly to say a bad thing about Hitler for fear he'd lose his readers and only changed his mind years later when he realized he'd lose even more if he didn't say something. He said his father was a phony egotist who only pretended to have convictions or compassion so as to keep people in his thrall, that he had written pages upon pages of diary entries that Hank had once snuck a peek at about how he loathed democracy, how the Jews were a thorn in Europe's side, and how, when Hank was a youngster, he dreamed of smooching his own son's privates. I told him that was rotten luck, that my mother was a hypochondriac who had been imprisoned by her own fearful imagination, and that my father was a real estate developer who was always away on business when I was growing up, and that there was a time when I would have been thrilled to receive any sign of affection from him, maybe even a kiss on the privates. Things only got worse after we lost Wesley, who had always been the favored son over sickly Richard.

So Hank and I were fine company: a couple of Negative Nancys bitching and moaning about our imperfect upbringings and unrecognized talents until we made each other bust a gut.

Hank taught me a couple of valuable lessons that year. The first was that you can't count on Hollywood. While a lot of writers, your man Dick included, thought that movie work would be our golden meal ticket and were bitter when it wasn't, Hank seemed to accept his failure there as a foregone conclusion. He said it was necessary to have another project of one's own, something serious and with truth behind it, to balance the impersonal nature of the film business. He'd done work with UFA before Goebbels swallowed it up and it was the same old story, whether in Berlin or Hollywood. "Never forget this, Dick," he said with a strange intensity. "You're a tiny replaceable cog in an industrial apparatus whose business is manufacturing illusions." I asked him what his own project was, and he told me it was a journal he'd recently started: *The Reckoning*.

"Catchy name," I said. "What's its drift?"

"Culture and politics. Beauty and justice. Schiller for the twentieth century."

"Is it bolshie?" I asked.

"Depends on what you mean," he said defensively. "Of course, my father would say it is."

I later learned from him that his father had initially been on *The Reckoning*'s editorial board, which gave Hank's operation enough clout and funds to get up and running, but just recently Hank had written a savage denunciation of fascism along with the "social fascism" of bourgeois liberal democracy and signed it from the whole editorial board rather than his own name. Papa Rauch demanded he publish a retraction, and when Hank refused, he wrote a piece of his own in *The Atlantic,* declaring his unwavering commitment to a modern humanism distilled from the liberal tradition, one *that would make no truck with the anti-historical barbarities of either fascism or bolshevism, as a certain young poet manqué is all too willing to do, a clear sign that his talent is no match for his outrage.* It was pretty clear which lame poet of a son he had in mind, since just before the piece was published, Theodor Rauch withdrew his name and financial support from *The Reckoning.* Many of his centrist, patrician circle promptly followed suit. And the journal was now in a financial pickle.

But Hank didn't tell me any of that back then. Instead, he just said of the journal, "Its sole aim is to put forth an anti-fascist aesthetics. Revolutionary in its outlook, of course, but it bows to no single ideology but the truth."

I told him that was the spirit precisely to my taste—that I was a freebooter at heart, and my only North Star was freedom.

"You know, Dick, there's more to you than people give you credit for."

"Why? What do people say about me?" I asked.

"Oh, nothing," said Hank. "You know how people talk."

"About what?" I pressed.

"Oh," said Hank, fingering his ear like he was not going to say what was actually on his mind. "Just that you're all derring-do and misadventure and breezy bravado. But they mistake you for your persona. They don't see the real you."

"What do you see?" I asked.

"I see a smart, energetic boy who rejects the soulless, grown-up world. A boy who wants to embrace the whole of life in all its wildness and share it with others because he's not quite sure how to embrace just one person."

That's when the nutty little Kraut smooched your Dicky like his sweetheart.

Three months later, I left for China on assignment from *Good*

Housekeeping. It was Hank who got me the gig, through his press-agency contacts. I had taken his advice and hoped some serious war reporting would wash the fecal taste of Hollywood from my mouth while I planned my next big adventure (I also hoped Roderick and I could make a bundle there with some of his surplus firearms). Hank said it would help people see that Richard Halifax was not just a madcap adventurer but someone truly engaged with his time, a manly man who also cared about his fellow man.

Before I left, Hank asked me to carry some letters for him to Shanghai. He said he'd been communicating with members of the émigré community there, soliciting pieces and subscriptions for the journal, and was eventually planning to come out there himself, but for the time being he was having a hell of a time getting mail through the Japanese lines.

At this point, Sensei Kanemoto interrupted my story to ask if I knew the contents of these letters.

"Not specifically, no. I'm not so weasely as to read another man's mail, Sensei. Like I said, they were correspondence for his journal, addressed to organizations like the League of German Writers in Exile or the World Committee Against War and Fascism."

"And where did you drop these letters off?"

"A bookshop in the international settlement: Zeitgeist Books."

"And were you being paid to carry these letters?"

"I'm no dummy, Sensei. Hank was a swell enough guy, but he wasn't expecting me to do it for free. I got a little cut for playing courier, and sometimes the clerk at Zeitgeist would give me letters to bring back to Hank in California or down to Bangkok, where I had a few friends among the Siamese swanky set."

It was a fine operation we had going. Hank was keeping *The Reckoning* in the black, sans Daddy's donations, and I was pulling in enough to keep me in style, traveling between Shanghai and Hankow in an armored Bentley and buying rounds for the press corps. In fact, Agnes Smedley got so used to a gimlet on my dime that she took to calling the drinks I stood her "Dicky juice." Yessir, between Hank's courier service and Roderick's guns, I was stacking up yuan like Lincoln Logs. And that's when I started thinking about building a Chinese ship and sailing it over the ocean. It was time to start dreaming in deeds.

"Dickee-san, you do realize who you were working for, don't you?" asked Dr. Kanemoto. "When you were carrying those letters, back and forth?"

"You betcha, Sensei. Dicky Halifax, privateer."

"And the Soviets."

"You don't say? Well, all I knew, Doc, was that Hank had helped me out, and I was helping him out, and we both were helping ourselves."

"I'm sorry, Dickee-san, but how does all this brouhaha with Hank Rauch, as you call it, relate to the Norden bombsight plans?"

"I'm almost there, Sensei," I explained. "Please bear with me." And that's when it struck me that maybe Roderick's last words on our life raft had been aiming to tell me about the Norden plans. Was there something about those plans he wanted me to know? Well, I guess I'll never find out what had been on Roderick's mind, and I preferred not to dwell on that grisly moment just then. Besides, Sensei had his own questions he wanted answered.

"See, in December of '38, Hank himself made it over to China on journal business. By then I was in Hong Kong just about full time, working on the *Soup Dumpling*. I promised myself I wouldn't return to American shores except by my own boat. Roderick was about to leave for home on a mandatory Christmas visit with his family when Hank's telegram arrived, saying he would be sailing into Hong Kong on his way to Shanghai. I told him to look me up and we'd have ourselves a grand old time. Learning of this, Roderick tried to persuade me to return with him to Kansas City to visit my ailing parents and let him cook me a Christmas goose. I declined, and he left in a sulk.

"When Hank showed up, I made him my surrogate sidekick, just as Roderick feared, and the two of us tore up the nightclubs and whiskey dens along Queen's Road. It began to dawn on me then that, one, Hank Rauch was a hopeless drug addict, and two, the poor sod had developed quite a soft spot for me. I'll admit I rather enjoyed being the sunburst in that brooding universe of his, and when he was wound up on the right cocktail of fluids and powders, Hank was a helluva lot more fun than Roderick. But things got shaky when Mother returned.

"To say Roderick was the jealous type is putting it mildly—he once served the aviator Jackie Thorndale a quiche filled with thumbtacks after learning he'd be my co-pilot on the voyage for *The Magic Carpet* and that the biplane couldn't accommodate a third seat. I assured him now that I had no designs on replacing him with Hank as my sidekick on the *Soup Dumpling*. 'After all, you can't just up and find another mother, Mother.' But Roderick was still fearful. I begged him not to lace Hank's food with anything sharp—thankfully, Hank took most of his calories intravenously or straight from the bottle. But short of poisoning, whenever Roderick felt his place in the Halifax galaxy threatened, he resorted to grandiose demonstrations of his worth.

"That was how we'd fallen into the arms-running business in the first place. Our adventures were always straining their allotted budgets, like Roderick's belly against his waistband, and Roderick saw an opportunity to raise funds for our travels by putting his profession to use. We sold two thousand hand grenades to Haile Selassie on our tour of Abyssinia—even got his regal mug on the cover of *Time* magazine. Not that either gave him the winning edge in the end, probably because we'd turned around and sold just as many grenades to a band of Italian *Arditi* (now, those boys know how to fiesta!). As a result, I came away with enough lire and bongo-bucks to keep the adventure going in style. The following year in Spain, thanks to Roderick's shadowy connections, we'd found a similar opportunity to cash in.

"So when Roderick returned to Hong Kong at the end of January, knowing that Hank and I had been having a fine time without him, I guess I shouldn't have been surprised to see those bombsight plans come spilling out of his girdle. The only problem was that the *Soup Dumpling* was due to set sail by April. We'd never have enough time to go back to the States, find the right fella at Norden to blackmail, get paid, and then get new travel visas to be back in time for the launch. Besides, I was already working on a fundraising lead down in Bangkok. And even after only a brief trip away, I'd noticed upon returning that Ming Fat's shipyard had assumed the somniferous air of a preschool at naptime and my crew had acquired fresh cases of the clap. If I returned to the States for a full month, the whole endeavor would go belly-up. So we decided we'd have to save our grand coup for after the voyage. But both Roderick and I were nervous about traveling with the plans. What if they got wet? What if we got stopped and searched by the Japanese?

"'For chrissakes, Mother,' I said, 'why didn't you just leave them safely tucked away in Kansas City? That's D-minus work on risk assessment.' Clearly he hadn't thought things through. He was blinded by the need to astound me with his treasure, like a dog that brings a dead squirrel to the foot of your bed, thinking you'll be thrilled. I admit I was impressed, but Roderick's heist seemed to create more problems at the moment than it solved.

"Then Hank knocked on the door to our suite. Roderick started scrambling to hide the drawings, but I said, 'Wait, Roderick. What if we send them back with Hank?' I'd been his courier for the last year; now he could be mine.

"Roderick grudgingly accepted, but when Hank saw all those diagrams we were hoping he'd carry back, he just shook his head in disbelief. 'You two need to wise up. Only an idiot would carry secret information like that halfway across the world.'

"Roderick scowled at him.

"'Well, what's the trick, Hank?' I said.

"'I'll need a camera, a darkroom, and a pair of scissors.'

"And that's what happened—my two sidekicks cracked their heads together and out came magic. Turns out Hank had a use for that hypodermic needle and bag of chemicals beyond just squirting junk in his veins. He boiled those plans down into the teeniest little photographs you ever barely saw. I swear, they were no bigger than a freckle or the hind end of a fruit fly. 'Microdots,' Hank called them. Said his friends from the Zeitgeist Bookshop messenger service had taught him the trick. Well, you better believe Roderick and I took note."

"So Hank Rauch returned to California with the Norden plans hidden on microdots?" said Dr. Kanemoto, his curiosity evidently piqued. "Is that right, Dickee-san?"

"Yessiree, Sensei. Slapped 'em right onto the duplicate of an old letter I had lying around."

And there's more to that story, boys, but I'll have to save it for another time. Dr. Kanemoto has just returned and sounds like he's brought a visitor with him. Assuming everything pans out like I'm hoping, I'll soon be a free man and you can tell your mama to slap a cake in the oven for my homecoming.

Yours till soon,
Dicky

14

HILDEGARD RAUCH

Yes, I know I promised I wouldn't go to the fair without you, but I made that promise thinking you would come back in a few days or a few weeks at most. It's nearly Thanksgiving. Stalin is looking carnivorously at Finland, the Germans keep sinking passenger ships, and it's hard to tell that Britain and France have declared war at all. Meanwhile, Poland has entirely ceased to exist, and despite the prevailing mood here of "too bad over there," part of me is still in Europe. It's only a matter of time before all the various fires converge and the entire world is engulfed. So I spent the morning furiously writing appeals to get visas for Klara and Gerhard, the Brenners, the Blochs, and the whole Hiersteiner family—the list is endless, and even if I spend all day every day to the exclusion of all else, it will never be enough. And then I went to Treasure Island to meet Walter.

Imagine my chagrin when I arrived, as agreed, beneath the Tower of the Sun and there waiting for me was Walter—with Nadia.

"There she is. Our overgrown Gretel."

"Hello, Nadia," I said, shooting Walter a look. "I didn't realize you were joining us."

"Well, I can't let Walter and you have all the fun without me. Don't you know how jealous I get?"

Had he told her? "I wouldn't have thought anarchists go in for world's fairs."

"*Au contraire.* This is important field research. A perfect window onto the distraction of the masses, where capitalism remakes the sensuous life of culture into a cult of exoticized consumption. Plus, I like to shoot the metal boats."

"There'll be plenty of time for shooting things," said Walter, "but we must go see Hilde's painting first."

"I thought we were going to the girlie farm," said Nadia.

"I doubt the painting gallery will be able to follow a visit to the Nude Ranch," I said.

"It's settled, then," said Walter. "Painting first, then girlie farm."

"Fine," said Nadia. "Then we shoot boats."

The Palace of Fine and Decorative Arts, as you would know if you hadn't eaten a pound of sedatives, is not a palace but a massive hangar along the water. A far cry from the Beaux Arts beauty of the Palace of Fine Arts from the last fair here, in 1915. It seems San Francisco has a knack for staging world's fairs whenever the world is at war. The last palace was too beautiful to tear down. This one, glass and steel and aluminum siding, looks like it will be easy to convert into an aerodrome or tank shed.

We walked past the permanent galleries, which I had visited in the spring, past the Italian Old Masters, down the hall of Decorative Arts. The Aalto glass was still beautiful, Le Corbusier's furniture still left me cold, and I was even more awestruck this time by the masks and carved totems from the Pacific Northwest. I caught up with Walter and Nadia in the exhibition of Modern Californian Painting, where there hung nearly a hundred new works.

"There's yours," said Walter. "Right between the Helen Bruton mosaic and the Bufano sculpture." Walter was the only one of us who had seen the fall exhibition. In fact, he knew every piece in it.

I took in my painting, there amid the work of other artists I admired—real artists, I thought, realizing I sounded like Mother with her "real Jews." It felt like a validation. Perhaps I, too, was one of these real artists. And yet, even though this was easily the most accomplished exhibition I had been part of, the moment itself felt anticlimactic. Here was a work that I had infused with my being, a labor that had consumed me and given my days meaning, and now it was just another thing. Another object in the world, one more artifact of the human struggle that would ultimately become a piece of garbage in the ocean.

"Not without talent, Hildchen," said Nadia. "Though I'm not surprised. Walter is always drawn to talent. Like a bee to honey."

I looked at Walter, who smiled dumbly, as though there was no veiled meaning to be had from Nadia's words. "And her woodcuts are just as good," he said. "I think Hilde has managed to keep Expressionism fresh and alive in transplanted form. You've embraced the freedom and emotional force of abstraction without abandoning the figurative realm. And it's as evocative and dreamlike as the best of the Surrealists yet doesn't succumb to their nihilism. Instead, it is relentlessly humanist."

"Really, Walter," I said, blushing. "That's too much."

"Yes, please, Walter," said Nadia, "I almost regurgitated my corn dog. Besides, everyone knows there's nothing on the planet stodgier than humanism. If any word makes me want to reach for my dynamite—"

"Now, now, dear," said Walter, "you promised you wouldn't bring up dynamite in polite company."

To get from the art gallery to the Gayway, we had to cross the international pavilions. As we walked through the courtyards of the Pacific World—with grass-skirted Hawaiians dancing the hula, a kangaroo petting zoo from Australia, and a troupe of xylophone-mad drummers from the Dutch Indies—Nadia took me by the arm.

"Is it not sad, Hildchen," said Nadia, casting her eyes toward the Japanese pavilion, "to see the world remade as an amusement park for Americans?"

A man in a headband was busy turning little cakes of glutinous rice over a grill, calling out his wares. "*Yakimochi! Oishii yakimochi!* Very tasty rice cake!"

"Perhaps it's the only way to see the world at peace," said Walter, walking directly behind us. "As a fiction."

"Precisely," said Nadia. "The seduction of the ersatz world. To distract from a world at war. A most powerful opiate. Just like the movies. Or, for that matter, paintings."

I did not feel like taking Nadia's bait. I was too annoyed with Walter for bringing her, with Nadia for being herself. But mostly I was annoyed with myself for having become so entangled with the two of them.

"Look," said Nadia, "here we have the Japanese busying themselves with their woodcuts and rice cakes, while just across the street there, where that pagoda is, are the Chinese, no doubt polishing jade and steaming dumplings, as though they haven't a care in the world. Everyone wearing the same forced idiotic grin of the salesman, whoring themselves out to hungry Americans. You'd never think that actually, at this very moment, that Japanese man's brothers are probably raping and bayoneting those Chinamen's sisters."

Given the current world situation, I agreed there was something perverse about this vision of international harmony. But was it not reality itself that was perverse?

"Why shouldn't these people here live their lives in peace?" said Walter. "They are on a fantasy island in California, not occupied China. Would you rather they start killing one another here at the fair?"

"At least it would be honest," said Nadia. "But honesty is the one taboo of capitalism. Do you know why? Because the truth is revolting. And the only honest response to a revolting truth is to revolt."

"Well, at least they had the good sense to put Peru between China and Japan—didn't let geography stand in the way of a good buffer." Walter pointed at a vaguely Incan-looking ziggurat, beside a man selling steamed corn. "At least I think that's Peru."

I myself felt like Peru, stuck between Walter and Nadia. Not because they were at war—not that I could tell—but because I felt like the foreign entity that had been dropped into strange, perilous waters. If only I had stayed on my side of the ocean and kept my hands off Walter's peninsula, I would not have the anarchist archipelago of Nadia encircling me.

We continued through this pastiche of Potemkin villages, through the South Pacific and Latin America, skirting Italy and France and cutting through the conspicuous void where our map told us Czechoslovakia was. Just a few days ago, in the real Czechoslovakia, the Nazis had executed more than a thousand students who had demonstrated against German occupation.

China, it turned out, was, as the placard boasted in a phrase that would have made you howl with laughter, *an authentic reproduction of a historical Chinese village*—a walled city with fake peasants tending fake rice paddies and women selling fake ducks in a fake bazaar. A sign informed us that around the corner at the concession plaza, *Real Peking Duck* could be bought and enjoyed.

"There's a bit of reality for you," Walter said, pointing at a young coolie pulling a fat blond woman in a rickshaw. "Maybe she's late for work at the Nude Ranch."

We left Nadia at the shooting gallery. She was determined to stay until she won a stuffed alligator and said she'd come find us at the girlie farm.

It was easy to find, because it was the only attraction on the Gayway—amid the midget rodeos, laughing jacks, crystal balls, dunk-tank clowns, race-cart apes, guess-your-weights, and test-your-strengths—where grown men were lined up, looking as giddy with anticipation as the sons they'd left behind at the roller coaster.

The Nude Ranch was not a ranch at all but a peep show inside an old Spanish saloon. Terra-cotta roof tiles, whitewashed adobe façade, and split-wood lettering that read *Sally Bent's NÐude Ranch*, with the palimpsest of the *D* still visible beside the added, jauntily angled *N*.

Miss Bent herself was preparing to perform, we learned, so Walter bought us tickets and we inched our way from the porch to the darkened panorama inside.

"I'm sorry I didn't tell you I was bringing Nadia," said Walter. "I hope it's alright."

"Why shouldn't it be alright?" I said, a bit too aggressively. "After all, she's your wife."

"I hope I haven't made things awkward."

"Don't be silly, Walter. Let's pretend last week didn't happen—"

"Yes, but—"

"—And remain just friends, without the fucking. Please, I really do need a friend, and not a lover with a wife."

"Very well, Hilde. Friends it is. Without the fucking."

Just then the line moved forward and a titanic bouncer at the door checked our stubs beside a sign that read: *No one under eighteen. No photography. No lewd talk.*

"You better pay attention, Walter. Or this man will wash your filthy mouth out."

The girls were in a walled-off outdoor corral, visible behind glass, as though in an aquarium or the diorama displays at the Völkerkunde Museum. Except these specimens, clad in matching cowboy hats, red bandanas, white belts, and sequined silver boots, were busy doing the work of the most dysfunctional ranch in America. Girls petting a miniature donkey, lassoing a calf, riding a mechanical bull, and, yes, milking a real goat, as well as a host of other manual chores of whittling, polishing, and painting. All while unrestricted by clothing, save for the standard burlesque wardrobe of pasties and thong.

"I think we should sue them for false advertising," said Walter. "Nude, my eye."

"They're about as nude as much as it is a ranch."

But the other customers didn't appear to feel swindled. Instead, there was a kind of reverent hush, punctuated only occasionally by that stupidest of all male utterances: the libidinous whistle.

Of course, after Berlin, it all seemed laughably tame. Not a single hole visible, let alone penetrated. Not even a peek. It was as pure and wholesome as the butter being churned by that buxom Eve with red curls coming out her cowboy hat.

But what was different from any live show I'd seen, and what fascinated me, was the purely voyeuristic nature of it. The women did not acknowledge the spectators at all. Instead, they acted like it was just another day of work at the ranch and went about their mundane, futile tasks as though cognizant only of their own enjoyment, which they faked remarkably well. It was a charade, of course, but not having to mug for an audience seemed to give them an air of dignity. They were subjects in a live painting, unaware of any frame or viewer. They spoke desultorily to one another, which couldn't be heard through the glass or over the banjo music being broadcast inside the saloon. It struck me that as seductive as the illusion of naked girls performing manual labor was for some, even more powerful was the illusion of people absorbed in their work.

The spell was broken when the official show began and this understated imitation of life gave way to the more familiar burlesque spectacle. "Ladies and gentlemen," announced a disembodied voice, "please put your hands together for the Belle of the Bubble Bath, the

Femme Fatale of the Fan Dance, the Tantalizing Queen of Treasure Island—Her Sexellency, the one and only Sally Bent!"

Out came a petite, curly-headed blond woman sitting sideways on bare horseback, her body covered only by an artfully placed fan of ostrich plumes.

After the show, Walter went to go find Nadia, who presumably had not yet shot her way into a stuffed alligator, and I approached the bouncer and asked if it would be possible to see Miss Bent.

"Sorry, lady, but Miss Bent doesn't see fans between shows."

"Oh, I'm not a fan," I said. "Nor am I really a lady."

The bouncer raised his single large brow at me.

"I'd like to talk to her about a . . . business matter. Something pertaining to Richard Halifax."

The brow remained raised, and I couldn't help but think that, absent an eye, he'd make a good Cyclops. "Wait here." He latched the velvet rope behind him and went into the saloon.

Shortly, he returned. "Straight back through the double doors, first door on the right."

I passed through the saloon, down a corridor of dressing rooms, and knocked.

"Come in," called a deep feminine voice.

"Miss Bent?"

"That's what the giant name on the door says."

I already felt like an idiot. I was nearly certain I had come to waste this woman's time and didn't really know what I wanted to ask her.

She was sitting at her vanity, topless, applying lotion to her arms.

"Thank you for seeing me, and I apologize for bothering you."

"Thanks *and* sorry, huh? Say, does it smell like shit in here to you?"

"Uh, no, not particularly. Maybe a little."

"Goddamn goat sprays pellets like a howitzer. And that cute-looking donkey? Diarrhea factory. Word of advice—if you ever open a nude ranch, get fake animals."

"I'll keep that in mind."

"Do the tits bother you?"

"The tits?" I realized she was talking about her own, which were marvelous. "Oh, no, not at all."

"Goddamn tassels chafe the shit out of my nipples. So, Tater said you had something business-related to ask me about Dick Halifax?"

"Yes, that's right."

"What's he to you?"

"Ehm, well, nothing really. Or, rather, I met him only once, but it was my brother who knew him."

"And who's your brother?"

"Heinrich Rauch." She gave no sign of recognition. "He goes by Hank?"

"Hank? Hank Rauch?" she said, trying the name out. "Doesn't ring a bell. Any relation to Theodor Rauch, the writer?"

"Yes. He's our father."

This spark of celebrity seemed to warm her to my presence. "No fooling? Isn't that something. And you are . . . Miss Rauch?"

"Yes. Hildegard."

She finally turned from my reflection in the mirror and stuck out her hand. "Sally Bent. Look, Miss Rauch, sorry if I was a heel just now, but I don't like talking about Dick with strangers. It's too damn sad."

"Of course." Then, deciding I had no other strategy but to be forth-right, I said, "Miss Bent, my brother is currently in a coma, and I'm trying to sort out his correspondence and business matters, which have fallen on my shoulders for the time being. Among them is a letter that Richard Halifax wrote to you from Hong Kong just before his voyage and sent back with my brother, along with an enclosed receipt."

I handed her the letter and watched as she read it. I noticed tears well up in her eyes, and she suppressed a laugh that threatened to become a sob. "Yep, that's Dick for ya."

"You've known him a long time?" I asked.

"Since we were kids. You'd never know what a sweet, fragile crea-ture he was. Like a half-drowned kitten."

I didn't mention that I, too, had once caught a fleeting glimpse of that creature. "So this letter doesn't . . . mean something important to you?"

"Important?"

"I mean perhaps something between the lines?"

"If you're insinuating whether I have other business interests than riding horses in my birthday suit, then—"

"No, that's none of my concern. I'm sorry, I don't know what I mean. It's just that for some reason my brother never gave this letter or receipt to you, and he seems to have thought there was something important in them."

"Well, it hardly matters—they're duplicates."

"What do you mean?" I asked.

"Dick had already mailed me both the letter and the receipt from Hong Kong."

This seemed odd. "Really? Are you sure?"

"Dick liked showing off his new mimeograph machine, so whenever he wrote me from Hong Kong, he sent copies in that purply-blue ink and kept the originals for himself."

"I see. And you're certain you received this particular letter?"

"Oh yeah. I remember cursing him when I got the bill for those damned suits. A write-off! After all the debt we were in, he and his goofy pal Roderick get bespoke suits made—not once but twice! And then he foists the expense on me. Jesus. Financially speaking, Dick sprang as many leaks as that damn Chinese ship of his. And guess who inherited his debts?"

"You?"

"Ding, ding, ding. Prize for the tall German lady. The moment the *Soup Dumpling* went down, everything spilled onto my lap. No boat, no Dick—all our backers pulled out, and I had three hundred prepaid fares to pay back, a year's worth of marina fees, this whole joint's construction, in addition to that bridge loan he told me I should take."

The tears were starting to bleed her eyeliner. "Yep, I'll be shaking my ass till I'm seventy—that is, if they don't smash my kneecaps first."

I didn't know how to respond, so I thought it best to leave. "Well, I'm sorry to have taken up your time, Miss Bent."

"Wait a minute. Your brother Hank—is he a pansy?"

"If you're asking if he's homosexual, yes. A proud one too."

"Because I just remembered that while Dick and I were putting together the cruises last year, and he was going back and forth between California and China, he said he had a sweet racket going with a German pansy."

"Racket?" I said, unsure of the word in this context. "Do you mean they were lovers?"

"Well, no, sweetie, sex wasn't exactly Dick's area of expertise, if you know what I mean." She held up her hand with her index finger drooping downward. "I mean they were running an operation together. You know, one of Dick's schemes to bring in cash. Though the cash never seemed to come in at near the rate it went out."

"What kind of operation?"

"Oh, he didn't say. Just that it was hush-hush and that it would be an extra financial cushion. All the more reason, he said, to go lavish on the pleasure cruises—the best champagne, the best caviar, a top-notch Negro swing band. And I believed him. Never thought for a moment he would do something so simple as die and everything would go to pieces. But, hey, that's life, huh?"

"Yes," I said. "It seems to have been designed to go to pieces."

15.

To: The Dicky Halifax Junior Adventurers Club
From: Herr Dickee-san
On the Frink Family Coconut Farm
Ward and Protégé of Drs. Kanemoto and Frink

Fall 1939

Dear boys,

Looks like I'm going to be a bit delayed getting home. Dr. Kanemoto assures me he's preparing for my eventual release, and my feet are healing more or less as expected, which is to say painfully and piecemeal.

But in the meantime, guess what, boys? Your man Dick has gone back to school! That's right: I now spend my days just like you, sitting at my desk, learning my lessons, and waiting for the lunch bell to ring. Only in my case, there are no diversions of chewing gum, pulling pretty girls' pigtails, or flinging spit-wads at the class fatty. Sensei Kanemoto and his colleague Herr Doktor Frink run a tight ship, like my old Latin teacher Mrs. Voorhees, who once skull-slapped a boy so hard she dislocated his eyeball. But the beatings here have mostly abated. Only when I slip into my old ways of talking does Sensei K. have to set me straight. I guess that means I'm starting to cotton on to their instruction. I suppose it's a good thing Nacho isn't here with me, since he's an incorrigible know-it-all and would surely earn beatings for us both. When I ask about him, Sensei Kanemoto assures me he's fine, though he won't say more.

As a reward for my studies, I've been given plush new quarters. No more blood-damp prison cell for me, boys! No sir, I'm living in high style in a hillside house on a copra plantation. Do you know what copra is? I'll give you a hint: It's that white fleshy part of nature's favorite fruit, filled with enough oily goodness to power a defensive end or fuel an airplane engine. The only catch is you gotta be agile enough to shimmy up the tree to pluck it and strong enough with a machete to crack it. Can you guess what she is, boys? That's right—a coconut!

After months of roughing it, I'm finally back to sleeping on a feather bed and eating three-square a day, with coconuts for breakfast, lunch, and dinner. The place is a real Saipanese settler's hovel, indicative of the island's recent history as a colonial hot potato, replete with Spanish mission colonnades, Biedermeier furnishings, and Japanese house clogs and mats.

This, I gather, is where Dr. Frink lives, or once lived, though I'm not permitted to go outside my wing. But I did catch a glimpse of an old family portrait in the hallway on the way in and spied what looks like a prepubescent Herr Frink, in short pants and a mop of platinum hair, surrounded by a dour family of sunburnt Huns. It was clear that the jowly mustached man in tropical khakis was Papa, the buxom Brunhilde in a light dress and tight bun was dear old Mutter, fronted by the three little Frinks, with a rottweiler at their feet. A Chamorro servant was stuck in the corner, waving a blurry palm frond to keep the sweat off them. But, incongruously, seated beside the children, like he was part of the family, was a dark skeletal fella in a loincloth. You could tell by his facial features that he was of Caucasoid extraction, but he looked like an Indian fakir with his tangled mat of hair and beard, skin black as an aborigine, and leg sores the size of tennis balls. Ugliest bastard I ever saw.

That is, until about five minutes later, when I was led to my new digs and, for the first time since I'd stepped aboard the *Soup Dumpling*, caught sight of myself in the mirror. Boys, I just about died of fright. They say that character is something internal, that who you are comes from within. But you don't have to be a thespian to know that if you change the mask, you change the character. And I don't believe the face looking back at me belonged to Dicky Halifax. Or, rather, whatever I had become in the aftermath of the *Soup Dumpling*, even if it was still called Dicky, was a different Dicky from the one with my old face. Does that make sense, boys? Or am I already raving like a skid-row lunatic?

Now, where was I? Oh, right: I was trying to tell you about my new school schedule on the Frink family estate. Every morning a guard rouses me from my Biedermeier bed, watches me drain the hair snake and splash water on my face while I scrupulously avoid my own reflection, then he marches me up to the third-story lanai overlooking the plantation, where Dr. Kanemoto and his colleague Dr. Frink give me my daily lesson.

Dr. Kanemoto, upon confirming that I was indeed the writer-adventurer I claimed to be, returned with Dr. Frink, who promptly invited me to come stay at his house. Dr. Frink is a specialist in what he calls *Lebensreform*: "a totalistic program for regenerating the individual, the race, and the planet." He professes to being a big fan of my work, which is quite a salve to the ole Halifax Confidence Muscle, bruised as it was after my ordeal. Dr. Frink says he believes someone of my racial stock and talents could be very valuable not just for America but the entire world. There's not much a man can say when someone compliments your stock, except a sheepish thank-you. But what got me to sit up and pay attention was when Dr. Frink said he believed my greatest achievements as a writer-adventurer were yet to come and that he wanted to help me realize this most organic part of me.

"This may be of little interest to a writer of your caliber, Herr Dickee-san," said Dr. Frink, "but I happen to have several powerful connections in Hollywood. Consul Gyssling in Los Angeles is a personal friend, and he has a direct line to all the major studios. Dr. Kanemoto tells me you were rather jaded by how things turned out with *Ulysses, Junior,* which, for what it's worth, I thought was simply marvelous. But if you ever have any wish to write or star in your own films again, I can easily open that door for you."

"Gee, Doc," I said, "I hadn't really thought about it." I was feeling pretty low about my looks at the moment, not to mention my future prospects in Hollywood.

"And, as goes without saying, you wouldn't have to suffer those terrible rewrites by mercenary script doctors. We pay the bills, we pull the strings. And if we want the great Richard Halifax to make a picture the way he wants to make it, thus it will be."

"I gotta say, Dr. Frink, that sounds swell, but—"

"Wonderful! But first, Herr Dickee-san, we need to regenerate your body and character."

I felt myself clench up at the mention of more body treatments, but Dr. Frink assured me in an avuncular tone, "Don't worry. None of this will hurt. The painful part is over. Dr. Kanemoto has gathered sufficient data to make a diagnosis, and from that diagnosis the two of us have designed a targeted treatment plan. Dr. Kanemoto, if you please . . ."

Dr. Kanemoto withdrew a typed sheet from his leather portfolio.

"Dickee-san," said Dr. Kanemoto, as he began to read: "You suffer from a narcissistic personality disorder. You exhibit a particularly American form of this ailment, to which men who feel great hostility to their mother and who worship a remote or absent father figure are most susceptible. Your stunted sexuality, manifesting as impotence and hypermasculinity, compounded by a latent homosexuality and transvestism, are byproducts of these childhood feelings of rage and abandonment, and they are bound up with a morbid preoccupation with death and the reaction-formation of a god-like defiance of it. This complex prevents you from forming real attachments to people or causes beyond yourself. You are, in your own words, 'a privateer.' The one exception to this solipsistic isolation is your need for an audience, in the form of both a legion of adoring readers and a sidekick. You cannot see yourself as the hero except through the validation of your young fans and the devotion of a loyal subaltern. This need is so great, and so tied to the feelings of guilt and grief for your lost brother, that you fill this void with surrogates, whether real or imagined. You also suffer from beriberi, a multitude of precancerous skin lesions, shock-induced alopecia, poor kidney function, endemic tooth decay, and are at high risk for sepsis."

"Thank you, Dr. Kanemoto," said Dr. Frink. "So, you see, Herr Dickee-san, before we can send you home in a manner that serves all of our interests, including yours, we need to address these pathologies.

Not eradicate them—lest you suffer total ego death—but simply mold them in a way that enables you to flourish in the new future our two nations are building together."

"Swell," I replied. I had tuned out most of what Sensei Kanemoto was saying—who wants to hear a boring lab report? But I sure got a kick out of how Doc Frink was addressing me: "Herr Dickee-san." A Teutonic twist on Dr. Kanemoto's own Jap-ified take.

The next time I went to the washbasin, I made myself look up into the mirror. "Herr Dickee-san," I said, speaking the name aloud. "A film written, directed, and starring . . . Herr Dickee-san Halifax." Say, that's not bad, I thought.

My lessons aren't what you'd imagine when you think of school. Which is okay by me, because your man Dick has already had enough geometrical proofs and sentence diagrams to last a lifetime. The last time I was in a classroom, back at Princeton, I was busy daydreaming out the window, planning to stow away on an oil tanker to Europe, then hitchhike from Lisbon to Samarkand. So I was much relieved when my two senseis said there'd be no cracking of either textbooks or Dicky bones. Instead, the sole reading on the syllabus would be the book of my life. "The only prerequisite, Dickee-san, is that you be entirely truthful. Otherwise, the regeneration therapy will not work. Understood?"

Of course I had already told Dr. Kanemoto my whole story, or damn near all of it, and he seemed to have filled Dr. Frink in on the shape of it, but now we've been going through each moment of my recollections and putting it under the microscope. Their method is gentle but persistent. Dr. Frink calls it his *Selbstauslegung unter Verdacht*, which, according to the Halifax Translator, comes out to something like an auto-hermeneutics of suspicion. And each session comes with a little dropper full of cactus juice called mescaline.

In short, boys, I've learned from my Kraut sensei that the self is not a fixed thing, like, say, a Christmas tree or a coconut. It's an interpretation. An interpretation by which we understand our experience of the world. But all of those millions of recalled moments, which make up the memory of our life and the sum of who we are, are themselves interpretations. In other words, our sense of self is a story we tell ourselves about things that have happened to us, integrated into a fantasy of who we want to be. And, like with any event and the stories we tell of it, there are always at least two sides to the story. Take the Trojan War: Were the Greeks the good guys or the bad guys? Ask Homer and Virgil, you'll get two different answers. Hell, not even Homer's so sure, and he's Team Argive all the way. What about Helen—abducted victim or adulterous slut? And are we talking about Odysseus the cunning, charismatic hero or the dirty cheat and diabolical pirate? Well, that's how it goes with the story of our self. You code something as good or bad, happy or sad, your fault or someone else's, you tell yourself that version of the story, and then you put it away on the memory shelf. Dr. Frink's method asks us to take a good second look at those stories and see if maybe there's another version we haven't told ourselves, maybe even one we don't want to tell ourselves. This line of inquiry soon gets you thinking, say, what if these stories are not truthful accounts of who I am but rather obfuscating narratives that conceal or distort the version I don't want to tell? What if the story of myself is really just running interference on a whole other self, whose testimony I refuse to take?

For example, my doctors helped me to consider how the United States government was culpable in my brother's untimely death. The story I'd told myself and others all these years was that the strangling angel, diphtheria, had descended from the heavens like a curse from the gods. Little did I know, until Dr. Frink enlightened me, that the antitoxin to the diphtheria bacterium was developed in Germany as early as the 1890s and used to treat human cases throughout its empire well before the First World War. The United States knew of this antitoxin, and even though Germany was happy to share, our government neglected to buy the serum out of sheer sour grapes, thereby condemning thousands of innocent boys like yourselves to an early grave.

This was just one of many important moments that Drs. Kanemoto and Frink helped me to reexamine and, in light of new context, reinterpret. My teachers also helped me understand that the fate of Earth itself now depended on curbing the destructive rampage of

America's decadent civilization, which had grown from the effluvium of European modernity and the excesses of Jewish-Capitalist-Bolshevist-Democracy.

"That is precisely what you are suffering from, Herr Dickee-san," said Dr. Frink after one of these lessons, which, by dint of sheer repetition and the effects of that strange cactus juice, were starting to sink in. "Your sexual impotence is a symptom of the malaise, masquerading as vitality, with which America pollutes the world."

I went a little red at hearing Dr. Frink talk about my condition so frankly. I guess Dr. Kanemoto had filled him in, though he was clearly misinformed about the cause. "I don't mean to contradict, *sehr geehrter Herr Doktor*, but unless you mean lake sports are a form of malaise, I'm afraid my condition is purely physiological. Motor blade snipped the wiener tendons, and that's all she wrote. I'll never know the inside of a lady."

"Come, come, Dicky. Haven't you learned enough to realize that the physical, psychological, and spiritual are all interlinked? It is my understanding that tendons eventually heal, provided the body is otherwise sound and in an environment in which it can thrive. Dr. Kanemoto, what is your assessment as to Herr Dickee-san's anatomical function?"

"Despite heavy scarring in the pelvic region, Dickee-san's generative organs appear wholly intact. Prostate is normal. Erections would have abated during the period of acute malnourishment before he came under our care. But I see no medical reason why they shouldn't return in due time, once his organism has regained its equilibrium."

"Well, I appreciate the optimism, Docs," I said, "I really do. But no one's beat this hair snake out of the grass since that fateful day on the lake."

Dr. Frink made a pouty face and looked at Dr. Kanemoto, who was frowning. "Dickee-san, are you doubting our expertise?"

Questioning my teachers' authority was the one lapse that could still get me cuffed. "No, no, not at all. If you can rouse my Holger Danske from his decades-long slumber, I'll be your liegeman for the rest of my days. How's that sound?"

Dr. Kanemoto gave a curt little grunt, while Dr. Frink stretched his legs and recrossed them. He relit his pipe, then turned his notebook to a clean page and took up a sharp pencil from his row on the table.

"Herr Dickee-san, tell us more about your relationship with Hank Rauch. He was quite in love with you, was he not?"

"Hank? Oh, I don't know. I suppose he had the hots for me in his sissy German poet sort of way, but like I told Dr. Kanemoto, Hank and I were just pals. We had a few laughs and looked out for each other, and, sure, every now and then he'd get too drunk and give me a smooch and tell me he was crazy about me and I'd have to explain to him I wasn't cut out for that sort of thing . . ."

"Why did Hank Rauch come to China at the end of last year? You told Dr. Kanemoto he stopped in Hong Kong on the way to Shanghai. Presumably he came to Hong Kong to see you, but what was he doing in Shanghai?"

"Like I told Sensei K., he was on his mission for the journal."

"You mean for his journal *The Reckoning*?"

"No, I mean he was going to get his father's journal. His diary. Theodor Rauch had lost a diary in transit while escaping from Vienna to California a couple of years earlier. Someone in Shanghai had found it, and Hank was going to get it back."

"He was going to recover it on his father's behalf?"

I laughed. "Far from it. Hank was going to get it so he could ruin him."

Dr. Kanemoto, I could tell, was bored by this line of inquiry, unlike Dr. Frink, who seemed genuinely curious and pressed me to explain.

I told him that after converting Roderick's Norden plans into microdots for us, Hank went to Shanghai. About a week later, he returned. He still had some time till his ship sailed, and what with Roderick's wrathful eye on him and me pulling my hair out to get Ming Fat to finish the *Soup Dumpling* without turning me into a regular customer at the soup kitchen, Hank decided to go up to Canton for a few days. The city was now under Jap control and reopened to journalists who wanted a peek at the fresh devastation.

"I need you to look after something for me, Dick, while I'm gone," he said.

"That's when," I explained to the doctors, "Hank handed me the diary and told me the whole story." Though, truth be told, boys, I was fudging the timeline a bit here, as well as a couple of other things in the account I was giving. "See," I said, "not long after his father had pulled his support from *The Reckoning* and written that nasty hatchet job about his son being a talentless hack, Hank received a letter from Shanghai. The letter was from a Good Samaritan of the international settlement who worked in the railway's left-luggage depot. Hank's parents had come through Shanghai on their way from Europe to California, and a valise bearing Theodor Rauch's name and the forwarding address of Hank's bungalow in Los Angeles had, in the wake of two years of war and the crush of hundreds of thousands of refugees, suddenly turned up. To Hank, still smarting from humiliation at the hands of his father, this was his ace in the hole. Not wanting to take any chances in the post, he'd arranged to pick up the journal in person, and now he was going to publish his father's diary, expose him as a hypocrite, and knock him off his pedestal. Not only that, he said he'd organized things through his friends in Shanghai so that, in exchange for publishing the diary, he'd be flush with funding for his journal.

"Well, I was pleased as punch for Hank. I told him I'd put Daddy's diary in the hotel safe and guard it with my life, and off he went upriver to the scorched and ghostly remains of Canton.

"When he came back, shaken with the horrors he'd seen—mountains of rubble, canals choked with corpses, a whole city reduced to dogs and beggars—Roderick and I had done him the favor of transferring his father's diary to microdot.

"'Roderick's a quick study,' I said, handing Hank an old receipt that we'd tweezed and glued the little specks onto. 'Thought we could repay you the favor.'

"Hank seemed surprised and a bit wary. 'And the original?' he asked.

"'Well, the thing is, Hank,' I said, 'I'm afraid there was a small fire in the hotel while you were gone. Some Chinaman on the street below hit the rice wine a little too hard and shot his firecracker off backward. But thank God we made the photographs beforehand—'"

135

"Just to be clear, Herr Dickee-san," said Dr. Frink, interrupting, "you're telling me Theodor Rauch's diary burned in a hotel fire, but you made photograph copies on microdot before it was destroyed?"

"That's right, Doc."

"And you gave the microdots to Hank Rauch to take back with him to the States?"

"Yep. Along with the dots containing the Norden plans. Hank took both back with him—one little magic piece of paper for him, one for Roderick and me—all in the guise of a mopey letter and receipt for a couple of suits."

I noticed the doctors exchange pregnant glances.

"And can you verify," said Dr. Frink, "that Theodor Rauch's diary did in fact contain material of a compromising nature?"

"That's putting it mildly, Docs. If the stuff that was in that diary ever saw the light of day, well, let's just say that would be the end of Old Man Rauch's time at the world lectern."

I could tell that I had gotten Dr. Frink's attention. His little rabbit ears had pricked right up at mention of Theodor Rauch's diary, and now he was puffing his pipe with excitement. So I was relieved when the good doctor didn't ask me to tell him more about the circumstances of the fire, since I hadn't quite given him the straight dope about my involvement with the diary.

Instead, hoping to distract them, I told my senseis how grateful I was to have unburdened myself and how salutary I found these sessions.

The thing is, boys, though I might not have been as honest as Abe Lincoln, I wasn't just blowing smoke up their white coats. I really did feel grateful. To Dr. Kanemoto for saving me from the chopping block, to Dr. Frink for putting me up in the family mansion, and to both for the thorough realignment they were giving me. I feel like I'm getting my pipes cleaned—some much needed Drano down the Halifax Braino.

Dr. Kanemoto has made a daily point of getting me to acknowledge all these kindnesses. It is important to feel the salutary burden of *giri*, he said, the debt that can never be repaid. "Remember, Dickee-san, the burden of gratitude that is *giri* can never be lifted, only expressed through submission and lifelong reverence."

136

I know their methods of unkinking Dicky must be working, because the taste of Roderick has stopped haunting my dreams. And even though my lustrous white hair is still coming out in clumps and my remaining teeth rattle in their gum beds and my skin is still scabbed and raw, my tics and spasms have become far more manageable.

I'm even feeling relaxed, thanks in part to my pill-and-needle regimen. Every night before bed, Dr. Frink's man-nurse gives me my pills and injections and off I go to Slumberland, just like Little Nemo, innocent as a babe and untouched by night terrors.

I do hope Nacho is alright.

Thinking of you always,
Dickee-san

HILDEGARD RAUCH

You've been lying to me. All this time you've acted like you're on the verge of destitution, when it turns out you have a benefactor. Or at least you did. You had everybody fooled—your subscribers and contributors, even Father for a time, even me. But I'm not so stupid anymore as to believe that you were the iconoclast you made yourself out to be. You, who told me the ethical life should be a wrench in the machinery of power.

I finally went through the correspondence that was among your retrieved possessions from the St. Francis, hoping for some clue as to what you were up to. Something I should have done from the start, rather than chasing down your nonsensical note to its dead end at the Nude Ranch. At first I found little that surprised me. Your subscribers—under the impression that, as an independent journal of the dissident freethinking left, *The Reckoning* was kept afloat only by the goodwill and generosity of those similarly shipwrecked—had enclosed small single-digit contributions eked out from their monthly budgets. Your writers were groveling for a pittance while apologizing for the degrading attachment to money that the logic of capital had foisted upon them. And based on the frequency of *just following up* and *if I may gently remind you* and *making sure you received my last letter*, your rate of reply while conscious seems to have been only marginally better than in your current state. Dorothy Parker was the only one who had the gumption to say she would come after you with both hammer and sickle if you didn't pay her for her last piece. Huxley wanted his name featured more prominently on the masthead; Döblin said you completely edited out the cinematic quality of his last story and that you owed him an apology; and Diego Rivera said he and Trotsky would soon be testifying before the U.S. House Un-American Activities Committee, informing them that the Mexican Communist Party was a Stalinist puppet and that harbored among the three hundred émigrés from the war in Spain were at least twenty-five known officers of the NKVD, many of whom would be attempting to infiltrate north of the border. Would you, they inquired, like to publish a transcript of this hearing?

But for every thirty or so letters of salutation, imploration, and excoriation, a slim mint-green letter from one Ellen Winters, of Malibu, California, appeared. Her folded notes, as you know, were brief, but they concealed quite substantial matters. Namely, a two-thousand-dollar check addressed to *The Reckoning* from the Anti-Fascist Writers League. I found two of these, dated the first of September and October, the checks still inside. Clearly you had seen these, as the envelopes were torn open. But then why did you, whom I have always known to make quick use of a buck, usually by dumping it into your bloodstream, not cash the checks?

Ellen Winters seemed equally puzzled, as her note with October's payment said, *The fight is still the same. Did you not receive last month's funds?* The thing that bothered me was not how haphazardly you had run your finances but the very existence of those checks. What was the Anti-Fascist Writers League doing paying you such astronomical monthly sums? And what to make of her final ominous note, dated October 10, this time without an enclosed check: *Please be reasonable, Hank. Solidarity is the only path forward. With or without you.*

Well, the answer is obvious: You had sold yourself to the Soviets, and only after Stalin's pact with Hitler came to light did your conscience begin to stir. Suddenly, that money must have felt like taking a payout from Berlin, and you realized what a dupe you had been. And, if I know anything about your defiant pride, at that point you'd rather have asked your poor sister for money (or simply reside in five-star hotels without any intention of paying) than cash those checks. Is this partly what prompted you to move to San Francisco at the end of the summer? I'm not so naïve as to think you moved here simply to be closer to me. So were you running away from something in Los Angeles?

The real question is, before this crisis of conscience struck you, what were you and Richard Halifax up to? Doing favors for the Comintern and receiving Moscow dollars in exchange? Was that the so-called "racket"? All while presenting to the world that you were a beacon of the freethinking left?

It makes me wonder whether anything like that still exists.

To: The Dicky Halifax Junior Adventurers Club
From: Herr Dickee-san
Finding the Bloom of Health Where You'd Least Expect It

Fall 1939

Dear boys,

After breakfast yesterday, my man-nurse, rather than bring me to the lanai for my usual lesson, laid me down on the chaise longue and gave me a keister shot. Then he took me out into the coconut fields, where Dr. Frink was waiting.

"*Guten Morgen*, Herr Dickee-san," said Dr. Frink. "Today we begin a new course in your regeneration therapy."

"Hot dog!" I said, licking my lips. I was feeling a pronounced sense of both euphoria and dry mouth. "Where's Sensei K?"

"Dr. Kanemoto got called away for the moment, but don't worry. You're in good hands here. Please meet your new teacher." He gestured at the trunk of a coconut palm, which I found puzzling—that is, until a bundle of hair and limbs suddenly dropped from high up in the tree and crashed to the ground beside me.

The bundle rose and revealed itself to be a man. The skinniest, shaggiest, sunburnt-to-a-purple-crisp of a man I have ever seen. My shock was even greater when I realized he was, in fact, the very same loinclothed specter I had seen in the Frink family photograph. His remaining hair was perhaps whiter, and his skin hung maybe a tad looser from his skeletal frame, but other than that, he was the man in the picture come to life.

"*Angenehm*, Herr Dickee-san," said the wild man, in a small growly voice. "I am Karl Dieter Schivelbusch, the exiled King of Kabakon."

At the time, those words meant nothing to me, other than that they seemed as incomprehensibly strange as the man who uttered them. And it takes a lot to make your man Dick gape. Remember, boys, I've traveled the world and veered way off the tourist's path. I've seen Albanian shepherds with ingrown teeth that poked through their cheeks and a Panamanian street vendor with a hydrocele so big he had to cart his scrotum in a wheelbarrow. But this man—a kind of tropical Kaspar Hauser, clearly a German by birth but one gone feral—looked like an excrescence of the South Seas jungle. His whole body was an open sore of yaws, sunburn, and beriberi. His teeth were slime-green, and he smelled worse than that klong next to the fish-sauce factory I once lived above in Bangkok.

"We've asked Herr Schivelbusch, given his expertise, to serve as your *Gesundmeister* and look after your diet and exercise regimen. His body went through a similar ordeal of extreme deprivation, from which he fully recovered, so we thought he could help. Being a family friend who lives nearby on the estate, he has graciously agreed."

"I'm sorry," I said, thinking maybe the ole Halifax Hearing Horn had failed me. "Did you say he's an expert in diet and exercise?"

"*Genau so*," said the talking scab before me. "I shall purge you of all the toxins of modern civilization, just as I have done with myself."

I stood there gaping, until I heard the internal voice of Sensei Kanemoto reminding me to acknowledge the tremendous burden of *giri* that had just been dumped on my back. "I am overcome with gratitude," I said, trotting out the lines I had been taught. "I shall accept your offer with honor, though I shall never be able to prove myself worthy."

"Why, seeing you two together," said Dr. Frink, chuckling through his pipe-clenched teeth, "you could be brothers. The likeness is uncanny."

I've already told you, boys, how hideous my own visage had become. But hearing others confirm it was even more demoralizing. It meant I wasn't simply being vain or seeing myself through some dysmorphic lens born of suffering. A third party—one who seemed to believe in my future in Hollywood, no less—had just confirmed my resemblance to this grotesque human ruin. I would have cried, but my tear ducts were still swollen shut.

My doctor departed and Karl Dieter, handing me a young coconut, instructed me to drink the juice. He then led me deep into the coconut grove, to a little clearing alongside a stream, where we spent the day in sunbathing and pedagogy.

Karl Dieter Schivelbusch, I learned, was the sole surviving member of the Order of the Sun, an erstwhile utopian colony in German New Guinea begun before the last war by a German pharmacist named August Engelhardt. Engelhardt had leased from the Reich several thousand acres of a copra plantation on the island of Kabakon and begun his program of nudism, sun worship, and a strict diet of cocovorism—taking one's sustenance exclusively from coconuts.

"Did you know, Herr Dickee-san, that the *Kokosnuss* contains several essential vitamins and more protein and fat than a five-hundred-gram beefsteak?"

Karl Dieter, I discovered, was fond of telling me such facts in the form of questions. And he relished schooling me in the nutritional properties of his beloved coconut, along with the doomed history of the Order of the Sun.

The utopians, consisting of seventy civilization-weary Germans who had shed their pants for a last-ditch attempt at the good life, soon began falling ill and falling out. Apparently, all the coconuts in New Guinea could not prevent sun poisoning, worms, or scurvy, and within a couple of years their island paradise was just a patch of sand with a bunch of hot, hungry Huns at one another's throats. By the time the war broke out and the Australians snatched the Bismarck archipelago from the Reich, the founder Engelhardt was living alone on Kabakon, utterly out of his gourd. He died shortly thereafter under Australian occupation, but his heir apparent, Karl Dieter Schivelbusch, had caught the last packet bound for Rabaul and fled to the Marianas, where he found refuge on the family estate of his cousin, Wolfgang Frink.

After Saipan was claimed by the Japanese, most of the German settlers were given the boot, but they let a few stay on as advisers to their new colonial administration. These included the Frinks, who had come to Saipan at the turn of the century, first as teachers and then as managers in the growing copra trade. They, too, were staunch advocates of *Lebensreform* and had been amenable to the Order of the Sun, or at least its ethos, while recognizing its unsuitability for family life. Their youngest son, Humbert Frink, spent his childhood with cousin Karl Dieter, shimmying up coconut palms and worshipping the sun until he went to the mainland, became a navy doctor, an early Nazi Party member, and then, if Karl Dieter's hunch was correct, a member of German intelligence, where he was valued for his knowledge of the South Seas, his link to Germany's forlorn imperial glory, his fluency in Japanese, and his pioneering research in psychiatric medicine.

"You should be honored that Humpi has taken a shine to you," said Karl Dieter, referring to, I gathered, Dr. Frink. "He's quite powerful in the current regime." Though how Karl Dieter heard any gossip from Berlin while crawling about the coconut fields on this far-flung crumb in the Pacific was beyond me.

"Yes," I said, the words falling out of me as though by reflex, "I feel an extreme burden of obligation to Dr. Frink that can never be repaid, only expressed through my everlasting submission and reverence."

Karl Dieter ignored me and, scurrying up a coconut palm, sent what I presumed to be our dinner tumbling to the ground.

"So you really can live exclusively off coconuts?" I asked.

"Oh yes," he said. Then added matter-of-factly: "But they will take you right to death's door. Just close enough for you to look in through the keyhole."

"But what was all that baloney about vitamins and protein?" I asked.

"*Keine Bologna*, Herr Dickee-san. I said they have *several* essential vitamins, not all of them. And the human body needs all of them, or else—well, you end up looking like us."

Again, the reference to our likeness pained me. "But Dr. Frink said you fully recovered your health."

"Yes. I have learned to find the bloom of health inside the flower of sickness."

Jeez, I thought, Nacho would have a field day with this guy. "Why don't you just eat a normal diet," I asked, "and find the bloom of health inside the flower of health?"

"Because there is deep philosophical truth to be gained from living close to death. Isn't that something you understand, Dickee? Humpi told me you are an *Abenteurer*—an adventurer, no?"

"Sure, I don't shy away from risk, but there's a difference between taking risks and intentionally courting death."

"And would you say that the voyage of the *Soup Dumpling* was anything less than the intentional courting of death?"

He was remarkably well informed for a coconut hermit, and his comment stung.

"Now, look here, Herr Kokosnuss," I said sternly, not about to be pushed around by a sentient abscess. "Mistakes were made, I'll grant you that. In hindsight, I should have been more patient. Maybe let Ming Fat have his say on the ship design. We probably should have kept to Pengelly's route too, alright? But it was never my intention to get anyone killed."

"Not even yourself?"

"What do you mean myself? I'm the only one who survived, dingbat!"

"What about your companion?" he asked.

"Oh yes, of course. Nacho too. Speaking of, I would like to see him."

"In due time, Dicky, in due time. But first we must get to the bottom of the Halifax Blackness." He gave me a sickening grin, revealing teeth like a row of broken headstones. "Would you agree that the voyage of the *Soup Dumpling* was a failure?"

"Of course," I said. "Any simpleton could see that. It sank in the middle of the goddamn ocean."

"But that's not why you regard this last adventure as a failure, is it? Not because your boat sank and others died, but because you secretly wanted to approach that threshold yourself and look through the keyhole. Perhaps even knock on the door and have death welcome you in."

"That's ludicrous!" I shouted. "You are a madman, and you've only just met me. All those coconuts have clearly turned your brain to mush."

"And what has *your* diet done to your brain, Dickee-san? Rancid rice and the flesh of your own best friend? How many essential vitamins did Roderick contain?"

145

This naked cocophile seemed to know me inside and out. His sickly face now assumed a demonic look, and as I stared into his eyes I saw only spirals, spinning vortices that sucked me right in.

"Dicky," he whispered, as though he were inside me or, rather, I were inside him. "Do you remember when you were young and sick, when the fever took you? Remember how, after months of longing to go outside and play baseball with the other boys, another desire suddenly took its place?"

I nodded, too terrified to speak.

"When the fever gripped you, you no longer cared about childish games, did you? You wanted only to follow the fever. To explore its warmth to the very depths. Do you remember?"

"Yes," I said mechanically, my powers of speech no longer my own. "I remember."

"You know deep in your heart that death is good, don't you, Dicky? That Wesley went there instead of you and that made you jealous of him. And ever since, you wish you could follow him, isn't that right?"

"Maybe."

"You wanted to die, but then something happened and your brother beat you to it. You hated him for it and you hated yourself for it. Because he remained forever a boy and you, Dicky, have had to endure the crushing, humiliating experience of being a boy forced to become a man. Isn't that right?"

"Yes."

"You have tried to remain a boy in a man's body, and for a time it brought you success, when people wanted to be reminded of childish escape. But now they're no longer interested. So you find yourself trapped in a persona from which there is no escape. Millions of boys just a few years older than you died bravely in the war. Your brother, Wesley, died tragically young, and don't tell me it was from diphtheria. We know what really happened. But you, Dicky, are condemned to live. Meanwhile, everyone else your age has married, had children, and is a respected member of the community. And you, Dicky, what are you but a living joke? Your boyish hijinks and devil-may-care attitude have not aged well. The same 'Look, Ma' grin, the same crude schoolboy humor, the same breezy bravado that in a forty-year-old man reveals only rampant fear and despair. These boyish trappings are as worn and grotesque as your own rotting skin. Isn't that true, Dicky?"

"Yes," I said. "It's true."

"And now you flee from death toward life, toward an impossible youth, toward what you lost at the bottom of Lake Tapawingo on that fateful day that not even your doctors know about. Isn't that right?"

"Yes." The first tears my body had manufactured in months began to stream down my face.

"But you can't run, Dicky, because life itself is what is dragging you toward death."

"Yes, I feel it."

"Life is what is killing you, Dicky, because you have not understood how it springs from death."

It was a sentiment that defied logic, and yet when Karl Dieter whispered it directly into my brain, it felt incontrovertibly true.

"And remember what you thought after you so brutally beat your friend Nacho—that you never understood why, if the world beyond death was peaceful and good, should we then consider the act of killing to be evil? How can the gift of death be bad when death itself is good?"

"I agree it is puzzling."

"If death is good, Dicky, then everything that flows from death is also good. Isn't that so?"

"I suppose so."

"Death is the sun, Dicky. All life comes from its black light, then returns to it. All life draws meaning and definition from death and its eternal black brightness. Don't you agree?"

"I do." Amid this state of rapture, there was the observing and recording part of my consciousness—the Halifax Secretary—that simply took note of these strange interrogatory proceedings in which I had become an empty-headed yes-man. But in the face of Karl Dieter's overwhelming grasp of my inner darkness, I had no choice but to assent. I was as awed as any slack-jawed Glaucon before his Socrates. The Kabakon King had cracked me like a coconut and exposed the raw hidden flesh of truth, just like Dr. Frink's hermeneutical method. Only the experience here was even stronger and strangely out of body. I couldn't be sure where in space either Karl Dieter or I was, where he began and I ended. I could have just as well been on an operating table or in a coconut tree. The moment I looked into those swirling spirals of his eyes, all sense of earthly borders vanished.

"Face that dark desire, Dicky. Peer into your yearning for oblivion, open yourself to the urge to not be, embrace your subterranean twin. Now, Dicky, speak the name of your secret shadow desire."

"Death. I love death."

"*Ganz gut*, Dicky. And if death is a good thing, and death is the source and destination of all life, then killing must also be good. Don't you agree?"

"Uh-huh."

"What you thought was a contradiction is in fact a profound truth. You were simply in error, isn't that right?"

"Yeah, I guess so."

"But now you understand?"

"Yes."

"Say it for me, Dicky, so I know you understand."

"Death is good. Killing is also good. To kill and to die are both good."

"You have seen into the truth of things, Dicky. Now you can cultivate the bloom of health from the flower of sickness, because you have found the rich soil of death. And now you can be a man, a real man, no longer clinging to the boy within. You can free yourself from the burden of death. The burden of Wesley's death, of Roderick's death, of all deaths past, present, and future."

"Swell," I said. Was there anything more splendid than this, boys, to feel liberated from the burden of death?

"And now, as a man, you could even *kill* with impunity, even with joy in your heart, because you see that death comes from a place of love."

"Okey dokey."

"You could, for example, kill a beloved friend, not because he's done anything wrong, not because the camp guards made you do it against your will like in that awful fight with Nacho, but because you love him and now you understand that his death would be a kindness. Isn't that right?"

"Uh-huh."

148

"*Na, wunderbar.* Let us now talk some more about your friend Hank Rauch."

The Coconut King said some more things about my pal Hank, then reached under my loincloth and, finding my shriveled ding-dong, gave it a reassuring squeeze.

The sensation sent an alarm bell right up into the ole Halifax Vagus Nerve, and I spun out of consciousness.

When I woke, I was in my Biedermeier bed. I felt dizzy and face-sore, like I had slept on my jaw the wrong way. But gradually I became aware of another sensation, something far more alien and wonderful. I peeked under the eiderdown and, lo and behold, your man Dickee-san was pitching a tent big enough to house a whole Boy Scout troop.

Feeling rather different but still yours,
Dickee-san

HILDEGARD RAUCH

This is the last time I'm coming to visit you. I'm serious.

If you ever want to hear from me again, then you'll have to wake up and explain yourself. And to think last time I was disappointed in you simply for having pawned your integrity to a rotten ideology. Now I know you were willing to pawn so much more.

It all started following another lapse of judgment in Walter's office. We were smoking in our underwear when I asked him what he knew of the Anti-Fascist Writers League.

"Oh, not much. Some Popular Front organization. I think it's run out of Paris. Or New York. Or Hollywood. Maybe all three."

"Do you think it's a Soviet front?"

"I don't know. Why?"

"My friend Salka said she thought as much."

"Well, I haven't heard that, but I guess it's possible. May I ask, why this sudden interest in the Anti-Fascist Writers League? Considering making a donation?"

"I'm sure I already have many times. Or was it the Anti-Nazi Writers League? Or was it the German Anti-Fascist League? It's all a blur—back when I was naïve enough to think the Popular Front actually meant something other than playing Stalin's game."

I then told Walter of my suspicion that you were receiving Soviet funds for *The Reckoning*.

"But your brother was no Stalinist, Hilde. *The Reckoning*'s whole ethos was freethinking socialism. *Marxist–Schillerist instead of Marxist–Leninist*—isn't that what he said?"

"I didn't realize you were one of Eiko's regular readers."

"Oh, I'll read the backs of cereal boxes or old receipts in my pants pocket. *The Reckoning* or *die Rechnung*—makes no difference to me."

Perhaps that was why he also, I noticed, had two issues of *Free Masses* on his shelf—the magazine Salka and Ravenswood had said was a more popular, execrable version of your own.

"Speaking of," said Walter, before I could ask his opinion on it, "whatever happened to that letter you were hung up on? The one you showed to Sally Bent?"

"It was strange. She was completely uninterested in it. Said Halifax had already sent her a copy of the same letter and receipt."

"Really? So you still have it?"

"You'll think I'm being silly, but I couldn't bring myself to burn it. There has to be something I'm not understanding."

"You know, that was probably prudent. Nadia once told me that there are ways of embedding information on film negatives so small that they just look like periods or the dot above an *i*."

I stared at Walter. "You haven't been telling Nadia about any of this, have you?"

"No, of course not."

"You swear?"

"Yes, Hilde, I swear. The only reason Nadia knows about this technique is because of how ruthlessly the anarchists were persecuted in Spain. They had to start disguising their correspondence. Anyway, I just thought of it now."

"You're saying that on that letter or receipt could be entirely different information, shrunk to the size of a punctuation mark? Hiding in plain sight?"

"Exactly."

"So how do I see the information that is hidden on the original?"

"Well, I'm not entirely sure. I'm no cloak-and-dagger anarchist. I don't suppose you want me to ask Nadia?"

"Absolutely not."

"Well, then, what about a magnifying glass?"

"I think there's a microscope in the photography department," I said.

"Even better. Do you have the Halifax letter with you?"

"It's in my office."

There were two students working in the darkroom, and the janitor was sweeping the hall, but the photography wing was otherwise empty. Walter was fussing with the microscope when I came in with the letter and receipt.

"I can't tell that there's anything on here," I said. "It all just looks like ink."

"That's the whole idea. May I?" said Walter, reaching for the documents.

He brought the letter up eye-level and tilted it to the light. "Hmm . . ."

"What?"

"Do you see how in some places the ink looks shinier, more reflective?"

I tried looking as he had. "I think so. But it looks shiny in several places."

"Perhaps it's a treasure trove. Let's try under the microscope."

"How do you use it?"

"You mean you've never used a microscope?"

"Why would I? Have you?"

"Would you believe I studied biology for two years in Prague before coming to my senses?"

"Never. My only biological study was when our Wandervogel leaders seduced us in the forest. No microscopes needed."

Walter placed the letter under the microscope, lowered the lens, and demonstrated how to adjust the focus. I put my eye to the oculus.

"Well?"

"I only see my eyelashes."

"An important scientific discovery."

"Shut up. What am I doing wrong?"

"It just takes some getting used to," he said. "Try not to blink."

"Why don't you try?"

"And why don't you have some more wine?" he said, handing me my glass from his office. "Perhaps it will relax your lids."

Walter took my place at the microscope, while I drank my wine and watched him adjust the focus. After only a few seconds, he drew a sharp breath.

"What? Do you see something?"

"I do."

"Well, what is it?"

"It looks like a diagram. A technical drawing of some kind."

"Jesus. What the hell was my brother doing?"

"I believe they call it espionage."

Just then we heard someone calling Walter's name in the hallway.

"Who is that?" I asked.

"It sounds like Nadia."

The shout came again, this time clearly audible and clearly her.

"What is she doing here?"

"She's here to pick me up. I let her have the car today. Sorry, I lost track of time."

"Go, go. Please, I don't want to have to explain anything."

"You'll be alright here?"

"Yes, of course."

He made for the door.

"And Walter? Not a word of this."

He pulled his hat down over his brow. "Secret agent at your service."

I heard Walter and Nadia leave the building after stopping by his office—was the smell of sex still hanging in the air?—then directed my attention back to the microscope. I couldn't tell what I was looking at other than a diagram of some machine, with gears and gauges and lenses, and a dizzying array of numbers and tiny labels in English, like *obverse housing unit*. I found several of these drawings masquerading, just like Walter had said, as periods, colons, and the tops of *i*'s and *j*'s, none bigger than a millimeter. Whatever these plans were, it was clear you weren't supposed to have them. But the inflated sums from the Anti-Fascist Writers League now made sense.

Then I remembered the receipt. It, too, had a sheen in certain places that looked slightly different from the matte texture of the ink elsewhere. I placed it under the microscope and focused on one of the decimals. Several eyelashes later, an image came into focus. This time it was a handwritten page. Though I could not make out any of the words at that resolution, I was already struck by an uncanny sentiment. There was something familiar about the shape and slope of the tightly looped markings on the page.

I rolled the dial to magnify the size and could tell that the writing was in German. Not only that but, as a sick feeling crept over me, I recognized the lettering. It was unmistakable. I rushed to read the words:

April 9, 1919

> *The bolshevik hordes have now proclaimed a Soviet republic in all of Bavaria—another revolutionary council of Jew-boy scribblers and degenerates, not unlike the Red Guard rabble currently holding Vienna hostage. Will be glad to see them all shot like vermin. Though I'm so disgusted with Allied imperialism that I'm tempted to join their charade—nationalist, Spartacist, what have you—and take to the streets, shouting, "Down with lying Western democracy!"*
>
> *Annoyed at Lisbeth for profligate consumption of butter. Made up for by the pleasure of seeing Eiko change today. His door was ajar. I spied him in profile and caught the slender grace of his torso as it tapered into the gorgeous arc of his buttocks. Is it possible to be in love with one's own son? I dream of tasting him . . .*

I felt the world spin. Frantically, I searched for another dot. Something to confirm or deny the madness I had just read.

May 5, 1919

> *I finally summoned the courage. Lisbeth was away, visiting her sister. Ildi outside in the garden. Never been so scared before attempting anything. And yet so aroused. I was hard as a hickory stick when I presented myself to him on the divan. Eiko, as if he'd long been expecting this moment, patiently waiting for me to make the first move, took me in his hands, and then in his mouth.*

I began to heave. I felt I was going to faint but made myself finish the page.

Then, quite suddenly, Ildi came in from the garden. There was no time to
dissemble. I was in the throes of passion, the two of us, father and son, like
two figures of Greek myth, entwined. I had no choice but to be bold and invite
her to join us. "Come, Hildegard," I said, "honor thy father and brother in
the temple of pleasure."

My eye came away from the microscope, and I remember seeing the ceiling roll over me like a giant brayer as I faded into blackness.

When I came to, I was back in Walter's office, with Moholy-Nagy peering down at me from the wall. His hand in the photograph was stretched forward as if to anoint me. I needed it—I was still queasy and my brain felt like it had been put through a mangle.

"Walter," said a gravelly Russian singsong voice just above my ear, "our sleeping beauty has awoken." Nadia was seated beside me, on the chair that only minutes earlier—or was it hours?—had held my discarded dress.

She laid a cool, bony hand on my forehead and stroked my wrist.

Walter came over and knelt down next to the sofa. "Hilde, how are you feeling? You had us worried sick."

"Uh . . . not great. What happened?"

"You must have inhaled too many photo chemicals in the darkroom when you were developing your pictures," said Walter, eyeing me to be sure I followed along with his story. "I came back to get some papers I'd left in my office and noticed the door in the photography studio was ajar, and when I looked in, I was shocked to find you out cold, communing with the linoleum."

"I see . . . yes. I guess I must have fainted."

"We should probably take you to the hospital just to make sure everything's okay."

At Walter's mention of the hospital, I instantly thought of you, and then I remembered everything. The microscope. The dots. Those horrible lies. The heat rose to my face, and I felt sick again.

"No, no, really, I'm fine," I said, sitting up and fighting through the dizziness and nausea.

"I didn't know you took photographs, Hilde," said Nadia.

"Uh, yes . . . well, I do. On occasion."

"I should like to see these sometime."

"Why don't you stay with us tonight, Hilde?" said Walter. "I can bring you back to campus in the morning. Or Nadia can drive you home tomorrow if you're not feeling up to it. Right, Nadia?"

"It would be my pleasure," she said.

"No, no, thank you, but really I can't. Walter, my things—" I gave him the same searching eyes that he had used with me in guiding me through our cover story. "Are they still in the photography studio?"

"Everything's here in your bag," said Walter, giving me an assuring nod.

The two of them insisted on driving me home, which I accepted because I'd missed the last ferry and my head was still ringing. I could feel the knot at the back of my skull throbbing in time with my pulse.

"I'll just see Hilde up to her flat," Walter said to Nadia, as she turned onto my block. "Make sure she doesn't conk out in the elevator."

He opened the back-seat door for me and walked me up to my building. "Hilde. Those documents—you should burn them immediately."

"Yes. I will."

"Don't let your curiosity get the better of you. Just destroy them and be done with it. That's my advice."

"Okay." I wondered if he had seen the diary entries too, or if he was just referring to those diagrams. But I still felt dizzy and unsteady on my legs and was concentrating all my energy on not fainting again.

"Shall I see you up in the lift, then?"

"No, really, I'm fine. You've done more than enough. I worry Nadia already suspects something."

"Don't worry about that. Everything's fine. Just take care of yourself, Hilde. And burn those papers at once."

I set my bag on the coffee table and then spent the entire night sitting there in the dark, brooding on what I had read on those little dots.

It was Father's writing, to be sure. I knew he'd kept a diary, though unlike you, I never stooped so low as to read it—apparently your devious snooping was not just an adolescent phase but the beginning of something much worse. And I had a pretty good idea of what this thing must be. I recalled his dire prognosis, after losing his valise in Shanghai, that if its contents ever fell into the wrong hands, "the effects would be catastrophic, even fatal." And here I thought he was being melodramatic.

And yet it was—at least in part—a complete lie. Or a fantasy. Perhaps a diary of secret wishes? Because while I cannot vouch for what Father felt toward you or even, God forbid, did to you (though I cannot believe it), I know as sure as I know anything in this life that he never summoned me, as a fourteen-year-old or at any age, to a night of sexual congress with him and you. But even if this diary was a record of his secret wish fulfillments—anti-Semitism, homosexuality, incest—I could think of no good reason that such a document would be in your possession, encoded in a bill for Richard Halifax's suits.

When the sun rose through my window, I decided to burn them. I know this is what you instructed me to do all along, which is why there was a great deal of resistance in me—the last thing I wanted to do at that moment was your bidding. And yet Walter was right: There was nothing to be done but destroy them.

I rose from the couch to burn your dirty secrets at the stove, withdrew them from the bag, but on my way to the kitchen was stopped dead in my tracks. It was the smell. The smell of the papers.

I knew the smell of mimeograph ink because I had spent hours at that infernal machine in the faculty lounge, making copies of handouts for my students. The aroma, warm and vinegary, was a consolation for the drudgery of the task. And though the ink at school was black like typewriter ink and not that telltale blue-violet, the smell of a freshly minted copy was unmistakable.

An hour later, I returned from the Emporium with a children's microscope kit, which, the clerk assured me, would allow me to see every paisley on a butterfly's wing.

It took me the rest of the morning to read through the manual, with its baffling diagrams, but eventually I got the thing up and running.

I put the papers Walter had given me beneath the glass, and just as I suspected, every period, every decimal, every dot atop an *i* was just an opaque blob of ink. They were copies. Fakes. The originals with the microdots—well, it was obvious who took them. My God, what a fool I was.

All our conversations in the studio, in his office, inviting me into their home, driving me to L.A., taking me to the fair. Was it all a ruse? Was he after the diagrams or the diary, or both? And how long had he and his witch had designs on me? Had he somehow known about these documents before I told him about your bewildering note? Or had he genuinely been my friend before seizing an opportunity and deciding to betray me?

The more I thought about it, the more I saw how the whole thing had unfolded right before my eyes. It was Walter himself who suggested the possibility of microdots—"Nadia once told me"—and still he managed to make it feel like it was my idea to look at them under the microscope. And then the wine—no doubt I had been drugged. It had all been a sinister setup. But why hadn't he just stolen them earlier? Perhaps he had tried and failed and so hatched this plan, even telling me that he had studied biology for two years in . . . Prague. He said he had studied in Prague. I had missed the connection at the time, but suddenly I remembered what Salka said that night on the beach. That she once knew a Walter S., a student radical in Prague, who later took part in the Hungarian Soviet before being killed by the Whites.

Perhaps her Walter wasn't shot after all, I thought.

You seem to be in good company, Eiko. Apparently I surround myself with liars and betrayers, and what's more, I'm stupid enough to trust them. And now whatever evil gears you set in motion and then tried to get me to stop—well, they now continue to turn. Thanks to you, I have given wing to our father's destruction. And I will never forgive you for it.

To: The Dicky Halifax Junior Adventurers Club
From: Herr Dickee-san
Unmoored

Fall 1939

Dear boys,

Not long after my vision quest in the copra fields, Nacho came to visit.

I was cautiously chewing my breakfast out on the lanai, still groggy from drugged sleep and preoccupied with the lead pipe under my kimono, the likes of which I hadn't known in over twenty years of wet noodledom, when who should come shuffling down the hallway but my beloved little wharf rat.

"Nacho!" I shouted, as the guards ushered him out. I stood awkwardly, tucking my johnson into my belt—a trick I learned in high school that will serve you boys well in the coming years—and grasped my young friend by his shoulders.

"Well, if it isn't my old sparring partner and trusty sidekick!" I said. "My, Nacho, you're looking fighting trim. Come, take a load off and help yourself to some coconut." I was trying to inject a little levity since, frankly, my young friend looked haggard.

Nacho lowered himself gingerly onto the rattan chair, blinking at his surroundings. I could tell he was shocked by my sumptuous living arrangements. "What is this place? And why are your teeth so new and shiny looking?"

"Are they?" I asked, fingering my front ones. They did feel uncharacteristically firm. "Must be the coconut diet."

"What's going on here, Dicky?"

"Don't worry, Nachito. You're safe here. It's the Frink family coconut plantation. And I've been having a whale of a time. All that was missing was you."

"I just assumed they chopped your head off once I stopped hearing your screams through the walls," said Nacho.

"So you *could* hear me! Why didn't you answer?"

"I guess I was still mad at you for starting that uprising in the mines and ruining my plans for escape."

"You mustn't mope, Nacho. It's unmanly."

"What the hell are they doing with you here anyway, Dicky?"

"I've been studying, and I'm undergoing regeneration therapy. But, Nacho, I prefer to go by Herr Dickee-san now."

He blinked at me a few times, then shrugged. "I guess it's no stupider than 'Dicky.' What the hell's regeneration therapy and why haven't they killed you? Or me, for that matter?"

I sensed he had not undergone the same therapeutic regimen as I had and was still his unregenerated little wharf-rat self.

I explained to him the course of study that my healers had led me through, as well as my robust diet of coconuts, mescaline, and pills, which were clearly restoring me to health, though I still preferred not to look in the mirror. "Oh, and several daily injections too. Quite invigorating. You wouldn't believe how much the good doctors have helped me."

"Dicky, these people are not trying to help you."

"Nacho, I know it's hard for you to understand this, being a poor half-breed orphan from the docks of Macao, but I'm an American celebrity. I told you it was only a matter of time before my fame reached the right ears and cleared up this misunderstanding. Dr. Kanemoto, whose benevolence is a debt I can never repay, realized who I am and then, along with the help of his colleague Dr. Frink, devoted considerable resources to healing me so that I can return home in the bloom of health. Now, as I've asked you before, please call me Herr Dickee-san."

"Then why were you screaming in the cell? Who was torturing you?"

"That wasn't torture, Nacho. I mean, not exactly. It was painful, of course, but healing hurts. Dr. Kanemoto aptly likened it to a visit to the dentist. Speaking of which," I said, rubbing my jaw, "kinda feels like I just went to the dentist . . ."

Nacho looked at me skeptically. No doubt he felt a little envious of all the attention yours truly was getting while he was left rotting in that cell.

"I want you to know, Nacho, that I've put in a good word for you with Drs. Kanemoto and Frink. I told them that I'll do anything they want, provided they let us go."

"Go where?"

"Back home to America, Nacho. Where else?"

"America is not my home, Dicky."

"Oh, you'll love it there. Maybe we can get you enrolled in a paralegal course or something that will satisfy your pointy little Jesuitical mind. Granted, we might have to do some side work for the Japs and Jerries, but it's a mere sliver of the eternal debt I owe the doctors for healing me. Besides, Dr. Frink assures me that he has powerful connections in Hollywood that can guarantee your man Dickee-san another stab at the silver screen."

"You told me you hated Hollywood and thought making movies was like working in the international drug trade."

"No, I never said that."

"You said it was 'a schlock farm run by greedy pimps and vindictive pansies' and that you would never again stray from your true vocation as a writer-adventurer."

"Who appointed you to be my stenographer, you little imp? So I want to make movies, okay? Is that really so shameful?"

"It is if you're willing to sell your soul to a malevolent foreign power."

"Nobody likes a scold at breakfast, Nacho. And you have no idea what you're talking about."

"They've done something to you, Dicky."

"In fact, if you must know, Nacho, they *have* done something to me. Now, I don't mean to be vulgar, but let's just say that my healing regimen has restored my full bloom of manly vitality, if you take my meaning. . . ."

Nacho looked at me blankly.

I pointed discreetly toward my lap, which, even though it was covered with my kimono, showed an appreciable bulge. A magnificent sight—

though, to be honest, the thrill of my restoration was beginning to shade into a throbbing, mildly dizzying ache.

"I'm virile once more, Nacho," I said, standing and unbelting myself as I turned to him in profile. "And it would seem in perpetuity."

Nacho recoiled in horror, no doubt reminded of similar contours that had marred his first week aboard the *Tonan Maru*.

"Don't worry, my friend. No need to bare your teeth—I mean nothing untoward."

Nacho backed away to a safe distance as he continued to stare derisively at my tumescence. "It's probably a side effect from all those strange drugs they're giving you. They obviously replaced your teeth and are using you for some terrible experiment."

"Funny you should mention it." I told Nacho that I had recently had a dream of that sort, right after my field trip with the Coconut King. In the dream, Drs. Kanemoto and Frink were standing over an operating table, arguing about what to do with me, and Dr. Kanemoto was furious that my teeth had been replaced without his permission.

"I thought we agreed, Dr. Frink, that he was not psychically up to the task of reintegration, to say nothing of his degraded physical appearance."

"Keine Angst, Dr. Kanemoto. The new teeth are simply a question of hygiene. Though, as you know, I've always believed there is enormous potential should he reclaim his original persona. Think of all the work he could do for us, all the people he knows. And he's such an idiot, he's virtually idiot-proof."

"You're forgetting that he was my discovery. I shared him with you, and now you're clearly undermining my efforts. I have no doubts your new friends in Moscow are behind this."

"Come, come, Dr. Kanemoto. I'm your grateful guest here, even if this island was once part of our own magnificent empire. I would never dream of subverting your designs, and I assure you, my country's pact with Stalin changes nothing between us."

"Talk about a nutty dream, huh?" I said to Nacho. "I knew I must have been dreaming nonsense when they started talking about an alliance between the Krauts and Russkies. But, nonsense or no, this steel ding-dong I woke up with is the real deal."

"Maybe they've surgically implanted a stick of dynamite in your penis and they're going to use you as a human bomb."

"What a sick, uncharitable imagination you have, Nacho. How does your hypertrophic brain go to such outlandish corners?"

"The Kempeitai do that kind of thing all the time. They have a whole facility in Harbin dedicated to it. I met a Manchurian who had been an orderly there, and he'd get drunk and talk about seeing men who'd had their esophagus surgically attached to their bladder so that they pissed out bits of chewed food, women who had plague bacilli implanted in their wombs so—"

"Stop! Good God, Nacho, my poor miserable friend, if only you could meet Drs. Kanemoto and Frink, you'd soon give up your suspicions—Wait, that's them there! See those two men walking up the drive? The little Oriental fella in the red-and-white medical armband—that's Dr. Kanemoto."

I went to the edge of the high veranda and waved to the doctors as they approached. They saw Nacho and me and lifted their hats by way of greeting.

"See?" I said. "They're smiling. No doubt they're coming to meet you and perhaps start you on the same regeneration therapy I've just completed. Lord knows you could use it."

"Dicky," said Nacho, still unappeased. "Your doctors clearly haven't cured you of your stupidity, because that armband is not medical. It's the uniform of the Kempeitai. Your benevolent doctor is an officer of the Japanese secret police."

"Haven't we been over this before, Nacho? You have an unhealthy amount of knowledge and it will only bring you misery. And for the last time, you churl, call me Herr Dickee-san! I'm a man, not a boy, and a man deserves respect!"

Annoyed as I was, perhaps he was right. I did recall having seen an awful lot of what I thought were Japanese doctors during my visits to Shanghai, usually escorting what I had assumed were ailing patients into covered trucks. And, though he didn't much talk about it, it was clear Nacho had suffered previous encounters with the secret police.

"Whatever they've promised you is a lie, Dicky. The Kempeitai don't help people. And that German is probably with the Abwehr or SS."

"Yes, Karl Dieter said something of the kind."

"Who's Karl Dieter?"

Suddenly I felt a little surge in my groin and up my spine, an electric current that shot straight from foreskin to forehead. "Never mind, Nacho. That doesn't concern you." I noticed that my senseis were now down below, looking up at us on the high veranda. "Come on, let me introduce you to the good doctors. Perhaps they can cure you of your congenital surliness."

I turned and tried to take Nacho by the shoulder, but once again he pulled back from me. "Get away from me, Dicky. I'm not going with you, and I'd sooner kill myself than let those doctors lay a hand on me."

"Always so dramatic, Nacho. Now, shrug off that chip on your shoulder and let's go."

I reached for him once more—and, boys, even though I've replayed the incident in my head a thousand times, I still don't know exactly what happened next.

Perhaps it was his horror of the Kempeitai, ingrained from past bitter run-ins, that jolted him. Or perhaps after so many whalers' wangs had been aimed at his face, he instinctively recoiled from mine. Whatever the cause, be it involuntary reflex or self-destructive impulse, Nacho leapt up onto the low wall of the terrace. Then, without so much as a sound, my newest, dearest sidekick and indomitable wharf rat either lost his balance and fell or, in an act of horrible self-annihilation, made good on his word and swan-dove twenty feet below to the hard Saipanese earth.

"No!" I screamed. "Nacho!"

It's possible he had intended to take the doctors out with him, for they just barely sidestepped his body as it crashed down between them. He landed with an awful thud, his limbs a collection of contradictory angles.

Dr. Kanemoto rolled Nacho over with a flick of his boot and examined him. He put two fingers to his lolling neck. "Is he alive?" I asked. Dr. Kanemoto ignored my question and, eyeing Dr. Frink, gave one of his little grunts.

"Herr Dickee-san," said Dr. Frink, the two of them now looking up at me as I stood frozen in horror at Nacho crumpled at their feet. "You are ready to go home. But it will be just you now."

Another shot to the keister is all I remember before this morning, when I came to in a car being driven down to the harbor. My doctors assure me Nacho is alive, though with grave injuries that will require him to receive care here while I go on my mission. I demanded to see him, but they said he was in the hospital, in a fragile state. "Well, tell him I'm coming back," I said. "Tell him not to give up. You hear, Nacho? I'm coming back for you!"

My doctors nodded politely. "Of course, Dicky. We'll tell him. You just get what we've asked for, and Nacho will be here good as new when you get back."

As I boarded the submarine, bereft of my sidekick, I felt anything but in the pink of health promised by my coconut mentor. In fact, your man Dickee-san felt like he was a hundred broken pieces held together by glue.

But he is coming home.

~D.

Part II

TRADE WINDS

The Testimony of Simon Faulk

20

SEPTEMBER 1940

I suppose it all looks a bit deranged from where you're sitting. And I grant that it is, though it made perfect sense at the time. What you must understand is that there is a deranging power to this man. That is why I believe he is so dangerous.

You want it from the beginning, I assume. But if you want to understand what happened in San Francisco, you need to know first what happened in Bangkok. And you can't really understand Bangkok without understanding what came before. That's the thing about beginnings—they harbor occult origins. I don't wish to be obtuse, but it's a genuinely vexing question, where to begin. I'm inclined to start with March 24, 1916, the moment these lines began converging, for that was the moment I knew my life would be a lonely, perhaps even a ruinous one. But I suppose you're not interested in that.

What you're interested in, of course, are my dealings with the German consul Fritz Wiedemann—who, by the way, could have been immensely useful if you people and those useless twats in the Foreign Office hadn't been such cowards. But Wiedemann is important only because his overtures coincided with—in fact, prompted—my quest for Richard Halifax. *My quest for Halifax.* God, it makes me sound like a madman, hunting a grail or a whale, when really he was just a damned writer. Not even a good one at that. Just a professional liar. Like us, I suppose.

In a fitting stroke of perversity, my leviathan surfaced the day Richard Halifax was officially declared dead, in October of last year.

I should have known then and there that it was too good to be true. But hindsight makes idiots of us all.

That morning in San Francisco began like any other last fall—bleary and forgettable. I was at my window, chewing a pencil, benumbed by a second gin and the dingy sky, dreaming as I often did of small brown feet on my back, when the burgundy face of my uncle poked into view.

It hovered above the passport-renewal forms that lay in a neglected pile on my desk and spoke to me in a breathy, Scotch-fumed whisper. "Simon, my boy! Just the lad I want to see. There's been a wee development."

Wee indeed, I thought. Not only was my uncle Paul, the consul-general, rarely in the office before noon, and usually then just to have his secretary remind him where he was lunching, but he had never, in these past six months, darkened the doorway of my sordid little office where I pretended to be a passport-control agent.

"I've just gotten word from Wiedemann. He wants to meet."

The pencil fell out of my mouth, and the brown feet pattered from my mind. "Fritz Wiedemann, the German consul?"

"No, Fritz Wiedemann the ruddy sausage vendor. Who else?"

"What does he want?"

"Well, he didn't say, naturally. The man's a right rogue. Slipped a note in my golf cleats while I was cinching up my girdle in the gents'. Had the tee time right after mine."

"Do you have it? The note?"

"Don't be daft, dear—I flushed it the moment I read it. But it said, *Arrange a meeting with those who can receive me.* If you ask me, he wants to defect."

"Defect? Why do you think that?"

"Oh, just a feeling in the gut. A scent of cloak-and-dagger in the air. But whatever he wants, it sounds like he has something to offer. Could be good news for you, son."

"Let's not go jumping to conclusions, Uncle Paul."

"Nonsense. This calls for a drink. Hermione!" the consul called to his secretary. "Some fresh ice for us thirsty boys, if you please."

Uncle Paul always wanted what was best for me. He was the only family I had left, which meant that I naturally responded by dampening his enthusiasm. But in truth I felt the same frisson of giddiness he did, and I was grateful for another gin to calm my nerves.

I knew I had to be careful not to give the German consul's note too much credence. Captain Fritz Wiedemann, after all, was an enigma. A thoroughbred Nazi and one of Hitler's nearest-and-dearest, suddenly dispatched to San Francisco last summer to take up the post of consul. He had been Hitler's commanding officer during the last war—rumors were he'd saved his life, which was already a mark against him. When Hitler took power, he popped back into the frame, first as secretary under Rudolf Hess, and then as Hitler's personal adjutant. Throughout the thirties, he was there at Hitler's side, smiling and nodding, his Guy Friday and Old Trench Chum, running errands, riding into Vienna, rolling into Prague, until, all of a sudden, he's relegated to a third-rate diplomatic post on the American Pacific. The reserve of drunks and bunglers who, for reasons of blood or debt, can't be entirely severed from courtly favor. So the question was, why? Did he and the führer have a falling-out? Or was his banishment only a cover? What was to say that Wiedemann was not still—as everyone including SIS, the FBI, and even *Life* magazine believed—Hitler's aide-de-camp who had come here to coordinate intelligence with the Japanese and plan for a war in the Pacific? Depending on one's motive and perspective, San Francisco could be an extraneous node on the far side of the globe or it could be the joint of the world.

Yet the role of Hitler's special-appointed California spymaster seemed too obvious. The Abwehr usually made at least a passing gesture at subterfuge. All the same, this sudden approach made me both excited and wary. Of course, ever since Bangkok, everything made me wary. But Wiedemann was too big a fish to ignore, a tuna that had just flopped into my uncle's lap while I was baiting minnows. So I spent the rest of the morning cabling with London, requesting approval to meet with the Nazi consul—a highly unusual request, given that our countries were already at war.

If I'm free to speak honestly, and I don't see what more I have to lose at this point, I had little confidence in the Service by then. It was, and to this day remains, in a shambolic state, grossly under-resourced for a war that everyone saw coming yet had still managed to take Whitehall by surprise. And that's only because they spent the last five years shading themselves in their rectal vaults. Section V, under Felix Cowgill's cranky, supercilious leadership, was no better off. Cowgill knew not a whit more about counterintelligence than any of the rest of us, though he clearly regarded me as a useless appendage.

It little surprised me, then, that by lunch I still did not have any answer from London. I spent the walk over to Edelweiss pondering the possibilities. If Uncle Paul was right and Wiedemann really did want to switch sides, it would be the first exciting thing that had happened to me in my postlapsarian existence. The intelligence yield could be huge. It might, I thought, even get me back in good graces. It might—my imagination now running wild—even get me . . . No. I had to stop myself from finishing the thought. There would be no path back to Bangkok. That fair city, and the woman I'd left there, had vanished behind a thick wall of San Francisco fog.

"You're late, Faulk. I thought you limeys were supposed to be punctual."

Before I'd even hung my hat, I knew it was going to be a long lunch. Special Agent Cliff Hader, head of the FBI's San Francisco division, was looking at me like the older brother I'd never wanted: a mix of condescension, camaraderie, and hostility.

"Blame my mother," I said, sliding into the booth. "A hopeless Italian."

"No fooling? Well, you hide the dago well. Can't even smell the garlic on you."

I smiled at this, less at the coarse jibe than at the misguided idea Cliff Hader had of my Venetian mother, she of the flaxen hair and translucent skin, who would have been ill for days if she so much as tasted garlic. And while I suppose I did "hide the dago well" these days, I had spent my adolescence in an English public school hearing otherwise.

I wasn't going to tell Special Agent Hader the real reason I was late, at least not until London had decided how they wanted to manage the Wiedemann situation. For the moment, it was my private little secret, and I relished not sharing it.

I ordered a lager and schweinebraten from the dirndled waitress and took in the beer hall's atmosphere, with Bavarian flags, bears rampant, and bankers hugging beer steins the size of small grain silos. Odd place, I thought, to hold a counterintelligence meeting, though admittedly convenient. We could interrogate the weekday lunchtime crowd, find someone with an *Ich liebe meinen Führer* pin beneath his lapel, and call it a day.

Conducting counterintelligence in the States had become a touchy affair that fall. My job, intended to be a remote sinecure to keep me out of the way, suddenly changed when Hitler invaded Poland. The FBI, which had a rather paltry counterespionage apparatus, finally realized their spy problem was a problem, and consented to our assistance. We'd help the Americans dig up German spies and, in doing so, make them feel the Nazi threat on their own soil, in hopes they might wake up and join the fight.

Except the Americans—or at least their appointed representative from the FBI—didn't seem terribly grateful for my help. Yet he still demanded to be kept apprised of everything I was doing. I can't say I exactly thrilled to these newly instituted lunch meetings either, as it meant that for at least an hour every week I had to watch Cliff Hader eat and talk, often at once.

"Well, shall we get to it?" I said. I'd learned from our previous encounter that Hader was inclined to small talk in the form of monologues, and unless I wanted to be raked over the coals of baseball statistics, the Chinese problem, or why American automobiles were the best, I had to hurry to head off any openings. "I'll go first."

The bulk of my work, when not maintaining my flimsy cover of stamping passports and issuing visas, consisted of keeping tabs on two spheres of espionage. The first was the homegrown Nazis of the German American Bund and its various tentacles in fascist-leaning cultural and business organizations. The Bund had a stronger presence down south—they'd recently filled Hindenburg Park in Los Angeles for one of their "Peace Rallies" meant to allow German aggression to proceed unchecked. But the Deutsches Haus of San Francisco was home to various Bund and Bund-affiliated events, most of which aimed at bringing the Reich to American soil or American dollars to the Reich. The second sphere concerned the activities of the German consulate, along with its Italian and Japanese counterparts. Wiedemann's consulate was mostly opaque to us at the time, though we suspected overlap between the spheres, and I was trying to catch glimpses by seeding informants throughout the various affiliates of the Bund and anywhere else a Nazi spy might decide to roost.

My achievements of that particular week, which I inventoried for Hader while he sucked at his Coca-Cola, included the following: I had recently infiltrated the San Francisco Alpinists Club with a German-born British national, who, thanks to visa problems, was now in my debt and posing as an enthusiast of the Strength through Joy program back in the fatherland. With any luck, his chatty treks up the hump of Mount Tamalpais would elicit like-minded feelings and further leads. Another informant, embedded in the German American Business League, had just reported plans of its many hundreds of small-business members to launch a boycott of Jewish companies. And my informant at the Deutsches Haus reported that two brothers from a San Francisco metalworks had been boasting about their plans for a terror campaign targeting prominent interventionists and émigrés. Idle fantasy, it seemed, though they claimed to be proficient in bomb-making. Finally—and this last bit I offered up more as an amusing anecdote than a credible piece of intelligence—O'Malley, my informant on the waterfront, had told me that a crabber deep in his cups in a Latin Quarter wine dump last week swore he saw a submarine surface off Stinson Beach and vomit up a man who, waving a samurai sword, plunged into the waves and swam ashore.

Hader sneered. "My brother-in-law is a crabber. Lyingest bunch of drunks you ever met. Make the Irish look sober by comparison. I honestly don't know how you all manage it—wasting your time chasing a load of horseshit."

"I'm afraid wasting time and chasing lies are the heart and lungs of our trade," I replied. That was precisely how I'd spent my last three months in Siam, only to be awarded with expulsion. Which was why I was now stuck in San Francisco, living out my exile in a sulky protest, with little to show for myself beyond a stubborn case of piles, a gin-soaked liver, and too many sleepless nights thanks to the horn wails and buzzing neon glow of the jazz club beneath my flat. Having spent years living contentedly amid the reeking canals of the Far East and the cut-throat warrens of the Mediterranean, I had found my private hell in the swank center of the Tenderloin. Or perhaps, I thought, it was here in this phony California beer hall, watching Cliff Hader sleeve-wipe his brow while he masticated his wiener schnitzel.

"Well, wasting time is not how the Federal Bureau of Investigation operates, Faulk. Better take note of it," said Hader, pointing his fork at me. "Of course, Hoover's willing to pick up Germans nosing around where they don't belong. And we got to keep our eyes on the Japs too, of course. But the real problem, as far as the Bureau is concerned, is the reds running around in plain sight."

Hader told me how the recent flood of émigrés from Europe were of a persuasion hostile to the American way of life and, drawn as they were to Hollywood and other communication media, they posed an especially outsized threat in the way your average potbellied, tuba-playing *Enkel Hans* of the local Bund chapter did not. That's why, he said, the Bureau's primary counterintelligence efforts were targeting "premature anti-fascists."

"Premature?" I asked, confused. This was in October of last year, mind you—we in England were already at war, albeit a phony one. Even Chamberlain and Lord Lothian, the leading lights of the appeasement crowd, had come around by then. "Is it really still too early to be concerned with fascism?"

"Think about it," said Hader. "All those homegrown reds who went to Spain and came slinking back sore losers. Or the ones from Germany and Austria who keep pouring in. Believe me, there are a bunch of bolshies in California posing as victims and refugees; meanwhile, they're free to hawk their poison on every corner."

Hader told me he had his eye on one of the more prominent émigré journals, *The Reckoning*—run by Heinrich Rauch, the son of the famous German writer. He'd put a tail on both Rauch and his sister, whose address in Russian Hill was listed as the journal's San Francisco branch office, and was hoping to leverage a factotum down in L.A. to get a look at the funding. "You follow that Jew money far enough, eventually it all turns up red."

Hader looked at me for a reaction, as though trying to gauge just where exactly British intelligence stood on Jews and reds or if he could detect a trace of either in me. "I'm sure the local Chinese have partisans screaming revolution too," he continued, "and who knows what the Japs are up to, but we still don't have an Oriental agent who can penetrate Chinatown. All our guys stick out like a, well, like a white guy in Chinatown."

I didn't volunteer that I was frequently one of those white men myself. Stalking the night for a trace of what I'd lost. Even then, six months on, I found it distasteful to be surrounded by a whole country of lumbering *farangs*. Of course, I liked being a white man, but that didn't mean I wanted to see them everywhere. Nor did I want to lord my whiteness over others, as they do in America nearly as much as in the colonies. This is what is so rare and wonderful about being a *farang* in Siam. You are not a usurper or a *sahib*, rather a welcome foreigner from the West. English, French, Italian—it doesn't matter. To them you are simply a *farang*. And after years of being seen by the Italians as hopelessly English, by the English as laughably Italian, and by most of my Scottish relatives as a bloody Sassenach, I found it a refreshing identity. But now in America I had become one of Cliff Hader's cartoon "limeys."

The problem with America—among its many problems—is that everything here is a cartoon. Big. Loud. Garish. Unlike Siam, there is nothing to discover, nothing to peel back. Even the much-praised beauty of San Francisco shouts in your face, like an artless burlesque show of "Hills! Bays! Bridges! Say, mister, ain't I pretty?" That's what passes for seduction: Mae West tits on a tap-dancing Shirley Temple. Fitting temptress for a nation of overgrown children.

I was about to slip off into a reverie of warmer days and memories of my own temptress, when the waitress tipped her laced cleavage down to my eyes and asked if I wanted another beer. I did. Even Hader, I noticed, was caught in its thrall and ordered another Coca-Cola.

I took advantage of the interruption to snatch the reins of the conversation and broach the subject of the German consul. "Did you happen to see the *Life* magazine profile on Fritz Wiedemann?"

"Yeah, sure. One of my guys clipped it for me. Why?"

"Just wondering what your impression was. Seems he's stirring up quite a moral conundrum for the society ladies in Pacific Heights. 'What would you do if you were seated next to Captain Wiedemann at supper?'"

"I wouldn't let my wife get within ten feet of him is what," said Hader. "He's a snake."

I felt a sudden pang of sympathy for Cliff Hader's wife, though I somehow doubted she was a society lady. "And have you found where exactly he's slithering about?"

"We've got eyes on him," he said cagily.

"And?"

"And what?" It was clear that the FBI did not intend these intelligence-sharing meetings to be a symmetrical exchange.

"Well, I'm just curious what you make of him. For example, he seems to want to have nothing to do with the Bund. At least that's his public stance. And it's to be assumed that he's here to bolster isolationism and suck money out of all the wealthy Roosevelt haters. Hence all the dinner parties on the peninsula. But we have sources who indicate that he's also at the head of a major network to encourage German nationals to return to the fatherland—or perhaps stay and do its bidding."

Hader shrugged. "We've been monitoring the immigration traffic. Lots of German nationals have been coming into SF from Japan, who then proceed on to Canada or down to South America. And lately we're seeing a wave of engineers embarking for Japan on German passports too. Wiedemann occasionally takes them out to dinner before they embark."

"That fits with our belief," I said, "that Wiedemann is here to stitch up the spy net across the Pacific Basin. The German Security Service already have an intelligence web on the Asian side—*die Orient-Gruppe*—from Tientsin to the South Seas Mandate, and we believe they're trying to link up with the Japanese network in California."

"Well, whatever he's doing, he has a big budget. We think he might be behind the recent attempts by a Swedish businessman to buy up the local papers—*Vallejo Evening News*, *Oakland Tribune*, he even put in a bid for the *Chronicle*."

"Really? And how do you know that?"

Hader explained that Wiedemann had what's called an inheritance fund. When a German national living in California or anywhere in the Northwest dies, the American dollars of his estate are turned over to the consulate. If he leaves his wealth to relatives in Germany, the beneficiaries in Germany are then credited with a corresponding sum in marks, paid out by the government, but the American dollars still go to the consulate.

"And doesn't Wiedemann have to send that money back to Berlin?" I asked.

"It appears not. Dead-German largesse seems to be piling up in Wiedemann's coffers. See, we figured we might get a look-see at where that pile of inheritance money ends up if we got the banks to mark the bills before disbursing them to the German consulate. But so far the only place we've seen them turn up is at this Swede's business dinners with a few newspaper publishers."

It was a clever move, I had to admit, but before I could inquire more about Wiedemann's illicit funds, Hader suddenly began to cough. It seemed a piece of schnitzel had gotten stuck in his throat. Not wanting to witness the offending morsel's expulsion or watch a man die from lunch, I signaled to the waiter for a glass of water and got up to go to the toilet.

I recall it was one of those peculiar American long-trough affairs, ideal for awkward shoulder-rubbing and genital-viewing. Perhaps to distract from the temptation of the latter, the day's paper had been unfurled above the urinal. And it was there in that vulnerable position, after months of conjuring him in my mind's eye with a smoldering rage, that I saw the face of my betrayer, beaming at me with his impossible smile. The man to blame for my expulsion from paradise: Richard Halifax.

As some small recompense from the universe, he'd been officially declared dead.

21

I was finally granted permission to speak with the German consul, and a meeting was set for the end of the week. *Promise him nothing and make him show his cards first*—those were my instructions from Section V. Along with the ever-so-witty reminder to *Keep your wallet closed this time and please do try not to get deported.*

Oh, such comedians you lot were back in London. I could just picture everyone cozied up around their pints in the bar of the St. Ermin's, roaring to the new recruits about what a twit I was. How was it that for years no one paid the slightest attention to the scant doings of the Service in Asia, yet somehow word of my failure in Siam had spread with an urgency unseen in the annals of espionage? Harry Steptoe had written me that summer to say he was sorry to have heard about *the Bangkok Cock-up*—as though it already had a fixed and indexed title in the lore of diplomatic bed-shitting. Steptoe said he felt awful about it, as well he should have done. Though *his* name, curiously enough, had not managed to attach itself to ignominy. Nor had the illustrious name of the man who played me for a fool, then disappeared at sea.

That moment I saw Halifax's name in the paper, I began brooding on him again. I wondered what his final thoughts had been before his ship went down. Had his life flashed before his eyes, as people say, or was his mind blank with terror? Or was there just enough space for a momentary thought? *Bloody hell. Damn it all. I'm sorry.* I had often wondered whether, back in 1916, my parents had time for these briefest of cognitions. The torpedo had ripped through the hull of their ship, cutting it in two. The stern remained afloat, while those in the bow were pitched into the sea. Some managed to climb back onto the floating remains, but my mother and father, along with some fifty others, were either crushed, incinerated, or drowned—perhaps all three. I liked to think they were given at least a moment, amid the panic and confusion, for a last gasp of understanding, a final acceptance of their fate before the steel came crashing down and the water filled their lungs. In the case of Richard Halifax, I hoped there had been that same moment of awareness, so that he could recognize what a damned fool he was and that he was getting his just deserts.

Does that sound vindictive? Well, it's only fair that you hear my account of what happened in Siam. Not that I think it will change your verdict. But you've asked for my testimony, so you'll just have to listen.

I had come to Bangkok in 1937 on a six-month loan from Singapore and immediately fell in love. First with the city itself—its canals, its cuisine—then, foolishly, with a woman.

Bangkok was a revelation. A city of sweltering grace devoted to the arts of pleasure, yet not in the seedy way of Shanghai, or the robber-baron clubland of Singapore, or the guilt-ridden West. It was a sovereign, floating city—like the Venice of my childhood—a city of carved wood and colored glass and delicately patterned roofs shimmering in the sun. Every sense unlocked a secret: the little alleys reeking of jasmine; the saffron streak of monks in barefooted procession with their alms pots; the rhythmic pounding of green papaya and chili at the *som tam* stand; the monitor lizard sunning on a rock outside the dock of an English haberdasher. It was also a city of brothel boats plying the klongs, with lithe, amber-skinned girls smiling outside the Venus and Mosquito bars. Upon arriving, I enjoyed a string of these dizzying liaisons, each time falling deeper under the city's spell.

I had left behind a broken marriage and an equally ill-suited position as a cog in the diplomatic service, following the grooves cut by my forebears. My wife was a picky eater who, like her friends the Mitford girls, had developed a taste for fascism. I was bad at obeying my superiors, incapable of writing internal reports without succumbing to long bouts of daydreaming, and as a result had become stuck in a dull domestic post, liaising between the Foreign Office and the Italian embassy. The most exciting part of my job was crossing St. James's Park, where I routinely thought of drowning myself in the lake.

Deliverance came in the form of a lunch one afternoon with Valentine Vivian, who, no doubt at the urging of my uncle, offered me an unofficial position within and beyond the Foreign Office, so to speak. An assignment to Livorno—no wives allowed. It was a dogsbody position, really, but for an undistinguished junior diplomat with a gentleman's degree from Cambridge and a rather blighted record from Harrow, whose only real skill was an unearned proficiency in Italian, it was my way out, and I took it. The next time I made it back to London, I was served with divorce papers. She'd found a motor-car racer from Derby—one of Mosley's crowd, who ate only steak-and-kidney pies—and I was free.

When I arrived in Bangkok three years later, after spells in southern Europe and a year flitting between Singapore and Shanghai, I had tasted the world's pleasures and had every intention to go on tasting. Until Anya. Then suddenly I was content to stop.

I first met Richard Halifax on the veranda of the Oriental Hotel. It was late January 1939, and I would have said then that, for the first time in my life, I was well and truly happy. It was one of those sublime Bangkok second dawns, when the fever-heat of day has finally broken and the body sybaritic of the city starts to stretch and yawn itself awake. A wan light rippled on the river as the waiter brought us a tray of Stingers.

I could scarcely believe that the man sitting across from me, with a set of American teeth as white as his collar, was the same man who, according to the papers out of Hong Kong, was planning to sail a toy ship across the ocean.

Halifax took a dainty sip of his drink. "Forgive me, Mr. Flint," he said, addressing me by my alias, "but you look familiar. Have we met before?"

"Only in passing. I believe it was at Prince Chula's wedding."

"Oh yes, of course. My apologies."

"Not at all. I don't have a memorable face." Sometimes I thought it was the one trait that made me well suited to this line of work.

"Well, the bride and groom outshined us all that day. You're friends of Lisba's people?" asked Halifax, presumably because the bride was English.

"No, actually, I know a friend of the prince here in Bangkok."

"Oh, really? Who?"

"Anya Amatyakul." I tried to say it nonchalantly.

"Oh, Anya! Of course."

"You know her?" I asked, though I already knew the answer.

"Sure. We met at the Royal Bangkok Club—she was swimming in the lane next to mine. Extraordinary woman."

On that point, Halifax was not lying. Whip-smart, with a wicked sense of humor and the most delicate features you've ever seen, Anya seemed to have been designed to bring me to my knees. She was half Russian, half Thai, the daughter of an adjutant to one of the minor princes, tutored by an English governess in Bangkok and corrupted at a finishing school in Paris. Occupying a role she never would have been allowed to play in the colonies, where being a half-caste was worse than being "a bloody native," she was at once a Europeanized member of the Thai nobility and, to the resident Westerners in the city, an emissary of Siam. I chose to ignore that some used the word "courtesan."

We had met at, of all places, a ramshackle food stall outside the British legation, where she overheard me trying to order noodles and had erupted in laughter. I turned to face my mocker, and there was a beautiful, smirking woman in a green silk dress. "You just said, 'I want to ride a cat.'" I was poleaxed then and there.

It had seemed simple: *ow pad kee mow khrap*. But in Thai, tone is everything. Perhaps it is true of all domains. Books. Women. Politics. Which is why I bristled when Field Marshal Phibun, modeling himself after other tone-deaf autocrats, changed the name of his beautiful country from "Siam" to the brutal and unsonorous "Thailand." It reeked of nationalism and soulless modernity—unlike Siam, which conjured an ancient land still vibrating with Sanskrit mysteries. In Thai, *Seyaaam* was a question, a gentle breeze briefly parting the veil. And Anya was not "Thai" but "Siamese," through and through.

Tone, I learned, was also paramount when it came to the American seated across from me. Since the prince's wedding, I'd seen Halifax from afar at various social functions—at the United Club, out at the horse track, at one of the many parties inside the British legation's plush grounds or at the riverside palaces of the English-speaking Thais. But never had I expected to encounter him in this context. For the Richard Halifax I knew—or at least I thought I knew—was a booby.

At those gatherings, Halifax was always regaling his audience with some hair-raising travel anecdote in which he played the role of dashing idiot, a combination of li'l'-old-me and Errol Flynn, with a touch of the schoolboy pretentiousness that university-educated Americans were often at pains to show to the rest of the world. He introduced himself to others as a "writer-adventurer"—which, in a world full of rapist-murderers and actor-directors, sounded like the most terrifying hyphenate of all.

It was Anya who had first told me that Richard Halifax was friends with several high-ranking Thai military officers from earlier escapades and that he had been coming to Bangkok for the last year on business from China. This was the first moment that made me wonder if there was more to this man.

The next moment came when I consulted Harry Steptoe in Shanghai about finding someone who could facilitate a deal of a politically delicate nature and the name that came back to me was, of all people, Richard Halifax.

"The writer-adventurer?" I asked, astonished.

"He's a deuce of a fellow, that Dick. I'll fix you two up."

But the man eyeing me over his drink at the Oriental was not what I had braced myself for. One-on-one, he seemed polite and genial, even a touch shy. At least, at first.

"So," said Halifax, "Harry Steptoe said I might be of some service to you?"

"Yes, well, what exactly did Steptoe tell you?"

"Oh, you know Harry. I believe the words he used were 'a Galehaut, a go-between, someone who can help Lancelot and Guinevere *avoir une liaison.*'"

"Sounds like bloody Steptoe. And you took that to mean . . . ?"

Halifax looked around him. We were the only ones in the far corner of the veranda, our only eavesdroppers the hovering mosquitoes and toads croaking along the riverbank below. "Harry knows I have friends in these parts and that some of these friends have large collections of rifles and machine guns. See, last week I was in Shanghai, tending to a similar shipment to the Kuomintang. Naturally, Harry and I lit up Nanking Road, or at least what's left of it. Anyway, he told me there was a consular attaché in Bangkok who was in the market for similar gifts to be delivered to the Siamese but not through the official channels. Does that sound about right?"

"More or less," I said through clenched teeth. Leave it to Steptoe to reveal secret intelligence operations to his drinking pals. Last time I was in his company in Shanghai, right after the Japanese took the city, an American businessman at the Mercantile Club approached me and asked if I, too, was "a spy like Harry."

"I hear that you know Major General Maiboon," I said to Halifax, hoping to learn more of his qualifications. The general was known to control smuggling routes along the southern gulf coast as well as in the north, where the borders of Burma, Indochina, and Siam dissolved into mountains and poppy fields as far as China.

"Sure, the man's practically an uncle to me."

"In what sense?"

"In the sense that I washed up on the general's lawn in Hua Hin, half-drowned from a swim in the gulf, and he and I have been thick as thieves ever since."

As he moved into story mode, I sensed Halifax shedding his inhibitions and undergoing some kind of a metamorphosis. He explained that he had attempted to swim the Gulf of Thailand a number of years ago, followed by an overland traverse of the kingdom from the Malay Peninsula all the way up through the foothills of the Himalaya in the north, and that General Maiboon had been his guide. "We hacked our way through the jungle, telling dirty jokes and laughing our heads off without understanding a word the other was saying."

"So you don't speak Thai?" I asked.

"I didn't at the time, but that trip cured me of my ignorance. *Pom pood thai dai yiam mak!* Of course, you'll know that if you've read *The Glittering Kingdom*."

"I'm afraid I haven't."

"Well, the critics don't agree, but I think it's one of my better ones.

A traipse through the ruined splendor of empires: Angkor, Ayutthaya, Sukhothai, all the way up to Dali."

"And it was on this 'traipse,'" I asked, "that you came to know the smuggling routes in the north?"

"I know it sounds crazy, but there are headmen up in those hills who've named their sons—hell, even their favorite opium pipes—after me. Why, last time I was up near Chiang Rai, I met a little Red Mussur boy who answered to the name 'Di-kee Hafash.'"

I didn't bother responding to this ridiculous boast. "Steptoe also said you have access to American and Dutch suppliers. What kind of numbers?"

"How many do you want?"

"How many can you get?"

"At least fifteen. Probably twenty."

I sat up in my seat. "You mean to say you can procure twenty thousand rifles?"

Halifax swirled the last of his drink and leaned back in his rattan chair. "Shouldn't be much trouble. My contact in Batavia is sitting on a pile of ten thousand old Mausers and Škodas that he'd love to unload. I can get the other ten from the Philippines."

"And ammunition?"

"I'll have to check, but I'm sure we can get a couple hundred cartridges per rifle."

I ordered another round of Stingers and explained that it was of utmost importance that the arms not be traced to the British. The deal required total secrecy, far more discretion than Harry bloody Steptoe had shown up till now.

In the last year, Field Marshal Phibun had tacked hard toward Tokyo. After centuries of dodging rape-minded suitors with only torn petticoats and a few scratches to show for it, Siam—singular in Southeast Asia for being a sovereign nation, yet friendly to British business and Western culture—was now being courted by Japan. Part of Japan's newfound imperial mission to "free" Asia, as they billed it, from its European oppressors. And unfortunately, with a spate of trade agreements and a cabinet full of pro-Japanese warmongers in the Thai government, the attraction appeared to be mutual. They saw an alliance with Japan, even as coerced junior partners, as their best chance of getting back territory taken by the French as well as sticking it to the Chinese at home, who, in their eyes, were a parasite on the Thai national body. And given the cramped quarters in which Siam found itself—squeezed between us and the French, and now the looming ambitions of Japan—I could hardly blame the wily little dictator for cozying up to the new bully on the block. It seemed it was only a matter of time before pale, bloated Britannia herself would be scorched by the rising sun.

Of course, my job was to prevent that from happening. A friendly, reasonably well-armed Thailand could be a bulwark to Japanese aggression. And Field Marshal Phibun, though sufficiently enamored of fascism to keep a life-sized signed photograph of Mussolini above his desk, was not so ideologically rigid as to turn down under-the-table bribes. With a long history of amiable commerce with Britain and rampant Anglophilia among the Thai nobility, Phibun expressed a wish to remain friends. He had let it be known that he was open to receiving gifts from us, especially the kind that could bolster an army, only he couldn't risk having Japan, or for that matter the French, know about them, lest they get the wrong idea. Moreover, if the pro-Japanese elements in Phibun's cabinet—especially propaganda minister Wichit, the self-proclaimed Goebbels of the Orient—got wind of the deal, then it might well set off another lurch toward fascism and the Japanese embrace.

"So it is critical that we have our hands clean," I explained to Halifax, "and that no one in his cabinet knows about the deal. You will be an entirely unavowed agent, facilitating an independent sale to General Maiboon."

Halifax shook my hand. "Lord's work you're doing, Flint. You can count on me."

Neither arms dealers nor writer-adventurers—let alone writer-adventurers who also deal arms—ooze trustworthiness. But, though it pains me to admit this now, I somehow felt like I could trust Halifax after that first meeting. I still don't understand how and I shall never forgive myself for it, but I think he must have charmed me.

More important, he seemed to have the right contacts. Steptoe, half-lunatic though he was, vouched for him, said the man had been consistently arming the Chinese, both the revolutionaries and the nationalists, for the past year. Anya even gave him her endorsement. While she couldn't speak to his facility as an arms dealer, she confirmed that he had the respect of Bangkok's international business community and smart set.

Just to make sure, the next time I golfed at the Dusit Palace in the company of General Maiboon, I sliced my ball into the same sand trap, giving me occasion to casually mention Halifax's name. Sure enough, the general laughed and waxed laudatory about *Khun Di-kee* and mimicked swinging machetes in the jungle together.

Halifax said he needed 20 percent as a down payment and would collect the remaining bill along with his 10 percent commission fee once the arms were delivered. This sounded reasonable, and no one in London voiced any objections—a point later forgotten in the legend of the Bangkok Cock-up—so I gave Halifax the go-ahead along with ten thousand pounds.

We met three more times that spring, but with the Oriental too conspicuous for repeat encounters, I relocated to shabbier quarters, in a brothel bar in Chinatown. It was in the second floor of a shop house on a *soi* off Yaowarat Road, filled with choleric-looking fruit stalls and bicycle repair. The neighborhood seemed denuded, the Chinese signs having been forcibly removed and painted over with Thai lettering, as per Phibun's new policy of "Thailand for the Thais." It was a bad time to be Chinese, just as it was a bad time to be a Jew. I wondered whether it would ever be a bad time to be British.

Halifax told me the orders were proceeding smoothly. And in fact, a shipment of three hundred rifles was received by General Maiboon in March, as a show of good faith. They were a bit more antique than expected—likely used to shoo the Spaniards from Manila forty years ago—but Halifax assured me the rest of the arms would be of newer vintage. In all, he had been able to secure twenty thousand rifles, with three hundred cartridges each, even more than his initial estimate and at the same price quoted. He had even managed to track down five Maxim guns in a Sumatra warehouse, pilfered from the army after the Great War but in decent working order, which he would be happy to tack on at minimal cost.

I paid the two bored working girls at our table to go dance with each other. "If you don't mind my asking," I said to Halifax, "how do you happen to have such a thorough network of these contacts in the East Indies and Philippines?"

"Now, now," he replied, wagging his finger. "You wouldn't ask the magician to explain his tricks, would you? But let's just say that in the course of my travels, I've learned that officers' clubs and bootleggers' bars are the surest way to get your bearings in a place. Doesn't hurt to have a resourceful sidekick either." But that was all he would deign to say on the matter.

A month went by. When Halifax finally surfaced in April, it was Thai New Year. We had both been soaked by roving street urchins, who rang in the holiday by gleefully dousing everyone within reach of their buckets, especially *farangs* in suits. We hung our dripping clothing beneath the steam-belt fan and talked in our underwear. Halifax had just come from Hong Kong and gave me an earful about a diabolical shipbuilder who was undermining all his wishes.

"Halifax, please focus. What," I said, enunciating, "is the status of the shipments?"

"Everything's fine, chief. Just a bit of a bottleneck. The Japs have all the Chinese ports blocked, as you well know, and it's wreaking havoc on the flow of shipping. Why, Roderick ordered an electric mixer in February and it's been stuck in Manila ever since."

"You'll forgive me if I don't give a toss about Roderick"—whoever that was—"and his mixer." I noticed with irritation that Halifax's persona was shifting again, from affable businessman to hapless, devil-may-care buffoon.

Just then a slender-limbed girl with exquisite breasts came to the table. "Still no want love?"

Remarkably, I didn't. I was completely under Anya's spell by then. I slipped the girl twenty baht and told her to buy herself a drink and a rest.

"They're going to think we're queers before long," said Halifax.

"They can think we're bloody Martians for all I care."

"But what if they mention us to the Japs? Two *farangs* who meet in a brothel and never sample the house goods?"

I didn't bother to explain that the mama-san was one of my informants. Unlike Harry Steptoe, I still believed in the value of secrecy.

"Have a throw if you like, Halifax. But see to it that the goods arrive in Songkhla posthaste. At the rate these Thai generals get reshuffled, Maiboon might not be head of the garrison there for much longer."

Our final meeting occurred a week later. Halifax clapped me on the back and said he had good news and bad news. "Which would you like first, old sport?"

All traces of the polite businessman I'd first met on the veranda of the Oriental were gone. "Tell me both this instant," I demanded, "and for God's sake stop 'old sporting' me."

"Well, chief, we Americans speak sequentially and like to conclude on a positive note, so I guess I'll start with the bad. The shipment's been stolen by pirates."

"Very funny."

"Boy howdy, do I wish I were joking. But those cutthroats in Mindanao don't have much in the way of a sense of humor."

"You're serious? Pirates?"

Halifax nodded.

"How many did they get?"

"All of them, I'm afraid."

"All of them? But I thought the majority were coming from Sumatra."

"I had them routed to the Philippines, where everything would be shipped together on a merchant vessel carrying rebar and aluminum piping."

For a moment I was speechless. Then very slowly I said, "You mean to tell me that twenty thousand rifles and five Maxim guns are now in the hands of a gang of Muslim pirates?"

"Well, nineteen thousand seven hundred to be exact, and I don't know the ins and outs of their faith, per se, but here's where the good news comes in: The American navy chased those sons a bitches down and sank their boat. Blew it out of the water, according to my source in Manila. So the rifles and Maxim guns *were* in the hands of those Moro scoundrels, but now they're safely at the bottom of the ocean."

"And this is your good news?"

Halifax shrugged. "I suppose it's more like a negation of the bad news."

I felt the rage spreading through my body. I went to the bar, ordered a triple gin, drank it down in one go, then calmed myself with lines of a snaking pattern on the silk runner beside me.

The whole thing had been a complete waste of time, and there I was, trousers round my ankles, both thumbs up my arse. Little did I know that was just the beginning.

My temper reined in, I returned to Halifax at the table. "You do understand that I'll need the ten thousand back."

"Sorry, chief, my understanding was that was a nonrefundable deposit."

"Halifax, have you been winding me up? Were there ever any guns?"

"Now, hold on there, Flint. I got those three hundred to you right out of the gate to show I was a fair dealer. But you should know as well as anyone that things sometimes go south in this business—that's all part of the adventure: contingencies and unforeseen acts of God."

"Piracy is not an act of God. Nor is trying to bunko the British government."

"Look, I understand you're sore. But that's no reason to go and accuse me of being a cheat. How many times have we met since you gave me that money? If I was just looking to make a quick buck off you, I'd never have come back to Bangkok."

"Fine. Then return the money and we'll call it bad luck and part on fair terms."

"I'm afraid I can't do that."

"You can't or you won't?"

"It's already been invested in the *Soup Dumpling*."

"What in the bloody hell is the *Soup Dumpling*?"

"My Chinese junk."

I slammed my fist on the table, which woke all the bar girls from their nap.

"If you expect me to go tell London, 'Sorry, lads, the deal's off—damned pirates, you know—and, oh yes, that ten-thousand-pound deposit has actually been put to work building a ridiculous vanity project called the *Soup Dumpling*,' well, then I'm afraid you are sorely mistaken. I know you Yanks think you're invincible and that the rest of the world exists as only a nebulous abstraction, but you will see that running afoul of the British Empire still has grave consequences."

I wondered if Halifax bought my threat. I certainly didn't. What grave consequences, other than my own professional embarrassment, could possibly come of this? The "wrath of the Empire" I had invoked was generally reserved for colonial peoples demanding food or freedom or other unmentionables and whose uprisings were more easily met with mustard gas or machine-gunning. But a con job by an American writer?

"What if I offered you something else?" said Halifax. "Something worth far more than a few thousand lousy pounds?"

I glared at him. "It's *ten* thousand pounds."

Halifax leaned in. "I don't suppose you've heard of a little machine called the Norden bombsight, have you?"

"What of it?"

"Well, I don't suppose your government would be interested in the plans?"

"You're telling me that you have a copy of the design plans for the Norden bombsight and that you want to give it to me?"

Halifax shrugged. "Call it a token of goodwill and a mea culpa for the shooters."

I stared at the man for several seconds, then burst into laughter. "Alright, now I know you're a liar."

"I could have them to you within the week."

"Oh, please, Halifax, this is too much, really. I suppose it wasn't hard convincing that loony Steptoe you were a gunrunner. And I'll admit, I half-believed it too. I thought, well, if Arthur Rimbaud can give up poetry to become an arms dealer in Africa, then why not that silly second-rater Richard Halifax in the Far East? And those rusty muskets you dug up were a good touch. But you've overplayed your hand here if you expect me to believe the plans for a highly guarded innovation in aerial bombardment have somehow wound up in the lap of America's most well-traveled nincompoop."

"You know," he said testily, "I think I see why the Japs here all laugh at England's spy service. Maybe *they'd* be interested in the Norden plans. Or, for that matter, maybe the Germans. They might not have such qualms about accepting valuable military secrets, even from so-called 'second-raters.'"

I could see that I'd offended the man, not by calling him a liar or a fool but by questioning the quality of his prose. Gunrunner or not, he certainly had the thin skin of a writer. But there was simply no way he had access to the Norden plans. The Americans guarded it like it was the holy grail of war secrets, swaddling it in hyperbole. *Will change the face of war forever, whoever possesses it will be assured of victory in the next conflict,* and such tripe.

But what if Halifax did have it? I didn't believe him, but you'll admit that crazier things have happened in the annals of espionage. Is it not common lore that Somerset Maugham was tasked in the last war with going to Russia to assassinate Lenin? When that mission failed, the king of the middlebrow bookshelf was said to have engineered the Czech uprising against the bolsheviks. Patently absurd, yet accepted among our ranks as true.

So what did I have to lose by accepting the man's ridiculous offer? I'd already sunk ten thousand pounds of the Service's funds into something called the *Soup Dumpling*. Why not agree to see these fairy-tale plans? And imagine if Halifax was not bluffing, if it came to light that I had not only refused the plans but because of my skepticism let them fall into someone else's hands?

"Wait," I called to Halifax, who was halfway out the door. "Stay for another drink."

And so a week later, I stepped off a sampan in Hong Kong's Victoria Harbour, where Halifax was to hand over the documents. But when I arrived at the bar of the Peninsula Hotel, there was no sign of Richard Halifax or the Norden plans. It didn't take long for me to learn that his ship, the *Soup Dumpling*, had sailed the day before. Half the city had placed bets on where it would sink.

I was of a good mind to give chase, perhaps catch him in Formosa and flog him within an inch of his life. But then I received an urgent cable at my hotel from Minister Crosby, ordering me to return to Bangkok at once. Serious accusations had been made against me.

It had been brought to the field marshal's attention by his ever-scrupulous minister Wichit that the British vice-consul was attempting to smuggle guns into the kingdom and arm factions within the Thai military, which would be understood as a provocation and insult to Japan. In other words, someone had set me up and leaked the deal to the Tokyo loyalists in Phibun's government. All the details of the purchase—number of guns, location of meetings, and my travel details from Bangkok to Hong Kong—were known. The only thing not disclosed was the name of the arms dealer. So who else could have been the source of the leak but Halifax himself?

Not only had he spun me around on lies while he emptied my wallet; he had also no doubt sold me out for a hefty bonus.

Fortunately, the lack of any hard evidence of the deal—General Maiboon must have dumped those three hundred moldering guns in the jungle as refuse—along with Phibun's and the British legation's vehement denial of authorizing any such transaction saved me from a full-blown diplomatic scandal. However, for being linked with the dirty rumor, which the Thai Japanophiles pressed to their advantage, I was never to show my face in the Kingdom of Thailand again.

The rum bastard had swindled me right and good. Other than a pile of old rifles from the last century, there had never been any guns and certainly no bombsight plans. Just a con artist playing his mark. He'd taken enough off me to fund his idiotic boat trip—had even lured me up to Hong Kong just to rub his victory in my face—and all it had cost was my happiness.

Not bad for a bloody clown.

22

You can perhaps now appreciate, in the aftermath of my professional disgrace and expulsion, to say nothing of the personal blow it entailed, just how much was riding on my meeting with the German consul Wiedemann. Following the debacle in Bangkok, Uncle Paul had made a place for me in his consulate—really the only place I was still welcome—where I could lick my wounds, stamp a few passports, round up some waterfront informants, and drink myself numb. And then all of a sudden I found myself on the verge of a possible intelligence coup that could have changed everything: brokering a defection from Hitler's inner circle. Or, alternatively, I could have been wasting my bloody time. As it turned out, both proved true.

Our first meeting took place last October at the Mark Hopkins. Having learned that Wiedemann regularly brought a girl to the penthouse, I booked a room on the floor below. As per your instructions, the FBI had no knowledge of our meeting. It was just him and me.

There was a gentle knock, and I went to the door. The consul in frame looked like Jean Renoir's image of a continental playboy, which apparently he was. Ascot, dark pinstripe suit, a Dunhill between his fingers, platinum watch dangling from a tan wrist. All he lacked was the monocle. But I could tell from his eyes he was nervous, and he entered the room tentatively, as though having second thoughts.

I tried to put him at ease and presented him with a full bar. "Can I get you something? Whiskey? Gin?"

Oddly, he chose a cordial. "The room is not bugged, is it?"

"You're welcome to have a look," I said, but this seemed to satisfy him. I handed him his Drambuie. We touched glasses and he emptied his in one swallow.

"Would you like another?"

"Mmm, yes, please. I do enjoy the honeyed taste of the Highlands." He had a fruity tenor voice, and his English, while fluent, was clipped and sibilant. In need of more honey. But he appeared to have shed his initial nervousness. As though crossing the threshold was the decisive action and now he was free to be himself.

I poured a second drink for both of us—gin for me; I couldn't stand the national syrup of Scotland, even if my father and Bonnie Prince Charlie were turning in their graves.

"I always have views to the north when I stay here," said Wiedemann, staring out the south-facing window. "The hills of Marin upon waking are spectacular."

I had noticed that everyone in San Francisco was always swooning with pride about how beautiful their city was, as though they'd built the bloody place themselves. Frankly, the headlands of Marin struck me as just a cluster of denuded lumps.

"Of course, those aren't the only spectacular hillocks I look upon here, if you know what I mean." Wiedemann mimed an enormous pair of breasts, just to make sure I understood.

This marked the start of a torrent of speech by the consul concerning his pleasures in the city, most of them amatory. In only a few months' time, he had become well acquainted with the city's trysting hotels, high-end brothels, and French restaurants, which, in San Francisco, do double billing as bordellos. In the course of this bewildering disquisition, he specified that he liked women with very big breasts or very small ones, "but not those humdrum middling tits," that he was tired of commuting from Hillsborough to the consulate downtown every morning and was looking for a place to buy in the city, and that he had recently been accepted as a member of the exclusive Olympic Club, whose golf course overlooked the Pacific and whose club sandwiches were by his reckoning "stupendous."

"Herr Wiedemann," I said, unable to take any more of his logorrhea, "if I may be so bold, there must be a more pressing reason you've asked for this meeting."

The consul seemed suddenly embarrassed again, like he had shrunk back into his shell. Then, after some moments' silence: "My government knows nothing of this meeting, and everything I tell you must be kept absolutely secret."

"Of course."

"You must understand that I am first and foremost a soldier. A German officer in the old tradition. I have been a loyal patriot my entire life, but the time has come when one must disobey orders in order to fulfill one's duty to one's country."

How many times had he said that in front of the mirror? "Please, continue."

"What I mean is, my days with the regime are numbered, and I thought I might offer my services. In order to save Germany from ruin."

"Numbered how?"

"I've fallen from grace. That's why I'm here. As you must know, San Francisco is not exactly a top-tier diplomatic appointment."

"I'm well aware. Though you seem to be rather enjoying yourself here."

"Oh, I am, marvelously so. So much that I don't want to go back to Berlin."

"Why is that?"

"Because I fear a guillotine in Landsberg Prison awaits me."

"And you'd be willing to help us instead?"

"In a word, yes."

"So you wish to defect to England?"

"Good God, no. London depressed me even in peacetime. I should hardly like it more once we start dropping bombs on it. No, I think life out west suits me."

"You do realize we have no power to grant you asylum in America."

"Of course. But maybe you could put in a good word with the Americans if you find my help to your liking."

"Perhaps," I said flatly.

"Or maybe you could find me somewhere nice in Canada," said Wiedemann. "Wonderful nature up there, I hear, and you know we Germans are real slavering Romantics when it comes to an unblemished forest. I also hear Montreal is rather elegant."

"And what exactly did you have in mind in the way of help?"

196

"Information, naturally. I've spent the last five years by Hitler's side. I've known him for twenty-five. I know how he thinks. I know what he's planning."

I was well aware of his proximity to Hitler, which was why I found it difficult to believe a word he said. "I am eager to hear what you know, Consul, but I must inquire first: What exactly was the cause of your fall from grace, as you put it?"

Wiedemann made an anguished face that gradually dissolved into that of the cat who ate the canary. "I fucked Ribbentrop's wife."

Provided Wiedemann was the stallion he billed himself to be, I suppose it seemed plausible. Though that did not necessarily make it true.

"And this . . . indiscretion with Frau Ribbentrop," I said, "was also your road to Damascus? Am I to believe, Consul, that you've had a change of heart about National Socialism?"

Wiedemann smiled and pried another Dunhill from his cigarette case. "The party was good to me for a while, as was Hitler. But power has corroded whatever sanity he had left. Each success makes him more delusional. I've known it for years. I suppose it's less a matter of a change of heart than seizing the opportunity before he drives us off the cliff."

"That's good, Consul. Opportunism suits you better than moral epiphany. Now, if I may ask, you said you could reveal something of Hitler's plans?"

"Certainly. He's going to invade all of Europe."

"That's hardly privileged information. He's already begun."

"Poland is just the prelude. He'll invade the West too. First France, then England. It's been in the General Staff's plan since 1914, though Hitler didn't think it would ever come to that. He never thought England would declare war, not after the way you let us have our way with Austria and Czechoslovakia. Now he's furious and hell-bent on punishing you."

"When?"

"I don't know. Soon. Probably after the winter."

"You mean spring?"

"Possibly. But, mark my words, it will happen. He will even attack America. North and South. Make no mistake, he is deranged, and only force will stop him. England and America must act together."

"Be that as it may, Herr Wiedemann, for your offer to mean something, I need details. Plans. Maps. Lists. Physical evidence. Names of German agents working here in America and abroad. Do you understand?"

"I told you, I've been banished. I'm not on the inside with the Gestapo or the Abwehr. Unlike some of us," he said, pitching his eyebrow at me, "my post here is purely diplomatic."

"I understand you're overseeing a rather large swath of said diplomacy that far exceeds California. You yourself have made several trips to Mexico in the last six months. And no doubt it's for diplomatic reasons that your staff has grown from seven members when you arrived to, what, nearly thirty now? I also hear you have a research group devoting a great deal of attention to the wilderness of Alaska. All purely diplomatic, I assume?"

He laughed. "Like I told you, Herr Faulk, we Germans and our forests . . . Did you know that Hitler has a team of scientists working on bringing back the Ur-creatures of primordial Europe, such as the pachyderm and aurochs?"

"Fascinating, though that's not quite the information that is going to earn you a defection."

"Well, I can't very well tell you all my secrets now, can I? Not until I've been given assurance in the form of documents, like a shiny new American passport."

"Again, you must be confused, Herr Wiedemann. I am the passport-control agent, but for Great Britain, not the United States."

"Like I said, I will settle for Canada."

"And I can tell you that no matter what treasure trove you promise us in exchange for your Canadian forest retreat, it will be met with a dismissive wave of the hand unless you've first established your credibility. Consider this the ante before the deal."

"Very well. I already told you about Hitler. What else can I whet your appetite with?"

"Let's start with your relationship with the Bund. Does your government really disavow them and their dreams of violence? Or is that simply a public pose?"

"I've never been more sincere about anything in my life. They're turds, utter turds—lower than the lowest dregs we filled the ranks of the SA with. They're far worse propaganda for us here in America than anything you lot are doing. Did you know that Fritz Kuhn came to see me in Berlin last year, seeking an audience with Hitler? Well, I had the distinct pleasure of telling him that he had no business wearing the swastika and that, by official orders of the führer, his organization was legally forbidden from using our emblems. Oh, you should've seen the look on that little turd's face! Of course, that hasn't prevented a few of the soft-brains from waddling up to the consulate and pitching me on ludicrous fantasies of collaboration. Rest assured, the only support they get is from the cement when they're thrown out on their ear."

He seemed genuinely disgusted, and his logic struck me as sound. If Germany's goal was to keep America uninterested in the war, then the Bund's terror plots could only cock things up for them. "Speaking of collaboration," I said, "what's behind Hitler's new friendship with Stalin?"

"A marriage of convenience. If you want to know the truth, we've been working with the Soviets long before Ribbentrop made things public."

"Is that so?" I said, trying to hide my surprise.

"Ever since the Reichstag fire. Of course, I don't know the ins and outs, but the Gestapo and the NKVD have been grinding the sausage together from the start. But even if your apparatus didn't know before, it's all out front in the shop window now."

"And what do your friends in Tokyo make of the pact? Seems hard to fight bolshevism together when the bolshies are now your ally."

"Oh, they were tetchy for a week or two, as you might imagine, but the Japanese are apt pupils. They realize what bodes ill for France and England bodes well for them in Asia. And perhaps America too."

"What do you mean?"

"Just go to the Komandorski Islands and you'll see German, Russian, and even Japanese scientists working together in perfect harmony."

"Doing what? Fortifying them?"

"I just process research grants, Herr Faulk. I'm afraid man of science is not one of my hats."

"The FBI thinks one of your hats is overseeing a German–Japanese spy ring across the Pacific, with millions of dollars in funds."

"Now, wouldn't that be nice? But their investigation must entail simply reading the lies the press writes about me."

"And the funds?"

Wiedemann gave another chuckle. "My intention in asking for this meeting, Herr Faulk, was to warn you about Hitler and lay the seeds for a possible arrangement. I have only myself and my experience to offer: I know Hitler's inner circle well; I know we have many commercial and diplomatic interests throughout the world. I can speak to these in far greater detail once the terms have been arranged and my safety guaranteed. But I fear my post here will be short-lived. Ribbentrop still has it out for me and, knowing that vindictive worm, he won't rest until he sees my head sliced off.

"England's chance is running out too, you know. It is not enough to have declared war. You must act. You must strike before Hitler brings the whole world into a war without end. He will destroy Germany. He will destroy Europe, England included. There will be only ruins."

He had clearly rehearsed these lines. But this grandiose moral warning was more fit for a lecture by Theodor Rauch than an intelligence report. And while I thought there was substantial propaganda value to be had from the defection of one of Hitler's inner circle, regardless of the intelligence yield, I knew I had to sell Wiedemann to the Foreign Office with specifics, not just vague promises. "We have plenty of Cassandras of our own saying the very same thing back in England, Consul. But if you want to be of distinct service now, if you want any hope of breaking free from your masters in Berlin, then you'll have to give me something concrete."

"I have been sent here by my government to promote peace, Herr Faulk. That is my only assignment. What else can I tell you other than that whatever looks like pacifism here ultimately serves the interests of Hitler?"

I let out a sigh to show my boredom. "It's getting late, Herr Wiedemann. I should let you get back to Hillsborough—surely your wife will be wondering about you." I stood as if to usher him out, waiting for my words to take effect and for the man to feel the chafe of his wedding band along with all his other overlords.

Wiedemann stared at the paisley carpet, fingering his ascot in thought.

"A curious man arrived last week at the consulate."

"Go on."

"I was instructed to receive him and issue him three thousand dollars and a new suit."

"And where did this curious man come from?"

200

"That's partly what made him so curious. He came from the Pacific Ocean—by a Japanese submarine."

I thought of the story my informant had heard from the crabber. "Where did he land?"

"On Stinson Beach."

"And what is this man doing here?" I asked.

"No idea. Presumably he has come with a shopping list. Information to procure, people to contact, et cetera. There seems to be an air of urgency and secrecy around his arrival. But, as I told you, I'm no spymaster, nor am I trusted with anything of importance. I merely facilitate."

"If you want to help your case, Herr Wiedemann, you'll make an effort to find out. In the meantime, where can I find him?"

"I don't know that either."

"And I suppose you spoke with this mystery man through a chink in the wall or with him covered in a blanket? Or do you actually know what he looks like?"

"That I do know," said Wiedemann eagerly, as though he'd been waiting for just such a question. "He is perhaps the strangest man I've ever seen. He looks very sick but with a veneer of health. His gums are mottled, yet his teeth are pearly white. His face looks scarred and pickled—no, not pickled, sugared. Yes, candied. Like a young boy wearing the skin of an old man. He has a white beard and eyelashes that are all white, though he has no eyebrows. He is also completely bald, save for a long white strand that he pomades into a ludicrous wave. Oh, and his fingers twitch and he walks with a limp."

At least this wreck of a man should be easy to identify, I thought. "And this St. Nicholas of Bedlam who's come ashore by submarine—I don't suppose he has a name?"

Wiedemann shrugged. "I know him only by the code name used to tell me of his arrival: KOKOSNUSS. As perhaps you know," he said with a giggle, "it means coconut."

"Is he Japanese, then, or German?"

"Neither," said Wiedemann, pausing to drain the rest of his cordial. "He's American."

was just beginning to imagine my path back from the dunce's corner when news of the Venlo catastrophe broke. Two SIS agents in Holland, reeled in by a pair of supposedly disaffected German officers looking for British support to overthrow Hitler, let themselves get abducted in the border town of Venlo and driven into the Reich, where they were put through God knows what torture and coughed up every bit of intelligence they could think of. But as if that was not bad enough, one of the men was carrying *on his person* a full list of the Service's operatives in Europe. I remember, upon hearing the news, a sense of relief that my humiliation in Siam had now been overshadowed by a cock-up of far vaster proportions.

On the other hand, the means of my redemption had vanished. Following Venlo, Wiedemann was declared strictly verboten. Anything looking remotely like an anti-Nazi overture—especially the proposed defection of a Nazi official whose top line in his CV consisted of being best mates with the führer—was to be regarded as a Trojan horse and left outside the walls to rot. Under no circumstances was I to treat the German consul as a viable asset, and certainly there would be no offer of defection. Instead, I was told to stick to my weekly meetings with Cliff Hader—joy of joys—helping to ferret out hidden enemies within, and to keep Wiedemann under surveillance from a safe remove.

As I said before, I have always had trouble with orders, prohibitions, and the like. A contrary impulse bubbles up, and I suppress it only with great difficulty. What's more, I couldn't shake free of that strange lead Wiedemann had given me. An American agent come to shore by submarine and bearing the idiotic moniker Kokosnuss.

Was it even possible? Could a Japanese sub reach the California coast and have enough fuel to return?

This was the question I put to my uncle at dinner one evening soon after the Wiedemann parley, while he was scouring the menu at Omar Khayyam's. Sir Paul Ferguson, after all, was not only consul-general but a former seaman and enthusiast of all waterborne craft since the days of Sir Francis Drake.

"Oh, quite easily, my boy," said Uncle Paul. "The Kaidais, the Junsens—they cribbed all the designs from us and the Germans after the war and then outdid them all in terms of range. They can zigzag round the globe on a pleasure cruise in those things. Godemiches of Poseidon, they are. I should wonder they don't pop in at the fair from time to time and say hullo to their cousins in the kimono booth. Now, let's order the tahdig, shall we? They burn a bottom not half badly here. Oh, and the lamb fesenjan—not up to Tehran standards, mind you, but on this far side of the world it'll have to do."

I rarely saw my uncle at the consulate, so our meetings, when not in the dining room of his palatial Queen Anne on Alamo Square, often took the form of meals out. "Good to see the consul dining out with his subalterns from time to time," he explained. "Shows everyone you're aboveboard and not off in the shadows putting your fingers in people's pies, which, one hopes, is precisely what you are doing."

Uncle Paul beckoned the waiter and gave him our order, along with strict instructions on decanting the burgundy so it would be ready to drink with the meal.

"Now, why do you ask?" he said to me once the waiter left. "About the submarines, I mean?"

"Oh, no reason. Just wondering how much Japan's might matches their ambition."

"I thought you might be looking to hop aboard one back to Asia."

"Not a bad idea."

Sir Paul tonged a fresh ice cube into his gin. "I'm afraid you've got quite a dose, my boy, haven't you?"

"What's that?"

"*La fièvre.*"

"You mean malaria?"

"Losh, that's nothing a bit of quinine won't sort out. I mean the bamboo fever. It's written all across your face. Ever since you've been here, you've looked like a donkey that lost its load. And if you can't be happy in this gay little corner of New Albion, well then, something's positively wrong with you."

"I don't believe they're pack animals by choice, Uncle Paul."

"What's that?"

"Donkeys."

"What does this have to do with bloody donkeys?"

"Never mind."

"I've seen men gone full bamboo after only a year's service in the Far East—doesn't matter whether it's China, Japan, French Indochina, to say nothing of our own colonies. Even knew a chap who got thoroughly seduced by the Philippines, if you can imagine. As soon as they return to the West, they're hit with a depression, like their inner flame's been snuffed out. Their eyes have a hollow look, their mouth fixed in a sneer for the land of their birth. The Orient has seeped into them, and now they're stuck in a sort of terrible limbo between two worlds. They're certainly not natives or colonials, yet nor are they quite Englishmen or Scotsmen anymore. That's why we take good care to import a bit of home wherever we go, a kind of amniotic sac for the diplomatic corps. Yet for the few poor devils in the Service who aren't keen on coloring inside the lines, the fever lies in wait.

"I saw it on you last spring when you arrived—thought to myself, that Siam's done quite a number on our Simon, and in short time. I figured you'd get your bearings soon enough, but you clearly have it worse than I thought."

"Yes, well, it's nothing quite so bad, Uncle," I said, lying. His diagnosis was precisely how I felt.

"Of course, there's always been a strain of romance running through your veins, hasn't there?" he said, buffing out a spot on his steak knife with the corner of a napkin. "Suppose all that Italian *belleza* will do that to a wee, impressionable lad, now, won't it? To say nothing of that rotter Corvo your parents let you run around with."

I once had a remarkable tutor in Venice—a half-mad indigent Englishman who slept in a beached gondola at the rowing club and called himself the Baron Corvo. And yet the man was not a pure impostor. He had a true fallen aristocrat's flair for art and history, especially when it came to extemporizing on the more grotesque and sordid of the city's annals: back-alley stabbings and seductions, ducal poisonings and the like. This dandified Socrates, in his threadbare coat and signet ring, used to lead me and a few other boys from the English grammar school on impromptu excursions around the city, instructing us in drawing and discoursing in a captivating, un-schoolmasterly way.

"Yes," my uncle continued, "La Serenissima left its mark on you, my boy. Always with a headful of dreams and adventure. In fact, when you were just a wean, you used to tell me you wanted to be an explorer like Marco Polo or Mungo Park. Do you remember?"

"Mm," I replied. How could I not remember, given that he'd reminded me of it at least a hundred times? My very name—Simon Alessandro Epifanio Ferguson—reflected the heroic Venetian and Scottish stock of my boyhood idols, Polo and Park, though the two strains, rather than blending, seem to have collided and canceled each other out.

"Didn't have the heart to tell you that you'd missed the last boat on the Age of Exploration," said Uncle Paul. "But I'll wager the Service is about as close as you can get to real adventure these days, what?"

"I suppose it's just that I still miss Anya."

My uncle looked at me blankly.

"Anya," I said. "The woman I was . . . well . . . seeing. In Bangkok. The one I told you I had considered marrying." I instantly regretted saying it.

"See, that's the fever talking, my boy. Precisely my point. Liable to make a man do the daftest things. Look, if it's the touch of an Oriental woman you're pining for, this city does not lack. In fact, there's a special bathhouse in Chinatown that I could show you—well, of course, we wouldn't want to go together, that would be rather awkward, but on your own you could . . ."

Like most of the men on my father's side, my uncle Paul was a worldly servant of the empire and a bit of a scoundrel. He had headed legations across the Orient—Mukden, Peking, Cairo, and Tehran—

leaving behind a thick trail of unpaid debts and bastards. It was the bond of nepotism that kept him above the fray, and it was to nepotism above all, thank God, that he remained faithful.

"Tut, tut, my boy. Kiss them, love them—you can even bloody well breed the local women, but marry them? Ha!"

Of course he was right—Anya never would have said yes. She was, I suppose, a courtesan, and I was a damned fool. I had become so intoxicated with her that I acted like a besotted puppy. Probably smothered whatever real affection she might have once had. The few letters I wrote from exile had gone unanswered, and one had even come back to me unopened. Whether it had been refused by a Thai government official or by her, I didn't know, but when I reread the sentimental dreck that had poured out of me, like pus from an infected wound, I thought about heading for the Golden Gate Bridge and having a leap.

Yet I still shivered whenever I recalled the time she held me between her oiled feet while taking me into her mouth, a pleasure so great I had in fact momentarily lost consciousness. Sex was only one of her many passions, which included cats, chess, orchids, ballet, ghost stories, Russian and French literature, Thai cookery, court dance, the *Ramakien* epic, Hogarth prints, Chinese tea, calligraphy, and, to my amazement, fencing. It was electrifying to know that at any moment we were together, locked in an amorous embrace, she could have run her épée right through me. Perhaps she should have done.

I promised myself that I would never mention anything about Siam in front of my uncle again. It just made me hate him. And I didn't want to hate my uncle Paul. I had been enormously fond of him as a boy. Coming around at Christmas with strange and wonderful gifts from across the world, then plunking himself down at the dining table; fueled by a bottomless glass of whiskey, he would burble for days in an unending stream of stories, jokes, and queer turns of phrase, spilling his drink and staining my mother's upholstered chairs. I didn't understand half of what he said, though as I grew older I realized most of it was nonsense, made-up colloquialisms that no one else said, as though he had been granted a special license by the OED to enlarge the lexicon.

It is inevitably sad to grow up and see one's relatives with adult eyes. Uncle Paul, the magical and beloved saint of my childhood, had become a garrulous, bigoted old drunk. I suppose he was always that, but I had once enjoyed the naïve privilege of finding it amusing. And after my parents died, my uncle had done his best to keep me afloat. I owed him so much. Yet still I found myself struggling to get through a dinner with him.

But he had been right about at least one thing—the tahdig was indeed not half-badly burnt.

After seeing my uncle into a cab, I walked through the Latin Quarter to the half-rotted wharves along the North Beach waterfront. At a tilted structure marked only by a sign that read *Uscita*—Exit—I ascended the rickety steps and ducked through the warped doorframe of the wine dump.

Inside, it reeked of turpentine and stale tobacco. The kerosene lamps, hung along ropes suspended from the rafters, rocked with the tide eating away at the foundation, such that I felt vaguely seasick in the dim swaying light. A few driftwood chairs and tables lay scattered on the sloped floor, as did a few customers. The rest of the patrons sat at the horseshoe bar, assembled from hogsheads and the weathered staves of an old ship, huddled over buckets of what was sold as wine. A far cry, needless to say, from Uncle Paul's burgundy.

The clientele were the kind one sees in waterfront dives the world over—stevedores, fishermen, pimps, and whores, the pathologically curious and pathologically drunk. All seemed indifferently welcome at the Exit. The man I had come to see certainly belonged to the final category. He was at the end of the horseshoe, elbow hooked round a pail of poison, the rest of him in a heap against the wall. Above him hung a stained print of Mantegna's Christ, as oddly foreshortened as the drunk below. The latter's mouth was agape, and his watery eyes in profile reflected the shifty orange glow of the lamplight. He looked to be either in the throes of epiphany or stone dead.

"Mr. O'Malley," I said, taking the stool beside him. "Are you still with us?"

Slowly he turned toward me, revealing the inked canvas of his face. "It appears I have not yet been called. The dust banquet of the under-world shall have to wait."

Like the margins of a daydreaming schoolboy's exercise book, every inch of the man's flesh was covered in a quilt-work of cartoons. The first time I saw this spectacle, it took my breath away. Now I was beginning to discern the crude artistry within the interlocking figures. Buxom mermaids, cigar-smoking cats, copulating dogs, dancing skeletons, fighting sailors, Indian war chiefs, Hottentot queens, and mustachioed strongmen—and that was only what could be seen on his face, neck, and forearms. They were the portfolio and calling card of the tattooist Avey Rabinowitz O'Malley, known the waterfront over as O'Malley the Tattooed Jew. "And what brings you here on this fair, effulgent evening, Mr. Fox?" he said, calling me by the alias that I used for informants. "Have you come to quaff the dago red?"

"Just a beer," I said to both O'Malley and the bartender, who had approached. "I prefer not to end up like them tonight." I nodded to the customers splayed out catatonic on the floor.

"Oh, don't be put off. They're having a ball. I myself have had many a proper night's sleep on those boards. I believe the rats have softened up the wood over the years."

The bartender plunked down a beer.

O'Malley rose from his corner. "Shall we adjourn to my office, then?"

"After you."

"Another puddle, if you please, Enzo. Have it delivered to my office."

The bartender retrieved the oversized tin cup—it really was a pail—and filled it from a spigot while O'Malley heaved himself from his stool and stumbled over to one of the tattered tables, where his ink and needles lay.

O'Malley was something of a local celebrity among the effluvia of the San Francisco waterfront. As the story by his own telling went, he stepped ashore in 1900 as a good boy from the small middle-class enclave of Belfast Jews, with thirty dollars and a letter of introduction to the architectural firm of Bernard Maybeck. But, finding himself in a demon city swarming with sailors back from war in Cuba and on their way to the Philippines for more, drunk with the recent victory over Spain and riddled with all the vices of the Barbary Coast, he fell headlong into a wine pail and a new vocation from which he never escaped. By the time the earthquake hit, Avey Rabinowitz O'Malley, the doe-eyed apprentice draftsman and apple of his mother's eye, had reinvented himself across the water as O'Malley the Tattooed Jew: artist of the San Francisco demimonde, wine-dump raconteur, and purveyor of all gossip that came in with the tide and scuttled among the wharfs.

"Have you given another thought to an O'Malley original, Mr. Fox? Perhaps a tiger on your chest? Or a John Bull beefeater across your back? My own sympathies lie with the ransomed Six Counties, of course, but there's no image or symbol I disdain for a paying customer."

"Perhaps another time," I said, as the barman delivered a brimming pail to the table with a message.

"You're eight deep tonight, O'Malley. You said to cut you off at ten."

"*Grazie mille*, Enzo. And so you shall—I promise I won't fight you this time."

"Yeah, right," he said, and shuffled off.

"I want to ask you about that crabber you told me about last month," I said. "The one who saw a submarine breach off Stinson Beach and a man swim ashore."

"Ah yes, that would be Liam. But I don't recall you being interested in Liam's tale last we spoke."

"Where can I find this Liam?"

"Behind the partition veiling our world from the eternal mysteries. That's where good Liam has taken up residence."

"What do you mean? He's dead?"

"Extremely so, I'm sorry to say. But we sent him off in fine style. Have you ever attended a crabber's wake, Mr. Fox?"

"How did he die?"

"As to how is anybody's guess. Rogue wave, riptide, a slippery bit of rock. But they found him washed up by the surf a couple weeks ago, head stove in like a cask of brandy on New Year's Day."

"So his death was ruled an accident?"

"Ah, I smell what you're stepping in, Mr. Fox. A conspiratorial turn of mind is what you have. And I'll confess that at moments I share it myself. Man sees a queer, mysterious submersible deposit an equally queer, mysterious man on our shores and, sure enough, the following week he ends up dead? I grant you, sir, that's the very dreadful stuff of novels, is it not? But it's also sadly the case that crabbers wash up with broken heads every season."

I pushed a ten-dollar bill across the table. "Tell me everything he said about the man who came ashore—and, please, Mr. O'Malley, spare none of the pertinent details, but let's do without the embellishments."

"Suit yourself," said O'Malley, palming the bill. "But Liam's tale needs no inflation. Though, knowing him, there's a fair chance he pumped in some extra air on the first telling. He said your man popped out of a submarine visible from shore. Lit by the moonlight, he was. Liam caught sight of his silhouette, then used his binoculars to get a closer look, till your man dove into the water and vanished. When he came ashore, the man shook himself off by the clump of rocks on the south side of the beach, peeled off his vulcanized rubber suit, and from his rucksack pulled, of all things, a Japanese short sword."

"How did Liam know it was a Japanese submarine?"

"He said he could make out the queer characters stenciled onto the top of the vessel. Kanji, I suppose. Mind you, it was one of those bright yellow-mooned nights."

"And did he say what this man looked like?"

"According to Liam, he was as bald as a melon, save for a long silvery strand swirled upon his head like a Danish sweet roll. And with teeth that glowed in the dark too. When this peculiar creature saw Liam spying on him, he chased after him, albeit with a fierce limp. That's how Liam was able to make his escape. And about this impairment he must've surely been telling the truth, since only a true gimper could be outrun by a lard-arse like Liam."

It was a ludicrous story, and yet in the salient details it confirmed the Nazi consul's own. A strange-looking agent had indeed come ashore. If his mission was as urgent and mysterious as Wiedemann claimed it was, I couldn't help thinking that if I caught this man in my net, it might just overcome London's reluctance about the consul's intentions and earn each of us our way out.

It is a truism the world over that men drop their secrets where they drop their pants. And while I tasked O'Malley with trawling for news of this stranger from his many contacts in the humbler brothels of the city, it was through the haughtier establishments where the moneyed classes spent their seed that I was keeping tabs on Wiedemann.

One of the consul's regular girls, a petite Levantine beauty with a gap-toothed smile named Marie, came from a service run out of a French restaurant called Enchantée, on the corner of Polk and Bush, a fitting intersection for such a business. Marie was more than happy to write down Wiedemann's postcoital boastings and pass them along to me every week for an extra twenty dollars. She seemed to relish being paid to use her brain. If anything, her reports were too thorough, with a full transcript of the consul's exclamations and pet names. I had told her these inclusions were not necessary, but she said it helped her memory to be as comprehensive as possible.

I arrived at the Palace of Fine Arts for one of our encounters, wondering both how it was possible to be so hungover simply from inhaling the fumes of O'Malley's wine pail and why this city preferred follies to real buildings. On the bench opposite the lily pond, I fished out Marie's report from the hollow slat, unfolded my newspaper, and read of her latest rendezvous with Wiedemann, while she, only five feet away, fed the ducks. I couldn't help but observe that her taut little bottom, straining against her gingham dress, was aimed straight over the top of my *Examiner*. Was it really possible, I thought, that I would one day reach an age or attain a state of equanimity in which I would perceive such a bottom with disinterest, as merely one beautiful bottom in a sea of beautiful bottoms, none of which were of any pressing concern? With Anya, I had genuinely believed, for the space of a few months, that her bottom alone sufficed. But now, deprived of it or even the dim hope of it, I was back to being buffeted by the infernal whirlwind. A relentlessness that depressed me as much as it kept me in its thrall.

I noticed in Marie's report that on her last visit with Wiedemann, he recalled his exploits on a Rhineland pleasure cruise in the company of Göring and Hess, where they had enjoyed *an orgy of Neronian magnitude*. He then complained of the drab offerings for nautical adventure here on the bay and said that he had been looking forward to *losing his virginity* on a genuine Chinese junk.

"What's all this about a Chinese junk?" I asked Marie, a sudden sense of irritation in my voice.

"It was supposed to be a pleasure cruise when Richard Halifax arrived last summer on his ship."

Even when spoken in her adorable accent, the name repulsed me. Halifax and his bloody *Soup Dumpling*. It seemed there was no escaping the man's legacy here.

"Wiedemann had reserved a spot," explained Marie, "but then it was canceled when Halifax drowned."

Hearing about his drowning calmed me. "So what is this *gauche riverboat* Wiedemann is complaining about?"

"The riverboat casino at Treasure Island. One of Sally Bent's operations."

"Who is Sally Bent?"

"The woman who owns Sally Bent's Nude Ranch."

"*Nude ranch*? I don't believe I've ever heard those two words put together."

"You mean you have not been to the fair?" said Marie, shocked.

I had not, though I admit the idea of a nude ranch did pique my interest.

Marie told me that Sally Bent was a former dancer and working girl, much like herself, just older, who ran a burlesque theater in the Tenderloin called the Music Box, with a bordello upstairs. Since the Treasure Island fair opened, she'd also run Sally Bent's Nude Ranch, the most popular attraction on the Gayway.

"Her girls say she runs a good operation," said Marie. "She splits the take even, doesn't work anyone to the bone."

"You sure know a lot about this woman and her business," I said.

"I used to dance for her," she said wistfully. "Only for a few months."

"What happened?"

"My heel broke under me and I snapped my ankle in two. Goodbye, dancing."

"Bad luck."

"Bad luck my eye. One of the other understudies, she cut my heel with a saw."

The cloak-and-dagger world was everywhere, I thought.

Marie said she wished she could go back to work for Sally, to join the non-dancing side of the business. She was sick of having to share 70 percent of her wages with Claude, the maître-d'-cum-pimp at Bistro Enchantée. "He's not even French," she said. "He's from Guernsey, but acts like he's Robespierre." Marie, I came to learn, was from a Maronite family in Lebanon, orphaned by typhus during the war, who had, through years of famine and displacement, bounced between French-sponsored schools and asylums in Beirut and Port Said, where, as the young and soon-to-be-widowed bride of a Greek peddler from Smyrna, she eventually found her way to America.

"Then why don't you leave Claude and work somewhere else?" I asked.

"He says if we try to leave, he will cut our noses off."

"I'm sorry to hear that." I pictured taking a saw to the miserable pimp's nose for her. Then I noticed the last line in her report. "Marie, what's this mean? *Meet with Faulk: Nov. 13—10 p.m.—Sutro Heights Cannon.*"

"He says he wants to meet with you then—by the cannon at the Sutro Heights observation circle. You know, the one above the Cliff House?"

"Wait," I said, confused. "What do you mean he says he wants to meet? *Wiedemann* told you he wants to meet with *me*?"

Marie crouched and fed the ducks the last of her breadcrumbs. "It is funny, no? I told him your name was Sebastian Fox, not Simon Faulk, but he said it was all the same."

"Marie, did you tell him that you were working for me?"

"No, silly, of course not. He just said it blasé, like he knows it all along."

I crumpled her report and threw it in the pond, where a pair of geese descended upon it. "Well, I'm afraid that's the end of this assignment, my dear. Your cover's blown. But if you want my advice: Tell that rat Claude to bugger off and find yourself a new job. You deserve better."

I took out an extra twenty and left it for her in the hollow slat.

Wiedemann was waiting for me on the ruins of the Sutro estate by the parapet above the Cliff House. The park was dark and abandoned, but the consul's profile was caught in the moonlight.

"Don't worry, Herr Faulk," he said, patting the cannon like a pet. "It's ornamental."

"This whole bloody city is ornamental."

"But soon real cannons will be in order. I promise you that."

"Is that just speculation, Consul, or do you have something you want to share with me?"

"After the silence following our last rendezvous, I was afraid my overtures were not being taken seriously."

"Forgive us for not finding your lot so trustworthy these days."

"I was afraid that nastiness in Holland had made your people clam up. And yet, Herr Faulk, here you are."

Yes, there I was, in spite of express orders to keep away from Wiedemann. No doubt you'll call it a lapse of judgment. And I'll grant you curiosity played a role, but really, I was just doing my bloody job. Even if there was no prospect of defection, he didn't know that yet. He could still be useful to me. And I very much doubted I was going to be kidnapped and smuggled across the border to . . . where? Marin? Berkeley?

"How did you know Marie was one of mine?"

"Lucky hunch. That, and I searched her purse. Quite a little stenographer, that one."

"Why am I here, Wiedemann?"

"I like watching the ocean at night, don't you?"

I did not dignify this with a response, as it felt frightfully like the preamble to a soliloquy.

"My FBI tail thinks I'm down there at the Cliff House, still at the bar. That's him in the gray Lincoln out front. Doesn't realize there's a back exit and staircase to the beach. We make that same mistake ourselves, do we not? Even talking to each other. We see the one side facing us and think that's the man, never bothering to find out what's in back, as it were. But surely, given your occupation, Herr Faulk, you must think differently. You expect that as a general rule the appearance is the lie. So with a man like me, you see an officer from Hitler's inner circle, no diplomatic experience, suddenly banished to a minor consulate on the Pacific, and you think he's obviously here on anything other than a straight diplomatic mission. So when I come to you offering my assistance, offering to share privileged information about the most dangerous man in the world, naturally you are suspicious.

"But what if the man you think I really am is also a mere façade? What if the loyal Nazi, the playboy, is all a front for something else? Of course, that's not to say I don't truly love little girls like Marie or enjoy a good cigar after my golf game. But what if I told you I've also been helping Jews emigrate for the last three years? And that I intentionally fell afoul of Hitler's circle through peccadilloes that were too severe to overlook yet not grave enough to be considered a threat? The only one who felt threatened by me was Ribbentrop, who, thanks to rumors I planted—not to mention what I planted in his wife—fears I have secret ambitions to replace him as foreign minister. Hence my banishment to this far-flung post nowhere near the orbit of power, where I can satisfy my libido ad nauseam. You see, Herr Faulk, as others back in Berlin see me, I am the man who can't help myself, a good honest soldier who simply has too big an appetite for nice things and nice girls. That is the part I have played because it was the part that gave me a way out."

"So I'm to believe your appointment here was by your own design?" I asked. "You manipulated Ribbentrop, slept with his wife, and lost favor with Hitler just so you could be in a better position to do what exactly? Come here to tell me that the whole time you've been carrying the führer's robes you've really been a covert philanthropist? I don't need to come to empty parks at night to hear that, Consul. If you want to play trench coats in the mist, if you want to build your case for defection, then you better tell me something worthy of the theatrics."

"I am only trying to establish a relationship, Herr Faulk. I need you to know why I am helping you."

"And I need proof that you're helping me." The consul was irritating me as much as the cold stone bench pressing on my piles. I pulled my collar up against an arctic gust blowing in from the sea and stood to go.

"That agent I told you about—the one called Kokosnuss?" said Wiedemann, unable to suppress a grin. "The American who came to shore?"

"Yes? What of him?"

"He'll be boarding a ship to Japan at the end of the week."

"Which one?"

"The *Asama Maru*."

"And what is he taking back with him?"

"I still know nothing of this man other than what I already told you. I was instructed to arrange his travel visas and to book his passage under the name Richard Wagner."

"Richard Wagner? How many ridiculous names does this man have?"

"It's actually quite a common name."

"And he already has a passport under that name?"

Wiedemann shrugged. "I simply had my underlings forward the prepared documents on to the Sir Francis Drake hotel."

"You told me last time you didn't know where he was staying."

"I didn't. I just follow the instructions that come over the wire."

"When does the ship sail?"

"Friday night. The eight o'clock for Yokohama via Honolulu."

Wiedemann stroked his chin in a theatrical pose. I feared another monologue was coming. "Something else on your mind, Consul?"

"Consider the following a gift to you and a measure of my credibility. Not only will Richard Wagner, aka Agent Kokosnuss, be on board the *Asama Maru*, but so will twenty-two officers of the German navy."

I shot him a look of surprise. "You mean from the *Columbus*?" I said.

This was, you'll recall, shortly after the German ocean liner *Columbus* had been intercepted by our warship off the coast of Virginia last year, trying to run through our blockade and make it back home to Germany. But rather than surrender the ship to us, the Germans scuttled it and the American navy, humanitarians that they are, rescued all five hundred of its crew and passengers.

"I thought they were being held in Ellis Island," I said.

"Your apparatus is slow. A few days ago, they were moved across the country here to Angel Island. The Americans have agreed to let our naval personnel travel to Japan on the *Asama Maru*, after which they will proceed to Germany via the Trans-Siberian rail from Manchukuo."

A boatload of enemy combatants were being secretly smuggled out of America, and—though hardly a surprise—the FBI had not bothered to give us so much as a hint.

"I imagine your government would be happy to intercept those officers once they are on the open sea and before they reach Japan," said Wiedemann.

They would be thrilled—that is, if it was real. But what if it was a hoax? A possible decoy stratagem to distract a British gunship? Or to antagonize Anglo–Japanese relations? There could be any number of reasons Wiedemann was lying to me.

On the other hand, if the intelligence was genuine, then it would be a feather in my cap. The German officers couldn't be detained on American soil, but they could certainly be stopped somewhere in the Pacific. Of course, I couldn't yet disclose that the tip had come from Wiedemann. If I did, London would likely ignore it as a trap and punish me for insubordination, with a transfer to Greenland. But if I attributed it to a different source, which was easy enough, then surely it would be verified by other channels. Some twenty Nazi sailors, plus whoever this mystery agent Kokosnuss was, caught sneaking out of the States with cooperation from the Americans. The catch would do nothing to bolster Wiedemann's case for defection—it was clear I'd have to let that matter rest for the moment—but it would make me look like the competent intelligence officer no one quite believed I was.

Only it required me to do the one thing I promised myself I would not do and that I had been expressly forbidden from doing: trust Fritz Wiedemann.

"If you're playing me, Consul," I said, rising again from my bench, "as God is my witness, I will find a real cannon in this city and strap you to the mouth of it."

Wiedemann held up his hand in oath and smiled. "You'll be throwing me a party soon, Herr Faulk. A going-away party to Canada, we hope."

"In the meantime," I said, "no more of these nocturnal park visits. We're not in some cheap thriller."

24

A week later the *Asama Maru* was intercepted off the coast of Japan. And shortly thereafter, the Nazi consul and I began attending the cinema together.

Our first date was at the Castro Theater, seeing Errol Flynn play an unconvincing cowboy in *Dodge City*. Wiedemann boasted about having attended several parties in Hollywood in the company of Flynn. "First-rate fellow. Has his own personal pimp, did you know? Last time I saw him, Consul Gyssling and I were at the Brazilian ambassador's birthday bash and out comes a parade of girls, not a day over nineteen and naked but for high heels, bearing silver trays of every drug under the sun. Marched right out to Flynn by the swimming pool, and, would you believe, by morning he'd skewered every last one of them. Gyssling says Flynn hosts naked dinner parties at his home around a special dining table equipped with spring-loaded dildos in the seats."

I reminded myself to make a note of this: Errol Flynn attends parties with Nazi officials. I would leave out the spring-loaded dildos.

"So," said Wiedemann, rattling some Milk Duds in his hand, "have I earned my seat at the table?"

He was evidently pleased with himself. The intelligence had been good, for the most part. The British warship *Liverpool* had intercepted the *Asama Maru* just before it made port in Yokohama, whereupon officers boarded the ship and detained all German males of military age, including the naval personnel Wiedemann mentioned. Meanwhile, Japan was crying foul over their territorial sovereignty being violated within miles of their own coast. But none of that was my concern. What mattered was that Wiedemann had told me the truth and, thanks to me, London received actionable intelligence. It is important you understand that.

Of course, according to the reports I submitted, the intelligence came from Wiedemann's golf caddy at the Olympic Club, overheard during a fictional eighteen holes between the German consul and his Japanese counterpart and corroborated with a fictional immigration clerk at Angel Island. As a result, there were now two additional agents on SIS's payroll, neither of whom actually existed. I realized I was treading on dangerous ground here—leading Wiedemann on with false hopes of defection, and lying to my superiors. Which meant that if I ever in the future decided to prove to London that Wiedemann was trustworthy by revealing him as the source for the *Asama Maru*, I would have to admit that I had fabricated the other sources and was therefore not to be trusted. A bit of a conundrum. But if the Nazi consul continued to provide valuable information that the Service, knowing it had come from him, would ipso facto have ignored, then wasn't my decision for the better? A noble lie made in the name of the higher good?

"Your information proved useful," I told Wiedemann in the cinema, "but defection is not an overnight deal. These things take time."

The consul signaled his annoyance with a groan.

"Besides," I said, "your Agent Kokosnuss? The great Richard Wagner? There was no sign of him on the *Asama Maru*."

"What?" He seemed genuinely surprised to hear this, as an object that resembled a wet sheep pellet came tumbling out of his mouth. "What do you mean?"

"I mean no one by the name Richard Wagner or fitting your description of the mystery agent was found aboard the ship to Yokohama." Neither by O'Malley and his contacts among the stevedores and ship stewards before she set sail, nor by the British intelligence officers of the *Liverpool*. "The man is still hardly more than a figment," I said, "a collection of grotesque physical characteristics and silly aliases."

"I just assumed he had been detained by your people on the *Liverpool* along with the others."

"Why would you assume that?"

"Because," said Wiedemann, "I received a cable from our people in Tokyo this morning saying he never arrived. You're sure he wasn't taken with the others?"

"Quite."

"That means he's still here. *At large*, as they say in the crime films. Maybe he's been waylaid. Or perhaps," he said with an air of amusement, "even gone rogue."

The next day, I called at the Sir Francis Drake to see if I could find a trace of Wiedemann's rogue agent. He had captured my attention in the form of annoyance—his ridiculous names, his brazen manner of arrival, the question of his doings here, and now his sudden veering from the script. Wiedemann had coated this hollow man with just enough intrigue and urgency that I had to bite down to find out what was inside.

A beefeater doorman, who looked as though he'd been peeled right off the gin bottle, gave me a cheery "Top of the morning, sir," in some travesty of a Cockney accent. Then he ushered me into a recent American take on the Elizabethan golden age. The opulence read more gaudy than glamorous, with pseudo-Renaissance murals depicting Drake, the Sea Dog, in *Terra Nova*, marking his territory. Further evidence that historical eras functioned in the States like paint samples or costume closets—choose your favorite, mix and match, discard when you grow bored. The whole country was a pasteboard fantasy masquerading as culture.

Mercifully, the receptionist was powdered and clad for her own century. I flashed my bogus insurance-assessor card at her and asked about a guest named Richard Wagner, pronouncing it as Wiedemann had, like the composer.

She consulted her log. "I'm sorry, sir, I'm not seeing anyone under *V*. Could you spell it?"

"How about Richard Wagner?" I said, now pronouncing it like an American.

"Oh yes," she said right away. "But I'm afraid Mr. Wagner checked out three days ago."

Of course he did. "How long was he staying here?"

"Since the middle of October."

The receptionist confirmed the strange physical description of the man. Tall and thin, pronounced limp, mottled face and white beard, though not exactly old-looking. He had registered under a German passport.

"Did he sound like a foreigner?"

"No sir. Mr. Wagner had a strained, scratchy voice, but he sounded American. If I had to guess, I'd say he was from the Midwest—like me. Though we hardly spoke. Barely left his room. Roscoe, the elevator hop, said he muttered a lot to himself. Maybe ask him."

The lift attendant recalled the man warily, like he was a bad dream he preferred to forget.

"Your colleague said he talked to himself," I said.

"Not too much I could make out, sir. Just a lot a nonsense."

"What kind of nonsense?"

"Something about his *giri*."

"*Giri?* What's that?"

"You tell me. Like I said, strange cat. Think he mighta had a screw loose. Maids said they found blood on his sheets."

The German consul and I met one more time that fall, the day the lines finally began to converge.

I came twenty minutes late and found the *Reichskonsul* in the back row of the Warfield, watching *Confessions of a Nazi Spy* and eating popcorn out of his fist.

"Bit on the nose, this film, isn't it?" I said.

"I missed this one when it came out last spring—couldn't see it in Berlin naturally. We're lucky they tacked it on today as a double feature to *Espionage Agent*. It's quite accurate. You should pay attention, Herr Faulk—might help you do your job. Popcorn?" He offered me the tub, but I declined. "I was beginning to think you'd changed your mind about our meeting," he said.

"I had a pest trailing behind me. Took a little time to lose him."

"One of those grim Bureau boys?"

"It appears so." I was not surprised to have the FBI surveilling me—after all, despite our spirit of cooperation, I was still a foreign agent—but it rankled me nonetheless. Doing their bloody job for them, and this was how they showed appreciation.

"Well, then, welcome to the club," said Wiedemann. "I've grown to enjoy my little cat-and-mouse routines with them. Perhaps you will too."

This rankled me even more—to be perceived as being in the same club as Fritz Wiedemann, the Hitler-appointed Casanova of California. And yet here I was again, putting myself at considerable risk to hear the German consul's sweet nothings.

"Of course, you have it easy compared to me," continued Wiedemann. "On top of the FBI, I'm still hounded by the press and those grubby little protesters. They virtually ruined my talk to the International Relations Council at USF the other night. Why, even——"

Wiedemann cut himself short and shifted his attention to the screen, where a man was shouting *I don't want to go back to Germany! I don't want to go back to Germany!*

"Hear, hear," said Wiedemann, suddenly sobered. "That will be me soon enough, Herr Faulk. See those goons there? They're Gestapo agents, hauling any less-than-fanatical German nationals back to the Reich. If only that poor little man had a stalwart officer of the British intelligence service working on his behalf. You know, you missed a scene where your colleagues arrested a frail old Scottish woman for writing letters—very daring. Though not quite as sharp as this sophisticated toad of an FBI man," he said, pointing at a pipe-smoking Edward G. Robinson.

I could tell after five seconds of dialogue that the film was a fantasy, since Robinson's character sounded several orders of magnitude more competent than his real-life counterpart, Cliff Hader.

"Are we here to study for our roles, Consul, or do you have something to tell me?"

"Something has come across my desk," said Wiedemann, "that I think you will find interesting. What do you know about Theodor Rauch?"

"The writer? Oh, not much. Decline of the Old World, sanatorium of Europe, that sort of thing. Of course, I've heard his recent broadcasts raising the war cry against your führer. Why do you ask?"

"Did you know he seduced his own son?"

"I don't believe he mentioned that over the radio." Though I remembered reading in the paper some weeks earlier that Rauch's son had overdosed on drugs in a San Francisco hotel and was currently in a coma.

"Well, soon you will know, along with everyone else. His diary is to be published next week in *Free Masses*, and it goes into great and sordid detail on the matter. He won't be making too many speeches after that."

I had read Rauch's *Twilight in Messina* as a young man, mandatory reading for all of us playacting at bohemianism in the twenties, which included most of the student body of St. John's College, until they threw off the cloak of aestheticism and swapped it out for communism. The one scene that had stayed in my memory was where the earthquake strikes at the precise moment the old lovestruck pervert touches the boy's shoulder. Heady stuff. "Is the diary genuine?" I asked.

Wiedemann shrugged. "Who knows? Who cares? I'm sure it looks real enough."

"This was your people's doing?"

"A bit of teamwork, as it turns out. One of the few things we and the Soviets can agree on is that Theodor Rauch's middling humanism is a voice neither of us can abide."

"You're telling me this so that I can do what exactly? Stop the diary from going to press?"

"That's up to you, Herr Faulk. Theodor Rauch is the most powerful voice against Hitler here in America. I thought perhaps you and your people might wish to protect the propaganda value of that voice."

He wasn't wrong.

"Personally," said Wiedemann, "I've always found Rauch and his whole family insufferable—in fact, I once helped Heydrich draw up clean copies of the kill lists."

"Was this before or after you were helping Jews emigrate?"

He snickered, as though amused at his own gross contradiction. "My only point is that I'm trying to be of service here. What you do with my information matters little to me, other than that it helps open my parachute."

"Mmm, yes, of course."

"Regarding that, I believe some kind of assurance is finally in order."

"In due time, Herr Wiedemann. As I've told you, these things can't be rushed."

I had every intention to go on milking him like a cow, though I sensed the cow was growing resentful. "Any word on your vanishing act, the so-called Richard Wagner?"

"Not so much as a peep. Perhaps he got cold feet and retreated into the vast American wilderness. You know, it's funny—it was Agent Kokosnuss who was supposed to bring us the Rauch diary to finish what the Soviets couldn't see through themselves. But now he's disappeared, and apparently one of their own agents has managed to retrieve it. It's all an intriguing dance, isn't it?"

Wiedemann seemed to delight in taunting me with this mystery agent.

"You told me at our first meeting that you had no idea what Kokosnuss was here for. I take it that was a lie? Or have you just enjoyed stringing me along so that I have to keep repeating his ridiculous name?"

"Well, I can't divulge all my secrets at once to you, can I? Besides, you said you were paving the way for my defection. And yet here we are, still watching movies together."

"Yes. And you told me you'd be recalled to Berlin at any moment, and yet here you are, still at the movies. Now, supposing I do want to prevent the publication of the Rauch diary, where would I find it?"

"I'd try the West Coast offices of *Free Masses*. If you act fast, the darkroom—otherwise, you'll find it on the cover of their next issue."

"And what about Theodor Rauch?" I asked. "With no diary to ruin him, will he now be free to live and work in peace?"

"Well, it goes without saying that we'll have to kill him."

I couldn't tell if Wiedemann was serious. "Is this another tip you're giving me?"

"It's a joke, Herr Faulk. Aren't you English supposed to have a robust sense of humor? Think about it: If Theodor Rauch was murdered, he'd die a martyr. The backlash would be terrible for us. Totally self-defeating. That's why they've invested so much in this diary. Kill the man with his own words, so to speak. Only those soft-brains in the Bund want to go blowing things up and mowing people down in the streets. Which would of course turn America against Hitler much faster than any of your people can hope to do it.

"Now," said Wiedemann, raking up the remaining kernels from his bucket, "I've decided that British Columbia is a better place for me than Quebec. You know, still America in a sense, still the West, but the part your people hung on to. I must say I was charmed by Victoria when we visited last summer. Lovely botanical garden and a marvelous tea service. Best scones and clotted cream I ever tasted."

"I'll put a note in your file," I said. "Must have flowers and decent baked goods."

"Good. Because it's the last tip I'm giving you until I'm given something concrete, like travel documents and an escape hatch. I'm starting to feel like I'm being led on, and I must say I don't care for it. Oh, look," he said, glancing up at the screen. "They've caught the spy and he's revealed his entire network. Don't you just love a happy ending?"

Wiedemann slunk out the side exit, leaving me with the patriotic denouement of a trial and a halo of crumbs in the seat beside me.

My thoughts returned to Theodor Rauch and what Wiedemann had said. Destroying Theodor Rauch's reputation would indeed silence his voice, but killing the man would have the opposite effect. Everyone would know the Nazis were behind it, and the ensuing reaction would likely do more to turn American sentiment against Hitler and for going to war than any dozen of Rauch's radio broadcasts on Goethe would ever do. By that rationale, I thought with a laugh, if anyone should be planning to assassinate Theodor Rauch, it should be us.

When I got home, Marie was standing outside my building, struggling to light a cigarette. She hadn't yet noticed me, and I hung back to make sure that she was not by coincidence waiting for someone inside the jazz club. But no one came out, and I noticed that even after she had the cigarette lit, she still kept her hand up to her face, awkwardly cupping her nose and mouth.

I approached without breaking stride, and as she turned I saw that she was holding a handkerchief dabbed in blood. "Go through the club all the way out back to the stairwell," I instructed. "Up three flights and I'll let you in."

"I'm sorry to come here like this." She was seated on my bed while I ran a washcloth under warm water at the sink.

"It's fine, really," I said. "But, Marie, how did you know I lived here?"

"Well . . . I followed you home one day after meeting by the duck pond."

"Why?"

"To see if I could, I guess. A kind of practice."

"Practice for what?"

"I don't know. Doing what you do."

"I see," I said, struck by her tenacity as well as my own obliviousness. "Well, you seem to be better at it than the FBI."

I gave her a glass of gin, knocked one back myself, then washed her wound. It was a shallow slice right at the base of her nose, where the septum met the channel of her upper lip. I felt slightly lightheaded, not at the sight of the blood but at the intimacy of the touch and the fragrance wafting off her shoulders.

"It should heal fine," I said, applying a small plaster I had on hand for shaving cuts. "Maybe just a tiny scar on the bottom."

I poured us another drink. "Did Claude do this?"

"I took your advice. I told him I was finished. He said if I try to quit again, he will chop it off."

"Don't worry. There won't be a next time for Claude."

"You're going to kill him?"

"Ah, wouldn't that be nice?" I said wistfully. "But didn't you tell me Claude is from Guernsey? Perhaps I'll settle with getting him deported. One of the few perks of being a passport-control agent."

I noticed that she had a larger faded scar just visible along her hairline. "Did Claude do this one as well?" I asked, gently brushing her hair back with my fingers.

"Oh, that? No. That was from my first week in San Francisco, five years ago—at the waterfront strike. A policeman saluted me with his blackjack."

"Wish I could deport him too."

She swallowed down the gin and smiled. "You are kind, Sebastian—or is it Simon?"

"Simon." Thanks to Wiedemann, she already knew my real first name, so she might as well call me by it.

"But, Simon, I didn't come here for you to be my nurse. I come for another reason."

"Oh?" Could she read my thoughts? Were there glittering heart-shaped pools in my eyes?

"Remember how you told me to watch for a man who is almost bald, walks with a limp, and has very shiny teeth?"

This jolted me from my erotic daze. "You mean you've seen him?"

"I think so. You see, I went to the Music Box to see Sally Bent, as you suggested me to do. I told her how I had danced for her once, and in fact she remembered me. So I ask about working for her in the upstairs or out on the casino boat. She says, come spring, if the fair reopens, there will be jobs at her Nude Ranch, but I tell her I don't like milking cows or feeding horses. And she says, 'If you want to sail the high seas, honey, then you gotta slop the hogs.' I tell her, sure, I'm comfortable with all the positions, though 'slopping the hog' is a new one to me. And she says, 'No, I mean if you want to work upstairs or on the boat, you also gotta work the ranch. All my girls do equal parts and get equal shares. That's partly why I'm so goddamn broke.'"

On top of Marie's natural thoroughness, the gin and the adrenaline had made her voluble. "What about the man, Marie?" I said, nudging her to her subject, though I was happy to have her sitting on my bed, looking into my eyes.

"Yes, I come to that now. And then while we are talking, the strangest-looking man I ever saw comes into Sally's office. He looks like he was cooked. Or perhaps confit. A very old young man or a very young old man. He takes off his hat and he has only this little ring of hair, no eyebrows, and his skin above his beard has so many spots, and he walks like there's broken glass under his feet."

"What did he say to Sally?"

"He comes into her office, with that big doorman behind him, and he says 'Hello, Sally, old girl. Did you miss me?'"

"And she says, 'Who the hell are you? Tater, get this creep outta here.'"

227

"And he says, 'Don't you recognize me, Sal? It's your old forest friend, Dick.'

"And Sally looks at him and then the blood goes out from her face and she turns white like this strange man's teeth and then she tells me I have to come back later."

The next day I went to the Music Box to talk to Sally Bent. Not only had Marie's physical description matched Wiedemann's agent Richard Wagner; she'd even heard him call himself Dick. But it was a Sunday and the Music Box was closed. I was cursing myself for not coming late last night after I'd sent Marie home, when suddenly an image in the alcove caught my eye.

The stairwell was plastered with posters of Sally Bent's old shows, most of them featuring a girl in the martini glass, the damsel in the bubble bath, the ostrich-feathered coquette kicking toward the stars. But one poster stood out. Instead of a naked woman, there was an illustration of an old sailing ship—a Chinese junk.

Treasure Island Pleasure Island—
After-hours at the Fair!

**Take an Evening Cruise with Sally Bent on Richard
Halifax's *Soup Dumpling*
Fresh from its Pacific Adventure.**

Below were pictures of Sally Bent, presumably, and a face that I knew all too well. The grinning visage of Richard Halifax.

Right then, the idea entered my consciousness through the back door and kicked me in the brain. "It's your old forest friend, Dick." The words Marie overheard the man speak to Sally Bent. What if Richard Wagner, aka Agent Kokosnuss, was . . . ?

That's when I knew it. I didn't know exactly how, and at the time it still made no sense, but some part of me knew it.

Richard Halifax was alive.

Part III

THE DEEP

To: The Dicky Halifax Junior Adventurers Club
From: Dicky Halifax
A Stranger in Ithaca

Springtime 1940

Dear boys,

You don't know how good it feels to be able to write you again.
There was a dark time when I didn't think it would ever happen—that
the vortex of the Pacific had spat me out only to suck me down into
a realm far worse than death, where our minds are scrambled eggs,
our limbs the playthings of a sinister fate, our voice a choked and
alien rattle.

That special mimeograph machine each of us keeps in our soul,
which records experience and prints it for others' eyes with only
the slightest variance in fidelity, had gotten thoroughly jammed. I
couldn't shoot out a single sheet, no matter how hard I cranked. In
fact, for a few months there, the whole Halifax operation had to shut
down in the face of a hostile takeover. I despaired of ever resuming
my life as the author-adventurer you know and love.

I'll spare you the blow-by-blow of my journey home, as it strikes
me there's only so much suffering young readers like you should
be forced to endure in one story, lest you become disturbed or,
worse, inured. And I won't have my boys flinging my letters into
the fire, out of either terror or boredom. So if you want to know
what it's like to cross the ocean on a submarine with a brain full
of regeneration therapies, a keister full of stupefying drugs, and

grieving the loss of your recently crippled sidekick, you'll have to look elsewhere.

When the hatch finally popped on that sea worm off Stinson Beach, I was steaming with cabin fever and a whopper of a headache, having ground down my new teeth into glistening nubs. I climbed out of the submarine, sucked sweet California air for the first time in over a year, and cried my eyes out. It was October, the height of Indian summer, and the smell of eucalyptus and fennel was just enough of home to make me realize the barren waste I'd become. I waved my cane in the air, howling like a madman, and made for shore. I wasn't much of a swimmer anymore, what with the number Sensei Kanemoto had done on my feet, and the water was cold as hell, but I could still float and thrash around well enough for the waves to carry me home.

While I was changing into dry clothes on the beach, a tubby fisherman spied me. Drs. Kanemoto and Frink had said it was imperative I not be seen, but I was too tired and foot-sore to give chase. Instead, I hobbled off to a cove that was familiar to me from sunnier days, when my friends and I used to come to picnic and tan ourselves on the rocks.

Back then, boys, I had been the toast of the town. I'd blow in on the heels of a long lecture tour, hoping to catch my breath and cozy up in my Russian Hill apartment. But I couldn't be home for two days before the tennis star Willa Reynolds and her cousin Fido, a swing-band drummer, would come roust me out of bed, throw me in her Plymouth roadster, and zip me out on a field trip. With the three of us digging into one another's hip bones and laughing our heads off, we'd usually burn down Highway 1 to Frank's Place at Moss Beach. There, a hundred feet above the surf, we'd watch the sunset over gimlets and crabcakes, having a roar of a time until Dashiell Hammett inevitably soured the mood by screaming at the waiter, punching his date, or singing "The Internationale." Sometimes we got treated to all three. But if it was truly one of those halcyon summer days that Northern California gets only four or five times a year, and scattered in niggardly fashion like the leg hairs on an old man, well, then we'd head north to Stinson Beach, and, armed with a gallon of Corpse Revivers and a cooler full of oysters, we'd tramp to our favorite cove, away from the crabbers and kiddos, and there in the company of other nature worshippers, we'd soak up the sun in our birthday suits.

One summer, I think it was in '31, my amigo Diego, wall-painter-*extraordinario*, joined us at the beach. I hadn't seen him since our Mexican adventure and my big swim across the Panama gap. When the canal authorities told me only documented vessels were allowed to cross, it had been Diego's idea that I declare my body to be the SS *Halifax*, tonnage 157 pounds. And sure enough, those fastidious bastards weighed me, tagged me, and let me cross for thirty-six cents. "See, Ricardo," he had said, "everything is possible." And sure enough, when he came out to California the next year, the bankers let him jazz up their lunchroom walls at the Pacific Stock Exchange, Willa Reynolds let him wiggle his Mexican paintbrush under her tennis skirt, and the bohemians at Stinson Beach hailed him as a conquering hero when one afternoon he managed to swallow an entire grapefruit, unpeeled; then, as a victory lap, wearing only his holster and a Dutch sailor's hat, he strode into the waves and fired his pistol at the gathering clouds. Diego had been right. Everything was possible then. Before the Rockefellers smashed his paintings and before I chased a rainbow down to Hollywood.

Sorry, boys. I've digressed. What I mean to say is: Curled up against a wet rock on Stinson Beach, shivering in the frigid wind on my first night back on Californian shores, I warmed myself with memories of those sweet sun-kissed days on that self-same sand.

When dawn broke, I hitched a ride to the city on the back of an ice truck. "Hobos in the back!" was all the driver said, slowing to a roll on the edge of town. This was the first test of my disguise, and while I was happy to pass with such flying colors, my ego registered the blow.

As directed, I went to the hamburger stand down the block from the German consulate on O'Farrell, where I asked the griddle man if he wanted to buy a watch. When he said no, as I had been informed he would, I ordered two burgers with extra pickles and onion rings. Boys, those greasy little shit-stain hamburgers were the first real food I'd eaten since coming off the coconut diet—I'd hardly eaten a thing on the submarine except for rye toast and tranquilizer tea—and, my God, I nearly died from ecstasy (and later from intestinal uproar).

Fifteen minutes later, a dapper fellow in a dark-green suit and white fedora walked in the door. He eyed me at the counter eating my burgers—I noticed that he flinched when he saw my face—and asked if I'd had a pleasant journey.

This was my prompt, to which I responded: "Smooth seas do not make good sailors."

And he replied: "Fear is the best wind for sails."

This, then, was my contact, the Nazi consul Fritz Wiedemann.

He ushered me into a back room behind the kitchen with a camera, tripod, and small bespectacled man, who told me to stand on the taped line and face him.

An hour later I had been outfitted with a passport bearing the depressing name Richard Wagner, an envelope containing three thousand dollars, my travel visa, and passage on the Japanese liner *Asama Maru,* sailing next month. Tucked inside the passport was a note that said: *Hank Rauch, #1212 penthouse suite, St. Francis Hotel.*

"I believe you have everything you need," said the Kraut consul. "I don't expect, or want, ever to see you again."

"Just one question," I said. "Do I look familiar?"

"Not at all. Why, have we met before?"

"No. Never mind."

I was noticing a pattern.

That's when things really began to go south. My doctors had made everything sound so simple: All I had to do was call on my buddy Hank, who apparently had moved up to Frisco over the summer, and get him to point me in the direction of those teeny-tiny documents: the Norden plans and Daddy Rauch's diary. Then the two of us would have a laugh like old times, he'd agree to keep mum's the word, I'd ship off back to Yokohama—and presto, I'd be good as new.

Hank Rauch opened the door to his penthouse suite and recoiled at the sight of me. Not even ole Hank, who'd spent hours fawning over your man Dick and drinking in my college-quarterback looks, recognized me. My disguise was flawless, but it made me feel awful.

"Yes?" he asked, perplexed.

"Hiya, Hank, did you miss me?"

"Who the hell are you?"

"Hank, it's me. Your old pal Dick."

He just looked at me, confused.

"Don't you see, Hank? It's me. Dick Halifax. Back from the dead."

His face dropped. "That's a sick joke. Now, if you'll excuse me," he said, trying to shut the door, before I blocked it with my foot.

"Hank, look at me. It's really me. I'm alive."

Hank began shaking. He turned and went back into the room and immediately made for his pills, swigging down a few with the bottle of vodka on his bed stand.

"You're not crazy, Hank," I said. "And I'm no ghost. I've just been in a tight spot for a while."

"But . . . you're dead!" He pulled the newspaper from the wastebasket. "See?"

Sure enough, there I was, looking grainy but handsome in a thumbnail photo in the *San Francisco Chronicle*, having been just declared dead by a jury of my peers in a Missouri probate court. But then I saw something that horrified me. "Page fourteen? They put me on page fourteen?"

I flipped to the earlier pages, which were all choked with world politics: debates about blockades, Chamberlain trying to bring Hitler to the talking table, Hitler planning his visit to conquered Warsaw, the Soviets swallowing up Baltic ports and leering at Turkey and Yugoslavia, the French fending off German raids on the Saar, Chinese bombings of a Japanese airbase in Hankow, Japanese casualties in a skirmish with the Soviets in Mongolia, and, of course, the biggest battle of them all, the 1939 World Series showdown between the Yankees and the Reds. On page three, there was a photo of German girls with pitchforks being sent from the city to go fetch the fall harvest. Did those rather plain be-kerchiefed *Mädchen* really take precedence over the official obituary of America's most beloved writer-adventurer? One who had mysteriously vanished at sea on the most daring adventure of his career? When I saw a three-by-three-inch ad for forty-nine-cent butterscotch that got more space than my death ruling, I got downright miffed. "These shitheads at the *Chronicle* must have gone soft in the brain!"

Hank was looking at me. "My God, is it really you, Dick?"

Once I'd finally convinced him that it was in fact me and I was in fact alive, Hank burst into tears. Then he started firing questions.

Drs. Kanemoto and Frink had advised me to keep my answers to a minimum here, though there was little risk of divulging too much, since Hank Rauch was a notorious drug addict and I was, in everyone else's understanding, dead.

"You must persuade Hank," my doctors in Saipan had instructed me, "using all the powers at your disposal. If, as you say, he loves you, then he will agree to hand over the microdots. You have the unique advantage, Dickee-san, of being both ransomer and hostage."

"How's that, senseis?" I asked.

"You will tell Hank that not just his life but your own life—which both you and he prize so much—depends on recovering the documents in his possession. If he does not give them to you, and you do not give them to us, then our legion of shadow operatives in California will hunt you down and kill you both."

"But . . . I thought you wanted to help me?"

"We do, Dicky. Of course we do. But we must be able to hold you accountable."

"And what about Nacho?"

"Well, naturally, if you don't do as we instructed, we will be forced to liquidate Nacho too. He's gravely injured, as it is."

It seemed the doctors did not quite trust in their own experimental regeneration therapies to rewire your man Dick, so now they were hedging with more customary methods.

All this I explained to Hank, as he sat on his bed in his hotel bathrobe, smoking one cigarette after another and looking at me in horrified disbelief. "So you see what a pickle I'm in, Hank?"

He sat there, silent. A dark look had come over him. As I said, boys, Hank's psyche was like the slopes of Fuji. A storm could roll in unannounced and suddenly blot out the sun.

"Hank? Did you catch all that?"

"You know, you have some goddamn nerve turning up here, asking me for that diary."

"What do you mean, Hank?"

"Did you really think I wouldn't find out what you did with it?"

"Find out what?" I said, though I had an inkling.

"Goddamn you, Dick!" He flicked his cigarette at me and began pacing the room, working himself up into a state. "All I know is that half the words in that diary you gave me in a microdot were not the ones my father wrote. How do you explain that? Huh?"

"What are you saying, Hank? You're not talking sense."

"I'm saying you forged them! You and probably that lunatic Roderick. I knew there was something fishy about that bogus story of the diary burning in a hotel fire and you being able to salvage only the microdots."

"I don't know what you're talking about, Hank. I told you: Some soused Chinaman shot a firecracker into the curtains."

"You expect me to believe that? Come on! What really happened, Dick? You forged my father's diary and filled it with outlandish lies, then destroyed the original so you could pawn off the microdot version on me. And then when I get back to the States, I start getting hounded by our Comintern contacts, who say you've already promised them the diary to publish in *Free Masses*. Am I close?"

I tried holding out, but the thing is, boys, he had me dead to rights. And the way Hank's forehead vein was throbbing, I felt like I ought to level with him.

See, Hank left his daddy's diary with me for the few days he went off to Canton. Naturally, I gave it a quick read. Now, Hank's original idea was simply to publish an excerpt of the diary in his own journal. But in advance of his visit, I'd had a bright idea and, through our friends at the Zeitgeist Bookshop in Shanghai, found a better buyer in the commie rag *Free Masses*. Based on how I'd heard Hank describe the parts of the diary he'd seen, I had sold them on it with the promise of some juicy nuggets.

But when I read that dull diary there in Hong Kong, well, I was none too impressed. I knew I had to add a little Halifax Elbow Grease to liven up the works. So I dusted off my handwriting skills and recruited Roderick to supply the *Deutsch*. He had been attending German language and cultural events ever since he was a tot, and his mother spoke to him exclusively in Hun. It took some wheedling—plus the promise of a big payout—to overcome his natural jealousy of Hank, but pretty soon the two of us got to work. When we finished, Roderick burned the original in the hotel trash can out on the balcony while he grilled a pair of steaks, and the grease fire really did manage to set the curtains alight. So the story about the hotel fire was true, at least in part.

"Alright," I said to Hank, who was still giving me the Kraut scowl there in the St. Francis, "so I jazzed a few things up. But only because your daddy's diary was just a bunch of idle wishes and weak-sister fantasies. Not one drop of real action in it. What's the big deal if I embellished a little here and there?"

"Big deal? Dick, you wrote total lies. You said my father fucked us!"

Like I said, I was trying to rev it up, and I suppose my writer-adventurer instincts to enlarge and improve simply kicked into high gear. I thought, if anything, Hank would dig it.

"I was just trying to help you, Hank. I figured, hey, if my buddy Hank wants to torpedo his own father, then he's gonna need more firepower than this thing, which reads like the naptime whispers of some prissy old bookworm."

"You promised it to *Free Masses* behind my back! That's not what I agreed to. And certainly not to publish lies!"

"Let me get this straight. You were willing to sink your father in print with his own words but not with ones I've seasoned with a little mustard—and for a nice pile of dough for us to boot?"

"They're lies!" he shouted. Hank reached for the vodka, poured himself a full glass, and chased down another handful of pills from his nightstand laboratory.

"Hey, Hank, go easy on those pills."

"You don't get to tell me what to do, Dick! You're dead!"

He took another swig, then collapsed on the bed and started to weep.

Damn me, boys, if it wasn't the saddest sight I ever saw. I went over to Hank on the bed and tried to comfort him. "I'm sorry, Hank. Really, I am."

"It's not only the forgery," he said, now in a low, sniffling tone. "My feud with my father . . . The whole time I was playing their game, even before I knew I was playing it. Even before I took their money and passed their messages. Shrugging my shoulders at the purges and the show trials because the fight against fascism was more important. Using that idiotic term 'social fascist,' spoon-fed to us by the Comintern, to discredit the liberals and democrats. What a *Klotz*! That sickening photo of the Red Army and Wehrmacht in a joint victory parade on the streets of Brest Litovsk—that was it for me. Too many lies, Dick. I'm just so sick of the fucking lies."

While Hank was talking with me next to him on the bed, sitting there in that feminine bathrobe with his hair all tousled, all fine-boned and smooth-skinned, well, it made me think of slipping into Sally's dress and of her dipping her legs into my pants, and suddenly my hair snake began to swell. My post-operation turgidity had gone into abeyance on the nightmare submarine ride, but now, as Hank leaned against me and I smelled the sweat and cologne coming off the back of his neck, it returned with a fury.

"Gosh, Hank," I said, trying to ignore my tumescence, "sounds like if I hadn't noodled around in that diary, you might have gone through with publishing it in your journal, and now you'd regret it."

Hank snickered. "I guess that's one way to look at it."

"Well, then, how about as a token of gratitude you let me have those microdots?"

Hank laughed.

"What's funny?" I said.

"Are you serious? Have you not just heard a word I said?"

"And did you not hear when I said I can't leave here empty-handed?"

"Well, they're gone," he said, fingering his ear. "I burned everything. It's over, Dick."

I could tell he was bullshitting me. Hank was a lousy liar with a blatant tell. In Los Angeles, he and I used to play poker with some roughnecks down at the San Pedro harbor, and as soon as the table noticed that Hank fingered his ear whenever he was bluffing, we took him for every penny he had.

"Hank, just do me this favor, and then we'll be square. We can even work on another picture together. Dr. Frink assures me we'll be free to do it our way this time. He says the Kraut consul down in L.A. calls all the shots with the studios, and all Frink has to do is get on the horn with him and say my name."

"Is that what they've promised you, Dick? Another stab at Hollywood? Do you really think they'll stop demanding favors after this? They'll wring everything they can from you, and then the moment you stop being useful, they'll ruin you. You know, I had heard a rumor about you in Spain and dismissed it as preposterous, but now I wonder if it's true."

"You know how rumors are, Hank," I said. "Come on, you know me." In truth, I felt a bit rotten about the Spanish job—Roderick had really stooped too low, even for him.

"It's just two stupid pieces of paper, Hank. Can't you see both our lives are on the line here? Not to mention," I said, taking aim at his heartstrings, "the life of a poor little crippled boy named Nacho, currently imprisoned on Saipan?"

Hank seemed unmoved.

"I can't just ignore my *giri*, Hank. If I don't get those dots," I said, "then we're both finished. I might as well have drowned out there in the ocean. And you might as well just swallow that bottle of pills."

Hank laughed again, his mordant gallows humor never failing him. "Well, Dicky, sounds like you're in a classic Halifax 'tight spot.'"

That's when he noticed me pitching a circus tent in my pleated pants. And things suddenly went to a confusing place that I can't quite recall or describe.

All I know is that eventually I got Hank to agree to give me both sets of documents: the Norden plans and the sordid family business about Daddy Rauch. He told me to come back to his room in two hours and he'd have everything there and ready, and at last the Japs and the Jerries and even the Russkies would all be happy and get out

240

of our hair once and for all, and I could make my grand second-act comeback, and Hank could continue publishing his journal, shouting high-minded slogans into the void, and he and I would go back to being just pals, and everything would be swell. The only costs incurred would be letting Emperor Hirohito eyeball some diagrams about American airplane gadgets and knocking that smug Olympian Theodor Rauch off his perch, exposing him as the dirty old pervert he was. Even in its impaired state, the Halifax Cost-Benefit Calculator had no trouble doing the math on that one.

But that damn fool Hank, even worse at balancing the books than yours truly, just couldn't do the reckoning.

When I went back to his suite at the appointed hour, the door was ajar. Before I even stepped inside and saw him lying there in a human puddle, I knew what had happened.

Hank had called it quits. A bottle of pills, a note, the whole works.

When the seas get choppy, boys, some people just don't know how to ride out life. The Papists say it's a sin to pull your own plug, and while I don't set much store by visions of spectral souls enduring eternal misery simply for having wanted to put an end to their torment here on earth, I do think it's unspeakably sad when life turns against itself. To say no to all possibilities, to live so utterly bereft of hope—it does seem inhuman. For what is humanity, boys, if not an absurd hope in the face of all evidence to the contrary? Is that not why that ole Manchegan Don makes us cry as well as laugh? We all saddle our nag and take aim at the mule train, so to speak. And if you think it's sad when the inevitable collision comes, then how much sadder is it to strip off the sallet and crawl into our deathbed and put an end to all our future adventures? No, boys, put your mother's pills back in her dresser and hurl yourself into life. No matter how hard things get, no matter the cost, live.

But it's hard to keep sight of this truth when the blackness grabs you by the lapels and belches in your face. When I saw Hank there, looking like Roderick on his seaborn catafalque, looking like Nacho face down and broken in the Saipanese mud, looking like Wesley—well, you get the idea—I lost my mind.

People talk about going crazy like it's a onetime deal, but I assure you, boys, sanity is like a long marble staircase in a Hungarian bathhouse, and once you lose your footing on a slippery patch, it's only a question of how far you'll fall and in what kind of pool you'll land. I don't rightly know when I first began to slip, though I reckon it started years before I drove the *Soup Dumpling* into the sea floor, since surely it was some form of diseased restlessness, and not just my hyperactive thyroid, that had impelled me to undertake such an expedition in the first place. But as for where I hit the bottom, well, there was no mistake.

It was in a room at the Sir Francis Drake, with rose-thorn wallpaper and green velvet curtains, two hundred feet above Union Square. Just up the street from where I saw Hank and all our loose ends splayed out on the floor. Hank was dead. Or so I thought at the time. Furthermore, I had no idea where he'd hidden away those papers with all our tiny treasures.

This was not how I had dreamed my homecoming would be. I'd thought it would be exhilarating to pass myself in disguise at haunts where I was once greeted by name. A temporary covert identity, as Sensei Kanemoto had explained it, would liberate me from old problems, from the old grooves of existence that I had outgrown but in which I nevertheless found myself stuck. "Your persona is like a suit, Dickee-san. Even the finest suits need time to rest on the hanger, or else they lose their form." Stepping into an alias would give me time to air out the wrinkles and stink lines in the suit of my old persona, so that it would be fresh to wear again later.

Besides, as I'm sure you'll agree, boys, the best parts of the *Odyssey* are when our hero's in disguise, either tricking the Cyclops or, once he's back home in Ithaca, pulling the wool over everyone's eyes, preparing to turn those suitors into gyro meat.

But it's no fun going incognito if you can't drop the guise and then glory in the reveal. If Odysseus, after skewering that grumpy ogre's eyeball, had just kept his mouth shut and preserved his alias, sure, maybe he'd have had a smoother homecoming, with fewer crewmates dead. But he'd never have proved to the world that he, Odysseus, king of pain and master of cunning, had lived by his wits and lived up to his name. He knew good and well that no bard wants to sing the adventures of some dolt named Nobody.

The result was that upon regaining my native shores I felt farther away from home than ever. Everything familiar had turned strange and threatening. Not only did people not recognize me; I had become a stranger in my own native land. And the one person I'd revealed myself to had up and jumped ship.

Part of what sent me into such a tailspin was being back in the town I'd once splashed around in like an emperor penguin. Let's say you were to take a page from the Halifax calendar circa 1934—a tough year for the nation, but a humdinger for your man Dick. Riding high off my round-the-world adventures and the hefty book deals and lecture tours they had spun, I was living the easy life up on Russian Hill, just before I got sucked into the Scylla of Hollywood and Charybdis of bespoke housing. My books had made me a household name, and now Dame Fortune and her twin sister, Future Movie Stardom, were lying splay-legged and ready. Little did I know, boys, those twins got teeth where you least expect 'em.

But neither dentition nor disappointment would have been on my mind back then on any San Francisco Saturday. No sir, after a three-martini lunch with my agent, Feakins, down at the Tadich, where we'd fill out my calendar of engagements and I'd regale him with A-1 book ideas, I'd grab a quick nap, snap on a fresh collar, and head out to the Barbary Coast for a first-class spree, whoopla-ing the night away.

We'd start the evening off fresh in the Latin Quarter with a Campari spritz at the Lido, where the drinks come floating by on little canals and the gondolier-waiters look like handsome dandies from an early Theodor Rauch novel. Then we tack weird into Finocchio's, drinking daiquiris while we watch the drag queens strut their gams and shake their falsies all while keeping their nuts tucked. By then we're feeling good, boys, and starting to feel a bit peckish, so we hop over to Izzy Gomez's for steaks the size of a catcher's mitt, washed down with lightning bolts of Izzy's home-brewed grappa. Or maybe we head up to Julius' Castle for a bottomless glass of Barolo and a plate of linguini alla vongole so big you could swim in it. As we eat, we look out across the bay at Alcatraz, thinking of Al Capone in his sad cell there, crying his murderous eyes out 'cause he can smell the garlic and olive oil wafting all the way from our table.

With a solid foundation laid, we're feeling damn good and ready for more. So we head down the old gauntlet on Pacific Street to Gay Nineties, where San Francisco's second wave of debauchery lives on in rebottled nostalgia. Here we drink punch, with whiskey or rum or both if you dare, then we take one of the taxi girls out for a spin on the dance floor. They've got our number, boys, literally! Ain't it fun to flash the charm and watch 'em melt? We could have them all, and the thrill of that mental conquest is far more satisfying than the complicated greaseworks between the sheets.

So we leave Betty or Helen with a quarter in her pocket and a quiver in her knees and head back into the night, this time with our posse of new bottlemates. One of them insists we throw down a bandolier of tequila at Sinaloa; another stumps for Taos Lightning at the Kit Karson; and a third says we'd be fools to miss out on a Fernet Branca Hanky Panky at the Fly Trap. We're in no mood to argue, so we do all three! Now we're feeling adventurous, and what better way to ramp up the fun than just down the street at the Music Box, where my old pal and sweet Kansas City gal Sally Bent runs a well-oiled burlesque show. What with all the knockers flying around, a couple of our friends have got the randy up in them and are itching to visit a Maiden Lane French joint like La Bavette or Enchantée, but we don't go in for that frilly, pimpish atmosphere, all Louis Quinze and weak-sister rococo with a sinister undercurrent. So we tell them, good news, fellas, Sally runs a little extra hokey-pokey upstairs, all honest corn-fed girls working for an even cut of the take.

Now, this is where your average spree can take a dip, boys, or outright dissolve, once the load is shot and the sleepiness sets in. So it's important to have something grand and irresistible still on the horizon, and that's why we've saved our visit to Forbidden City until now, for the two o'clock all-Chinese floor show. The Orientals know how to create an air of mystery, boys. They respect ritual. They trim their toenails and pluck their eyebrows and they sit on straight mats. Above all, they delight in sophisticated pleasure. You just watch Lady Li turn from a beautiful courtesan into a butterfly on the floor of

Forbidden City while nursing an opium-laced highball and see if you can keep a dry eye.

That's the grand finale, boys, and now we can go home to bed, feeling proud of what we accomplished. Our saucer count is stacked well into the teens, we've come face-to-face with the sublime mysteries of the East, and we're still standing. There's no shame in throwing in the towel now. But if there's any gas in the tank, if any of you hearty boys want to make it to see the sunrise, then come with me. We'll drink brandy-laced coffee at the Red Caboose until the first rays of morning come over the bay, and then we'll stumble our way to the Aquatic Park. That's right, boys, we're going for a swim! This is what separates the good-time Charlies from the real conquistadors. When your testicles hit your adenoids and the bright tight feeling spreads all across your chest, that's when you know you're truly alive. Hell, we feel so good, we could swim out to Alcatraz and towel off right in front of Scarface himself. Instead, we turn around at Black's Point, backstroke our way to the beach, marveling at the pink dome of crepuscular light and thinking, Gosh, fellas, ain't life something? Back on land, we wring out our briefs, stuff 'em in our pockets, and head to breakfast at Roger's, where we salute the new day with eggs, bacon, pancakes, and a Bloody Mary the size of an ancient kantharos. That's how we'd tear open this town, boys, and burn it down to cinders.

But none of that was on offer to me there in my room in the Sir Francis Drake, two hundred feet above the world, where I watched from my window as Hank's tallowy corpse was taken away in the ambulance. Nobody would have recognized me. Not Dan at the Red Caboose, not gregarious ole Izzy Gomez, not even crusty Julius, with his sharp dago eye.

I couldn't even think of venturing out. The idea of people on the street shuddering at the sight of me was unbearable. At the same time, the walls were closing in. I felt more imprisoned than I had been in Sensei Kanemoto's torture-chamber-cum-rehabilitation-cell. At least there I had the hope of coming home. But now I was home and completely alone. Cut off from everyone and everything. I had scared poor Hank into taking the plunge, and I had no idea how to fulfill the mission my doctors had set me, since I had no idea where he'd stashed those documents. They sure weren't in his hotel room—at least as far as I could tell, for what was to say Hank hadn't transferred those tiny microdots from one piece of paper to another. They could be on anything bigger than a punctuation mark. I was already at loose ends, and the thought of going out hunting around for a handful of semicolons made me feel all the crazier.

On top of that, the longer I delayed, the more likely Sensei Kanemoto's Black Dragons and Dr. Frink's murderous Bundists were to hunt me down. I don't know if they were serious or had just planted the idea to scare me, but in my addled state, the idea took root and assumed monstrous reality.

In short, I became a shut-in. The worst kind of sickly weak sister you can be. Just like my mother had been, just like I had been when I was a young boy like you.

If you cut yourself off from life, boys, the mind and body fester. You will start to believe things no healthy brain could entertain. These ideas will poison you, literally, taxing your organs and curdling your blood, so that you indeed end up becoming the invalid you once feared you were. It's an evil self-fulfilling prophecy, and once the rot sets in, only the most heroic act of rebellion, against a will that has otherwise become hell-bent on self-strangulation, can undo it. It requires a power akin to grace, though not one I ascribe to any bearded divinity. It's gotta come from you, boys, from the sand deep in your guts.

Too bad, then, that I was fresh out of sand. With Hank dead, and along with him all hopes for my glorious resurrection and the film career I'd been promised, evil thoughts were free to run wild across my brain.

Things got so bad that I became convinced that one of the last things dear Nacho had said to me—that my doctors had surgically implanted a time bomb in the ole Halifax Hair Snake—was true. This, as you may recall, was one of his hypotheses regarding my sudden tumescence. Looking back on this now from the vantage point of restored sanity, I can safely say that Nacho was just being his morbid self. But trapped in my room, my gray matter reduced to jelly, bereft of any sidekicks, cut off from all my fans and readers, including you precious Junior Adventurers, and still reeling from that bewildering engorgement at Hank's place, I began to give full credence to this idea.

Who knows the number of weeks I spent in mortified preoccupation, alone in my room, conducting numerous experiments on this most mysterious of organs? I felt like I was nineteen again, in the months after the accident, poking and prodding in despair. Was it possible a small incendiary had been lodged within? A cigarette-sized stick of dynamite? A Vienna sausage–shaped lump of gelignite? Or had a full stick of TNT been implanted there, which would have explained my dramatically turgid state, and then subsequently been absorbed by the body, only to be deployed again later? Could such a thing happen? Could the penis in fact . . . swallow?

I did hear a faint ticking sound, and while I was not limber enough to place my ear much lower than my nipple line, I'm pretty sure it was coming from the bedside clock.

Meanwhile, the room-service trays were starting to pile up, and I refused to let the maids in to clean. Eventually, the exploratory surgery I had refused to countenance became the only remaining option. You know how the worst idea you'll ever have, boys, as soon as it's named, as soon as all your fear and revulsion attach to it and you run from it as fast as you can, repulsed that such an idea even sprouted from your brain, is really the first stirring of destiny? Because the moment you say "anything but that" and run the other way, then the countdown begins, for now it's got you by the ankle and you're entangled. It's only a matter of time before the idea obsesses you, seduces you with its repulsiveness, until you realize that your horror was simply a conscious expression of what you secretly wanted most, and as with the infernal souls clamoring on the banks of Acheron, fear turns to desire and spurs you on.

There are only so many times you can drive your car across a bridge before letting the imp of the perverse jerk the wheel and take the plunge; or look at a sharp pencil before you surrender to the impulse to jam it in your eye; or regard that dangling, useless, confounding, all-consuming appendage, the seat of all your worth and worthlessness, before you embrace destiny and take a knife to it.

Yes, boys, things had gotten very bad indeed. But, thankfully, when I took the steak knife to myself, I made my cut along the vertical axis and managed to avoid lopping the sucker off.

The sudden pain, blood, and evident absence of explosives scared some much needed sense into me. I wrapped my bleeding hair snake in a washcloth and ran to the nearest pharmacy for rubbing alcohol and gauze. "You were wrong, Nacho!" I remember shouting to no one in particular. "No bombs in this penis!"

When I returned, the room had been cleaned. I dressed my wound, howled from the sting of the antiseptic, and, lying on fresh white sheets, imagined myself convalescing in hospital. A nice seven-year stay in a sanatorium—that's what I needed, like a character from a Theodor Rauch novel. Picturing myself on a mountaintop terrace, doing my daily horizontal on the chaise longue, swaddled in a starched white comforter and sipping consommé from the spoon extended by the steady hand of my male nurse and sidekick Nacho Fu, I felt a delicious calm come over me. It was a comforting image, and I could have dwelled in it for days. What's more, thanks to my knife work, my erections seemed to have abated.

But the paranoia returned.

The maids had been in my room. Who or what else had been placed there? What if my bed was booby-trapped? Or the shower nozzle filled with face-melting acid, or the toilet packed with buckshot? Then I thought of the stack of cash the Nazi consul had given me. Three thousand dollars seemed like a suspiciously large sum for a modest month-long stay, and I'd only used a few hundred to keep the hotel management off my back. But what if the money was in fact some sort of surveilling device? Or coated in a toxic residue designed to make me go insane? In a panic, I flushed the bills down the toilet, taking care to shield my face from the buckshot.

That's when I knew I couldn't stay. If I did, it would mean certain death, whether at the hand of killer housekeepers or myself. I needed help. And the sole person I could think of turning to was in fact running a burlesque theater just ten treacherous blocks away.

Sally Bent, bless her heart, was good enough to take me in. Now, I've already told you boys all about Sally and me back in Kansas City, so I won't bore you by repeating what a sweet sister she was. She must've been confused as hell by my turning up at her door, just like Hank had been, but she bit her lip and nursed me, one step at a time, back up the long staircase to sanity.

Sally stashed me in the barn of her Nude Ranch at the closed fairgrounds, where I spent the winter in a fetal position. Each week she'd bring me groceries, and sometimes she'd stay awhile and relive old memories with me. After my night of the long soul in the Sir Francis Drake, I felt even more adrift, such that I despaired of ever slipping back into the old suit of myself. I was, I told her, even entertaining thoughts of filling my pockets with gravel and sinking into the bay, back under the sea where I belonged. "I'm Nobody, Sally," I would say. "No hero, no sidekick. Neither alive nor dead. Nobody."

Trying to pull me out of my funk, Sally would recall our old times together as kids and those magical two years of playing hooky in the forest between our houses. It was hard to believe the buxom, powdered lady stroking my hand had once been that skinny-limbed gamine I had found so beguiling. She reminded me about the time we climbed the prairie elm and ate watermelon and I drank the juice that ran down her leg and dripped from her toes to the branch below. About the time we dared each other to go to Union Station and sneak onto the first train that was leaving and ended up in St. Joe, where we drank root beers at the cemetery overlooking the river. About how my mother used to have fainting spells in church and my father, shaking her awake, would hiss between clenched teeth, "Regina, stop being such a goddamn actress," which became one of our recurring sayings.

Sally also reminded me how we hooked up years later, in Chicago, our childhood friendship already a distant memory. "Remember, Dick, it was in '29, just before the crash. I was dancing in a tits-and-trombones show in Towertown when I saw the marquee across the street with your name blazoned across it: *An Evening with Richard*

Halifax: From Timbuktu to Tenochtitlán. Little did I know that before long I'd be shaking my fanny on the wing of your airplane five hundred feet in the air."

She did her best to bring me back to myself, good old Sally, and though it helped some, I spent those rainy winter months in her barn feeling like a ghost.

The funny thing was that, even though I felt a million miles away, I was curled up on a couch not a hundred yards from where I should have docked last spring. The *Soup Dumpling*'s berth was just around the corner from her barn. In fact, if things had worked out the way they were supposed to, Sally and I would have been plying the bay and lining our pockets.

Instead, I learned that Sally was in arrears to some of the less scrupulous loan sharks in town and was busting her hump to get out of the red. Of course, it was my shipwreck that had landed her there. The bridge loan she'd taken out to pay for the slip at the fair—a full year in advance she'd had to pay—had pulled her under; the riverboat casino was hosing her with exorbitant rental fees, and, even with the Nude Ranch raking in a rich harvest, she could barely pay enough to keep her knees intact.

"Debts?" I said, surprised. "But you should be fixed for life, Sal."

She regarded me cautiously, as one does the insane. "And why is that?"

"'Cause I took out a massive life-insurance policy on yours truly. And you were my prime beneficiary."

Sally looked like she was about to burn her wig.

"No one contacted you?"

"No."

"I guess those bastards don't go out of their way to pay up."

"You were only recently declared dead, Dick. No one knew what happened to you. They looked for months before giving up hope."

"Well, now that it's official, you just gotta call up Lloyd's of London and demand those Dicky dollars."

"But, Dick . . . you're alive. You realize that, right? You're alive. You don't have to hide."

"Dick Halifax is dead."

"No, he's not. He's right here—the same man with all the memories we've been reliving. You were that boy, and that boy is still you."

"He existed once, but I don't know how to go forward with him."

"There's just one way, as you yourself told me: chin up and tits out."

"But, Sal, what about the Black Dragon hatchet men and . . ."

"Anyone who thinks they own you, Dick, is in for a rotten surprise. Take back what's yours."

It was a swell thing to say, but I wasn't able to hear it. "You really don't want that insurance money, huh, Sal? It's over fifty grand."

Sally's jaw crashed to the floor. "Did you say fifty grand?"

"Yeah, I was smart enough to take it out before I announced the voyage of the *Soup Dumpling*. Got a swell rate too. And it's all going to you, Sal. I left the digs down in Laguna Beach to Roderick and Hank—thought it would be funny to look down from heaven on the two of them fighting, but my reaper's curse mowed down that idea—so maybe you can get the house too."

Sally looked confused. "Wait a minute. Do you mean Hank Rauch?"

"Poor ole Hank," I cried, burying my face in my hands. "This whole mess is his fault."

"What do you mean?"

"I mean if Hank Rauch had just given me a couple of stupid pieces of paper instead of killing himself, I wouldn't be here now, leaking tears on the floor of your barn. Instead, I'd be in Tokyo, laughing over steaks and geishas at the Ginza Lion while my senseis helped me reclaim my life and career."

"I see . . ." she replied absently. Then, after a few minutes' silence, she said, "Dick, you should know: Hank Rauch isn't dead. He's in a coma."

"What?" I shouted. "Hank's alive?"

Now it was my turn to burn my wig—which, by the way, was something I desperately needed. Whatever remaining strands I had tried to muster into a pompadour were looking pretty paltry. It was time to face the music that I was as good as bald, which is a humiliating daily memento mori that will come for many of you boys by middle age or even sooner. And vain as it may sound, I would have given my left arm to keep the hair on my head. So cherish that fine lustrous mop while you have it, boys. Run your hands through it fifty times a day, and never wear a hat unless you have to.

"But, Sal, that's incredible," I said, referring to the news about Hank. "How do you know?"

"I met his sister just before the fair closed. Right before you showed up."

"Hildegard? What did she want?"

"Oh, nothing. She just introduced herself after a show."

"I see. Nothing else?"

"No," she said guardedly. "That's it."

Later that evening, just before she left, Sally said she thought maybe being declared dead was something I could turn to my advantage.

"What do you mean?"

"Well, don't you remember how you used to complain that your fame felt more and more like a straitjacket? How the constant travel was becoming the very drudgery and rat race you vowed to escape, and how on the lecture circuit you felt like a marionette being pulled by the strings of an invisible puppet master of your own creation?"

I nodded.

"And that you longed to live a quiet life somewhere, free to write whatever you wanted in peace, not beholden to some congealed public persona? Remember, you told me that if you could do it all again, you'd sell the house and find some silent rocky perch on the coast to live like a hermit scholar. Mount Athos on the Pacific, you called it. Nothing but stone and light and clean white paper for writing."

It was true that I'd said all those things to Sally over the last few years. Every new adventure I thought up was supposed to break me free of these feelings of constraint and stagnation, and yet somehow they just left me feeling all the more trapped. Though, if I'm perfectly honest—and I have no reason to lie to you, boys—my idea to chuck it all for the hermit's cave was perhaps more an expression of frustration and fantasy than an actual life plan.

"Well, now's your chance," said Sally. "You can live the simple life you've longed for. Just with a different name."

"Yeah," I said. "Maybe you're right." I could tell what Sally was thinking, and even though I agreed, it still stung. Now that my corpse was worth fifty grand to her, she liked me better dead.

Sally bid me good night and said she'd be back on Monday to check on me.

That night I wandered out beyond the Gayway and strolled the world pavilions, empty and somber in the moonlight. As I limped my way through Chinese pagodas and Japanese torii, past Peruvian temples and Easter Island idols, across the Florentine statuary and chrome coffee machines of Italy and the hexagonal turf of the cheese-and-bicycle tour of France, I felt like the last man on earth.

It was a relief to know Hank was still among the living, albeit perhaps as a vegetable. And, thankfully, the worst of my paranoia had abated. But I also felt as sad and forlorn as I'd felt the whole winter. The rains were coming to an end, and Sally told me that workers would soon return to Treasure Island to prepare for the reopening of the fair in spring. That meant I'd have to move on from Sally's barn, and I had nowhere to go, and nothing to do. My only hope for freeing myself from the tremendous *giri* that my doctors had placed on me was currently in a coma, in a state of indefinite hibernation, which is exactly how I felt. And it was clear that Sally, sweet as she was, didn't think much of the idea of me coming out of it, now that she knew about the insurance money. As soon as I stopped being dead, she'd go back to being worse than broke.

There on the darkened island, watching the roving beacon of Alcatraz sweep across the red towers of the bridge, I saw with clarity the true nature of the voyage of the *Soup Dumpling*. It had been an act of desperation. A joint venture of all the wrong motives: to stay in the spotlight; to pay for my costly house; to prove my youth as a rebuttal to my aging reflection; to convince myself, my publisher, and the exhausted public that boyish adventure still had a place in their hearts; to somehow be less lonely in the world, even though every trip I took and every book I wrote sank me deeper into my own abandonment. I kept throwing myself at death to prove once and for all to that sickly moribund boy in his bed, looking at a color plate of a Chinese junk in *The Treasures of the Orient*, that I was not him, because he dreamed in his bed, while I dreamed in deeds. But the death-bound boy in my mind could never be dislodged. No matter how many adventures I had, no matter how desperately I chased life and hammered my fantasies into reality, he would always be there, calling me to the shadow world, pulling me to the deep.

My poor little wharf rat Nacho had been right: The *Soup Dumpling* really was the stupidest expedition undertaken in the entirety of human history. And I, Richard J. Halifax, should have drowned out there in the Pacific. Everyone would be better off for it. Despite my doctors' best efforts, they had not succeeded in regenerating me. In pulling off the old mask of myself, instead of uncovering the real me beneath, they'd revealed nothing but raw nerves and sinew. I felt the pain of my ordeal and the weight of my past more than ever. And rather than looking toward an open horizon to fill with new adventures, I now saw only darkness.

The sole insight from my regeneration therapy was what the coconut demon Karl Dieter had told me in that vivid nightmare while my teeth were being replaced: that, having cultivated the bloom of health from the flower of sickness, I could kill an old friend with impunity, because life came from death and death was the great blessing of life.

It was now time, I decided, to kill that old friend.

I went to the shoreline and lowered myself onto the shoals. I reached down into the rocks and began filling my pockets. The adventure was over. The black waters of the Pacific awaited.

That's all for now,
Dicky

Part IV

ASHORE

Herb Caen, *San Francisco Chronicle*, April 13, 1940

Fair in Forty: Lights Will Go On for Second Season

Treasure Island, Take Two

It's official, folks. Our days of dreary hibernation are soon over. After a stormy winter, the Pageant of the World Pacific returns to Treasure Island this May.

While the fair's prospects at a second run looked shaky when the curtains went down last fall, with lackluster profits and a fresh war in Europe, she lives to see another year. And though the international pavilion will be thinned out and the calendar shorter, this year's fair, like the phoenix atop the Tower of the Sun, emblem of our city's rise from the ashes of adversity, will shake her tail feather and soar.

Fun in Forty

Many of the delights of learning and leisure you remember from last year will still be on offer, only bigger and better. The hit show "Cavalcade of the Golden West" will now be galloping through the centuries of the entire country in full panoramic panoply with "America! Cavalcade of a Nation." The University of California's science exhibit will now feature a cyclotron, smashing atoms to the amusement of young and old. And, if the forecasts for the Gayway are to be believed, the lines for the Nude Ranch will snake all the way to Peru.

But, just in case that doesn't get our fair rivals in New York quaking in their boots, the Fun in Forty has more up its sleeve. Benny Goodman will be swinging through town for a series of concert dates. And the Aquacade—yes, you heard me—the Aquacade is coming to Treasure Island. Their splash of a performance at Flushing Meadows last summer was just a warm-up for their spectacular synchronized song, dance, and swim routine in a massive new indoor pool with bright lights and crystalline waters.

I've been assured by fair director Mr. Vandeburg that every arch, column, and fountain on the island will be twinkling with so much color and light, you'll think you've hopped inside a kaleidoscope. At time of writing, millions of California flowers are being woven into a square mile of the most beautiful carpet you've ever smelled. And presiding over this splendor will be our trusty gal, Dame *Pacifica*, an eighty-foot vision of world peace, on a fine pair of stone legs.

Artists Al Fresco

But *Pacifica* is not the only giant at this year's fair. Famed Mexican artist Diego Rivera will preside over the Art in Action exhibit, where he plans to create one of his controversial frescoes. Will it be met with cheers or chisels? Stay tuned.

A continuing four-month show revealing the backstage side of art, Art in Action will be the central theme of the Palace of Fine Arts, aka the aluminum shed. A number of notable artists of the West are participating. Helen Forbes will paint in tempera; Maxine Albro in oil; and Dudley Carter, known to last year's fairgoers for his splendid work on the Shasta Building, will demonstrate how to sculpt with an ax. Just watch out for the wood chips.

Local foreign artists will also be present. Bolivian-born cartoonist Antonio Sotomayor will draw his outlandish caricatures; Czech printmaker Max Pollak will crank out the graphic arts; and Austrian painter Hildegard Rauch, daughter of the illustrious writer Theodor Rauch, will capture the face of the fair in portraiture.

See you at the summer fair, folks. Don't forget to wear a coat!

HALIFAX ALIVE?

Man Claiming to Be Dead Author-Adventurer Found on Farallon Islands

SAN FRANCISCO, CA. APRIL 15 (AP)—

A man claiming to be the writer and adventurer Richard Halifax was rescued by the coast guard this Tuesday on the Farallon Islands, thirty miles west of San Francisco. Last fall a Missouri court declared Halifax dead after his ship *Soup Dumpling* disappeared while attempting a trans-Pacific crossing. No trace of the vessel or its crew was found.

Until yesterday, that is, when the coast guard was alerted after a birdwatching cruise sighted a man on the uninhabited island, waving his arms in distress. The man, who showed signs of extreme physical duress and was clad in only a pair of cut-off blue jeans, claims he drifted ashore after escaping in a lifeboat from a Japanese whaling ship. He is currently receiving medical treatment at Mount Zion. Authorities have not disclosed further information.

Meanwhile, as news of his alleged reappearance spreads, dozens of Halifax's fans have gathered outside the hospital to cheer the long-lost adventurer's miraculous survival and belated homecoming. Among them is the Mexican painter Diego Rivera, who has arrived in San Francisco to paint a mural at the Treasure Island fair this spring. "If anybody can survive a shipwreck and float his way home, it's Ricardo. I've seen him swim the Panama Canal like it was a heated pool." Rivera said he's confident the man is the authentic Halifax. "I can't wait to give him a bear hug and buy him a drink."

To: The Dicky Halifax Junior Adventurers Club
From: Dicky Halifax
Saved by My Loyal Readers

Springtime 1940

Dear boys,

I left you with a real cliffhanger there, huh? On the verge of calling it quits and filling my lungs with bay water. I bet you thought your man Dick was a goner.

And so I would have been, but as I took my first step out into the frigid tide, I heard a voice. At first I thought it was a voice whispering that it was time to go find Wesley. But then a second voice chimed in.

"Look, that dumb son of a bitch is about to go for a swim."

"No, you blockhead, he's about to off hisself! He's got rocks in his pants. Look!"

They were shouting to each other in stage whispers.

In the presence of others, I suddenly felt embarrassed, and my moment of dire resolution passed.

It wasn't the first time I'd sensed another presence out there on the island, skulking around the Gayway in the dead of night. During my first month there, I had seen a lone figure through a crack in the barn. No doubt one of the Black Dragon hatchet men or Bund assassins that my doctors had threatened me with. I watched as he poked around the ranch and even heard him rattle my doors while I lay there stone still, not daring to breathe until the specter gave up and returned to the place in my imagination where he'd taken up permanent residence.

Now, startled out of my desperate act, I turned to look for the voices and saw two squat forms up on the Gayway.

"He's spotted us," cried the voice. "Quick, let's scram!"

They ran and so did I—I thought in opposite directions—but as I scrambled over the rocks and rounded the corner back to the barn, I was knocked ass over teakettle. I scrambled to my feet, ready to fight, thinking I was likely a goner but at least I'd get in a few good licks. So imagine my surprise when I saw before me not a Black Dragon hatchet man or some ice-eyed killer from the Bloodlands of Europe but two little plug-ugly pip-squeaks, each no more than four and a half feet tall and with cheeks still plump with breast milk.

The funny sight of them, along with me all keyed up from nearly having necked with the grim reaper, made me giggle. "You boys must be in one fine hell of a hurry," I said. "In this dim light, going at that speed, I mistook you for a pair of bowling balls."

"Guess that makes you the pin, Pops!" said one of the boys, as he stomped on my foot, then yanked his compadre by the collar. "Quick, Slop, run! Don't let the creep catchya!"

But the boy addressed as Slop remained rooted where he stood, staring at me, mesmerized.

"C'mon, Slop!" his partner shouted. "I said scram!"

But Slop, nonplussed, continued to stare.

I was starting to feel self-conscious, assuming he was entranced by my hideousness, when suddenly he said, "You're Dicky Halifax."

I was thunderstruck. "What did you say, young man?"

"You're Dicky Halifax. Stinker, lookit, it's Dicky Halifax."

"You blockhead," said Stinker, the one who'd been anxious to skedaddle. "Dicky Halifax is a pile of shark turds at the bottom of the ocean by now."

"Nope. Just look at him."

Both of them gave me a thorough eyeballing. "Now pretend all those nasty spots and freckles on his skin weren't there and it was fresh as a May field. And that he still had eyebrows and that his eyes were a brighter blue and not caked with yellow gunk like a dirty piss trough and that his lashes weren't all white and ghostly like cobwebs. And that he still had a full head of hair instead of that nasty little rattail coiled around the top like some greasy burner on the stove."

"Alright, young fella," I said. "I think he gets the idea. But hats off to your facility with simile."

"Gee, now that you mention it, Slop," said the other boy, "he does kinda look like Dicky. Say, mister, is you or isn't you Dicky Halifax?"

"He is, Stinker. I'll stake my shoe rag on it."

"Well, mister, is you or isn't you?"

"I . . . I . . . I . . ." But I couldn't face it. I was too ashamed. Too far gone. "I'm afraid you boys have me mistaken for someone else. I'm just a weak-sister hobo trying to catch a few winks in this barn."

"See, Slop, I told you. Dicky Halifax is deader'n a doornail. This guy's just some ugly old bum."

I saw the disappointment break across young Slop's face, and it almost killed me. He turned, shoulders hunched, and began to shuffle off behind his friend.

Then suddenly he looked back and said, "You said 'weak sister.'"

"So, what of it?"

"You know who says 'weak sister' more than anybody?"

"Who?"

"Dicky Halifax."

"Well," I said, "he can't be the only one."

Now he narrowed his little plug-ugly eyes at me and stomped back to the barn where I was standing.

"Have you ever flown in an open-cockpit airplane?"

"Well, sure."

"Did you ever get caught sneaking into Mecca while dressed like a Mussulman?"

"As a matter of fact, I did."

"Did you once lose your underpants to a hungry fox while swimming in Lake Titicaca?"

"Guilty as charged."

"Did you ever outrun a boatload of Malagasy pirates by posing as a French naval captain and commandeering a gunboat?"

"I'd be lying if I denied it."

"Did you and Diego Rivera once play handball with an effigy of Roderick's head at the ruins of the royal handball court in Chichén Itzá?"

I couldn't take it any longer. I'd been shaking like a leaf the whole time this little squirt was asking his questions. Each one revealed him to be an ever more adept reader of the Halifax oeuvre while at the same time calling me back to myself, drilling through the obscuring layers of my doctors' therapies and my own deep funk. At the mention of Roderick's head, I dropped to my knees and started leaking tears all over their little hobnailed boots.

Have you ever seen a picture of St. Sebastian, boys, torso rippling and pierced by arrows, in the throes of an anguish so exquisite it turns to ecstasy? Well, that's how I felt when this little inquisitor put the screws to me: utterly transfixed.

"You got me pegged, my sweet, dear boys," I cried. "Don't believe everything you read in the papers. Your man Dick is alive!"

"What's with all the eye juice, Dicky?" said the one called Stinker, who was a bit of a hard case.

"Oh," I sobbed, "just an ocular condition I picked up overseas."

"Dicky," said the one called Slop, "me and Stinker here are your biggest fans. We shined shoes six days a week and collected cigarette butts from the sidewalk just to buy a subscription to the Dicky Halifax Junior Adventurers Club and get your letters from the *Soup Dumpling*."

A fresh eruption cascaded down my cheeks. "Bless your heart, boys. That's mighty good of you."

"Yeah, but all we ever got was a couple lousy letters before you set sail from Hong Kong. We weren't too sore about it, on account of thinking you was dead and all. But now that you're alive, we feel kinda gypped."

"I've been writing you the whole time, boys, honest, I have. It's just that after the *Soup Dumpling* went down in the typhoon, I had a hell of a time getting the mimeograph machine to work. And the postal logistics posed an even hairier problem."

"Gee, Dicky," said Slop, who was the sweeter of the two, "your ship really went down in a typhoon? Tell us about it, won't ya?"

And so, boys, I spent the whole night telling these in-the-flesh Junior

Adventurers about the harrowing ordeal I've been chronicling for all of you. If Sally had helped me up the first couple of steps from rock-bottom insanity, it was these salt-of-the-earth San Francisco shoeshine boys, Slop and Stinker Sinclair, who dragged me the rest of the way.

The Sinclair boys, I learned over the course of our retreat, were both eleven years old, and although they resembled each other like brothers, almost twins, they were cousins. These bucktoothed, round-headed little plug-ugly look-alikes were, like your man Dick, expert at getting themselves into, then out of, tight scrapes. Their fathers—the Sienkiewicz brothers from somewhere beyond the pale who, at Ellis Island, had been rechristened Sinclair—had come out west, where they made a mint in the coffee business before they went broke in the crash and both blew their brains out. Now their mothers, orphan sisters from a bogswater in Ireland, ran a boardinghouse in the Mission, but they were always at each other's throats, hurling accusations of nefarious smells and unholy vapors while they laundered bachelors' soiled sheets and tyrannized their daughters. This left the Sinclair boys, Arlo and Charlie, who'd been rechristened by the Market Street shoe-shining community as Stinker and Slop, free to spend their days either sweatin' at the shoe box and earning a few dimes or laying off and getting into mischief.

The latter is what brought them to the darkened fairgrounds, specifically the Nude Ranch. "We was hoping to see one of them nekked ladies, Dicky," said Slop.

"But can't you see the fair's closed, boys?"

"Yeah, sure, that's why we came. We couldn't get in when it was open. We tried sneaking in six ways to Sunday, but every time that big galoot would catch us and throw us out on our ear. We thought maybe the nekked ladies was living in the barn in the offseason."

"No, boys, I'm afraid they've all gone home to rest. I've seen nary an areola all winter."

"Aw, nuts," said Slop.

"Say, Dicky," said Stinker, "why are you living here in the nekked ladies' barn anyway?"

"I've been keeping incognito and convalescing."

The boys looked at me blankly, like I had just spoken in Portuguese. It made me miss Nacho, who, even as a non-native speaker, had an ample vocabulary. "It means I've been lying low, boys."

"You mean you're hiding out? Like a bandit? Or a pirate?"

"Something like that. In fact, I was even after some hidden treasure."

"Treasure? Did you hear that, Slop? Dicky's after some buried loot."

"Is that why you've come here to Treasure Island, Dicky?"

"Well, gee, I guess so. I hadn't put that together, but you're right, Slop. I guess that makes me a regular Ben Gunn—ragged, marooned, and half off my rocker. Only it seems my treasure's gone missing."

"Is it a chest of doubloons like Captain Flint buried?"

"Yeah, do you know where it's buried, Dicky?"

"Yeah, Dicky, can we help you dig it up?"

"Yeah, and get a little cut for ourselves?"

"Now, now, boys," I said, heading off their barrage. "This treasure's a little different. It's not buried so much as hiding, and rather than Old Flint's gold coins, it's a set of teeny tiny photographs."

"Is it pictures of nekked ladies?" asked Slop.

"You boys got a real dose of the randy, huh? But, no, it's not naked ladies. Just some important documents."

At the sound of the word "documents," both boys nearly fell asleep.

"Well, Slop, we better scram," said Stinker with a yawn. "If that nob finds his boat gone in the morning, he'll report her stolen, and then we're toast."

"You boys stole a boat?" I asked.

"Nah, just borrowed it. The Fort Mason marina's chock-full of 'em at night."

"Say, you boys got sand. Do you know how to pilot a skiff in the open water?"

"Sure, we done it plenty of times. O'Malley the Tattooed Jew taught us. He even took us out all the way to the Farallons once."

"Yeah, but he got so blotto on the way out, we had to sail back without any help."

"That's fine, boys. Just fine. Sounds like I could have used you on the voyage of the *Soup Dumpling*."

"Gee, Dicky, and how! That would've been a hoot. We would have made sure you never sank."

"Yeah, Dicky, if you had us with you, that typhoon would have turned tail and run back to China where it came from."

And that's when I got the glimmer of an idea.

These Junior Adventurers had awoken something in me, rescued some hidden ember within. That voice from my childhood sickbed, the one that spoke with an oracular authority, now cleared its throat and repeated what Sally had said—that no one but me owned Dicky Halifax and that there was only one way forward: chin up and tits out.

No matter what anyone tells you, boys, it's always best to be yourself. Let the world know who you are and dare them to do their worst. And me, well, I'd had enough of skulking around incognito, living in a dark barn on an abandoned island, looking like some luckless wight called Richard Wagner, and crying about a few lousy microdots. Suddenly I saw the path unfold before my eyes, the path that was always available to me and that only I could claim.

"Say, fellas," I said to my new juvenile-delinquent sidekicks, "how would you like to take a top-secret Junior Adventurers voyage with Captain Richard J. Halifax?"

"Whoopla!" they crowed in unison. "When do we leave?"

"First thing tomorrow, boys. It's time your man Dick washed ashore."

And so began the next phase of my adventure. I'll tell you all about it soon!

Yours,
Dicky

27

HILDEGARD RAUCH

I really had washed my hands of you. The whole winter I refused to address a word to you, refused to come look at you untroubled in your sleep. I genuinely worried that if I did come, I just might take the pillow from behind your head and suffocate you. Now, staring at you in your saintly repose, considering what you did, what you made me party to, the thought of smothering you still crosses my mind.

But, then, that would be finishing what you intended. And I don't feel like giving you the satisfaction. Besides, I can't go to jail, not yet—I have to paint in the spring fair alongside Diego Rivera.

The organizers have taken a page from Sally Bent's Nude Ranch and invited me to be a part of the Art in Action exhibition, where the public will watch us as we work. A window into the artistic process, as the curator puts it. More like a peephole. Instead of exhibiting our art, we ourselves now have to become exhibitionists. Of course I said yes.

I'm sure you're jealous—which is precisely why I'm telling you. Everything I've heard about Rivera leads me to think I should wear lock-buckled overalls as a security measure, though I'll be offended if he doesn't at least make a pass.

I've also agreed, reluctantly, to be Father's interpreter when he comes to speak at the fair's opening ceremony in May. Of course he's delighted, because it means I'm one step closer to becoming his amanuensis. Which, thanks to that repulsive diary page I read, is a more sickening prospect than ever.

Ever since I put my eye to that microscope, I've told myself a thousand times that those words were a lie. I know they are. But, while I know the scenes there are false, did Father really write them? Yes, the handwriting looked like his, but that could be forged. And the language? Well, it was certainly not the signature prose of Theodor Rauch. Then again, Father's style is the result of extremely slow contemplation and revision, which is hardly how one would write a private diary. What if it was some appalling fictional world he had concocted for his own pleasure? What if his civilized aplomb was a kind of counter-posture, a moral cork that kept those terrible desires from bursting out? So, what of it? It was a private diary, after all, not meant for my or anyone else's eyes, and he had every right to express private thoughts in private, no matter how dark and antisocial, without expecting that his son should take possession of it or that his daughter should ever read it.

There is only one person to blame for that, and that person is you.

The only person I hate more than you right now is myself, because only someone as stupid as me could have followed your breadcrumb trail of madness and then fallen right into the trap of Walter and Nadia (they are also candidates vying for the Hilde's Most Hated List).

They're spies and thieves. There is no other conclusion to draw. They stole the papers with the microdots that night in the photography lab and left me with counterfeits, expecting me to burn them and remain none the wiser.

Walter thought he had put the whole thing over on me. He telephoned the morning after to check on me and asked if I'd burned the papers. I lied and said yes. I had been so stunned at his betrayal that in the immediate aftermath I was too shocked to confront him or speak in more than monosyllables.

"That's good, Hilde. Your brother's mess is finally out of your hair now. Listen, are you sure you're alright?"

"Yes. Fine." It was like I was on the other side of the room, watching myself speak.

"Well, then, I'll see you on campus next week—I have to go down to Los Angeles tomorrow to hold the donors' hands. I tell you, Hilde, stay out of the museum world. It's all hind-licking and telling old women how stunning they still look so they'll add another zero to the check."

"Yes. Fine." I had become an automaton. Walter's attempt at our former playful banter now fell dead in the chasm between us.

"Goodbye, then, Hilde."

That was the last I spoke with him. He was not on campus the following week or the week after that. The chair of the department said he had been asked to stay on at the Fisher Museum in L.A. to consult full-time for the spring and that he would be taking a temporary leave from Mills. But when I called the University of Southern California and asked the secretary of the art department for the extension of Walter Seidler, I was told the same: Dr. Seidler had taken a temporary leave.

No one answered the Seidlers' telephone in Berkeley either. I thought about going over there but then realized it was useless. Whatever Walter had done with those documents was already done.

I was so furious—with you, with Walter and his witch Nadia, with myself—there was nothing to do but paint. In fact, the only reason I'm able to look at you now is that I've exorcised the worst of my rage in a frenzy of work. Thankfully, Mother and Father went east for the holidays, including a New Year's Eve party at the White House, so there was no need to pretend strep throat or influenza, as I couldn't bear the thought of facing them. Instead, for a full month while school was in recess, I saw no one—no students, no colleagues, no family, no friends, no hospital visits. My only interactions were with the grocery clerks who handed me the food, coffee, and cigarettes that kept me alive. I was, for the first time in a long time, well and truly alone. Which, it turns out, was precisely what I needed. All my anxiety and anger crystallized into a ruthless sense of purpose.

I painted and I brooded. I heard the New Year's celebrations outside my window and wondered at the strangeness of the tallied years. When scrutinized, a year—like a word repeated ad nauseam—quickly becomes absurd. One thousand nine hundred and forty: a unit of time measured in reference to the birth and subsequent execution of one single stubborn Jew. A man born, we are told, so that he could be murdered and the rest of humanity left to mark the time until his return. Is not each passing year an homage to this original senseless act of killing? Nevertheless, people still kiss and cheer, still wear pointy hats and drink champagne.

When classes resumed at the end of January, I continued to paint, rising at dawn to work for a few hours before school and then again in the evenings. I was a furnace fired on caffeine, nicotine, and turpentine. Sleep became the brief interval in which I worked out problems of composition and color in my unconscious mind, and when I lifted my brush first thing in the morning, I was immersed. I lost myself in the rhythm and textures of my contracted world, narrow as an anchorite's cell yet infinitely capacious. And as the images took shape on canvas, they expressed a sense of anguish I never could have spoken aloud.

By the end of March I could sense I was almost finished with them. The tension within me loosened ever so perceptibly. I even began thinking about taking a trip to Death Valley to see the wildflowers, which had come late this year.

Then one evening last week I arrived home after a long day that found me more irritable than usual. As was my habit, I turned on the six o'clock CBS news service and listened to Murrow's report from London and Shirer's from Berlin while I ate a paltry dinner and smoked. After hearing about Denmark's swift surrender and Norway's doomed fight, I went back to mixing my paints, leaving the radio on in the hope that Burns and Allen would lift my mood.

I was in the act of making skin tone—folding in a streak of vermilion to the burnt ochre and titanium white—and waiting for George to start flirting with Gracie when another news bulletin interrupted: Richard Halifax was alive, found on some rocks just off the coast of San Francisco.

I looked down at my palette knife trembling with twin flesh, and I knew that your predicament was not yet through with me, nor I with it.

Which is why I've come here. Richard Halifax is two floors above you, and despite what I told myself when I left this morning, I wasn't heartless enough to ride the elevator past your room without coming to look at your stupid, silent face. But now it's time I talk to someone who can give me some answers.

28

SIMON FAULK

I spent the winter searching for my white whale, but I searched in vain. He had breached for a moment, only to disappear back into the deep. But if he was there—and some part of me knew he was—eventually he'd have to surface.

After Marie's story last fall, I went to question Sally Bent, but she was a cool customer and gave me nothing. She said crazy men wandered into the Music Box all the time. She promised to keep an eye out for the man I was looking for, then sultrily blew smoke in my face and had her enormous bouncer see me out. I used Marie, now on Sally's payroll, as my eyes and ears at the Music Box, while I ventured out several times to the shuttered fairgrounds on Treasure Island. But all I'd found there were a couple of young boys, catching toads and setting off firecrackers beneath them, and they scurried off at the sight of me.

I felt everything slipping away. Wiedemann refused to meet again unless defection was granted. And my irritating twin specters—the mystery agent Kokosnuss aka Richard Wagner, and Richard Halifax, an irrational connection based on nothing more than a passing association in my brain—haunted me. The more time that passed, the more I thought I was mad to think such a thing.

There were only two bright spots that winter. The first had been the black-bag job of recovering the Rauch diary from the office of *Free Masses*. I'd followed Wiedemann's tip, not because I cared about protecting Theodor Rauch from humiliation, deserved or not, but because stopping a plot to ruin the most illustrious voice in the fight against Hitler would certainly aid my work here and increase my currency with London.

The *Free Masses* office was in a run-down neighborhood south of Market Street. I went in the middle of the night and brought O'Malley with me as a lookout. He managed to defuse an argument between two vagrants and sent them across the street to fetch a bottle from the Hotel Utah, while I climbed the fire escape and elbowed my way into a second-floor window. Inside, my torch illuminated a drab office with swollen manila folders stacked to the ceiling and peeling portraits of the mandated idols—Marx, Stalin, and an ugly bloke with a chinstrap beard who might have been Abraham Lincoln. Given Wiedemann's cagey answers in the cinema, it was unclear what his role had been in stealing this diary, other than some sort of joint operation between his people and the Soviets. But, sure enough, his intelligence had come through again, and in the darkroom I found hanging on clothespins several pages of Theodor Rauch's dirty laundry. Very dirty indeed.

The Rauch job was the only bit of real action I'd had in years, and it had given me an old taste of adventure that made me nostalgic for my younger self. It was all slipping away. *Then the hour, irrevocable*—a phrase from a novel that years later still chimed in my brain. I was already older than my parents were when the hour had tolled for them. There must be something to do, I thought. Some achievement that could stanch the bleeding of time.

I suppose I should have handed the diary over to London right away, but I decided to sit on it, saving it for the right moment when I might broach the prospect of Wiedemann's defection again. It was December, and the memory of Venlo was still too fresh; the gates were locked shut. But they couldn't ignore the man's value—or my own—forever. Eventually, they would get over their gun-shyness and reconsider. Needless to say, I was wrong.

My other sunny moment was stamping that miserable pimp Claude's passport as null and void. It was simple. I contrived to have O'Malley's stevedores engage him in a tavern brawl and get him tossed in jail for the night, whereupon his expired visa was discovered and the nasty maître d', freshly beaten to a pulp, was deported back to his rock in the channel.

I did this kindness for Marie out of genuine sympathy, not calculation. But she had, perhaps out of gratitude or courtesy, begun showing her appreciation according to the arts of her trade. And pleasurable though these caresses were, they also made me feel sadder and lonelier afterward. I felt I should either start paying her or fall in love with her, as I had done so foolishly with Anya. But love was not something I knew how to will on command. It was either waiting around the corner for you, ready to gut you, or, as was more often the case, it wasn't.

I was just settling into what seemed a long gray depression, born along by a river of drink, when I heard the news: Richard Halifax had returned. Found on the Farallon Islands, not thirty miles from San Francisco.

It was like a sign from an otherwise mute universe, an uncanny omen. I knew then that my theory had to be true, but I wanted Fritz Wiedemann to confirm it.

I found the Nazi consul at Alfred's, entertaining a table of Germans beneath a lurid painting of a matador. I watched them from the corner of the bar, hiding behind an oversized gimlet. They seemed to be having a jolly good time, with ten-ounce martinis, twenty-ounce rib eyes, and a magnum of Veuve Clicquot.

My attempt to open a path for Wiedemann's defection with London had just fallen flat again, this time definitively. I thought perhaps enough had changed by April—a new "C" at the head of the Service, Hitler's invasion of Norway, and surely France and England soon to follow—that the offer might be considered by the Foreign Office in a new light. So I made one more futile stab and solicited my uncle's help. We were met with a swift and resounding "no." And just in case there was any equivocation, a message from Cowgill reminded me: *You've been told before to stay away from Wiedemann—now leave it alone!*

When the *Reichskonsul* excused himself to go to the lavatory downstairs, I waited a minute, then followed after and sidled up beside him at the urinal.

He spoke without turning his head or so much as his eyes to me. "I figured after three of those sizable cocktails you'd like to relieve yourself, Herr Faulk. Thought I'd do you the favor of taking the lead."

"Very considerate," I said. "Though I was rather enjoying your merry evening from afar. Any special occasion?"

"A going-away party, in fact. Two chemical engineers and their wives, relocating to Japan from Mexico."

"Taking anything interesting with them? Souvenirs from the New World?"

"Far be it from me to know. Though even if I did know, Herr Faulk, I don't see what business I would have telling you. After all, you—what is the phrase the American kids use? Ah, yes—stood me up."

"And yet you're still here in San Francisco, Consul. What was all that talk last fall about the ax falling at any moment, Ribbentrop on a rampage and out for your head?"

"It's all true. It's just that things are moving slower now with the war. But, mark my words, I'll be recalled before the year's out—perhaps sooner, since yesterday I forgot to send birthday greetings to the führer. Which in Hitler's inner circle is tantamount to rebellion."

"Does that mean your offer still stands?" I asked.

"I was led to believe my offer held no interest for your people."

He was not wrong. Nobody was interested in Fritz Wiedemann's defection. It was not happening, it would not happen. All I wanted from the consul that night was an answer to a single maddening question. So I told him, "On the contrary, Herr Wiedemann, your offer interests us enormously. But the war makes things slow on our end too. There's just one thing I need to know first."

"Oh no, not this tired old tune. I told you—not a word more until I'm given a concrete guarantee."

"It's a simple yes or no. If you tell me this, you can be holding a British passport and be on a ship to Vancouver by next week."

Wiedemann shook himself vigorously, then zipped his fly. "I'm listening."

"Your agent. The strange-looking one who came ashore last October by submarine under the alias Richard Wagner? It's Richard Halifax, isn't it?"

Wiedemann smiled. "Who?"

"Richard Halifax—the missing writer who just washed up on the Farallon Islands. He's bloody Kokosnuss, isn't he?"

Wiedemann giggled at the washbasin. "I'm sorry, that name makes me chuckle every time I hear it. But I'm afraid I haven't the slightest idea who you're talking about, Herr Faulk."

The next day I stumbled into the Tadich Grill, where Cliff Hader was in the corner booth, scowling at me over his lemonade. "Lose your razor, Faulk, or are you infiltrating the dockworkers' union?"

The waiter approached and I ordered a martini and the Dover sole. The food was certainly better at the Tadich, but whatever semblance of *Gemütlichkeit* we'd shown each other at our earlier beer-hall meetings had by spring been worn down to a paper-thin veneer masking mutual contempt.

"What's the news with Richard Halifax?" I asked once the waiter had left. Hader was conducting the inquest on Halifax's reappearance, to determine whether this man was in fact the same one who had been ruled dead. I hadn't slept since learning he'd washed ashore.

"You've really got your shorts in a twist over this, huh?"

"It's him, isn't it?"

"Look, Faulk, as of now, technically, it's inconclusive. The dental records don't quite match, but they're old, and Halifax said he got a bridge put in while he was in Hong Kong. Sally Bent swore in her interview that the guy's a fraud and that the real Halifax is dead, but then again, she has every reason to say so since she's the primary beneficiary on his life insurance. His parents are too frail to travel, and the mother's senile, but the father does believe the photo we sent is that of his son. And he confirms the birthmark on his waist and the two congenital hammertoes on his feet. Halifax's agent, Fred Feakins, also says he's confident it's him. He put a number of questions to him about their past, which Halifax answered satisfactorily. Same goes for Diego Rivera, even though he's a lying bolshie troublemaker."

"And what do you think?" I asked.

"I'd say it's him, no question. The doctors say his body's been through hell—starved, broken, poisoned by the sun. Fits with the story he told about getting picked up by a Jap whaler, then, somewhere near the Aleutians, cutting loose in a lifeboat and drifting all the way here. Damn lucky, if you ask me. And tough as nails too. I know you

Brits don't go in much for compliments, but you gotta hand it to the guy. He's got a real pair on him—and, lucky for him, they float."

"It's him, Hader. He's Kokosnuss."

"He's what?"

I was going to kill myself if I had to say that name again. "The foreign agent who came to shore by submarine last fall. It's Halifax."

"Oh Christ. This theory again?"

"Just listen. One, in October of last year a strange-looking man— nearly bald, bad skin, shiny teeth, pronounced limp—is spotted coming to shore on Stinson Beach from a submarine breached near the coast. Two, my source within the German consulate confirms that an agent matching this description came to shore in precisely this manner, under the alias Richard Wagner. Three, in November someone who looks just like this man is spotted by one of my informants at Sally Bent's theater, the Music Box. Four, just a few days ago, Richard Halifax, having disappeared in the Pacific last spring, now mysteriously bobs to the surface—where of all places?—on the Farallon Islands, a stone's throw from the city. And, five, what does Richard Halifax look like? According to the papers, an utter wreck—nearly bald, permanently damaged skin, with a pronounced limp, and, as you've just confirmed, with new teeth. Now, doesn't that strike you as a bit more than a coincidence?"

"It strikes me as a pile of horseshit—you got a crabber telling a waterfront drunk about a nighttime submarine sighting and a dance-hall whore seeing a Tenderloin street bum and an anonymous source in the German consulate that you still won't reveal. Sounds like all the other 'tips' the Bureau gets about who killed the Lindbergh baby or where Amelia Earhart is living. Meanwhile, you're fully loaded by lunchtime, smell like a brothel, and with that five o'clock shadow, you look like you could work at the wop butcher shop."

"*Bauco de un American, te me par un petoeo del me buso del cueo,*" I replied in the colorful Venetian of my childhood.

"What the hell's that?"

"Just an old proverb from my mother's side. It means, 'God bless the FBI. It's such a delight working with them, but need I remind them that I don't work *for* them?'"

"You really are a prick, aren't you, Faulk? Look, if this source of yours at the German consulate really exists—though, since you refuse to share his name with us, I'm beginning to think he's a DT hallucination of yours—why doesn't he just confirm your crackpot theory that Halifax is a secret agent from the deep?"

I cursed Fritz Wiedemann and the dead end he'd become. I felt my rage—toward Wiedemann, toward Hader, toward Halifax, toward all the useless twats in London—coming to a boil. I knew I was in danger of doing something rash and forced my mind to focus on the patterned wallpaper.

It was a trick I learned from my old tutor Corvo, and one I've used to calm myself whenever I become distraught. He called it "the line therapy"—demonstrated when, during the course of his impromptu lectures, Corvo digressed into opaque matters concerning his life and those who had wronged him, which seemed to include all of the London literary establishment, the Roman Catholic Church, and the cursed city of Aberdeen. Recalling these bitter memories, he would grow profoundly agitated, his face a deeper crimson than his signet ring. Then, becoming aware of his disturbed state, as confirmed by the startled looks of his young companions, he would administer the line therapy. It consisted simply of following the lines of any ornamental motif, which could be performed just about anywhere one looked in the city, until a state of equanimity was attained. "You will find, *raggazi*," the baron told us, "that lines quiet the mind. If you travel them patiently, you will free yourself from preconceived forms and come to know that everything in this curved world is line and that all lines eventually converge. That is the secret to drawing well, and it is also the secret to a life free from disturbance."

The waiter arrived with the fish and I, having regained my calm, ordered another martini.

"I'd like to interview Halifax," I said.

"On what grounds?"

"I met the man several times in Bangkok last year. I can help confirm if it's him."

"He's still in the hospital recovering—the doctors say we have to limit his visitors."

"Yes, well, I'm not exactly asking your permission, and if you refuse, I will have Ambassador Lothian lodge a formal complaint for obstructing our inquiry."

Hader gave me a confused look, which is what I was hoping for. "Inquiry? How is Richard Halifax's reappearance a matter of British diplomatic concern?"

"How?" I said. "Oh, let me count the ways. Well, for starters, his unfortunate ship the *Soup Dumpling* sailed from the British port of Hong Kong, and it just so happened to be carrying British citizens aboard. Among them: Halifax's captain, Pengelly, who was injured early in the voyage before returning to Hong Kong and is filing a civil suit against him for breach of contract."

"But—"

I held my finger to Hader's objection, as I had, for maximum irritation, saved the real evidence for last. "But most important: One of the missing crew, presumed dead—a university student named Peter Stephens, of Milton, Massachusetts, formerly enrolled at Dartmouth—just happens to be the son of an Englishwoman, and it appears young Stephens himself was born in Rhodesia, which means that he, too, is a British citizen. Which means, given Halifax's miraculous survival, a wrongful-death lawsuit is surely in the offing. So, yes, rest assured, I *will* be speaking to Richard Halifax. Just as soon as the nurses say he's able."

Hader grumbled into his flounder. "Better get a handle on the booze, Faulk. One of these days you're gonna fall on your face."

Soon thereafter I received a call from O'Malley, saying I'd better come round for a pint, or better a pail, as he had quite a whopper of a tale to relate and it would take plenty of liquid to swallow it.

I arrived at dusk and O'Malley was already three pails deep, regaling the rest of the bar with a rumor about an IRA man who'd gone off to Spain to fight fascists and never come home. "According to Seamus, who works in a brewery in Buffalo, Frank Pike is living in a cabin on the banks of Lake Erie and driving an ice truck. 'Hand to God,' he says. And that means something, mind you, coming from Seamus. He spent three years in the priesthood. Ah, Mr. Fox," he said, addressing me. "Pull up a stool and we'll fill you a pail."

"Why don't we go for a walk instead," I said. It was my best chance of keeping the man some semblance of sober.

"Oh, fine. He's a great one for strolling, this one," said O'Malley to his bar mates, in a stage whisper. "Fears sitting on account of his hemorrhoids."

We walked along the piers, awash in shouts and nets as the first of the fishing boats went out for the night. O'Malley threw his long tattered scarf around his neck in a flourish, accepted a cigarette, and told me about a pair of young acquaintances of his who'd recently given him, as he put it, "a giraffe of a tale. But one I thought I'd better share. For, despite the paltering sound of it, Mr. Fox, it bears a startling conformity to certain particulars."

"Very well, then. Let's have it."

"Well, you must first know that the lads in question are shoeshine boys. They spend their days in the street, not the schoolhouse. Atop that, they're half orphans, God bless 'em, which is just to say that they have a thick feral streak in them; one may go so far as to call it a streak of criminality. Nothing heinous, mind, but the boys have a rather liberal regard for laws concerning private property and civic ordinances and the like."

"They're thieves, then?"

"On occasion, but that's missing the point. You see, Mr. Fox, I knew their fathers, may they rest in eternal peace, and I saw the path their families set out for them, and then I witnessed how, in the wake of such loss, that path went crooked. I have no doubt that had not tragedy befallen them at such a tender age, they'd now be good little altar boys at St. Ignatius or studying for their Bar Mitzvah at Temple Emanu-El. As a result, I see something of myself in the lads and have taken it as my duty to oversee their moral education, as it were. I taught them how to draw funny faces and play dice, how to throw a proper punch and take one on the chin, and schooled them on which peelers were mean and crooked and, in the event of retreat, which alleys were dead ends. I also instructed them in the art of fishing and sailing, this being one of the finest natural bays in all the world."

"I'm sure their fathers are looking proudly upon your efforts, Mr. O'Malley. Now, how exactly does this pertain to my concerns?"

"I was just getting to that, Mr. Fox. You see, given the aforementioned skills and proclivities, the Sinclair boys have developed a habit of piloting boats that don't belong to them. And recently they've taken to boasting that they borrowed a vessel for a trip out to the Farallon Islands with a famous passenger aboard."

"Wait, you don't mean . . . ?" I couldn't articulate where my mind was leading me.

"They claim they were the ones who deposited Richard Halifax ashore there. Left him on the island, as per his request."

"Where did they meet him? When? Tell me everything."

"They say they found him hiding out on Treasure Island at the end of March. Filling his pockets with stones, he was. Claim they saved his life, and nearly at the cost of their own. You see, on the return voyage the lads washed ashore down by Fort Funston, caught in rough seas with a tangled sail. They were a bit shaken and not much inclined to speak about it at first. But once the papers told of Halifax's miraculous survival and rescue, well, the boys felt sore at being left out. Started saying they knew Dicky Halifax was alive before anyone else did."

I knew it all along. And yet I was dumbstruck. To think those times I wandered Treasure Island, shuttered in winter, he really was there, hiding in the shadows.

"I know it seems like the kind of spoof young boys love to tell," said O'Malley, "but, well, the way they described Halifax sounded just about the size of your mystery man. Limping with a cane, mottled face, wojus little rattail of a toupee, all that. Figured I'd pass it on. Of course, they'll deny every word of it if anyone comes questioning them."

"Did they say where on Treasure Island they found Halifax?"

"As a matter of fact, they showed me a pair of torn ladies' undergarments that have become their prize possession. Said it came straight from a magical place called the Nude Ranch."

That night, with an enraged sense of purpose, I stomped up the steps of the Music Box, past the poster of the Treasure Island pleasure cruises, and into the office of Sally Bent.

She sat sidesaddle on her desk, smoking.

"You've been lying to me, Miss Bent."

"How the hell did you get past Tater?" she asked.

"I started a fire in the trash can outside your building."

"Well, I might as well offer you a drink till he comes back and throws you out."

She melted off the desk and poured us each two fingers of rye.

"How long have you known he's alive?"

"Who?"

"Don't play cute, Miss Bent."

She gave me my drink. "I do better with names, Mr. . . . what was it again?"

"Fox. How long have you known Richard Halifax is alive?"

"Oh, you're still hung up on that? Like I told the Bureau guy just the other day, I don't buy that phony they found in the Farallons." She sat back on her desk with her legs poised like pistons. "As far as I'm concerned, Dick Halifax is dead."

"You'd like to think so, wouldn't you? I do imagine it will be painful losing that insurance money. Now, let's try again. When did you start hiding him on Treasure Island?"

"Treasure Island? Where'd you get that idea?"

"From the two witnesses who met him there, right on the premises of a certain Nude Ranch with your name on the sign."

She drank in silence.

"Miss Bent, you've already perjured yourself to the FBI. If you force my hand and I turn these matters over to them, you'll likely go to prison. Not to mention the mountain of unwanted scrutiny you'll bring down on your friend Richard Halifax. If your intention is to protect him, then being honest with me is your best option."

"Who the hell are you anyway and what do you want with him?"

"I told you—I work for an international insurance firm, and I want only a full accounting. But I can and will cooperate with the FBI if need be. On the other hand," I said, pulling out a roll of bills, "I have five hundred dollars for anyone who can provide accurate information."

She eyed the money, returned to the sideboard, and refilled her glass. She drank with her back to me, then topped it up again. "Something's wrong with Richard. He's got a screw loose."

"When did he first come to you?"

"Last November. Just after the fair had closed."

"Why?"

"Why? Because he was completely out of his head—shaking and talking nonsense."

"Why did he come to you specifically?"

"He said I was the only one he could turn to for help."

"You've known each other a long time?"

"Since we were kids."

"And he didn't want anything in particular from you?"

"I told you, Richard needed help—food, shelter, a friend. He was a total wreck."

"Why did you lie to the FBI when they questioned you?"

"What was I gonna say? Who, Dick Halifax? Yeah, that's him, and, oh, guess what, he's been hiding in my barn all winter?"

"Did he say why he had come back in secret? Surely you must have asked him."

"He couldn't bear to talk about it. All he said was that he was no longer in control of himself, that it wasn't safe to be in public. He said people wanted him dead."

"Who wanted him dead?"

"I don't know. He said everyone—Germans, Japanese, maybe Russians too."

"Why did they want to kill him?"

"I'm telling you, he's not well."

"Did he ever say anything about how he got here? Who sent him back? Who he was working for? Anything like that?"

"No, he wouldn't talk about it. But someone must've brought him back from the ocean."

"I want you to tell me everything, Miss Bent, from the moment you encountered him to the last time you saw him."

She tipped back the rest of her whiskey, then told me how he came to her last fall.

"Once I got over my shock, I tried to ask him what the hell happened.

But he wasn't fit to answer. He said the ocean was a charnel house, that only a sick son of a bitch would call it the Pacific. I mean, I'd seen Dick down before, he had his spells of doubt and melancholy, but the man before me was an abused animal.

"The fair had just closed for winter, and no one even knew if it would open again, so I stashed him in the barn. I said that if he kept quiet, no one would disturb him and he could lie low there as long as he liked. I didn't tell him that 'long as he liked' meant either until the fair reopened or until, as I feared would happen first, I had to put him in the booby hatch.

"Every time I visited him and brought more provisions, he pleaded with me not to go. But I still had businesses to run, girls to manage, and the constant juggling of dollars. Finally one day I'd had it, so I just explained to him I wasn't his mother and he wasn't a baby and that I had other things to worry about, including the pile of debt caused by his disappearance.

"That was how I learned Dick named me as the beneficiary on his life insurance," Sally explained. "And it was at his urging that I contacted Lloyd's of London to collect on the claim."

"But he'd have to be dead for that to work," I said. "Does that mean he didn't plan to reclaim his identity?"

"He says he wants to go off and live the quiet life of a hermit, right? That he's through being Dicky Halifax, that foreign agents are after him, and that as soon as he gets his strength back, he's gonna go hole up in a plush cave somewhere like the Count of Monte Cristo and write his magnum opus. The same night he tells me about the insurance policy, he says to me, 'Isn't it funny, Sal, how the course of our life can change with a single piece of paper? That check from Lloyd's will erase all your troubles, and me, well, if I had just gotten my hands on a coupla lousy pieces of paper, I'd have been the toast of the town again.'"

"Why did he want these pieces of paper?" I asked.

"He said they contained secret treasures that would free him from his *giri*."

I recalled that the lift attendant at the Sir Francis Drake had mentioned the same word. "What does that mean?"

"Search me. It was just part of the nonsense he kept repeating. He said if only he could have done something great with his life, then his friends wouldn't have died in vain. But when I asked him to explain, all he said was, 'Don't you see, Sal? My own life is being held hostage from me. And I won't get it back, not until the world knows Daddy Rauch is a kiddie-fiddler and the Japs know how to make a Norton.' Now, how's that for nuts?"

I shot to my feet. "Is it possible he said Nor-den, with a *d*?"

"Yeah, sure, I guess. Why?"

My God, I thought. Could it possibly be true? Not only was Richard Halifax the foreign agent Richard Wagner, but the Norden plans were real too? Had the rum bastard been telling me the truth all along?

"Did he say any more about these papers? What information they contained? What they looked like?"

"No. But there was something else. You see, not long before Dick showed up at my door, a German gal named Hildegard Rauch—daughter of the writer—came round with a letter that Dick wrote me, thinking it might be something important. Something to do with her brother and Dick. I don't really know."

"Did she give you this letter?"

"No, I already had a copy, because Dick had mailed me one. But then when he told me about how his life hung by these slips of paper, well, it got me thinking. Maybe it had to do with that letter."

"You didn't ask him?"

Sally Bent flicked her cigarette into the brass spittoon beside her desk and let out a sigh.

"I see. You didn't tell him about the Rauch girl's questions because you didn't want him to find that letter. Because that would have thrown a wrench in him being dead and you striking it rich."

"Congratulations, Sherlock. You cracked the case."

"I should like to see your copy of that letter."

"I'm telling you it's nothing. It was just an ordinary letter. And a suit bill from Hong Kong."

"All the same, I should like to see your copies of both." I wondered if, despite Sally Bent's silence, Halifax had still found his way to the Rauch girl and those documents. "Just one more question, Miss Bent. What do you think prompted Halifax to resurface?"

"Beats me. All I know is that I came to the ranch at the end of March with some groceries and a bottle of champagne for Dick and me to share. I had just gotten notice that my insurance claim was accepted and the payout would be mailed soon. But when I got there, he was gone, and the wall safe in my dressing room had been emptied.

"I figured he just needed a few hundred bucks to start over somewhere and had set off without saying goodbye. But two weeks later, I saw his name in the papers and I wanted to kill him."

29

HILDEGARD RAUCH

At first, I thought I'd gone into the wrong room. I checked the name on the chart. It said *Halifax, R.*

God, how different he looked. Perhaps, as some alleged, he really was an impostor and the real Halifax still dead. Whoever this man was, it looked like he'd endured centuries of suffering. Whereas you—even though with each passing week the doctors say your chances of waking lessen—resemble a frozen distillation of yourself, like a portrait in a locket.

"Hello, Richard," I said softly.

He had difficulty turning his neck, so I went to the foot of the bed to meet his eyes.

"We met once in Addis Ababa. I'm—"

"Hildegard. Of course." He spoke in a raspy voice, with great effort. "What a fine surprise."

It was him. The voice was different, the hair gone or shock-white, but sunken in their caves were the same icy-blue eyes I'd been drawn to in Ethiopia.

"I told the nurse I was your cousin." I had also brought her a chocolate cake to grease the wheels, just in case she recognized me from your wing two floors below.

"Now, wouldn't that be nice?" said Halifax. "To have Rauch blood running through my veins."

"How are you feeling?"

"Oh, pretty swell, all things considered. Just glad to be home."

"Richard, I won't disturb you long, but I need to ask you something."

"Well, I'm not going anywhere till the docs get these seagull parasites out of my guts. So pull up a chair and ask whatever you like."

I drew close and sat beside him. "Were you and Eiko—that is, Hank—were the two of you engaged in . . ."

"Jeez, Hilde, that's a fine hell of a thing to ask a guy right off the jump. Me and Hank are just pals. That's all."

"I'm not talking about sex, Richard. I mean China. I know about the papers you gave him with the microdots—on a letter you wrote to Sally Bent and a bill of sale from a tailor in Hong Kong. I need to know what you two were involved in together."

Halifax's eyes seemed to glow in their holes for a moment. "Gosh, Hilde, seems like you're already pretty well informed."

"Why did my brother have those documents?"

"Why do you ask? Are you telling me that you have them now?"

"Please just answer my questions first. Why did Hank have them?"

"Well, it was Hank's idea, Hilde. I just went along with it."

"Went along with *what* exactly?"

"You're going to make me say it, huh?"

"Yes."

"The plan to wreck your father."

It was as I had feared, but the words still knocked the wind out of me.

"What was he going to do, blackmail him?"

"He was going to publish it."

Even worse than blackmail. "Where? In *The Reckoning*?"

"No. *Free Masses.*"

That was the magazine Salka and Philip Ravenswood had disdained. The same one I had seen in Walter's office that night he stole the microdots. "Why didn't my brother follow through with it?"

"Beats me. I mean, I've been out at sea all this time. I guess I just figured Hank did publish them. So you're saying he didn't?"

"No, he didn't."

"Do you have those microdots, Hilde?"

"No. They're gone."

"Both of them? The letter and that tailor's receipt?"

"Yes."

"Well, where'd they go? Who has them?"

"They were stolen."

"By whom?"

"Does the name Walter Seidler mean anything to you?" I asked. I felt the blood rise to my face as I said his name.

"Seidler, Seidler . . . You know, as a matter of fact, it does. Just between you and me, a couple years back I took some messages from a Walter Seidler to a bookshop in Shanghai. Messages your brother asked me to bring."

"About what?"

"Oh, just boring notes about keeping track of people and money. Finding receptive voices and pockets in need of lining."

My belated suspicions about Walter were finally starting to fall into place. "So, you and Eiko were running messages for the Comintern?"

"You know, you sound like Sensei Kanemoto," said Halifax. When I asked what he meant, he winced, then said, "Never mind," and with a forced smile continued, "So you're telling me this Walter Seidler stole my papers? What's he to you?"

"Just someone I thought was a friend," I said. "I thought you were my friend once too, Richard. But I take it you, like Hank, were making money off this plan to destroy my father?"

"No, Hilde, you've got it all wrong. That diary business—that was all Hank's idea. I was just lending him the paper for his microdots. Hell, if you're gonna blame me for that, then you might as well blame the tree that supplied the wood pulp for it."

"Did you know the diary was a fake?"

"Fake?" said Halifax.

"My father never touched us!"

"Hey, that's none of my business, Hilde. But Hank sure seemed to think it was real. He even said, dirty as it was, the diary, especially the later entries, had some of your father's best writing."

"That's absurd."

"Suit yourself," said Halifax sulkily, as though hurt by my disbelief.

"Sally Bent said you and my brother had a 'racket.' What did she mean?"

"Boy, you've really been poking around, haven't you, Hilde?"

"Answer the question, Richard."

"I don't know what Sally was talking about. Honest. Maybe she was referring to me running some messages for Hank to Shanghai the last couple years. That's all I know."

"She said you told her last spring that you were planning to have a big payout soon, enough to help fund my brother's journal and your expedition."

"Well, that's what I've been trying to say, see—the diary was Hank's business. But those other dots with the machine drawings, that's my affair. And I entrusted Hank to carry them back from China along with his own stash. He promised to keep them safe for me until I got home. But you're telling me they're really gone too?"

"What were those drawings of, Richard?"

"But how did you even get them, Hilde? Did Hank give them to you?"

"He told me where to find them, and then I lost them. Now tell me what they were."

Halifax demurred.

"Look, Richard, I'm not with the police or FBI. And if I report on you, I'll be reporting on my own brother. But since Eiko roped me into this mess, I think I have a right to know the truth."

"They're just some technology plans Roderick lifted from a place called the Norden Company. But you'd be amazed how much some people care about them."

"And now that you're finally back, you still want them?"

"Bingo."

"Well, too bad. They're gone."

"That's a shame. 'Cause some angry people are going to be even angrier to hear that. And I fear Hank's gonna have some explaining to do when he wakes up from that long nap of his."

The nurse appeared in the doorway. "Your cousin needs his rest, miss."

I turned to go, my mind burning anew with your betrayal and my own naïve hand in it. But then another thought came screaming to the surface, sending me past the corralling arms of the nurse and back to Halifax's bed.

290

"Richard," I said, standing over him, "how did you know that Eiko is in a coma?"

"You said so."

"No, I didn't."

"Oh, I know—it was the nurses who told me," he said. "A bunch of chatterboxes. I tell you, I can't get through a ten-minute sponge bath without hearing all the gossip." Halifax flashed a smile at the nurse. "Isn't that right, sweetheart?"

As the nurse ushered me out, I tried to make sense of what was obviously a lie. You've been under for six months, and he's only just returned. So how could he possibly know, unless . . . I stepped out of the hospital into daylight, and suddenly it all came crashing down on me.

Your letter had said it all:

You know I don't believe in Ghosts, but I've just spoken with a Dead Man. It's Dick—him, but not him. I'm scared. If anything happens to me, something you must see to . . .

He was there with you. That night. He's been here all along.

ƒIMON FÁULK

I was pacing the hospital hallway, wondering how it would feel to knock a man's teeth out, when Cliff Hader called me in.

Against the starched white of his pillow, Richard Halifax looked less like the irritatingly handsome charmer of my memory and more like a grease stain upon which a few strands of hair had gotten stuck. He still had his teeth, true, but the rest of the man was a ruin. What more could a punch do?

"Mr. Halifax," said Hader, "this is Simon Faulk, with the British consulate."

I had spent a year envisioning this moment. Even when I believed him dead, I dreamed of finding him and giving him his comeuppance. In all my fantasies, I always began with "Hullo, Halifax. Remember me?" Which, now that the moment had arrived, is precisely what I heard myself say.

Halifax raised his swollen eyelids and gave me a blank look. "Sorry, mister, I'm afraid I don't."

This response had not been in my script. "We had, ahem, some business dealings in Bangkok around this time last year?"

"Is that so? And what did you say your name was?"

"You would have known me as Sebastian Flint. But my name is Simon Faulk."

I saw Hader crinkle his brow in disdain at the idea of an alias. Or perhaps he just didn't like mine.

"Faulk, huh?" said Halifax. "And what was the nature of our business, Mr. Faulk?"

He was taking the piss, I was sure of it. "I'm afraid that's classified, but surely you remember. We met at the Oriental Hotel? On the veranda? And several times thereafter in Chinatown?"

"Gee, I'm sorry, Mr. Faulk. I guess the ocean's done a number on my noggin."

"You're telling me you have no recollection of our interactions in Siam?"

Hader shook his head not so subtly in contempt.

"Isn't it called Thailand now?" said Halifax.

Perhaps I could punch a grease stain after all. "So you can recall the recent name change of a country, but you don't have the slightest recollection of me?"

"Sorry, chief. Don't take it personally. I had lots of dealings in Bangkok, like I said, and that sea breeze has blown a big hole through the ole brain-ium."

"Get on with it, Faulk," said Hader.

I took a deep breath, resisting the now-palpable urge to put my thumbs into his lying eyes, and proceeded with the questioning. "How did you end up on the Farallons, Mr. Halifax?"

"It's like I told Agent Hader last time, I floated there on the lifeboat. The same lifeboat I escaped from the Jap whaler in. The same one that smashed up on the rocks and that I burned for firewood."

"And why did you escape from the whaler?"

"I was tired of cleaning the latrines. And, if I'm frank, being used as one."

"How long were you stranded on the island?"

"I didn't have my calendar on me, but I guess it was about two or three weeks."

"And in that time, you saw no other vessels?"

"Sure, I saw a bunch, but none of them saw me. I must've looked like just another sea lion from way off."

"What was the name of the Japanese whaling ship you were on?"

"Something *Maru* was all I caught when I was making my getaway in the lifeboat."

Every bloody Japanese ship ended with the word *Maru*. "And where did you make this escape?"

"Well, I didn't have my sextant, and the Jap captain wasn't too forthcoming either, but my best guess is I was up near the Aleutians. Like I told Agent Hader, once they picked me up from the wreckage of the *Soup Dumpling*, we went south all the way to the Marianas, and then, as far as I could tell, we made a big swing north, all the way toward Alaska. But it was open water the whole time. Plus, I had a head full of mush and a body that could barely endure all the scrubbing, polishing, and back blows assigned to it. It was only once I'd gotten enough rice and fish guts in me to get my wits back and I saw we were near land that I decided I'd take my chance in the lifeboat. Thank God it had that cask of drinking water in it, 'cause the current swept me right past the islands on a southeastern express until I crashed into Seagull Rock. Why, if the boat hadn't smashed up on the shoals there, I'd have drifted straight through the Golden Gate."

Hader looked at me impatiently. "We've already been through all this, Faulk."

"So you deny having returned to San Francisco at the end of last year, before you were found on the Farallons?"

"Sorry, chief, I must still be a little shaky. Are you asking if I already landed in Frisco and then went back out to Bird-Shit Island to live off seaweed and cockles for two weeks?"

"That's right."

"Why would I do that?"

"Because everything you just told us is a lie. You didn't escape from any whaling lifeboat."

"I didn't?"

"No. You arrived on Stinson Beach, courtesy of a Japanese submarine, last October." I looked into Halifax's eyes for signs of faltering and detected only the slightest fluttering of his whitened lashes.

"Gee, that's news to me."

"You then went to the German consulate, where you met with Consul Fritz Wiedemann and were given three thousand dollars and a shopping list. Isn't that right?"

Out of the corner of my vision, I noticed Cliff Hader turning red.

"You must be mistaking me for someone else," said Halifax, "'cause this hospital bed is the first bit of California terra firma I've touched in well over a year."

294

"Not true. You've been living in San Francisco for the last six months under the alias Richard Wagner. The first month you stayed at the Sir Francis Drake, and even though you took care to rarely leave your room, both the lift attendant and the receptionist remember you. You were supposed to board a ship to Yokohama last November. The German consul gave you your ticket and travel visas. But you never showed. Instead, you went to your friend Sally Bent at the Music Box theater and spent the winter living in her barn at Treasure Island. You remained hidden there until just a few weeks ago, when you recruited two young thieves to sail you out to the Farallon Islands, where you miraculously sprang back to life."

Halifax said nothing. Cliff Hader looked at me, and I realized right then I was sunk.

"Do you have anything to say to these accusations, Mr. Halifax?" asked Hader.

Halifax put on a pained look and made a considerable show of effort before he spoke. "Well, sir, Agent Hader, that is some doozy of a tale. I'm still trying to wrap my head around it. I sure wish I could have seen my old friend Sally Bent sooner, like Mr. Faulk here thinks. The fact is I haven't seen her in the flesh since the summer of 1938. But you better believe I'd have given my left leg to be cozied up in her girl barn on the Gayway this past winter and not shivering in a cold puddle of Jap sailor piss."

"Does that mean you deny having met with the German consul, Fritz Wiedemann?" said Hader.

"Unless he was dressed up like one of those sea lions, sir, I don't believe I've ever made the man's acquaintance."

"I have multiple witnesses," I said, "who can confirm Richard Halifax's presence in San Francisco and on Treasure Island in the months and weeks prior to his supposed landing on the Farallons."

"Alright," said Hader, stepping between the bed and me and nudging me toward the door. "I think we'd better let the patient rest now. Thank you for your time, Mr. Halifax. We'll let you know if we need anything more."

"You bet, fellas. Anytime."

In the empty vestibule by the lift, Hader cornered me. "What the hell was that?"

He was so close I could smell his rancid coffee breath. "What?"

"You said you wanted to talk to Halifax as part of a consular inquiry regarding the sinking of the *Soup Dumpling*. And instead you trot out this lunatic theory of yours?"

"I told you, I have multiple witnesses—Halifax is lying. There's—"

"Answer me this: Do you have material evidence or eyewitness testimony to prove that Richard Halifax met with Wiedemann in the last six months?"

"Well no, not exactly, but—"

"Then you don't have a goddamn thing. Get this through your thick skull, Faulk: This is not your show. Halifax is an American citizen on American soil. We've confirmed his identity, he's been through a hell of an ordeal and come out on the other side. You are a foreign agent, allowed to operate here only insofar as your work is of help to the Bureau. If you have some information that you think is pertinent to our counterintelligence efforts, then you tell me in private, and I'll determine how to proceed. Understood?"

I felt like a schoolboy again, back in short pants, being scolded and beaten by my superiors. For daydreaming in class, for muttering curses in Italian, for stabbing a boy in the neck with a compass.

"In the meantime," said Hader, poking a meaty finger right in my chest, "stay away from Richard Halifax."

I went in search of a drink and came to a dodgy bar called Pal's Rendezvous. There I had two gins in rapid succession and ruminated over a third. The bar was dank and devoid of sunlight, with a fetid yellow rug on the floor and only a few committed morning drinkers. It was a much needed antidote to the antiseptic white glare of the hospital and the bloody botched operation that had just taken place there.

What was I thinking? That Halifax would confess? That Cliff Hader would slap the manacles on him, and I would look on with pride at justice served and my score settled? It became glaringly obvious in that moment that I had made a mess of my life.

I looked up at the intricate wood carving above the bar and forced my eyes to follow the undulatory lines of the inlay. I imagined I was shrunken to the size of a flea, tracing the lines in a labyrinth, following them to their inevitable point of convergence. Gradually, my temperature fell from a rolling boil, as I lulled myself into a kind of trance.

Corvo's line therapy had saved me from reaching the end of my rope countless times. Though on occasion, before I could truly calm myself, I first had to snap.

If only I hadn't snapped in one particular instance, my parents might still be alive. The only reason they were crossing the channel that day in 1916, while millions were dying nearby in the mud, was that I had injured a boy at school—the little bugger deserved it—and they had come to London to prevent me from being expelled.

I wished that my father hadn't succeeded in talking the headmaster around. Instead, I could have returned to Italy with my parents, as I so desperately wished to, and then perhaps they would have embarked on a different day or from a different port. Or, even if we had crossed on the *Sussex* that same day, perhaps we would have sat in the stern, and then they would still be alive. Instead, they were gone, and I bore not just the eternal loneliness of the orphan but of one who at the age of twelve had condemned himself as a parricide.

As I sat there in that dark pub, tracing the lines of the woodwork, thinking about my destiny and my tutor's words—*all lines eventually converge*—it suddenly occurred to me. I had been going about this all wrong.

Twenty minutes later, back at Mount Zion with Cliff Hader nowhere in sight, I retraced my steps down the wing, waved to the nurse at the desk, saying I forgot my hat (which was stuffed inside my jacket), and returned to the room of the recuperating hero.

This time, I grabbed him by his hospital gown and slammed my fists into his chest. "Still don't remember me, Dicky, old boy? Well, let me jog your memory!"

I took him by the throat and clamped down on his windpipe.

At last Richard Halifax gave me a genuine look: of terror, pain, and, yes, recognition.

"You wound me up in Bangkok, thinking you'd never see me again. But every now and then, destiny and justice happen to align."

Halifax tried to speak, but only choked sounds leaked out.

"You still owe me ten thousand quid for the imaginary guns. Remember the ones you promised me in Bangkok and then never delivered?"

"I'm saw . . . weee," said Halifax in a toadish gurgle.

"Oh, do you think an apology is what I'm after? No, Dicky, old boy, it's far too late for apologies. Besides, your words have no value. Actions are what count. And it's your actions that have brought us together. Setting me up, luring me to Hong Kong, and then, just before you leave, slipping a word to someone in Phibun's cabinet about the arms deal. The only part you didn't divulge was that the whole thing was, as you planned it, a figment from the start. And I bet you got a tidy payment for leaking the deal too—so let's call it another ten thousand, shall we, just so the numbers even out. Now that's twenty thousand pounds, which if we convert to dollars, is, oh, let's say . . . fifty thousand."

Halifax was turning a deep violet, the veins in his forehead throbbing.

"Does that sound like a lot, Dicky? Well, thanks to your little swindle, I can never set foot in Siam again—no, excuse me, you're right, *Thailand*. Ugly name change, you'll surely agree, yet still a beautiful place. But guess what? I'm barred from the country for life. And you know something? I rather liked it there. Could have seen myself growing old there. Had a nice woman too. But all of that's gone. And now I'm here, chasing after the likes of you. So let's add on another fee for severance, or reparations, call it what you will. And, well, let's just say for the sake of simplicity that the total bill comes out to one hundred thousand of your finest American dollars. Does that sound like a fair sum, *chief*?"

The writer-adventurer's eyes looked like they were about to pop from his skull, when I finally loosened my grip.

Halifax wheezed and hacked as he sucked for air.

Hearing his distress, a nurse poked her head in. "Is everything alright here?"

"Oh yes, Nurse, I believe a pea just went down the wrong pipe." I pointed at the tray of gelatinous hospital lunch at the patient's bedside. "Isn't that right, Richard?"

Halifax gave the nurse a thumbs-up before convulsing in coughs.

"See?" I said. "Tickety-boo."

Once the nurse left, he tried to say something, but no sound escaped from his mouth. "What's that, Halifax?" I said, leaning down close. "Something on your mind?"

"I don't have a cent to my name," he said in a rough whisper. "Let alone a hundred grand."

"Oh, come, come, Dicky. I don't expect you to pay it off in one lump sum. I expect you to be in my debt for life. Besides, Fritz Wiedemann says you received a generous stipend from him, and I know he has quite a substantial budget. I suggest you begin by asking him for another handout. Let's start with ten thousand dollars."

Dicky shook his head. "I don't know what you mean."

"What I mean is very simple. You get ten thousand dollars from your Nazi paymaster and then you give it to me. Or else I'm going to ruin you. You see," I said, counting on my bluster to carry me through, "Cliff Hader was very intrigued to hear the general outline of my allegations this morning. Which I kept intentionally vague, and which I can make fall apart if you choose to cooperate. However, if you choose not to, well, then I'll get very specific, and America's beloved writer-adventurer and miraculous survivor Richard Halifax will be exposed not only as a fraud but a fascist spy. Just imagine— what will all your young fans think when they find out you're doing dirty work for your overlords in Tokyo and Berlin?"

Halifax shook his head again. "Even if it were true, they'd never believe you."

"Oh, they will, once I give my witnesses over to the FBI and to all the newspapers. Your dear friend Sally Bent, who now despises you; those poor little orphan shoeshine boys, the Sinclairs—such talkative boys, and with excellent memories too—and there are others, including the German consul himself. Yes, Dicky, I know what you've been up to. I know about the Rauch diary. I also know you're promising the Japanese the very same plans you teased me with in Bangkok."

Halifax actually seemed surprised that I knew this. "What do you mean?"

"Answer me this, and be very careful how you answer, because if you lie to me this time, I really will kill you: Are the Norden plans real?"

He took a moment to catch his breath. "Of course they're real. I wasn't lying about that or the guns. They really were stolen by pirates. And I really was going to give you the plans in Hong Kong, as agreed, but, you see, we had an issue with one of the crew's visas and, well, we had to pop over to Formosa to sort things out with the Jap authorities, but then by the time we came back you were gone. Hell, I hate to say it, but if anyone ratted us out in Bangkok, it was probably your gal."

I felt myself go hot in the face. "What are you talking about?"

"Your girl, Anya. You knew she was cozy with the Japs, right?"

"That's a damned lie."

"You didn't know, huh? Well, it was just a rumor I heard anyway . . ."

I felt the urge to throttle him rising and gathering force, but I was determined to keep my composure. "Do you have the Norden plans now?"

"Not on me, chief. No pockets in this hospital gown," he said, smiling. "Not even a backside."

"Do you know where they are?"

"No, but I know who last had them. Gal by the name of Hildegard Rauch."

"Theodor Rauch's daughter?"

"That's the one. She had an old letter of mine, with the Nordens stuck on as microdots."

This confirmed Sally Bent's story about the Rauch girl.

"Want me to ring her up and ask about them?" asked Halifax.

"Don't you say a word. Those plans are mine now, understand? Consider it part of your debt-repayment plan."

"Fine," he said. "They're all yours. So you get the plans, the ten grand, and then we're square, right?"

I laughed. "Hardly, *old sport*. Don't you see how this works? I own you now."

To: The Dicky Halifax Junior Adventurers Club
From: Dicky Halifax
Back from the Dead

Springtime 1940

Dear boys,

People don't like it when you return from the dead. They've gotten used to the idea of you being gone, and your intrusion back in their lives is unwelcome. It forces them to move you from one category, dead—generally thought permanent—back to another, alive, and they resent the mental drudgery of refiling. Plus, a whole lot of unresolved questions and grievances, to say nothing of the pending lawsuits, suddenly bubble up to the surface.

Oh, sure, I made the papers for a day. And I could see a small crowd of fans outside my hospital window down on Divisadero cheering my return, my old pal Diego among them. But he had a wet fresco to go dab, and at the first sign of bad weather, which in San Francisco is hourly, the rest of them scattered.

I'm guessing you boys already know about my miraculous public appearance—who doesn't?—but since you're all subscribed Junior Adventurers and this adventure isn't quite over, I'll give you the straight dope.

The Sinclair cousins, Slop and Stinker, who you'll recall are my plug-ugly shoeshine boys and your fellow dues-paying club members, had restored me to myself and inspired me with a plan to rejoin the ranks of the living.

We had a lark of a ride out to the Farallons. Slop and Stinker picked me up before dawn in a gaff-sloop pocket yacht, freshly purloined from the Marina harbor, and the three of us set out like we were off for a weekend picnic. Once we ducked under the Golden Gate Bridge and lit into open ocean, I got the shakes pretty bad and had to be restrained, what with the ole Halifax Memory Bank dredging up the terrors of my recent bout at sea. But Slop poured some rotgut down my throat while Stinker kept a steady hand on the tiller, and I was myself again in no time. We had a stiff breeze the whole way out, which kept our sail full, and the sun even managed to poke out from behind the clouds. It was smiles all around, fortified by some hard salamis the boys had pinched from home. We shared our spoils with a school of dolphins that swam along beside us, the whole lot of us cackling like a bunch of chuckleheads. We were still telling one another dirty jokes when we sighted the islands. "Land ho, boys!" I cried, using my salami like a spyglass.

Stinker steered the boat to a sheltered cove, while Slop and I unloaded a big bladder of drinking water, a quiver of salamis, a cigarette lighter, and the rest of the rotgut.

"Well, boys, I suppose this is where I get off."

"Aw, Dicky, tell us another limerick first," said Slop, his eyes filling with tears. "We got all day to get back."

"Alright, young fella, but just one more. I don't want you boys getting caught in the open sea come dark. Let me go out on an instructive note and pass on some advice in the form of a cautionary tale. Also, take note of the artful enjambment:

"While pissing on deck, an old boatswain
Fell asleep, and his pisser got frozen.
It snapped at the shank,
And it fell off and sank
In the sea—'twas his own fault for dozin'."

"That's a clunker if ever I heard one," said Stinker, always the critic.

"So the message is don't fall asleep while peeing?" asked Slop.

"That, and to remain alert at all times," I said, "especially when your ding-dong is on the line. If I can impart one piece of wisdom to you, boys, let it be that."

I asked them for one more favor: to get ahold of a phone directory and swing by Hildegard Rauch's place sometime when it was vacant and see if they could spot any pieces of paper matching a particular description.

Then I patted them both on the head and gave them twenty dollars each, along with a pair of ladies' underpants that I'd found in Sally's barn. "A token of my appreciation, boys. Fresh from the Nude Ranch. You pulled your man Dick out of a pickle and I'm forever in your debt." The Sinclair boys gasped, then immediately tugged at the silk thong till it tore in two—a crotch for Slop and the ass for Stinker.

Before they shoved off, I swore them to secrecy with a blood oath, which may or may not result in hepatitis in the coming years. I told them that if they blabbed about their role in Operation Drop-Off Dicky or about having seen me earlier at the Nude Ranch, then I'd have to come to their mothers' house, tell them that their sons were spineless loose-lipped rats, and demand my money back with interest.

"But I know none of that will come to pass, because you're stand-up honest boys, loyal sidekicks to a man." I hopped over the bow onto the rocks and pushed them off. "So long for now, boys. Godspeed and bon voyage!"

I trusted that the Sinclair boys got home safe and abided by our pact of silence, but I began to fear they did so all too well. They were supposed to tell the coast guard at Fort Point that they had seen a man stranded on the island while out on a fishing expedition with their uncle, which would then trigger an immediate rescue mission. Whether my sidekicks fell down on the job or the coast guard simply didn't believe them, which is too often the plight of the young, I can't say. But the result for your man Dicky was nearly fatal.

I had expected to be stuck for only a couple of days on the Farallons, which is a generous, romantic-sounding name for a heap of wet rocks in the frigid crosswinds of the Pacific. And lest you think it's a peaceful refuge suitable for spiritual reflection, like some marine hermitage or floating Walden, know that it reeks of seal shit and is livid with the unceasing screams of gulls, cormorants, and some wretched waddling fowl that looks like a penguin's imbecile cousin. There's not a dry patch anywhere to be found. And some of those seals, especially the ones with a big old dingus on their face, are downright mean. Suffice it to say I didn't sleep a wink those first few days, and I was divested of my salamis within a matter of minutes. My lighter was of no use either, as there was nothing dry to burn, and the wick itself got waterlogged after the umpteenth surf spray. So it was just me and my bladder of water, which I slowly sucked at while I waited for the rescue boat to appear.

Three days came and went. My bladder was already running low on day four when a seagull came and punctured it. Now I was really in the soup, boys. After all I'd been through, I was going to die of thirst on a pile of stones within yodeling distance of home, and after I'd already made it back. What a dope! I was so angry that I lunged after that damned gull and tore its smarmy little head clean off its trunk.

And that was how I stayed alive, boys. Fifteen days on gull blood and cockle meat. It was enough to sustain me, but the cold and the wind and the wet, and then the short bouts of the blinding sun—well, you know how it goes.

It occurred to me that ever since I'd sprung to the surface on that bunk bed from the wreckage of the *Soup Dumpling*, I'd been reliving the horrors of privation and the loss of a beloved sidekick. It didn't matter whether I was in a Saipan penal colony, a swanky San Fran hotel suite, the shuttered barn of my old friend's girlie farm, or now on the wet rocks of the Farallons with my beard stained a vivid bird-blood red. In all of them, I was alone. Forsaken by Wesley, then Roderick, then Nacho, then Hank, then Sally, and now my young pals Stinker and Slop. A whole parade of friends come and gone. All the striving and glory, all the quick-thinking and hard-nosed survival—what did it earn you in the end but anguish? And no matter how tightly you hugged your sidekick, one day they would abandon you, and then you'd face the great immensity alone. There is no peak you can conquer, no sea you can cross, no person you can love, that will alter the stupefying loneliness of existence.

Such were my dying thoughts on the Farallons, boys. I know I've said it before, but I was truly ready to lay down my load and finally surrender my breath to Blasé Mother Nature or Vindictive Dame Fortune or whatever mean old bitch is at the helm of this whirling orb, when the birdwatching boat appeared.

I was saved yet again. Only this time your man Dick was truly coming home—as himself.

But even though I've succeeded in shedding my disguise and reclaiming my name, I'm still far from free. As a matter of fact, I currently have more people making demands on me than ever before, as well as violating basic standards of decency when it comes to visiting a convalescent in hospital.

I'm not sure how many flags the good ship *Halifax* can fly—after all, I'm a freebooter at heart—but will be sure to write you again just as soon as I've untangled myself from the rigging.

Yours,
Dicky

HILDEGÁRD RÁUCH

I started following Richard Halifax the day he was released from the hospital. My plan was to confront him, to tell him I knew he was a phony and liar and threaten to go to the police if he didn't tell me the truth of what happened between you and him. But I kept waiting for the right moment, and before I knew it I was following him. Somehow the promise of this activity gratified me. I thought if I could just observe him in his natural element, he would eventually reveal his true colors.

I watched him dart in and out of stores around Union Square, acquiring garment bags, now sporting a rather obvious toupee, still looking frail and disfigured, with people on the street giving him furtive looks. I followed him from his hotel to various bars, where he never stayed long and seemed to drink alone. He moped all the way down Market, pausing often to catch his breath, to an office building on Spear Street. Twenty minutes later, he came out sobbing. I was beginning to feel more sorry for him than enraged, when he adjourned to a grimy chili parlor opposite the German consulate. Was he meeting someone there? I wondered. If Halifax really had been in the hotel with you that night six months ago, how and when did he come home? And what had he been up to here? My mind began spinning with possibilities. But just when it seemed something momentous and revealing might happen, with Halifax passing through the doors beneath the swastika, he instead got into a cab and headed west. By the time I hailed one, I'd lost him.

Obviously, I have a lot to learn about being a tail. Perhaps I should ask my own tail for tips, as I've learned to all but ignore the Packard that still periodically keeps tabs on me. Maybe we could team up.

I had dinner in a quiet Chinese restaurant, then walked home. I was fishing out my keys when suddenly a man stepped out from the shadows of my building and blocked the door.

"Good evening, Miss Rauch."

Startled, I leapt back into the alcove.

He was a severe-looking man, with tired eyes peering out from under his hat brim. "I'm sorry, I didn't mean to frighten you."

"What do you want?"

"I want to help you."

"I don't know you."

"The name's Fox. I work for an insurance agency. May we speak inside?" He had a British accent, and I could smell the gin on his breath.

"Certainly not. And, just so you know, there's an FBI man watching us right across the street."

"You mean the bloke in the gray Packard? No, he knocked off to the diner about fifteen minutes ago. I'm sure we have a little time until he returns."

"Then say whatever you have to say right here," I said, refusing to show him my fear.

"Very well. It's quite simple. I have something in my possession that I think you might want." The man handed me an envelope.

"What's this?"

"Have a look."

I opened the flap and withdrew three photographs. They were prints of pages from Father's diary—one of them was the same page I had seen on microdot. "Where did you get these?"

"Let's just say that if I hadn't intervened, they would have dramatically boosted the sales of *Free Masses*. And I imagine your father would find it rather difficult to continue making speeches or publishing books."

So Walter and Nadia had brought them to the same magazine that, according to Halifax, you were going to publish them in. "And you intervened why? So you can come here and blackmail me?"

"Quite the contrary. I have no ill will toward you or your father, Miss Rauch. As I said, I'm the one who thwarted the publication of this diary."

"And yet I sense you have more than charity on your mind."

He gave a tight smile. "I'd like to propose an exchange. Sally Bent said you came to her last fall with a letter from Richard Halifax, addressed to her. That letter is all I want."

"Well, she's wasted your time. I don't have it anymore."

"That is a pity."

"So if I don't have the letter, then what—you won't give me the diary?"

"I'm afraid not. And then it's possible your father's dirty secrets might fall into the wrong hands."

"Then you're not proposing an exchange at all," I said. "You're threatening me."

"Yes, I suppose you're right. I guess it is blackmail."

"You know the diary's a forgery, right?"

"It doesn't really matter, does it? If it's believable enough to get into print, it will be enough to destroy your father's reputation and silence his voice. I imagine it will make things difficult for you too."

Headlight beams flashed over the hill as my tail drifted back into his parking spot down the street.

"I'll give you until the end of the week," said the man who called himself Fox. "You never know, perhaps the letter you say is lost will have turned up by then, and we can both put our minds at rest. In the meantime, those copies are yours to keep."

When I came up the steps, I saw that the door to my apartment was ajar.

I paused at the threshold. Had the Englishman been in there before I returned, or was someone else waiting for me? I thought I could hear something coming from inside, like a quiet slurping. Grasping my keys so that a jagged spike poked out from my fist, I used my foot to nudge the door open. "Who's there?" I shouted.

"Ah, there you are," said a scratchy female voice I recognized immediately. "I was wondering when you'd ever get back."

I peered around the doorway and there on my couch, her feet up on my coffee table and drinking from my mug, was Nadia.

"Spend the evening with a nice boy? Or perhaps a nice girl?"

"What are you doing in my home, Nadia?"

"Waiting for you. What's it look like?"

"You broke in?"

"Of course not—the door was open. Though it looks like someone else broke in before I got here." I looked behind me and saw the shelves ransacked, the drawers disemboweled. My canvases were scattered across the kitchen floor along with all your mail. The canvas closest to my foot was smudged with dark thumbprints that looked like pine tar or shoe polish.

I was on the verge of tears. A lit fuse had begun coiling through me, and in a few seconds something would explode. "You should leave now," I said to Nadia.

"Oh, Hildchen, I came to give you an apology."

"What are you sorry for?"

"Me? Nothing. But it's for Walter. I think he did something awful to you."

"And you were part of it too, no?"

"I don't even know what *it* is, my dear. All I have is what was in his final note: *Apologize to Hilde for me. Tell her I really did consider her my friend.*"

"What do you mean final note? He's . . . ?"

"Dead? Yes, probably. He was recalled."

"Recalled?" My confusion delayed the pending explosion of tears, but I felt suddenly lightheaded and sat down on the couch beside her.

"To Moscow, dear. The Comintern is collapsing. Stalin's turn toward Hitler means the Popular Front is now not only outdated but a dangerous relic. Walter scrambled to stay afloat, but . . . well, you can swim for only so long. His cover was blown. His network in Shanghai was infiltrated. Could have been Germans or Japanese, or just as well someone in the Cheka."

"And what about you?"

"What about me?"

"Aren't you also working for the Soviets?"

Nadia spat in contempt. "Pah! I wouldn't lift a finger for those criminals. But I knew Walter was with them—running around in his little mask, moving money around all his fine-arts charity fronts and literary-journal dollhouses."

"Including my brother's."

"I believe so, yes."

"Did he realize you knew about him?"

"Of course. And he knew things about me that I hadn't told him. Yet by the time we learned these things, we were already together. So we had each other's secrets to keep us safe. Things we knew not to discuss, and the assurance of mutual destruction if we did. A happy bourgeois marriage, I suppose." She said it with a laugh, though I could see her eyes go glassy.

"Was his passion for art a cover too?" I asked. Somehow that seemed even worse than faking love.

"You know, the sad thing is, Walter would have been quite happy simply being a scholar. Perhaps in another age."

I said nothing. Walter did once have a choice, just as you did. Just as Richard Halifax did. One had no choice in being crushed by the jaws of history, but you could choose not to become one of its teeth.

"I should clean this up," I said, rising to my feet. All I wanted was to take a hot bath and melt into it. I knelt on the kitchen floor and examined what looked like a shoe-polish rag. Strange, because I haven't polished my shoes in years.

"I'll help you, my dear," said Nadia. She dried her eyes on her shirt-sleeves and unwedged herself from the couch. "Now, did the thieves steal any of your paintings? These . . ." she said, gesturing at the ones leaning against the wall in the kitchen, "are quite provocative."

"No, that's not what they're after."

Nadia cocked a thick eyebrow at me. "Then what, pray tell, *are* they after?"

"So you really don't know?" I asked.

"As I said, Hilde, you were Walter's project, not mine."

"You know, Nadia, I think it's time I ask the questions and you answer them. Why did Walter steal those documents from me?"

Nadia sighed. "I can tell you only what little he told me and what little more I know. You see, dear, Walter was technically part of an organization called the Fourth Directorate, Soviet military intelligence, but, as he was an intellectual, well connected to artistic and academic circles, his domain was of course cultural. But he and his network—in the Anti-Fascist Writers League here in California and the Zeitgeist Bookshop in Shanghai—had come under increasing suspicion of late for harboring Trotskyite counterrevolutionary motives. No doubt his marriage to me didn't help in that regard. Walter and his group were on thin ice and they knew it. Now, I gather your brother had something that was deemed important, perhaps something that he himself refused to surrender, which ended up in your hands and which Walter was compelled to relieve you of. But you shouldn't take it personally, dear. It was just part of his job. In fact, whatever he stole may well have signed his own death warrant."

"What do you mean?"

"I mean that Walter's mission was a failure. He told me so himself in the cryptic language we used with each other to complain about work. He said that one of his objectives had been undermined—stolen before it could hit the target. The other, he said, had turned out to be a fake, and because of it, 'no target would ever be hit.'"

I tried to puzzle out what this meant. The first objective could refer to Father's diary, which ended up in my blackmailer's hands. Hadn't the Englishman Fox said he prevented the diary from being published in *Free Masses*? But the diary was also fake. Of that I was sure. But what about the diagrams?

"Did he say what was a fake?" I asked. "A set of technical drawings, perhaps? Diagrams for some kind of machine?"

"It could be. I gathered from his insinuating language that it might be some kind of military technology. He also said someone had played a nasty joke on whoever got their hands on this document, and now the joke was on him."

So were the diagrams I had seen under the microscope—the ones

Walter stole and both Halifax and the Englishman Fox now wanted—also fakes?

I laughed at the absurdity of the thought.

"Something funny, dear?" asked Nadia.

I was too exhausted to do anything but tell the truth. I told her about my blackmailer, who wanted what were apparently a set of fake drawings.

"And what, may I ask, is he threatening you with?"

I laughed again, this time at how shameless she was. "Let's just call them what they are: lies. Lies that will harm my family."

"But lies you would like to have back in your possession?" said Nadia.

"Yes," I said warily. Did she know about the diary?

"Then why not do the exchange?"

"Because I don't have the fucking diagrams, Nadia! Remember, your fake husband and my fake friend stole them from me?"

"There were many aspects of our marriage that were clouded by deception, Hilde, but I assure you Walter really was my husband and we really did love each other."

"Did he tell you we slept together?"

"Of course."

"And you're not angry?"

"Why should I be? He was working."

"I see. And is that why you are here now? Because you're working?"

"No. I'm here because I feel sympathy for you, Hilde. You are a good-hearted girl who has reached for the sky but stuck her hand in an airplane engine."

In that moment, I wished that Walter had just been an art historian, as he had once wanted to be. And that you had just been a writer, as you once wanted to be. Then I could have been free to just be a painter. It would have been quite enough for all of us.

"It strikes me," said Nadia, "that if this Englishman wanted to do something nasty with these documents of yours, then he already would have."

"Yes, that occurred to me. But it also occurred to me that if he thought it was valuable leverage, he would have made copies anyway."

"Exactly. So there is no guarantee to anything you do. You cannot fully protect your family from the world. You cannot save your brother from himself; you cannot prevent others from seeing and believing lies. You can only use your extremely limited capacity to steer the world in the direction you wish to see it go. And now you are presented with a choice. A man is trying to blackmail you in order to obtain from you drawings that he believes you possess and that you in fact do not. What shall you do?"

"I don't know."

"Let's put this another way," said Nadia. "He wants a set of worthless drawings that got my husband—and your friend—sent to an anonymous death or some frozen hell worse than death. And guess what? You know how to make drawings. You even teach people how to do it."

Gradually it dawned on me what she was driving at. "You mean give him a forgery? A forgery of a forgery?"

"Now you're catching on."

"But I have no idea how to shrink a drawing onto something like a microdot."

"Ah, Hildchen, you poor naïve little *Künstlerin*. It's a good thing you're friends with someone who does. Now tell me, this Englishman, did he mention the name Richard Halifax?"

It was no surprise to hear that Richard Halifax and the Englishman were somehow entangled, but I was surprised to hear the name spoken by Nadia, as I had not said anything about him to her. "No, why?"

But before she could answer, the telephone rang.

"I meant to tell you," said Nadia. "It was ringing for some time before you got here."

"I'm surprised you didn't answer it. You seem right at home." I set the rag on the counter and answered the phone.

"Am I speaking with Miss Hildegard Rauch?" said a woman's voice on the line.

"Yes. This is she."

"Ms. Rauch, I'm calling from Mount Zion Hospital. Your brother has just woken from his coma."

To: The Dicky Halifax Junior Adventurers Club
From: Dicky Halifax
Back in the Saddle

Springtime 1940

Dear boys,

As soon as I got out of Mount Zion, I did what anyone who'd spent the last year shipwrecked, imprisoned, and hospitalized would do: I went shopping.

I hit the Emporium, where my resurrected credit line got me a new cream suit and pair of patent-leather spectators. Then I slid over to the makeup counter, where the gals slapped enough greasepaint on me to join the circus, but they pretty well covered up my blight. After that, I headed up to Bertie's Wigs on Mason, where I found myself a wavy sandy-haired rug that looked just like my old playboy's slickback, and I had Bertie glue that sucker down tight.

Stepping out into clear American daylight, finally looking more or less like myself and with all my major nutrients replenished, I felt like a million bucks with a permanent limp. I didn't see any assassins on the rooftops, and as far as anyone could tell, I was no longer bald, pocked, and scarred and no longer harboring dark thoughts of genital mutilation. Your man Dick was back.

I had a long list of errands to see to—like making good with Sally Bent and catching up with my plug-ugly sailor sidekicks—but first among them was a visit to the Kraut outpost, to see where matters stood. I staked out the German consulate from the chili parlor across the street. An hour later the dapper consul emerged, carrying a small leather gym bag. He slid into the back seat of his Mercedes-Benz, and I hopped in a cab and followed after.

The consul got dropped off at the Sea Cliff Tennis Club. As luck would have it, I'd been a member there for years.

"Welcome back, Mr. Halifax," said the front-desk guy, only somewhat reluctantly, after I pointed to my photo on the wall of fame. I tipped him ten dollars for recognizing me and asked to borrow a set of tennis whites and a racket.

I figured I'd have to stalk the courts and buttonhole the consul during a water break. But as luck would have it, I didn't even have to leave the men's locker room. Walking past the steam sauna, I heard an angelic tenor bouncing off the walls in German.

I stripped down, spun a towel around myself, and headed into the foggy den of the Lorelei.

I could just make out the consul's form through the steam. It was only the two of us in there.

"That's a fine set of pipes you got."

"Thank you. The acoustics are very generous in here."

"I bet you lure a fair amount of sailors crashing against your rocky shore."

The form leaned forward, cutting through the fog to see me. "Ach so. Yes, in fact that is true." I imagine with my makeup steaming off me and my wig glue melting so that my head mop slipped off-kilter, I looked more like when I'd first met the consul. "And on rare occasions," he said, "some sailors even crash twice."

"Is that so?"

"Yes. Once on Stinson Beach, and then again on the Farallon Islands."

"I know that wasn't exactly as planned, but—"

"You were supposed to sail back to Yokohama months ago. What exactly are you playing at?"

"The thing is, Captain, sometimes the sailor's gotta call his own tune."

"So am I to report that you have mutinied and withdrawn your services?"

"I didn't say that. I just need to do things my own way. As me. I'm not cut out for skulking around under an alias."

"That was just supposed to be for a few weeks, you imbecile," said the consul rather grouchily. "I hope you understand that unless you find a new way to demonstrate your worth, you'll be viewed as a loose end."

"Roger that, Capitán. I just need more time."

"Speaking of which, another loose end of yours has just sprung up."

"What's that?"

"Heinrich Rauch. He's awoken from his coma. Seems you made a botch of things all around."

"Hank's awake?" I cried. "Hot damn!" Of course it was music to my ears to know good ole Hank had bounced back from that nasty suicide attempt. I felt pretty awful about how things had gone down that night.

"The same goes for any other loose ends you have. *Tie them up. Or it will be you who's tied up, Herr Dickee-san.*"

I suddenly saw the Coconut King's swirling eyeballs pierce the fog and flash before me. At the same time I became aware of a quickening sensation beneath my towel—the first recurrence since my home surgery in the Sir Francis Drake. Smiting my lap with both fists, I tried to quash my tumescent paranoia.

I rubbed my eyes to clear the stinging sweat, and sure enough, when I looked again, Karl Dieter and his vortices had vanished. All I could see was the Nazi consul stretching out on the bench, with a clear shot of his frankfurter and beans.

"Did you hear me?" Wiedemann said, annoyed. "I said, when you get up, make sure you shut the door tight, or it makes for a drippy sauna."

Had I misheard him the first time? Had he, rather than issue an ominous ultimatum about tying up loose ends while addressing me as "Herr Dickee-san," simply told me to "shut the door tight" to avoid a "drippy sauna"?

"Now, if there's nothing else," said Wiedemann, "I'd like to relax . . ."

With my paranoid hallucination-and-engorgement passed and my senses restored, I now remembered what I had come to do.

"Come to mention it, there is one more thing." I told the consul how I was being shaken down for cash by a British agent sniffing under my tail. "He says the last time you two met, you ratted me out."

"That's ridiculous," said Wiedemann. "I never said a word about you."

"Well, he says he's got a pile of evidence linking you and me together, and he's threatening to turn us both over to the FBI unless I turn on the money hose to the tune of twenty grand."

The consul sat up. "He said that?"

"Yep. Tells me he's building a big case against us both."

I could see now the Kraut consul was sweatin', and not just on account of the steam.

I came away from the tennis club with the two things I needed: a cash infusion, which I received later that day, plus a confirmation of my hunch. The consul had denied tattling on your man Dicky but in doing so confirmed that he and the Englishman had indeed met.

See, boys, that sour limey Faulk or Flint or whatever he was called thought he had me by the shorthairs. But the problem with a fella like Faulk is that he was prone to indignation—feeling like the world owed him something. And whenever he got indignant, he said more than he should.

That's precisely what had happened in Bangkok. In explaining to dumb-dumb Dicky who not to tell about the gun deal, he had exposed his own weakness. That allowed me to make a few extra baht off him by luring him with the Norden plans while I ratted him out to the Jap-lovers in the Thai dictator's cabinet. I even had the pleasure of bringing him up to Hong Kong, just so he could eat my dust, so to speak, when he arrived to find only the confetti-strewn wake of the *Soup Dumpling*.

Now, in boasting to me at the hospital of how much he knew about my incognito return home, Faulk also intimated that he was on a firsthand acquaintance with the Nazi consul. I didn't know if that was an official part of whatever his dirty work was here in America, but I had a hunch that two consuls of warring nations shooting the breeze with each other was valuable information. And in the game of life, boys, where Dame Fortune is just one spin away from canceling your book deal and sending you back to Kansas City to be a middle-school English teacher, you have to turn others' weaknesses to your advantage. So I tucked that info away in my brain for future use and went about reclaiming my life.

I found new digs on the top floor of the Chancellor on Union Square, only a block from my nightmare residency at the Sir Francis Drake but a whole world away. I was determined this time not to succumb to paranoia, though I still kept a watchful eye on the rooftops, around corners, and inside public restrooms for any signs of Jap snipers, Aryan hitmen, or, for that matter, Sally Bent's big goon Tater.

Given how I'd recently pulled a fifty-thousand-dollar check out from under her, I was worried Sally might want your man Dick dead. Ole Sal was no cold-blooded killer, but money makes people do crazy things. Relish those years when chewing gum and baseball cards are the only currencies you care about, boys—once you get the hunger for greenbacks, you're on the treadmill to hell. And while I had earmarked a good chunk of my new allowance to give to Sally to help smooth things over, I figured it was best to give her a wide berth for now.

Besides, I told myself, my celebrity was my best protection. Who was gonna have the moxie to gun down America's returning hero and most beloved writer-adventurer? No sir, the time for black thoughts was over. I was back, Hank was alive, and Frisco was once again mine.

I went to have a drink at Izzy Gomez's to celebrate, but Izzy was out sick with cancer and I didn't recognize any faces among the regulars, nor did they seem to recognize me. So I hiked up to Julius' Castle, where, to my delight, after only a little prodding, Julius remembered me and bought me a drink. But it was no Barolo this time, just a cheap, vinegary Chianti. Then, without even asking me for an account of my miraculous survival, he immediately started talking about the war. The mood was glum, and all anyone felt like doing was chewing on headlines. I had been a headline too, just a couple of weeks ago, but nobody seemed to remember that or much care.

Needing a guaranteed boost, I decided to drop in at my agent's office on Spear Street. I figured it was time to get the ole Halifax Word Factory fired up again.

The Feakins Agency had nursed me from a shy cub on the school-cafeteria lecture circuit into a red-meat raconteur who could fill

318

Veterans Auditorium with fainting room only. I'd made Fred Feakins more money than any of his other authors and speakers combined, and now that I had survived the great disaster of the *Soup Dumpling*, I was excited to see the look on Fred's face when I pitched him the book version of my adventure tale. Dollar signs would light up in his eyes like a slot machine, and he'd break out the champagne in anticipation of another Halifax coup.

But no corks were popped that afternoon. Instead, Feakins said that, harrowing as my ordeal must have been, the war was turning harrowing ordeals into dime-a-dozen dross. "They're blowing up ocean liners now, Dick. Nobody's got an appetite for hearing how your *Soup Dumpling* sank. In fact, most people think you kind of had it coming. Sorry, kid."

I was crushed. I moped my way back up to Union Square, where I sat and watched the pigeons take dumps on tourists. It only cheered me a little, but I now discern in it a lesson, boys, which is the following: It's okay to feel sorry for yourself when the world drops a steaming load on your shoulder, but sooner or later you just have to wipe it off and seek out clearer skies. Because it's always sunny and birdless somewhere.

And sure enough, just this afternoon there was a letter waiting for me. It was from a group called the German American Business League, inviting me to come speak at their Friday Frühstück series. It's not exactly Carnegie Hall, and the pay is well below my usual rate, but as I recall from my first speaking gig at the Arthur Avenue orphan asylum, you gotta start somewhere. Besides, I'm not sure if this is something cooked up by the Nazi consul—it sure isn't the work of my deadbeat agent!—and I'm keen to avoid being thought of as one of Wiedemann's "loose ends" that may or may not need tying up.

But what matters most, boys, is that I'm back on the lecture circuit and back in the saddle.

Your pal,
Dicky

34

HILDEGARD RAUCH

Propped up against the pillows, you turn to me, staring like a fish in an aquarium.

"Well . . . how was Hades?"

"*Oh, what a time I had with Minnie the Mermaid, down at the bottom of the sea.*"

"Eiko . . ."

"*I lost all my troubles down amongst those bubbles. Why, she was just as sweet as could be.*"

"Eiko, please . . ."

"We were there together, Ildi. A sea of pure blue tranquility like you could only imagine . . . You were hugging me, and together we just floated in a delicious weightlessness. But then you let go and turned away. Then the cord was caught around my neck and I began to choke. I knew the only way I would survive was if I crawled out and escaped into the world above. Seems like it took me years to make it back."

"Six months and ten days, to be precise."

"So the nurses tell me. And the world's still here."

"For now. Though Hitler's trying his best to end it. He's already invaded—"

"Sorry, I don't think I'm ready for the world report yet."

"Very well."

"I know you're angry with me. I could hear you fuming in my dreams."

"I was worried I would never get to be angry with you again. . . . Look, I'm sorry you were in such a desperate place, I truly am. And I wish I could understand it, but I don't. I doubt I ever will. All I know is that your pain causes me so much pain. You've broken my heart so many ways in the last six months that swallowing all those pills was just the beginning."

"The pills?"

"Oh, Eiko, I can't do this with you now. Look, I know about you and Richard Halifax. And unless I've gone crazy trying to make sense of everything you left in your wake, I know you saw him the night you scribbled that letter to me. So what exactly did he say to you that made you so distraught that you couldn't bear to live anymore?"

"I don't know what you mean."

"Please, Eiko. It was in your suicide note."

"I never wrote a suicide note."

"You did. I read it. A full typed page. *I can't live in a world without Dick.* Sound familiar?"

"Not a bad line, but not mine."

"Your memory is still foggy."

"No, I do remember. It was Dick. He made me take those pills. He must have written that note afterward."

"You're saying Richard Halifax forced the pills down your throat and then staged it as a suicide?"

"I don't know. Maybe."

"Eiko, tell me the truth. What are you saying? Did he try to kill you?"

"I don't know what he did after I lost consciousness, Ildi—all I can tell you is what happened before everything went black."

"Then tell me everything."

"He came to my hotel room. The papers had just declared him dead, but I swear it was him. He looked awful, he was totally deranged, but it was Dick."

"He wanted the microdots?"

"Yes. How did you know?"

"That's a whole other story. Go on."

"He said his doctors demanded them. He said he had to complete his mission and go back to Tokyo so that he could finally return to Hollywood and achieve the kind of literary and film career he was destined for."

"What on earth does that mean?"

"Like I said, he was deranged. But he made it sound like he had been sent at the bidding of the Germans or the Japanese or, I don't know, maybe both. He kept saying that if he could just bring them what they wanted, then they would give him back the keys to his old life. That the Nazi consul in Los Angeles could open the doors for him at all the studios and make him a star. So, when I told him that he was out of his mind and he could go to hell, well, that's when he threw me down on the bed and . . ."

"And made you take those pills?"

"No. That's when he made love to me."

"What? You mean he forced himself on you?"

"No, no. It wasn't like that. It was just, the passion shifted and my fear and anger turned to desire, and for the first time Dick reciprocated. At least at first."

"So, what—you fucked each other and then he tried to kill you?"

"That's when it gets blurry for me. It was all very sudden."

"Think, Eiko. What happened?"

"I don't know. We were in the throes of it when I felt something come crashing down on my skull."

"He hit you?"

"I don't think so. I don't know. Maybe I hit my head on the wall? In any event, I must have passed out."

"But that's impossible. When did he feed you the pills? When did you write me that letter on the hotel stationery—the one that came to me in the mail?"

"Oh wait, yes, I remember now. I remember being conscious, but just barely. I couldn't open my eyes. I couldn't speak. I couldn't move, but I remember being aware that Dick was putting pills in my mouth. Pouring them down my throat with vodka."

"To be clear, he was trying to kill you?"

"I don't know. Maybe. I don't think so. All I know is that after some time, I came to. But my head throbbed terribly and I was very woozy from the pills. Dick was in the bathroom; I could hear him talking to himself. He sounded insane—something about the bloom of health in the flower of death, about coconut farms, about the debt that can never be repaid. Everything was a delirium."

"Why didn't you run out of the room?"

"There was no chance of me going anywhere. My legs already felt like concrete. I could hardly stand. I tried to make myself vomit, but I didn't have the strength. I could hear Dick still talking to himself in the bathroom, so I reached for the phone and tried to call you."

"Why me? Why not call the police?"

"I don't know. I only knew I needed help, and you were the first thought that came to mind. But when you didn't answer, I used all my remaining strength to scribble that note to you, then called for a bell-hop. I was just able to put it in an envelope and slip it under the door. And then I fell."

"He hit you?"

"I don't know—all I remember is falling. Falling backward. I just kept falling, down into a bottomless ocean."

"So you're saying when Halifax returned to the room, either he hit you or he didn't, and then he thought you were dead and tried to make it look like a suicide?"

"I guess so, if you say there was a suicide note. All I know is that I didn't write one. . . . Look, I know how it sounds, Ildi. But I'm telling you the truth. . . . Do you believe me?"

"I don't know what to believe, Eiko. You've been dreaming for the last six months."

"You found the papers in Father's library, right?"

"Inside Zweig's *Joseph Fouché*."

"Thank God. And you burned them?"

"I wish more than anything I had."

"So that's why you're mad at me."

"Why did you do it, Eiko? Do you really want to destroy our father?"

"Why didn't you burn them like I told you to?"

"Because I needed to understand! I couldn't obey a command like a machine without first knowing why. And now that I understand the meaning of those documents, I don't think I can ever look at you again without hating you."

"It was his idea, Hilde."

"Whose?"

"Dick's! You have to believe me."

"Why should I?"

"Because I'm telling you the truth. Look, I just wanted to get my hands on the diary. That's how it all started. I got a letter from Shanghai. Someone had found Father's valise and had written to the forwarding address that was on the luggage, which was to my bungalow in Hollywood. This was right after he had publicly humiliated me in print and condemned my journal to failure. I was furious. I was hurt too. All I could think about was how Father said that if that diary ended up in the wrong hands, the results would be catastrophic. And I knew some of it was indeed damning. Well, that sounded pretty good to me then. So I responded and arranged for the diary's retrieval. It was time for Father to stop hiding behind that prim, aloof image of his. If he was going to publicly sabotage my hopes for being a writer, well, then maybe I would threaten to show the world the real thoughts behind the Grand Old Humanist and High Priest of Literature. That's all it was. An idea."

"But, Eiko . . . our father never touched us."

"Of course not. He never so much as even hugged us. And now you know why."

"What are you saying?"

"He had thoughts, Hilde. Thoughts that fathers should not have for their sons."

"But his diary wasn't yours to read in the first place! Are we to condemn the man for his private thoughts?"

"Of course not. But I can condemn him for his reaction to those thoughts. Don't you think it explains why he was so aloof, why he regarded me in particular as such a threat? I attracted him and it revolted him."

"But what about those horrible lies? You say there is some truth to it, but what about the lies?"

"That was Dick's doing. I had no idea what he was up to. You see, before my trip, I had been asked by the Anti-Fascist Writers League to pass along messages to a certain bookshop in Shanghai. They paid well, and all I had to do was carry messages. Well, when my trip got delayed, Dick offered to be my proxy. He was the one who, without my permission, told the Comintern agent in the Shanghai bookshop about

Father's diary and set up a deal to have it published in *Free Masses*. Then, after I had retrieved the diary, I left it in his care in Hong Kong for a few days while I went upriver to Canton to report a piece. When I came back, he handed me the diary in microdot form and said the original had burned in a hotel fire—a total lie. Only later did he admit to me that he had 'jazzed it up' and that the money we'd get from *Free Masses* would keep my journal well in the black. I said, 'What do you mean, jazzed it up? You added all sorts of horrible lies! Lies about my father seducing my sister and me. Lies about my father wanting to murder my mother because she was a nasty Jew and because she was all that stood in the way of him turning his home into an endless parade of Nordic boy flesh.'

"He said Father's diary was filled with a few lurid thoughts and fantasies, but that if I really wanted to sink his ship, thought had to become action."

"And then what did you do?"

"Well, naturally, I was horrified."

"But even once you knew it was a forgery, you still kept it. You hid those disgusting lies in our parents' home."

"That was just to bide my time. I didn't know what to do. I tried not to think about it while I waited for Dick to get home so I could confront him. Of course, he never came home, or hadn't yet anyway. Meanwhile, the people who had been supporting me and my work—"

"You mean your Stalinist paymasters in the Comintern."

"Yes. Them. Well, they were anxious for me to follow through with handing the diary over so it could be published. But I kept putting them off. I delayed until I heard about Stalin's pact with Hitler and then . . ."

"That's when you recovered your conscience."

"I started receiving threats. I was told that if the diary was not handed over soon, then grave repercussions would follow. Well, I'll tell you what, that certainly curbed the self-destructive urge. No greater spur to life than knowing someone wants you dead. So before I left L.A., I hid the microdots of the diary in Father's library. I suppose I figured it was safest there and that's where it should have been all along."

"But what about when you told me you were only one unmet fix from offing yourself?"

"I guess I wanted you to feel sorry for me. I sensed you'd grown tired of me, and I was fishing for pity. And some cash. I felt terrible about what I had set in motion. But I did not swallow those pills to escape, Ildi. I swear to you. All I know is that when I started falling, my only hope was that you would get to those papers before Dick or anyone else did and prevent my mess from outliving me."

"Instead, I've only made a bigger mess."

"I guess we're more alike than either of us thought."

ꙅIMON FᴧULK

My idea for getting even with Halifax first took shape in the dark clarity of Pal's Rendezvous, in between those hospital visits. The premise was established there. What followed was just the reasonable conclusion.

I knew Richard Halifax was a fraud and an enemy spy, yet I had no way of using this knowledge to unmask him. It had become clear I would not convince Special Agent Cliff Hader of his guilt, at least not based on my current shaky roster of witnesses. Sally Bent would cling to her original story in futile hopes of keeping her insurance money; the shoeshine boys, as O'Malley warned me, would deny everything; the old lift attendant at the Sir Francis Drake would keep his head down; and Wiedemann, naturally, barring a British-funded new life in Canada, wouldn't admit a thing. Marie might be willing to testify, but to what? A likeness to a man who would surely look different the moment he was released from hospital and given a chance to groom himself? Hader was right. It was pure bollocks.

What's more, I could tell Hader was charmed by Halifax. And it took only minimal powers of detection to know he was less than charmed by me. That meant tangible evidence of Halifax's guilt was required to make Hader see beyond his prejudicial view. And if the past evidence was insufficient, then I would need future proof of his guilt. In other words, if I couldn't prove that Richard Halifax was already a Nazi agent, I would just have to turn him into one. And here my dead end, the Nazi consul Fritz Wiedemann, could be of help to me.

I recalled what Hader had told me at one of our meetings last fall: Wiedemann's inheritance funds were filled with bills marked by the FBI. This money had so far only turned up at dinners used to broach the illicit purchase of area newspapers, but Bureau informants in various Nazi-aligned organizations were on the lookout for them. Presumably, if Wiedemann agreed to fork over such a hefty sum as ten thousand dollars to a single agent, it was because he was drawing from this off-the-books account.

This is why I made Halifax bring me money from Wiedemann. I have no reason to lie at this point. I would admit to greed, but the truth is I didn't care about the money—after all, it wasn't my *money* that Halifax had stolen, just everything else: my happiness, my dignity, etc. Of course, I was not above stowing some of that cash in my floorboards to spend in the future, once I was beyond the purview of the FBI. A most venial sin in our profession, where venality is all but expected, but one I now have cause to regret.

By the middle of May, of the ten thousand dollars Halifax brought me as part of his debt-repayment plan, six thousand had gone back out in envelopes containing thank-you notes signed by Richard Halifax to suspected Nazi-front organizations, all of which were under FBI watch. In doing so, I had established a paper trail between Halifax, Wiedemann, and the homegrown Nazis that Berlin supposedly disavowed—a body of evidence that Cliff Hader and the Bureau would no longer be able to ignore.

It worked like this: My informant in the German American Business League, on my orders, suggested to his fellow members that they invite Richard Halifax as a guest speaker at their weekly Friday business breakfast. He assured them the writer-adventurer was, wink-wink, "particularly sympathetic to the spirit of German American business." The Nazis all winked back approvingly, happy to keep up the appearance of a real cultural organization. The next week, Halifax came to the Deutsches Haus and told them one of his potted adventure stories until their eggs went cold, and everyone went their merry way. The next day, the chair of the German American Business League received an envelope containing a signed thank-you letter from Richard Halifax— his signature forged by me from the affidavits he'd signed upon his return, testifying to his identity—along with two thousand dollars of Wiedemann's bills as a charitable donation.

I should have had enough to trap Halifax with this association alone, but I would leave nothing to chance. I wanted to overwhelm the FBI with evidence of his Nazi connections. So Richard Halifax received an invitation to another Deutsches Haus event, this time to the Nordic Choral Singers Society, then to the Germanic Association for Peace and Freedom. After each lecture, special envelopes of appreciation were sent, which, as mentioned, were observed by the FBI informants currently embedded in these groups.

Halifax, of course, thought he had been invited to speak at these events on his own merit, when the truth is, the world had long ago moved on from his tiresome antics and the whole thing was designed by me.

You can now appreciate my stroke of insight when, at lunch one day at Omar Khayyam's, my uncle mentioned the need for a last-minute speaker at the opening ceremonies of the Treasure Island fair at the end of May. He had spent the last bottle of Shiraz complaining of the numerous demands that the second season was making on the consulate in preparation for British Empire Day, especially given that the advisory committee he sat on was at pains not to have the Fair in Forty be another flop.

"I haven't hit the green in a week. Can you imagine? My short game will go to the dogs with that kind of neglect. And now fresh disaster has struck. Her eminence Gertrude Atherton has diverticulitis and has withdrawn from speaking at the opening ceremony. Not that I'll shed a tear for the old fuss muffin, but we're in dire need of a replacement."

The lamb kofta arrived to our table, sizzling and fragrant with sumac, ending my uncle's litany. "Oh, listen to me grumbling about my burdens when there's meat like this before us. *Lord be Thankit!*"

Up until this point, I had been only half-listening to him. I was preoccupied with Hildegard Rauch. I hadn't much faith that my proposed exchange of documents would bear fruit, but it was worth a shot, even if I felt a touch slimy playing the role of blackmailer.

"Who are you going to invite to replace her?" I asked my uncle, in a desultory attempt to keep the ball in the air. "Gertrude Atherton, that is."

"Well, that's just it, laddie. I've been doing what I can to infuse some 'Johnny get your gun and show that dirty Hun' sentiment into the proceedings, without appearing to engage in outright propaganda, mind, but the committee was counting on Lady Atherton to balance the interventionist leanings of our other keynote speaker, Theodor Rauch. Which I'm proud to say was my doing."

The name Rauch made me perk up. "I must say, I'm surprised Theodor Rauch accepted. A world's fair seems a bit beneath someone of his Olympian stature."

"Nonsense. That old laurel hound accepted as soon as we told him he was receiving a Spirit of Adventure Award. The man travels around the country collecting doctorates and trophies and plaques in exchange for a few rousing words about humanity."

I didn't remind my uncle that he himself had cooed over the very same award when the fair organizers bestowed it upon him last year.

"You know how these celebrity types are, my boy—they simply crave adulation."

That was the moment a dark corner of my brain was suddenly bathed in light, and the words just spilled out: "What about inviting Richard Halifax to speak?"

"Halifax? You mean the shipwrecked adventurer who just washed ashore?"

"Precisely." I'd realized that I could apply my formula for trapping Richard Halifax on a far grander scale. It would not only sink him in spectacular and public fashion; it would also move the needle on my real task here: to expose Nazi intrigues and bolster American support for the war. Of course, I couldn't claim credit for the idea myself. Fritz Wiedemann was the one I should thank. For he'd given me a way to do my job and have my revenge all at once. It was just as Baron Corvo had told me when I was a boy: *All lines eventually converge.*

"That reminds me," said Uncle Paul. "The Stephens family is crying bloody murder. They're claiming Halifax should stand trial for gross negligence. But you really think he's fit to be a speaker?"

"Of course. Lawsuits notwithstanding, Uncle, he's captured the public imagination. He'd be quite a draw, I should think."

"Really? I hadn't realized that . . ."

"Oh, certainly. Great adventurer, waylaid by fortune and shorn of his ship, still makes it home across the Pacific a year later. Quite a miraculous tale. Unbelievable, really."

"Mmm, yes. Does have something of the mythic about it. Full circle, as it were."

"And hard to think of a better man than him to represent Pacific unity. I was going to say 'the face of Pacific unity,' but after his ordeal, I'm afraid he's rather lost his looks."

"Oh dear. Is he ghastly?"

"Nothing a toupee and some stage makeup can't fix."

"Well, I must say I think it's a fine idea. Splendid, in fact." If Uncle Paul liked an idea, he warmed to it immediately, until it became his own passionate wish.

Three days later I was waiting by the bus stop across from the Deutsches Haus. The Golden Gate International Exposition's advisory committee had invited Richard Halifax to speak at the opening ceremony and—as I knew he would, for the desperate vanity of the man was as dependable as the rising of the sun—Halifax had accepted. Resisting the temptation to scratch my fake beard, I watched the Bundists file out from their noonday meeting. Presently, my informant came out and lifted his chin toward a pair of men in front of him—one a fat man in short sleeves, the other a rail-thin ferrety bloke in a chambray coat. They looked like they knew more about eating hamburgers and catching rats than they did about making bombs.

I trailed the two Bundists to a metalworks shop on South Van Ness. The half hour's walk in raised-heel shoes had already given me blisters, and my spectacles had slipped down the bridge of my nose at least a hundred times. But, ridiculous as I looked, for the kind of job I had in mind, the disguise was necessary.

I entered the garage and found the fat man, now in coveralls, bent over some kind of a lathe making a deafening screech. Sensing my presence, he stopped what he was doing and turned off the machine. "Sorry, mister, we're closed today for orders. You'll have to come back tomorrow."

"I am an associate of *Reichskonsul* Wiedemann," I said, disguising my voice in the accented English of my mother. "And I am told we share similar interests."

"And what might those be?" said the ferret, who'd just come out from the office.

"Sabotage. Mayhem. The murder of prominent Roosevelt worshippers and Jews."

The two men exchanged glances. "I don't know nothing about that, mister," said the fat man. "Sounds like crazy talk."

I set three thick stacks of Wiedemann's bills on a workbench.

The ferret went to the garage door and lowered it.

"Are you familiar with the writer Theodor Rauch?" I asked.

They both nodded.

"Good. I want you to kill him."

36

HILDEGARD RAUCH

You were standing in the kitchen with my triptych of paintings lined up against the windows. Alive. Awake. You'd slept on my couch the night before, and this morning I had observed the miracle of you opening your eyes. And even though I am no longer at your bedside, filled with worry and hope and rage, I still can't stop addressing these thoughts to you. I've never kept a diary, but the unsent, unread, even unwritten letter might be the most honest form of communication ever invented.

I handed you a mug of coffee and watched as you took in the paintings.

"What do you call it?" you asked.

"*The Geminicide.*"

The first showed two fetuses in the womb, in an amniotic yellow haze, one strangling the other. The second, on a cerulean-blue field, twin children in profile, face-to-face, each with their dagger thrust in the other's chest. And the final one, set against dark jade and ivory, adult twins male and female, both of them in the bath, legs entwined, with all four of their wrists slit.

I had drawn on my old studies at the Berlin city morgue and the pathological-specimens wing of the Charité Hospital. Though I had done those over ten years ago, there was little need to consult them, as they had been living vividly in my mind ever since. But unlike the sickly visceral pink of Dix's lust-murders or the dizzying Dutch angles of Grosz's death scenes, my twin murders were muted, otherworldly affairs. Rather than cast a light on the gory world outside, these scenes were illuminations of the interior realm. The children were naturalistically rendered, yet with a kind of medieval gauziness and simplified iconography, with flaxen hair and milky blue-white skin. Their green-eyed gazes met, lips slightly parted, locked in the eternal embrace of oblivion.

The paintings were not, I had come to realize, simple fantasies of rage toward you. They were as much expressions of my fear: that you were destroying me, that I was failing you and letting you die, that you were trying to destroy our whole family all because of the rivalry between you and Father. But neither of these feelings—the anger or the fear—could have existed outside the ether of love.

That feeling of roots, of continuity, of some kind of a warm refuge in the world, I now understood, could only be attained with you—my miserable, vengeful, self-destructive brother. That was why I was so scared, why I hated you so much for trying to abandon me. Because, quite simply, I loved you.

Of course I always knew I loved you, but the force of the revelation was in how I thought of myself. I grasped that, despite my reputation, despite my own self-image, I was not cold or callous or aloof. On the contrary: I was a creature driven by love.

An insight so obscenely self-evident and dangerously close to schmaltz that it made me cackle. How many paintings would I have to do before I had the revelation that I was also a creature who needs to eat and shit? But corollary realizations followed.

The High Priest's cool demeanor was not mine. The two of us were, in fact, different, though it was entirely possible that beneath his own aloofness burned an inner passion that was so precarious—or unspeakable—that it had to be protected and hidden away. Without the tension, without the undetonated charge, perhaps there would be nothing to sublimate, no powerful current beneath the placid surface of his prose. He had written somewhere that art was the compromise between respectability and the madhouse. While Father is undeniably a great artist, and I believe it gives him real pleasure to live his life in total devotion to his art, I am also quite sure he is miserable. But does devotion to a calling necessarily come at the expense of love and compassion? I don't know the answer, but I am going to live as though both are possible.

I also finally realized just how cruel it was for Father to belittle you in print. It is one thing for critics or fellow writers to tear one another down in public, and it is commonplace for parents to diminish their children's creative ambitions in private, but for the two domains to collapse into the act of a father publicly ridiculing his son's talent, well—there is something *incestuous* about it. It is a violation of one's duties as a father.

"They're beautiful," you said after observing the paintings in silence. "And frightening. Just like my coma dream."

I could tell you meant it. Though I still wasn't sure I believed everything else you had told me—that your attempted suicide was really Richard Halifax's deranged coital or postcoital assault, or that publishing Father's diary was all his idea. I want to believe you, I really do. And I believe you enough to feel unnerved knowing Halifax is out walking the streets, unsure of what designs he still has on you. That is why I insisted you stay with me—I've even put a moratorium on my one-night-only guest policy.

I worry that, despite everything, you still have feelings for him. When I urged you to go to the police with your story, you refused. "I'll say only this and say it only once," I told you before we left the hospital. "If even half of what you told me is true, then it should be crystal clear to you that Richard Halifax is a fraud and a maniac. He hurt you, Eiko. He maybe even tried to murder you. There. That's it." That was all I had said. And I don't know what more I can do.

Standing in my apartment, back among the living, you drained the rest of your coffee. "So, shall we get to work?"

"You're sure you're feeling up to it?" I asked.

"Never felt better." You fetched the blackout curtains, thumbtacks, trays, and two five-gallon buckets and retreated to my closet. It had been emptied of all my things and was awaiting its new incarnation as a darkroom.

I laid out a compass, protractor, and mechanical pencil across my desk and, propping up my model diagram on a stand, set about drafting my first forgery. I of course had no idea what the Norden bombsight was or what it—or, rather, its fake counterpart—even looked like, other than my dim recollections of the drawings that night in the photography wing. But I hoped that at a passing glance it looked similar enough to the guts of my children's microscope—the one I'd bought in order to detect the fakes Walter fobbed off on me—with all its baffling instructional diagrams. At the very least, the two contraptions both had lenses and something called an "obverse housing unit." With the drawings photographed and shrunken onto a sad letter from Richard Halifax to Sally Bent, which we typed from memory, I prayed it was close enough to pull off.

I was taking Nadia's advice about trading lies with the Englishman, though I was declining her assistance. While I wanted to believe what Nadia had told me about Walter, about their marriage, about her genuine sympathy for me, a lurking skepticism remained. I still didn't know who she really was or who she worked for—some shadowy anarchist network is presumably what she wanted me to believe—but asking her would not likely yield the truth. And now that you were back, you could develop the photos and make the microdots yourself. It was better this way, the two of us cleaning up our own family mess together.

Two days later I met the Englishman Fox at a nearby bar, where we swapped envelopes under the table. He tried to make it feel like it was a date rather than blackmail, which was pathetic and no less nerve-racking. But, by some miracle, he accepted the microdots. And that afternoon, Father's diary was finally where it belonged—up in smoke through my chimney. All this madness for a fake diary and a fake set of plans. So much flailing and grasping at detritus. So much life consumed in the pursuit of nothing.

That same night, Nadia showed up at my door. I assumed she came to offer her assistance with the Norden plans—or had she smelled the scent of the burning diary?—but she had other matters to discuss.

"Is it true you will be accompanying your father at the opening ceremonies on Treasure Island?" she asked.

I was, albeit reluctantly. After the business with the diary, it was hard to imagine facing Father, let alone playing interpreter and chaperoning him and Mother around the fair. And yet, partly out of my anger toward you this winter as well as my own cowardice, I had still said yes.

"Ah wonderful. You see, I wish I could attend too, but in fact my comrades and I are having a celebration that day. One of our own is being released from jail after twenty-four years of false imprisonment. Perhaps you've heard of the Preparedness Day bombing?"

I told her I'd seen the headlines. The governor had pardoned those convicted of an anarchist attack in the city back in 1916.

"Precisely. But really, that's neither here nor there. What I want to talk to you about is Richard Halifax."

That name curdled in my ears. Then I recalled that Nadia had also brought up Halifax just before I received the call from the hospital saying you were awake. "What about him?" I said, unable to hide my contempt.

"I hear he will be speaking at the opening ceremony alongside your father, Diego Rivera, and Governor Olson. Quite a motley lineup, I must say. Now, tell me, didn't you once say that you know Halifax?"

I didn't recall telling Nadia, though it must have come out during their Halloween party, after my mind had been taken over by gin. "We met only briefly."

"You know," said Nadia, "I met Richard Halifax once too. In Spain. And, judging by the tone in your voice, I believe we hold similar opinions of the man."

Nadia then told me that Halifax had come to Barcelona during the war to raise money for the republican side. "This was when every left-leaning celebrity with half a bleeding heart came over to chant Popular Front slogans. Most of these fools meant well enough, even though they were too blind to see that the very people they championed were being gutted by their supposed comrades in the Comintern and that every *¡No pasarán!* muffled a Stalinist bullet to the neck of a real revolutionary.

"Even in this atmosphere rife with bad faith, Richard Halifax distinguished himself. He and his photographer went round to the hospitals filled with wounded republicans. On the face of it, it looked very gallant, if a little gross. Halifax posing beside the maimed and amputated in their hospital beds, clenching his fist and flashing all thirty-two of his white teeth in solidarity. He was the toast of La Rambla that week he was there, standing people drinks at the Hotel

Continental, charming the pants off the foreign correspondents, including myself. He claimed the donations were already pouring in and that, once word got round to *The Saturday Evening Post* and *Ladies' Home Journal* and *Collier's* and *Boys' Life*, plenty more would be on the way. I was stringing for the *Vanguard* at the time and had my ear to the ground, but as far as I know not a single cent ever made it into any republican or revolutionary organization's hands."

"So he was a con man?" I asked.

"No, no, Hildchen. He was far worse than that. You see, I later learned, through my other channels, that the photographs Halifax had taken beside wounded Germans from the Durruti Column had been given to the Gestapo and used to target their families back in Germany. Hundreds of people ended up tortured and in the Lager thanks to him. And you know what their fate will be, if they're not already dead. No, my dear. Richard Halifax is not just a con man. He's scum.

"Now, tell me, Hildchen. All this bad business about your brother and his microdots, and Walter's thievery, and this Englishman blackmailing you—be honest: It has to do with Richard Halifax, doesn't it?"

"How do you know all this, Nadia?"

"I told you, dear, I have some friends in Shanghai. The true revolutionaries are scattered far and wide, but we're still here. Rumors have come my way that Richard Halifax was plotting, with the help of the Comintern, to publish a diary of your father's. Something rather terrible and damning. And I wager if it involved Richard Halifax and your father's diary, it likely involved your brother too. And if it involved your brother and the Comintern, then that's likely also what Walter was mixed up in, and the blackmailing Englishman as well. I know only enough about Halifax to know his total lack of scruples, and where there is something unsavory afoot, he is likely at the center of it."

I was as astounded as I was wary. The more I knew of Nadia, the more I doubted she was working for a network of stateless, uprooted anarchists. Yet how truly radical she would be in this world if she was simply telling the truth. "What do you want, Nadia?"

"What if I told you that you had a very special opportunity to get even with Halifax? For your brother. For the anti-fascists whose families were sent to concentration camps because of him. I know you are a bourgeois little *Künstlerin*, Hilde, but I also know you care for your brother and you once supported the people of Spain and deep down you are revolted by the injustice of the world. Isn't that true?"

"Yes. But what do you mean, 'get even'? What are you asking me?"

"I'm asking you to stand up for your family and for justice. Not with words, not with paintings. Just the simplest act. The purest expression of direct action. To strike a blow for the humanity you say you believe in—to put a stop to Halifax and all his future betrayals. Right there on the world's stage."

ſIMON FÁULK

The plan was a simple stitch-up, which these days is all the rage. The Japanese blew up their own railway line to justify the invasion of Manchuria. The Red Army, just last fall, shelled their own territory in Karelia and then made a rather flimsy attempt to pin it on the Finns. And there is ample suspicion that Hitler did something similarly tricky in that alleged Polish attack on the radio station in the German borderlands, giving him his excuse for invading Poland. So why couldn't I assassinate Germany's greatest living writer and voice of embattled humanism and make it look like it was the work of the Nazis?

Just like Wiedemann had once said, killing Theodor Rauch would be the perfect bit of negative propaganda—what the anarchists used to call "propaganda of the deed"—to drum up American sentiment against Germany. The idea was just the kind of bold and devious trickery the newly installed Churchill would have loved, though of course he couldn't know I masterminded the whole thing. Officially, I would perform only the humble role of exposing the plot in the nick of time. There was no need to actually kill Theodor Rauch, you understand. That was never my plan. Obviously, the effect would be more dramatic and therefore better if I had done, but I was no cold-blooded murderer. No, all I had to do was set enough of a tangible conspiracy in motion so that it could be known and stopped, with a clear line of evidence to the chief culprit: Richard Halifax, Nazi agent and assassin.

I had told the Bundist metalsmiths that the device should be small, as small as possible. Something that could be detonated at a set time while Rauch was at the lectern and not injure any others. "Perhaps you could fit it in something like this," I'd said in their garage, pulling out of my bag the Spirit of Adventure trophy that had sat on Sir Paul's desk—a slim chrome figure with large wings and an uplifted chest on a thick broad base.

Using the Golden Gate International Exposition letterhead purloined from my uncle, I then wrote to Halifax under the guise of a fair organizer, informing him we would like to custom-design the figure on the trophy he would be receiving at the opening ceremony—could he please visit the trophy makers' shop to have his dimensions and profile taken? A few days before the fair's opening, another letter was sent, this time requesting that he come to the plaza of the Federal Building on Treasure Island so that they could conduct a sound test and be sure that the lectern was of suitable height; oh, and please feel free to have a look around. The whole time, Halifax remained an unwitting dupe. I had Halifax at the bombmakers; Halifax poking around the stage at the fair, unauthorized, just before the opening; not to mention all of Halifax's recent visits, speaking fees, and sizable donations to various German cultural organizations—all documented, and with the breadcrumb trail of what were presumably Wiedemann's marked bills. Richard Halifax had become my little windup toy, mechanically putting the noose around himself. *How's that for a tight spot, Dicky?*

I had only to sound the alarm, add my evidence to what was already being tracked by the FBI, and voilà. My plan was to divulge the Rauch bomb plot at the last possible moment, just so that I could see Halifax pulled from the stage by federal agents and unmasked before the public.

I found myself imagining Halifax's arrest at the podium and the headlines of shock and outrage that would follow. I'll admit that I had become consumed with the idea of his ruin. Perhaps it was bordering on obsession. But I never lost sight of my mission. It was, I maintain, still in the name of the greater good. With one well-placed explosion, I could singlehandedly change the course of public opinion in this country. And if the Americans entered the war that summer, we could very well stop Hitler dead in his tracks.

I was so intoxicated with these thoughts that I had to remind myself that I was going to expose the plot before the bomb actually went off and anyone got hurt.

It all would have worked too, if only I hadn't blundered into the trap. I suppose Uncle Paul is right and I really am a romantic at heart. As well as a damned fool.

A week before the fair's opening, I went to a room in the Golden Gate Motor Inn, where Marie was lying on the bed in her underwear, with her stockinged feet up against the wall. She had her head in a magazine, the Dorsey Brothers blaring on the coin-operated radio, and she looked up for only an instant to register my presence. I should have known something was amiss. But then, I was never quite sure where the two of us stood. She was still a working girl, and I was still paying her as an informant. But whether these other services were simply gratis transactions or a sign of something more between us, I didn't know. The cruel, baseless idea that Halifax had planted in my mind about Anya—that she was the one who disclosed the arms deal to the pro-Japanese Thais—well, I didn't believe it, but I also didn't want to believe it. I fetched two glasses from the bathroom and cracked open the fresh bottle I'd brought.

I was feeling especially pleased that day. To my great surprise, my gamble on Hildegard Rauch had paid off; she really did have the Norden plans, and thanks to Wiedemann's tip, I just so happened to have the perfect leverage to extract them from her. We met in a tavern on Polk Street. I had ordered her a martini in hopes of making our exchange as civil as possible, but she came in eyeing me with disdain, handed me an envelope, and stayed only long enough for me to go to the loo to check with a magnifying glass that several characters on a maudlin letter from Halifax to Sally Bent indeed contained little drawings. When I returned and, holding up my end of the bargain, gave her the envelope with the prints and negatives of her father's diary, she left without a word. Oh well. I wasn't out to make friends.

I stowed the document in the consular safe until I could arrange a diplomatic courier to take it directly to London. I was, after all, playing with fire—stealing state military secrets from my assigned host country. But so long as I kept the Americans in the dark, the Norden bombsight plans would be the bright-red cherry of my redemption atop the knicker-bocker glory of Halifax's ruin. Why, even the hills of Marin, now green with spring, had begun to charm me.

I was just about to toast to our good fortune when Marie, who'd had her head buried in that magazine the whole time, suddenly leapt up and said, "Sally gave me the weekend free. Why don't we go on a trip together, Simon, just you and me?"

"A trip?"

"Yes. Not as, you know . . . business. But as . . . lovers?"

"Oh, I see." Her proposal floored me. I suddenly realized that I'd been protecting myself.

My God, I thought. Perhaps I could fall in love with Marie. Her small golden body, her thorough inquiring mind, and that sweet little accent and gap-toothed smile—what was not to love?

"Well, I think it's a marvelous idea. But where should we go?"

"Reno."

"Reno?"

"Yes. It's in Nevada. In the mountains, but full of glitz. We can go dancing."

"Well, why not? Let's go to Reno."

We had what I thought was a lovely time together, even if the love-making didn't quite add up to love. But on the drive back, Marie, who had been quiet and withdrawn ever since we checked out of our hotel, said in a sullen voice, "There is something I must tell you, Simon."

"What is it?"

"Fritz Wiedemann contacted me before we left San Francisco. He says he wants to meet with you tomorrow."

I found the consul in the back row of the Esquire, laughing as Laurel and Hardy bumbled around a sailboat.

"You always miss the setup, Herr Faulk. This man, the fat one, is driven crazy by the sound of horns. Unfortunately, he works at a horn factory. So, to cure him, the skinny one takes him on a sailing trip."

"I was surprised you contacted me through Marie," I said, now disgusted to think of them together. "I didn't realize you were still seeing each other."

"I could say the same for you."

"Yes, well, presumably that's not what we're here to discuss."

"I imagine not."

"Well, I'm all ears."

"As am I, Herr Faulk."

"Does this mean you've had a change of heart and are willing to help?"

"I would ask you precisely the same question."

"My God, man, just come out with it. What do you want?"

"You know very well what I want, Herr Faulk. But I've heard nasty rumors lately. So why am I here?"

"You're the one who called this bloody meeting, Wiedemann."

"What are you talking about? You did!"

"No, you damned fool, you did!"

Suddenly we were blinded by a flash of light.

"What the hell was that?"

"Was that a camera flash? You bastard! What are you up to?"

"Did someone just take our picture? Are you trying to set me up?"

"Hey, you back there!" shouted a voice several rows up. "Put a fucking sock in it!"

To: The Dicky Halifax Junior Adventurers Club
From: Dicky Halifax
The Toast of Treasure Island

Springtime 1940

Dear boys,

If there's a message to be gleaned from my adventure, let it be this: With a little bit of talent, a dash of luck, and a whole dump truck of grit, you can claw your way back onto the dais.

For the last couple of weeks, your man Dick has been capturing audience hearts in speaking engagements at a lively downtown venue: the Deutsches Haus. Sure, it's a bit Krauty for me, what with the mural of George Washington and Adolf Hitler saluting each other, and all those crooked little four-leggers flanking the podium. And the thought of being surrounded by possible Bund killers who might view yours truly as a possible loose end did give me the sweats at first. But there's been no sign of anyone gunning for me. Besides, you can't argue with decent acoustics and an attentive crowd, especially for a daytime gig. My throat muscles are loosening up, and I'm starting to feel my way into the material. I'm channeling the spirit of Shackleton and Scott, with a sprinkle of Stevenson and Poe, tentatively titled: "In the Soup! An Odyssey of Shipwreck and Survival on the Pacific."

As for that miserable drip Faulk, I paid off my debt to him and he seems content to leave me alone, at least for the time being. On top of that, I got a nice bit of cumshaw from the transaction, since the Nazi consul didn't so much as blink when I said I needed twenty grand.

Though now I know why.

See, boys, it all started one morning when I strapped on my shiny new spectators and took a stroll down to the Market Street shoeshine stands. I didn't see much polishing afoot, but I did find my little plug-ugly sidekicks, the twin cousins Sinclair. They were sitting on their boxes, chewing tobacco and poring over a Tijuana bible.

"Hiya, boys, how much for a shine?"

The boys eyed each other uneasily.

"What's wrong? Aren't you glad to see me? You know, I wouldn't be here if it weren't for your help. Though I fear you boys might have forgotten to notify the coast guard, as we discussed."

Suddenly, Slop looked like he was on the verge of tears. "Aw, gee, Dicky. Promise you won't be mad?"

"Don't sweat it, fellas. I'm still in one piece. Of course, I don't think I'll ever get the taste of gull blood out of my mouth, but I won't hold a grudge."

"No, Dicky, it's not that."

"Don't, Slop!" said Stinker. "Don't do it!"

"Don't do what, boys? Look, if this is about your rummaging around Hildegard Rauch's place and coming up empty-handed, don't worry. It was a long shot, anyway. I'm afraid that treasure hunt was a dead end."

"No, it's not that either, Dicky. It's much worse."

"I told you not to, Slop!"

"Well, what is it?" I asked. "Nothing's so bad it can't be fixed."

The tears began to leak down Slop's cheek, merging with the tobacco drool already dribbling down his chin. "I'm sorry, but I gotta tell him, Stinker. I can't live with myself if I don't."

"Tell me what?"

Stinker sighed in resignation, then came out with it himself. "We might've accidentally said something to someone about sailing you out to the Farallons."

"Ah, I see." Of course I already knew full well about their betrayal, ever since Faulk blasted the news to me with his gin-stink breath while I was laid up in hospital.

"Are you gonna tell our moms, Dicky?" asked Slop.

"Well, boys, that was part of our bargain, wasn't it?"

"See, I told you we shouldn't've said nothin', you blockhead!"

"Aw, gee, Dicky, we're awful sorry. It's just that all the papers were welcoming you back as a hero and we were so happy for you, we couldn't hold it in. It was like keeping a sneeze locked up—it felt like we were gonna bust."

I felt bad for the little gossips. And though I had been serious about them keeping their traps shut, I could hardly blame them. Besides, I had a bigger threat facing me than the boasts of a couple of street urchins, whose legal testimony, should it ever come to that, would be worth about two warm farts. Instead, I needed their help.

"I forgive you, boys. I know how hard it is not to share the story of an incredible adventure. And I won't tell your mothers, even though I should."

The little rats melted with relief.

"But I will have to request another favor of you."

"Anything, Dicky," said Slop. "We can steal, rob, draw funny pictures . . ."

"Yeah," said Stinker, "and drive cars real fast, and sail boats, and siphon gas, and sneak into the movies, and—"

"How are you boys with a camera?"

Ten minutes later, a Leica had been procured from an unsuspecting tourist, and my young sidekicks and I were skipping our way to the corner of O'Farrell Street. We camped out at Dixon's chili parlor across from the Kraut consulate and watched the swastika swaying in the California breeze while we waited for Wiedemann to show his face. Nine bowls with extra onions later, the Nazi consul came out to his car, looking debonair as always.

"There, boys, that's your man. Did you get a good look?"

They nodded in unison, the two of them with identical rings of chili round their lips.

Then we went over to Montgomery Street, parked ourselves opposite the British consulate, and did the same until the Sinclair cousins got a good eyeful of that British pimple Faulk.

"Alright, boys, remember those two faces. Now, go practice with that camera, and I'll be in touch soon. When you hear from me, I'll be expecting you to be ready to let that Leica rip."

"You betcha, Dicky," said my Junior Adventurers. "We won't let you down."

I gave them a hundred bucks to keep them in my thrall and sent them on their way.

I headed back to my hotel to catch a quick nap before lunch, but blow me down if I didn't find the little urchins, not fifteen minutes later, waiting for me outside with crabbed looks.

"What kind of con you running, Dicky?" said Stinker.

"What do you mean, boys?"

"We mean you scammed us!"

"Maybe he didn't know," said Slop, always the charitable one. "What Stinker means, Dicky, is the dough you gave us is bogus."

"Bogus?"

"Yeah, like counterfeit. See, we went to Gary's Tobacco to load up on supplies, and when we slapped that hundred down on the counter, that old bastard Gary gave us the evil eye. Then he pulled out a magnifying glass and looked at the bill, then held it up to the light, then gave it a sniff, then cleared his throat and made a little 'uh-huh' sound. Then he took the hundred dollars and he tacked it on the wall above the register. 'What gives, Gary?' I says. 'Ain't you gonna give us our change and bag up our haul?' And he says, 'That there's a counterfeit bill, you little hoodlets. And if you ever come back in my shop again to buy so much as a licorice stick, I'll sic the peelers on ye.'"

"Gee, boys," I said, truly surprised at this revelation. Nobody else around town seemed to have the acute eye of this Gary. "I had no idea. You think your man Dicky would've intentionally chumped you like that?"

"See, Stinker, I told you it was an accident. Right, Dicky?"

"You better believe it. Imagine how I feel now, knowing I'm flush with Monopoly money. I'd offer you boys another two hundred for your troubles, but I bet the whole stash is bunk."

"So you ain't gonna give us any real dough?" asked Stinker.

I could smell a shakedown, so I said, "Tell you what, boys. Why don't I just go to your mothers and tell them what a pickle we've gotten ourselves into and see if they have any ideas—"

"No, no, Dicky, it's okay! Never mind!" And off they scampered, the little ingrates. Meanwhile, my head was teeming.

So that explained why Wiedemann had been so loose with his dough—he was feeding me falsies, the old fox. Which meant I was passing on fake dollars to Faulk. Well, that was alright by me. In fact, it suited my plan just fine.

See, it stuck in my craw that Faulk thought he now owned me. Sure, I bilked the guy in Bangkok, and it was only fair he try to get even, but keep me in his blackmail dungeon forever? I didn't much like that. Your man Dick is his own boss. Sure, I'll hire myself out for a gig or repay a favor if need be, but I don't work for anyone but myself. On a similar note, I didn't much like that Nazi consul giving me ultimatums in the sauna while I was treated to a front-row view of his dudelsack.

Now, with my Sinclair boys out practicing their photography, I set about getting a little leverage with which to extricate myself from the clutches of the two consuls.

As you boys know, I'm an inveterate snoop with a keen memory for faces. I once followed a critic who had savaged one of my books for two weeks around Manhattan until I caught him cavorting with a streetwalker in Central Park, snapped a photo, and sent it to his wife. And that trick had given me an idea.

So I spent a few days bloodhounding after both Faulk and Wiedemann. It was easy to do, and at a safe remove, since each had an FBI tail hanging off his rear like a string of cans on the matrimonial getaway car. I slapped on my homburg and sunglasses, hopped in my dark-blue Chrysler Imperial, and joined the parade. And wouldn't you know it, on each diplomatic route, whether German or English, I kept seeing the same little olive-skinned, gap-toothed brunette coming and going from both consuls' quarters. It was a face I knew, and before long I puzzled out that she was the very girl in Sally's office that night last fall when I barged in there like a madman. Well, it hadn't taken more than a few days of peeping to figure out she was doing the two-backed beast with both Faulk and the Nazi consul. Even a little wiener-sucking.

I recalled how Faulk had nearly blown a gasket after I suggested that it was his Siamese courtesan who'd tipped off the gun deal to the Japs. Not true, of course. That was Roderick's stroke of genius, which I was happy to act on. But I liked that it rankled Faulk, and that gave me another idea.

So I cornered this tawny beauty one day outside the Music Box and used all my persuasive charm to convince her to be my go-between. I gave her a sob story about how there was a big misunderstanding about me between the two consuls and I just needed to get them together so that I could sort out the whole mess, but they couldn't know I was arranging the meeting or else they'd never agree to it. I could tell she was skeptical, so I also told her that I remembered bumping into her at the Music Box last fall when I wasn't quite feeling myself. And that, I said, was a dangerous coincidence. "I don't know if you or Sally Bent said anything about me to your friend Faulk, but I'd wager one of you did, since he seemed pretty certain of my visit that night. And, gosh, that puts you gals right in the jaws of the tiger. Unless, of course, you can convince the tiger that you're his friend and he can trust you." Well, that did the trick, and she agreed to tell each of her paramours that the other wanted to meet. I told her she was a smart girl and a good friend and that I now felt like I could trust her. I shoved a wad of bills into her hand and said that as a reward for playing ball, I wanted her to enjoy a weekend in Reno on my dime. "In fact, I already booked a room for you and your special friend Faulk at the Riverside. Under your name, Marie."

I had lumped Sally in with my threat to sweet Marie, but the truth is I would never hurt a hair on ole Sal's head, even if it was she who'd spilled the beans about me to Faulk. In fact, I decided it was high time I put things right between us.

I dropped in at the Music Box before the evening shows and presented myself to her bouncer Tater with a hail-fellow-well-met clap on the back, a barrage of palaver, and a fifty-dollar tip. This got me upstairs.

"Knocky knocky," I said, entering her office. "Look who's back from the dead . . ."

Sally looked up from her accounts book. "You must be braver or stupider than I thought."

"Aw, come on, old girl. Turn that fifty-thousand-dollar frown upside down."

"If this visit is supposed to make me want to kill you any less, it's not working."

"Sal, what was I supposed to do? Pretend I was dead forever just so you could keep the insurance money?"

"Works for me."

"Alright. Alright. I get it. You're sore."

"You stole three hundred and seventy-one dollars from my safe. I want it back."

"How 'bout I do you one better?" I unfurled five grand from my Wiedemann bonus and fanned it out on her desk.

She eyed it skeptically. I hoped not too close.

"And that's just the first payment. I'm gonna help dig you outta the red, kid."

"What's the catch?"

"What do you mean, catch? No catch. I got you into this jam. I'll help get you out of it. We're a team, Sal, you and me."

"Should I ask you how you got it?"

"Government work, Sal. Let's leave it at that."

"Oh, Dick."

I could tell I'd finally melted her a little.

"You should know I ratted you out to some limey claiming to be an insurance agent. Told him I'd kept you in the barn all winter. I could say I told him 'cause I was worried about you, which I was, but I also needed the dough since you'd screwed me."

"I figured as much, Sal. No hard feelings."

"He didn't really seem like a guy able to hold you down, anyways. You always find a way of rising to the surface, don't you, Dick?"

Her words made my eyes suddenly fill with tears. "That's the Halifax curse, Sal. Gettin' out of tight spots . . ."

"Oh, Dick, I didn't mean it that way. . . . I wasn't talking about Wes—"

"No, no, it's okay," I said, a hot tear streaming down my cheek. "You've got me pegged."

Dame Fortune must've been looking kindly on me for making amends, because when I got home, the receptionist at the Chancellor handed me a letter marked *urgent*. It was in a periwinkle envelope written in a fine calligraphical hand from the Golden Gate International Exposition.

They were extending a warm invitation, along with a handsome fee, to be a keynote speaker at next week's opening ceremony of the 1940 Pageant of the World Pacific on Treasure Island. Not only that—they were giving me something called the Spirit of Adventure Award, in the form of a custom-designed trophy.

"Hot damn!" I yelled. "Now we're talking!" As luck would have it, I'd be taking the stage with my good buddy Diego and, get this, Hank's hated old daddy himself, Theodor Rauch.

It made me think of Hank, and then I got to feeling blue. I had tried to go visit him in the hospital, but when I got there, the nurses said he'd already been released. No one answered down at his place in Los Angeles either, and when I phoned his sister, Hilde, she hung up on me. Twice.

I can't bear Hank being sore at me and want to set things right. If only I knew where that nutty German was hiding. But I know we'll find each other at some point.

I called the St. Francis, in case he'd returned to the penthouse, but reception said no luck. Which was just as well by me, since that place gave me the creeps.

In the meantime, I guess I should take in the moment and celebrate. I've made it home and back into the spotlight, with my own name and on my own terms. Hell, I'm going to be the toast of Treasure Island, just like I hoped to be when we first set sail from Kowloon Bay.

What's more, no Black Dragon hatchet man or Brownshirt assassin has come after me for my failure to deliver on the Norden plans or the Rauch diary. Whatever I heard Wiedemann say in that sauna must have been just a silly brain residue from my harrowing ordeal, like those strange, powerful erections. I'm happy to say they're under control now and my doctors in Saipan are beginning to feel like characters in a nightmare soon forgotten. While I guess that means a second shot at movie stardom via Dr. Frink's inside track is as out of reach as those damn microdots are, it's probably for the best. I'll conquer Hollywood on my own or not at all.

In fact, come to think of it, Hollywood can go fellate itself. My thoughts have been returning lately to those Daddy Rauch diary confessions—some of my finest stuff, even if I was only a ghostwriter. Anyway, it got me thinking I might try my hand at something in the romance department next. After seeing how my Junior Adventurers eyed that Tijuana bible and nearly tore each other asunder over a pair of Nude Ranch underpants, I figure there's a fortune to be made in the skin mags.

Yours as always,
Dicky

Part V

HORIZON

HILDEGARD RAUCH

May 28, 1940

Dear Eiko,

You may not have heard the news yet in your desert retreat. I'm enclosing the *Chronicle* clipping, since I didn't think you'd believe it if you heard it only from me. I hardly believe it myself, even though I was there. And, while I worry this will agitate your nerves when really you should be resting, you ought to know what happened.

I have to work my way up to it, as it unfolded that day, or else it makes no sense. So please sit back in your sun chair and accept this feuilleton à la Hildegard Rauch. . . .

Three blasts announced the opening of the 1940 Pageant of the World Pacific at Treasure Island, and though there would be no more fireworks that day, they would not be the last explosion.

At nine o'clock in the clear of a May morning, they burst over the water in star-shaped clusters, and the goddess *Pacifica*, towering over a weary and pleasure-starved humanity, stretched her stone arms again in welcome. A Hawaiian cavalcade of ukulele inaugurated the ferry entrance, and through the auto entrance came a ribbon of refugee flamenco dancers from Franco's Spain, clapping and twirling their way to the Court of the Seven Seas. The Carnation electric milking machines began to hum and suck, the sumo wrestlers cast purifying salts across the dojo of the Japanese pavilion, and the Ferris wheel on the Gayway, freshly oiled, turned its first of the year's revolutions. Since its last spin, Hitler had swallowed half of Europe, forcing the

Allies to retreat to the English Channel, where it looked like they would soon be drowned. But even in the face of death, the festivities must go on.

As the throngs headed to get their fill of legs and breasts at the Estonian fried-chicken stand and Sally Bent's Nude Ranch, hungry eyes with more-sophisticated palates flocked to the Art in Action pavilion to watch Diego Rivera start work on his new mural: *Pan American Unity*. Big man though he was, he clambered up and down the tiers of his scaffolding with the grace and speed of an acrobat. Already, forms were coming to life on the first fresco, filled with dialectic tensions. Beneath a soaring San Francisco diving belle, in a vision of the near future or perhaps an alternate present, sleek gray battleships aimed their prows beyond the Golden Gate.

All this Rivera brought to life while wearing a giant pistol on his belt, which did not seem like mere bravado, considering that gunmen had just sprayed his Mexico City home with bullets in hopes of sinking one in Trotsky.

These observations of the artist at work were, I'm sure, not lost on the High Priest, who, given his mollusk-like pace of secreting literary pearls, seemed impressed. I had just introduced him and Mother to Rivera, who insisted they call him Diego—to no avail. "Do these ships mean, Señor Rivera," asked Father, pointing at the painting, "that you are one of those rare communists who advocate for America's entry into the war?"

"One of the great virtues of being a heretic," said Rivera, "is that I have no line to toe but my own." I translated for Father, who still really only understands English if it stays put on the page.

The two ill-matched titans—exuberant firebrand painter in overalls, and the High Priest looking prim in his starched collar and cuff links—exchanged compliments through me, having somehow found themselves in the same lifeboat amid the current shipwreck. Father spoke proudly of his South American ancestry, and Rivera shared an anecdote about having passed a pleasant three days in a New York City jail thanks only to a copy of *Walpurgis Night*, which lay beside the toilet and so engrossed him that he paid no attention to the discomforts of the stifling cell. "The pages came in quite handy once I was done reading too," he added. This last statement so bemused Mother and

Father that they muttered an excuse about having to make their way to the Federal Plaza, for they were expected on the dais at six. As I escorted them away, Diego said he had enjoyed watching me work and gave me a wink.

It was nerve-racking to work before the ogling public, let alone ogling celebrity painters, like some monkey at the zoo. But the pay was good and the camaraderie of other artists outweighed my misgivings. I thought of those girls at the Nude Ranch, who created a compelling illusion by ignoring the crowds altogether and going about their artificial farmwork. *Just work*, I told myself. That's what people want to see. Not you mugging or acting self-conscious. Just blur out those distractions and lose yourself in the work. So I saddled my easel, so to speak, and got down to it. I was, however, thankful to be wearing more than nipple tassels.

But the distractions that day did not come from the crowds or the bustle of the fair; rather, they came from my own hovering dread. Dread about even having to see Richard Halifax again, who would soon be sharing the stage with Father. Dread, too, that our forgery would be discovered by that Englishman Fox (surely it would be discovered by someone soon) or that some other copy of the diary we consigned to the flames would surface elsewhere and that this time we would be powerless to stop its lies. Dread, as the High Priest walked the fairgrounds with me at his side, that beneath the lies there was, as you insist, some truth in those pages. Dread about whether I would have the courage to act.

By six-thirty, the crowds began to fill Federal Plaza. It was still warm and windless out, a true rarity here, and the bay looked as placid as the Lake of All Nations, adorned with gondolas and swan-shaped pedal boats. The evening sun floated above Mount Sutro, shooting its dying rays against the massive Covarrubias murals of the Federal Building. We waited in the cool of the lobby, behind the rostrum, with a pitcher of iced tea courtesy of the Lipton pavilion and a plate bearing the identifying label: *yacht club sardines*.

Mother tried to break the silence by criticizing my striped shirt. "People will think you're a fisherman, dear."

"Heaven forbid, Mother. Have a yacht club sardine and I'll return the compliment."

Father was looking intently at one of the young Stepin Fetchits, a handsome dark-haired youth. Mr. Vandeburg, the fair director, came by, barking orders to the boys, something about mopping up a flood from the Aquacade near the sound system and double-checking that the cables onstage were grounded.

I watched Father stop the handsome youth, touch him lightly on the wrist, and ask if there was any lemon for the tea. Given that he never drank a drop of it, I imagine he just wanted an excuse to make contact. It must have been agonizing how he kept himself choked off. It has been a devastation both for him and for you. You were doomed to be part of his fantasy realm, a haunting tempter of his shadow self, which prevented him from accepting the reality of you as a flesh-and-blood son, let alone fellow artist.

If you have suffered from being an object of unholy longing and scorn, then what, in his eyes, am I? A nonthreatening replica, I suppose, a remarkable appendage, an amusing offshoot, and, if he had his way, his girl Friday and full-time translator.

"Father," I said, after the boy had left. "There is something I have to tell you."

He and Mother looked at me alertly, as though they could sense the momentousness in my voice. "Today is the last time I will be your interpreter. Mother's English is perfectly decent. Or, if she's not up to the task, you can find someone else."

"But, Hilde," said Mother, "I thought we agreed that you would come down when—"

"No. I will not do it anymore. This is it. And my decision is final."

"Very well," said Father. "I suppose you're too busy with your painting. Is that what this is about?"

His remark annoyed me, which made it easier to broach my next point. "It's you who are too busy."

"What on earth does that mean?" said Mother.

"It means that I find it appalling that you never once visited Eiko in the hospital. For six months he was there at death's door. But you couldn't take the trouble, not once, to find the time in your holy, inviolate schedule."

"Oh, please, Hilde," replied Mother, "what good would it have done him? He was asleep the whole time, and now that we're here, he's left town."

Part of why I sent you off to the desert was so that they could not get the satisfaction of fitting you in now. It was too late. "It is not a question of utility, Mother, but decency and love. All he wanted from you was love," I said, looking at Father. "What you did to him in print—humiliating him like that—was unforgivable. It was the act of a petulant child and bully, not a father."

"Hildegard, you are behaving like a perfect hysteric right now—and just before your father has to speak."

"You are the ones who act like children! The world is a mess, life is chaos, and yet you insist on living in a cocoon of your own egotism, all while you pontificate on the fight to save humanity."

Suddenly Richard Halifax walked past the glass doors, laughing with Diego Rivera. He turned to us and flashed a huge smile that made me shudder.

I later realized, upon exiting the building, that the lobby was totally obscured from view and that he had only been looking at his own reflection.

We were brought to the stage, to a box of seats on the dais, thankfully without a spare moment for pleasantries or recriminations. Mother and I were seated to Father's right. On his left were Rivera, Halifax, and the governor of California, Culbert Olson. Mr. Vandeburg quickly reminded us of the order of speakers, who would introduce and bestow trophies on whom, and what cues from the band would follow.

Flanked by Miss Streamline and Miss Star-of-the-Sea Tuna, fair director Vandeburg welcomed the crowd to "the start of the most magical summer on the most magical place on earth!" The crowd went wild, and the 30th Infantry Band launched into Sousa's "Hands Across the Sea," after which Governor Olson presided over the raising of flags of state and country.

While the band played, my eye was drawn to a familiar figure offstage in the distance, over by the sound system. I could have sworn it was Nadia, though I could see only the back of her and I remembered she had told me she couldn't come to the opening day. She was talking with a dark, petite young woman—perhaps Greek or Turkish or Arabic—who was facing me with a beautiful gap-toothed smile.

Hearing the governor introduce Diego Rivera, I returned my attention to the stage. "Please welcome a man and artist truly larger than life, whom we are honored to have back here in San Francisco, our great world city on the Pacific, immortalizing this historic moment in paint." But when I looked again at the sound system, the two women were gone.

Upon returning to his seat, the governor turned to Father, one white-haired patrician to another, and said, "That's one crazy Mexican. Saw him making it with the Aquacade girl in the left-luggage room."

Diego had been instructed to leave his pistol offstage and to keep his words brief and free of politics. How do I know this? Because he said as much, before beginning a long tirade against the murderous forces of tyranny. "Tyranny feeds on the worship of false idols," he warned, "be they the swastika, hammer and sickle, or dollar sign. But all of them aim at the destruction of freedom, which is the basis of any art and civilization worthy of the name. Do not be fooled into thinking those threats are only over there, comrades. Those threats are here too, sometimes in the minds of our own neighbors and supposed friends." I later learned from Rivera that his fellow painter David Siqueiros had manned one of the machine guns in the recently attempted attack on Trotsky.

Finally, as the audience began to squirm in their metal chairs, uncomfortable at being exhorted by a known communist and rallied into a war against fascism that only about half of them were willing to acknowledge, let alone support, Rivera segued to Halifax, whom he had been tasked with introducing.

"I know the world would be a braver, gayer, and freer place if there were more men like my friend Ricardo Halifax, or, as many of you know him, Dicky. We thought we lost him somewhere out there in that big blue water, but I must say I never doubted for a second he was still alive. Dicky is like a piñata—the more you beat him, the more sweet things come out. He is like a heat rash in summertime—just when you think he's gone, he comes back. He is like our beloved *cucaracha*—no matter what happens, no matter how much death and destruction rains down upon him, he survives. And guess what, my friends? Here he is!"

Rivera brought Halifax to the podium, to scattered applause. As he strode by me, I again felt my spine turn to jelly.

I barely heard a word of his speech. Something about adventure, Dame Fortune, and how with a little American grit a man can survive anything. I kept picturing him forcing those pills down your throat, writing those lies in Father's diary, the better to destroy him. The same man who had lain chastely in my bed in Addis Ababa and wept into my pillow while telling me about his dead brother. What an absurd mystery human life is.

When Halifax returned from the podium to receive the congratulations of those of us on the dais, I stood and moved toward him.

Up close, I could see that his face was deeply covered over with pancake, the sweat beaded into flesh-colored crumbs along his upper lip and jaw. And above his ear at his hairline ran a long sliver of yellowish tape and what looked like little beads of glue.

"Hello, Hildegard," he said. "I hear Hank's back on his feet. I've been meaning to drop in on him, but your telephone doesn't seem to work too good."

"You stay away from my brother, Richard. I know what you did."

"I'm not sure what you mean . . ."

"You're not just a liar," I said in a voice audible to all those on the dais. "You're something far worse. You're a lie."

"Gee, Hilde. That's not very—"

"I almost fell for the fake suicide note you wrote after you tried to kill him. But you know what? My brother never loved you. I don't think anyone has ever loved you, Richard, and I don't think anyone ever will. Here," I said. "You left this in my hotel room years ago. But I don't want anything to do with you. And I engraved it so now you'll always know it's yours."

He took the cigarette lighter and examined it—beneath the initials *R.J.H.* was scratched in big damning letters the word: *SCUM*.

I had turned down Nadia's proposal, of course. I was no assassin, and the last thing I wanted was to be further embroiled with her and whatever forces, anarchist or not, she represented. No matter how much I had come to despise Halifax, I would not be the teeth in the jaws of history. But I would tell the truth.

I had told Nadia that she and I had visions of justice that would never align and that we had nothing further to discuss. And, except for her uncanny likeness by the sound system, that was the last I have seen of her. I even went by the Seidlers' house in Berkeley yesterday to satisfy my curiosity, but the place was vacant.

Meanwhile, everyone on the dais was staring at us with alarmed interest at the delay and whatever of my words they had overheard. Father was still waiting to be called to the podium. Mr. Vandeburg cleared his throat, and with a nervous laugh that tried to dispel the confusion I had cast, he rushed out to the stage to introduce the High Priest.

More confusion followed, as Halifax was meant to have returned to the stage to present Father with a Spirit of Adventure trophy identical to the one he'd received from Rivera. But now he was slumped in his chair, alone at the end of his row of empty seats, holding both trophies and the cigarette lighter in his lap. He looked like a man who'd just lost his home in a fire and escaped with only those three cherished possessions. After Mr. Vandeburg discreetly tried and failed to get Halifax's attention, he gave up and went on to introduce Father on his own and without any trophy.

When I took my seat, Mother whispered in my ear, "Whatever has gotten into you, Hildegard? What did you say to that man? Something about Eiko?"

"Never mind, Mother," I said. "It doesn't concern you."

I was still vibrating from my confrontation with Halifax and was only dimly aware of Father's speech, "What Peace Requires," which was proceeding along the usual lines of "democracy and culture, and the need for a new energizing myth to unite humanity."

Intent on not looking at Richard Halifax anymore or ever again, I focused my gaze on the crowd. A collection of mostly white faces in hats looked up at the High Priest, some kindly and attentive, some perplexed. A few were yawning or worrying their programs in their laps. But one face, in the fifth row by the aisle, was utterly rapt. His eyes were glued to the stage as though he was hanging on every moment. A sickening feeling crept over me as I recognized that face.

It was the Englishman Fox. My blackmailer. Had he already discovered that the Norden diagrams I gave him were fakes? His gaze was toggling between Father at the podium and Halifax on the dais, when suddenly I saw four men in dark hats and suits pluck him from the crowd and haul him away.

There was a murmur around the disruption as the Englishman protested, shouting something about Halifax, I think, but it was quickly drowned out when Father, reaching the moral climax of his speech, said the lines from *Faust* I will now never forget. They stand in my memory as the fuse, the words that lifted us from our seats and into a smoke-filled confusion.

But stand ashamed at last, when thou shalt see
An honest man, 'mid all his strivings dark,
Finds the right way, though lit but by a spark.

As you well know, I don't believe one can kill or maim one's way to justice. I think Plato was closer to the mark—justice is a kind of harmony of the soul. And in a world so profoundly out of harmony, I believe we have only a limited power to restore a sonorous order. The best we can do is gather a small corner of that chaos into meaningful form in hopes of stealing a glimpse of beauty and truth.

Yet I also believe another, vaster force is at work within this mess. Call it poetic justice or historical irony, but sometimes the collision of chance does far more than intention to redress the moral imbalance of the world. Of course, in this particular case, justice looks more like a grotesque farce, and I can't help but wonder if I was somehow an unwitting party to it. I'll let the attached clipping fill you in on the rest.

I do hope you've come to see Halifax for what he is. I myself, despite loathing the man, will confess to feeling a lingering sympathy. If not for him, then for the lost boy who got trapped inside.

Will join you in the desert soon. I hope you are finding strength in the dry life down there and that the writing is going well.

With love,
Ildi

San Francisco Chronicle, May 26, 1940:

EXPLOSION AT TREASURE ISLAND

Writer-adventurer Halifax injured in blast
at fair's reopening ceremonies.

SAN FRANCISCO, SUN., MAY 26—

A small explosion interrupted last night's opening ceremonies of the 1940 Golden Gate International Exhibition on Treasure Island.

The blast injured Richard Halifax, the writer-adventurer who recently survived a disaster at sea following the sinking of his ship the *Soup Dumpling* on a trans-Pacific voyage last spring. Mr. Halifax, after being declared dead by a court last fall, was found in April on the Farallon Islands, stranded but alive.

At 7:30 p.m., the eminent German writer and voice of Europe-in-exile Theodor Rauch was delivering a speech before a crowd of thousands in Federal Plaza, when a sharp report was heard, followed by the eruption of a small fire on the dais where Mr. Halifax was seated. Onstage with Mr. Rauch were Governor Olson, Mexican painter Diego Rivera, and Mr. Halifax, all of whom were speakers at the evening ceremony "Pacific Unity and World Peace" to mark the opening day of the fair's second year. President Roosevelt's radio address, which was meant to coincide with the lighting of Treasure Island for the season, was postponed until further notice.

Authorities have yet to determine the cause of the small explosion, though a full investigation is underway. Cliff Hader of the Federal Bureau of Investigation, San Francisco Division, said his department is pursuing all possible leads, which include: rumors of a plot against Governor Olson for his recent controversial pardoning of anarchist Thomas Mooney, convicted of the 1916 Preparedness Day bombing; a Nazi-led conspiracy against Theodor Rauch; a Stalinist attack on Diego Rivera; and faulty wiring in the PA system.

Halifax is currently in the hospital, where he remains in serious condition. No other injuries were reported.

To: The Dicky Halifax Junior Adventurers Club
From: Dicky Halifax
The End of the Adventure

Summertime 1940

Dear boys,

Remember these words and keep them in your thoughts: Every penis is a time bomb, and so is the man attached to it.

You never know when you'll be out for a Sunday stroll or sitting on the dais grinning like an idiot, nervously fingering a cigarette lighter, when—bang—it's kablooey o'clock and you're suddenly headed for the burn ward.

I mean this metaphorically, though in my case it proved all too real. Looks like Nacho was right after all: Those evil doctors Kanemoto and Frink must've stuffed an exploding cigar down my hair snake. Damn. And here I thought I was out of my mind when I nearly castrated myself back in that dark hotel room. I suppose if there's a lesson here, boys, it's *assume the worst and dig deeper*.

No sooner had I made my grand public reappearance at the fair, waving to the crowds like a conquering hero, than I found myself back in my old room at Mount Zion, hospital bed still warm and stamped with the trim contours of yours truly. Only one small part of me was missing.

Well, a few pieces if you want to get technical. But let's not dwell on the negative, boys. That wiener-and-ball-sac was twenty years useless anyway—that is, until I started getting those terrifying erections that were almost the end of me. So good riddance! If you ask me, it was a stroke of luck that it was burned to a blasted stump and the docs replaced it with an equally useless but generously apportioned tube of rump flesh and back skin. A show dong, if you will. Strictly ornamental. I won't be winning any beauty awards with it or fathering any future Junior Adventurers, but, hey, it fills out a pair of bathing trunks pretty nice and the pee still comes out a hole or two. Hell, if I'd known that medical science had figured out how to fashion fake ding-dongs from butt meat (and apparently the Krauts pioneered the trick a few years back), I'd have cut loose and started fresh ages ago.

All in all, this stint in the hospital was far better than the last one. Not only did I wake up with an ersatz sapling in my shorts—a pretty decent trade for my lost Spirit of Adventure trophy, immolated in the blast along with that nasty cigarette lighter Hilde Rauch gave back—I got a new job to boot.

How did I get this new job, you ask? Well, boys, just before opening day at the fair, I went round to the Civic Center and paid a visit to the FBI. Sporting a face grave with patriotic concern, I laid a real doozy of a tale at Special Agent Hader's feet.

I told him I didn't want to jump to any conclusions or do his job for him but I simply wanted to present him with a concerning pattern I'd noticed, which I felt was my duty to share. He told me to go on, and I told him, as outlandish as it sounded, I had reason to suspect there was a rogue British agent colluding with the Nazi consul right here on Californian soil. Boy howdy, that got his attention! And what proof did I have, he asked. Well, I said, I'd first encountered the vice-consul Faulk in Bangkok, where, under the name Flint, with a drink in each hand and a dusky underage courtesan on each arm, he'd been boasting about his off-license business ventures in the region: selling arms to the communists in China, running them through the jungly mountain passes of the Siamese north, and smuggling opium along those same routes south into Burma and Thailand. This was why I'd pretended not to know the man at the hospital, because he was so utterly distasteful to me and the polite company I kept.

"If I recall," said Hader, "Faulk claimed to have had business dealings with you in Bangkok."

"He would certainly like to think so, Agent Hader, though one could hardly call them that. They were more like business harassments. You see, when he found out my dear departed friend Roderick was a safety inspector at the Norden plant in Missouri, he tried bribing him for the plans. We ran the other way, naturally. In fact, we later heard from a British attaché in Hong Kong, just before we set sail, that Faulk had come into some ignominy in Siam and was going to be expelled. Now, I say this not to incriminate the man on hearsay but only to let you know why I regarded Faulk so warily when our paths crossed again in San Francisco."

"Yes, of course. Please go on, Mr. Halifax."

"Well, you were there for his baseless accusations of me at the hospital after my harrowing ordeal, so we needn't go into that, but shortly after my release, Faulk cornered me one night in my hotel bar at the Chancellor. Unsurprisingly, he was inebriated—I imagine you've noticed his predilection for drink—and in what I can only assume was an appalling lapse of professional discretion, he began boasting about having finally gotten his hands on those same top-secret military plans. Not only that, he said he was selling them to the Germans for a boatload of cash. Well, his criminal boasting was such an affront to my patriotism that I took it upon myself to have the scoundrel followed and catch him in the act."

Here I handed Agent Hader the photograph the Sinclair boys had taken of the two consuls inside the cinema. I thought Laurel and Hardy's "Saps at Sea" seemed like a fitting occasion for their rendezvous. Half the film roll had been pitch black, three shots were obscured by thumbs, and one appeared to be of a woman changing in a window. But there was one gem among them that showed the two of them, Faulk and Wiedemann, *in conversatio flagrante*, both their confused faces lit by the glow of the silver screen (and a high-powered flashbulb).

Was not that man, I said to Hader, pointing at the picture, the infamous German consul, a regular in the society pages and the once-intimate of Adolf Hitler himself? And was not that man beside him, his mouth distorted in speech, the British vice-consul Simon Faulk? The same man who had, with gin-fermented breath, leveled unhinged allegations against me while I was convalescing in the hospital? "The same man," I said, "whom I happened to follow across state lines, where I observed him escorting a young *mademoiselle de la nuit,* a known consort of the Nazi consul Wiedemann, to a love nest in Reno, Nevada, for what I can only suppose, based on the photographic evidence here, here, and here, was the express intention to engage in illicit acts in gross violation of the Mann Act."

Well, boys, I had a feeling, based on Hader's reaction to my medley of photos, that my story had gone down pretty well with him. But I didn't know the upshot of it until I landed in the hospital again and Cliff Hader came round to see me.

He thanked me for bringing my concern about Faulk to his attention. The feds couldn't search Faulk's office at the British consulate, on account of diplomatic immunity, but on the suspicion of carrying out immoral acts across state lines, as per the terms of the Mann Act, they were able to search his apartment, where they found nearly four thousand dollars in counterfeit bills. "Interestingly enough," Hader explained, "these same counterfeit bills have been circulating around town in the last couple of weeks, most of it in the Tenderloin within the radius of both Faulk's residence and the Deutsches Haus, a suspected Nazi base of operations."

The FBI naturally shared the photograph of the Faulk–Wiedemann tête-à-tête with Faulk's superiors in London, who disavowed any such knowledge or approval of these interactions between their man and the Nazi consul. The Brits even sent one of their own to take a look inside the consular safe and demonstrate that the spirit of trust and cooperation between our two countries still prevailed, especially given the added embarrassment that Faulk was the consul-general's nephew. "Who knows what all they found there and kept to themselves?" said Hader. "But one thing they shared that had been in Faulk's possession was a set of photographs of a diary attributed to the writer Theodor Rauch."

"You don't say? Any good?"

"What?"

"The diary? Was it a swell read?"

"Oh," said Hader, confused. "Well, I'm not at liberty to speak on that. The Brits are convinced it's a forgery, but let's just say Director

Hoover's a great collector. Never throws away a piece of paper. And since Rauch seems just a little too worked up about fascism and his daughter has been seen palling around with an anarchist agitator, he'll no doubt be adding it to his files.

"Speaking of which," said Hader, "the other file they found in the safe and shared with us was a set of technical drawings, just like you told us Faulk had been boasting about."

"You mean the Norden bombsight?"

"Yep, though it turns out those plans Faulk had were fakes. If they'd been real, you can bet your ass the limeys would have just kept the plans for themselves and never told us about them. But as it was, they were only a bunch of drawings of a toy microscope. Guess Faulk was trying to con the Germans with it."

"I'll be damned," I said, shocked. Had Roderick pulled a fast one on me? I suddenly remembered Roderick's unfinished final words, cut off when the grim reaper gave him the hook. "There's something I should tell you about the N—" Had that little weasel been about to admit to me he'd faked the Norden plans? Had the whole thing just been Roderick's desperate bluff for attention, afraid that Hank was moving in on his turf?

Well, I was damn lucky I hadn't succeeded in getting ahold of those plans and brought them back to Tokyo, only to be told they were drawings of a toy. The Japs would have turned my lights out then and there. Just goes to show, boys, that sometimes failure is the best ingredient for success.

So what had become of my English pest, the so-called Simon Faulk?

"Deported," said Hader. "We detained him after we found the counterfeit bills he had stashed in his floorboards. Damn shame about diplomatic immunity. Matter of fact, we collared him at Treasure Island, just before your, um, accident. So sorry, by the way."

The FBI's investigation had concluded definitively that it was a current from the ungrounded wire snaked under my chair that had climbed up the metal chair leg and caught the spark of my cigarette lighter. Of course, I knew what really happened, but I wasn't about to go into detail about Drs. Kanemoto and Frink or my residency on Saipan with Karl Dieter the Coconut King.

"At any rate," Hader continued, "Faulk was pretty far gone by the time we busted him. The booze had wrecked his thinking—paranoid fantasies and the like. Started hollering about how you were a Nazi agent trying to kill Theodor Rauch. He seems to have taken a sick interest in you ever since you two met, and I guess it grew into an obsession."

"Well, I'm damn sorry to hear it, Agent Hader. He probably was a nice fella once. But I'm afraid it's not the first time someone's come undone in the face of my celebrity."

"No, I imagine not. We at the Bureau get all sorts of perverts stalking famous people, jerking off in the bushes outside Joan Crawford's house or sending death threats to Ernest Hemingway."

"Oh, really?" I said, sheepishly, recalling a bout of epistolary weakness a few years back. "Who on earth would do a thing like that?"

"By the way," said Hader, pulling out a tattered copy of my first work for young readers, *The Codex of Wonders*. "I meant to ask, would you mind signing your autograph for Cliff Jr.? When I told him I met Dicky Halifax, he just about hit the ceiling."

"It would be my pleasure." Hader handed me the book and his pen and I signed.

"Just one last thing, Mr. Halifax," he said, after taking back the book and pen. "It seems," he said, fishing some papers out of his breast pocket, "that you've done a few speaking engagements at the Deutsches Haus in the past month. Is that right?"

"Oh, yeah, sure," I said, suddenly on high alert. "See, they sent me an invitation and I figured I'd get my lecture chops back up with a few gigs on the breakfast and luncheon circuits."

"And did you happen to write any letters to the German American Business League or the Nordic Choral Singers Society or the Germanic Association for Peace and Freedom?"

"No sir. Can't say that I did."

"So these were not written by you?"

Hader showed me the typed letters. Down at the bottom was a decent forgery of my John Hancock, but it wasn't mine. "No sir, Agent Hader. That's a B-grade forgery if you ask me. See how the *f* wobbles and tilts just a little too far left compared to my own?"

Hader compared my autograph on his son's book with those of the letters. "And you didn't enclose any cash donations with these letters, Mr. Halifax?"

"Most emphatically not, sir. I'll admit I don't keep a tight cinch on the Halifax Purse, but one thing I've never done is give money away for nothing. Strikes me as un-American."

"Couldn't agree with you more."

"If you don't mind my asking, Agent Hader, what's this all about?"

"We suspect Faulk was trying to tarnish your reputation—part of his aforementioned obsession. The letters with your forged signature included large cash donations of those same counterfeit bills we found in Faulk's possession."

"Well, I guess 'the enginer was hoist with his own petard.'"

Hader gave me a look like a man rusty on his *Hamlet*, then tucked away his letters and rose from his seat. "I'll let you get your rest, Mr. Halifax. I just wanted you to know that it was your tip that saved this country from a great deal of potential harm."

"Glad it could finally be of service," I said, trying not to think on the harm that had come to my own irradiated tip.

Which brings me back to my new gig in government service. See, boys, curiously, my stock rose dramatically after the bombing incident. Even my spineless agent Feakins came slinking back to get his 15 percent cut of the Dicky boom. Just goes to show you can't predict the whims of the market or Dame Fortune. Their hands are not only invisible but spastic. 'Cause while no one much cared that I made it home after the wreck of the *Soup Dumpling*, folks thrilled to the fact that I had made it home only to survive another near-death incident in a world's fair explosion in the vicinity of my groin (though thankfully the details of my operation remain . . . private). I had become a kind of icon of survival, I suppose, the man who congenitally courts death but just won't die, or, as one small-minded critic put it, "a real-life Looney Tune."

On account of this powerful public image—along, no doubt, with my solid work to help Cliff Hader ferret out foreign enemies among us—not long after my surgery I received a visit from two fellas named

Bill: one short and Scots Canadian, one tall and Irish American, both manly as hell. The two Bills, Stephenson and Donovan, said they were working on a hush-hush kind of outfit between America and England, something FDR and Churchill had been cooking up behind closed doors so the bureaucrats couldn't get wind of it. "We're looking for real adventurers, Dicky. Guys with guts, guys who know their way around the world, guys who can rub shoulders with the enemy and get close enough to steal their wallet. Someone who can think on his feet and keep smiling when his back's against the wall or his johnson's blown to kingdom come. Someone who's not afraid of fighting dirty and making it look fair. Hell, maybe even a fella who's comfortable speaking at a breakfast for fascist businessmen or a Nazi lunch of Schubert enthusiasts. Someone who looks like he's listing one way, enough to attract the attention of the FBI, while really, as we're prepared to assure Cliff Hader and Mr. Hoover, he's on the team of the good guys. In short, Dicky, someone who's not afraid of tight spots. So, kid, what do you say?"

Well, boys, there was only one thing to say, and that was: "Swell!"

Once I got out of the hospital, the two Bills launched me on a goodwill campaign. Officially, I'm a global ambassador of the Golden Gate International Exposition's Pageant of the World Pacific. But I'm also keeping my ear to the ground for the Bills—which as you know, boys, come not just in American and Canadian currencies but also in Reichsmarks, rubles, and yen. I swear, boys, once you turn double agent, there's no telling how many more times you can keep turning. Sometimes I feel as downright spinny as a dervish.

See, that snapshot of Faulk and Wiedemann at the movies together may have been enough to keep the Nazi consul off my back, but, as he assured me the last time I went to call on him, it was not he who called the shots.

"You can blackmail me all you want, Herr Dicky, but your failure to deliver on promised goods will not be overlooked by my superiors. As for me, I'm being reposted to Tientsin. So while your fate doesn't concern me in the least, I'm afraid your head is still on the chopping block."

He didn't have to tell me twice. And while I couldn't quite figure out where Wiedemann, that slippery sauna creature, stood—had he been meeting with Faulk because he was a turncoat or was he working some kind of game?—I knew one thing for certain. If those doctors back in Saipan could stitch up a timed explosive device inside a man's private parts, hell, anything was possible. These fellas meant business, and it had been foolish of me to think that, once I'd reclaimed my name, I could just shrug off my burden of *giri*.

"The Norden plans and Rauch diary were lost to the wind," I told Wiedemann. "That ship has sailed. But surely there must be something else I can do to pay off my debt?"

"Well, we would have liked to see Theodor Rauch destroyed. But, frankly, my government's not interested in the Norden bombsight. Between you and me, we already stole the plans two years ago. It's the Japanese who are hungry for it, but we haven't yet decided if that's something we'd like to share."

"You don't say," I said, my head spinning. Had my late sidekick Roderick, that dirty Hun-lover, gone behind my back and unloaded the real Nordens onto the Krauts long before he set this whole mess into motion? Was that what he had been on the brink of admitting to me before death whisked him away?

"Well, Fritzy," I said to the consul, "surely there's something I can do that will please everyone. But whatever it is, you better tell me quick, 'cause I'm bound for Mexico City next Tuesday, and after that Hawaii."

Yessir, I'm back on the road, reliving old memories and making new ones. Just last week I was climbing up the temple ruins in the Zócalo and munching on hot tamales, like I did years ago with my buddy Diego. He's still up at Treasure Island painting his mural, but he gave me a spare set of keys to his place in Coyoacán. I lent them to a dead-eyed Belgian fella I met in a bar, who told me he'd read all my books, including *Steppe Lively!* about my rail journey across the Soviet Union. He was on his way to do some mountain climbing—and from the look of his ice ax, he meant business—but said he would love to first pay his respects to Trotsky, if only he knew where he was hiding. I said, "Say, funny you should mention it; Diego's place is just up the street from the bearded old troublemaker—why don't you drop in and say hi?" I hoped that act of kindness would help placate anyone in Stalin's camp who still bore Hank and me a grudge for fumbling the Rauch diary.

This week I'm in Honolulu, where yesterday the navy took me on a tour of the seaside. Your man Dick got some beautiful snaps of Pearl Harbor, with those fine American battleships—all 102 of them. I think Dr. Frink will, in true German form, be quite taken with the sublime landscape, while Dr. Kanemoto, a bit more of a hard case, will greet them with a resounding grunt of approval.

Such is the life of a privateer, boys.

And lest you think I'm hiring myself out just to live the high life or pay the legal settlements to the wrongful-death suits brought by the families of the *Soup Dumpling*, know I'm still making good on my promise to help my old friend Sally Bent crawl back into the black. I wish the two of us could go back to simpler times, back to that little strip of woods where we used to swap clothes and share our dreams about who we'd one day become.

But that forest is long paved over and lives only in our memories, a shadowed cove of truth and innocence that will forever keep us linked. I just hope for the sake of Sally's knees that her loan sharks don't have ole Gary the tobacconist's eagle eye and spot that first batch of bills as bogus.

This morning, while I was breakfasting on the lanai and taking in the waves of Waikiki, the waiter brought me out a tray of fresh coconut. The sight of it made me choke up with tears, and suddenly I was sobbing like a paid mourner at a Chinese funeral. I thought of my dear cabin boy Nacho Fu, back there in Saipan, lost in a hell pit beyond the coconut groves.

Now, I know what you boys are thinking: *Dicky, aren't you on your way back to Saipan to rescue Nacho? Isn't that what you've been busting your hump to do all along? Isn't reuniting with your beloved sidekick what gives heroic shape to your harrowing ordeal and makes all your compromises and betrayals understandable, perhaps even forgivable?*

Well, boys, now that we've reached the final letter of your subscription service to "The Voyage of the *Soup Dumpling*," and seeing as you boys are nearly grown up after all we've been through together and I've already told you things I never told another soul, I guess I ought to level with you.

Remember when the prison guard made Nacho and me fight and I saw him lying face down in the mud and thought for a minute he was dead before he sprang back to life, at least until he catapulted himself off the veranda, where instead of breaking his neck and dying, he only broke his back and was gravely injured? Well, boys, sometimes what happens in reality is not good for what happens in stories. Especially stories for young readers like you.

Same goes for dear old Roderick, I'm afraid. Cannibalism on the high seas, sure. But outright murder? That won't do. Not for a hero you're rooting for. Sometimes the truth needs a little noodling, boys, and the precise details of who died when or how—what we might call the blunt world of historical facts—are sacrificed for the larger, more poetic truth of art.

Sometimes we can't even bear to tell the truth to ourselves. That's right, even when there's only one listener, some stories are so painful they still need doctoring. Like my brother, Wesley, for example. Gosh, it sure is easier to believe that diphtheria is what carried him off. No one to blame but the strangling angel herself. Because then you just have to reckon with the grief. Not the guilt. And it's the guilt that drags you under, isn't it, boys? The guilt is what carves a hole in your chest and makes you run the lengths of the earth trying to escape it. The guilt is what makes your parents retract all traces of love, so that even when they hug you it feels like they're spittin' in your face. The guilt is what compels you on the lake one summer afternoon, six months after his death, to put your manhood in the path of a motorboat propeller. Because he drowned and you didn't. Because he cramped up while you two were swimming Lake Tapawingo late in the season—he had said it would be too cold, but you called him a weak sister—and you went to help him and he started thrashing around, until suddenly he was dragging you under too, and it was going to be one or both of you.

No amount of living can wash away that stain, boys. In fact, I think all you can do is keep reliving it, drawing concentric circles round that same black hole. Just like the vortex that sucked down the *Soup*

Dumpling. Yessir, the Japs know their stuff when they talk about *giri*, the debt that can never be repaid.

That's why every hero needs a bard to sing his song. Because behind the hero's mask is a sucking blackness. Without Homer, Ulysses is just a no-account pirate and pathological liar, raping and killing his way home on a big wave of tall tales. And as both writer and adventurer, hell, I'm working a double shift. You boys came here for an adventure story, which is quite a different thing from the adventure itself. You know what they call the adventure without the story, boys? Life. And who the hell wants plain old life? Talk about a baggy narrative with a stinker of an ending.

How lucky, then, that you Junior Adventurers got to take part in this adventure through my story and not through the fifty-two bones of your feet or the saltwater scars in your lungs or the scorched and massacred field of your pelvis or the torn place in your chest where all your lost sidekicks live. Nacho was not my first sidekick or my longest or even my best, but—like Wesley, like Roderick—some little shard of him is lodged in my heart, like the sharp corner of a potato chip stuck in your gums, condemning me to eternal anguish. Perhaps that painful feeling is what they call love.

But let's not end on such weak-sister sentiment. Behind every great man is a boy with a hole in his heart. But you won't impress any doctors or win any friends by sitting on your duff and crying, "Woe is me, look at my hole!" Instead, you gotta go fill that hole with adventure. Let the winds of Aeolus whistle through it on the Ionian. Let an alpaca sneeze into it on the slopes of the Andes. Hell, let a pretty girl or boy or one of those pretty in-betweeners you see at the Inside Out Club in Shanghai take you out dancing and kick through it with their high heels. Or, even better, find a legion of loyal young readers, a pack of fearless Junior Adventurers who keep you afloat with dreams of eternal boyhood while you tilt your stern toward morning and sail through the Golden Gate, bound for the glorious horizon.

Yours in adventure forever,
Dicky

P.S. As soon as I get back to California, I'm off to find my old pal Hank. I didn't get a chance to patch things up with him before I left. Truth be told, I fear he might still bear your man Dick a grudge.

See, boys, just between you and me, Hank didn't exactly try to turn his own lights out back there in the penthouse of the St. Francis. In the heat of the moment, and with me suffering from the side effects of that terrible wiener bomb my doctors implanted, Hank got the wrong idea and something happened between me and him. And, well, in the wrestling match that went down, Hank knocked his skull real bad against the marble headboard (what kind of jerk uses marble as a headboard?). And your man Dick, unused to those kinds of proceedings, lost his own marbles. I thought Hank was dead. I couldn't hear him breathing—likely on account of my own hyperventilation and ear-ringing—so I panicked. I thought I had murdered him, unwittingly fulfilling the prophecy of my diabolical coconut mentor, Karl Dieter. So I reached for the pills on Hank's nightstand and poured a few down his throat so as to make it look like an overdose. In hindsight, I should have recognized that if he could swallow, then he was still alive. But like I said, boys, I was off my gourd. So I typed up a suicide note to make the whole deal look convincing. Said some real nice things too, about how much Hank loved me. Thank God I didn't overdo it on the pills and only sent him to dreamland for a few months.

Yessir, that was quite a tight spot we were in, me and Hank. But in the end, wouldn't you know it, everything worked out swell. I don't have to hassle Hank anymore about those infernal microdots and I can rest assured this hair snake of mine won't cause me any more trouble. And assuming Hank can keep his trap shut about all those nutty things I said concerning Drs. Kanemoto and Frink—lest I have to think of him as one of Wiedemann's loose ends—he and I can go back to being just pals, like we were before. God knows I could use a new sidekick.

Word is he's drying out in some tony hideaway down in Death Valley. Sounds like Hank's kind of place. Whoopla!

41.

ſIMON FÁULK

I suppose there's nothing more to say for myself. That man works his way into your mind like a cloying melody and gradually drives you mad. But I'm telling you, I took every precaution.

I notified the FBI about the Bundists' bomb. I called in the threat anonymously and gave them specific details as to the trophy's description, the location, and the time it was due to go off. "Seven-thirty," I said. "During Theodor Rauch's speech at the fair. Right there at the podium." Is it my fault the threat was not taken seriously? And of course the FBI covered up their own negligence, blaming the explosion on some kind of electrical mishap. Preposterous. You see, I issued express instructions to the Bundists to set the bomb for 7:30 p.m.—*on the 26th*. Not May 25th, the evening of the opening ceremonies, but rather a whole day later. I figured that would give the police and FBI ample time to disarm it, no one would get hurt, and everyone would laugh at what imbeciles the Bundists are—can't even get the date right on their own time bombs. But those idiots must have second-guessed me and thought they were correcting my error in changing the time.

Imagine my outrage, as I sat waiting with delicious anticipation to see Halifax taken down onstage by a rush of federal agents, when Cliff Hader and his goons not only failed to stop the bomb plot but arrested me instead. For what? Driving across state lines with a woman for immoral purposes! The Mann Act? Nobody told me about the bloody Mann Act! All the rest—the money from Wiedemann, which turned out to be counterfeit rather than the marked bills from his inheritance fund that I was counting on the FBI informants to catch, all my meetings with him, the Rauch diary, the Norden plans, even the bomb plot—was circumstantial and misinterpreted. I've explained it all to you. And while I admit to acting in an insubordinate manner and to ill effect, I will not admit to intentional wrongdoing. My motives were pure, though my judgment may have been clouded. Clouded by a disturbance, a pestilence, an ineradicable scourge that goes by the name Halifax.

I stand before you, gentlemen, ready to submit to whatever punishment you deem fit, though I will insist that my honor remain intact. So damn your eyes and fire when ready!

* * *

"Fire when ready!" he shouts again. But the men before him do not fire. Instead, they dab a cool, damp bundle of leaves over his forehead and give him a drink of bitter tea.

When he next awakes, his tribunal has morphed and resolved into two brown men in blue patterned tunics, kneeling beside him in the jungle.

"Where am I?" he asks.

He is given another sip of tea, and gradually he remembers. . . .

A week ago he disembarked from a sampan in Toungoo, hired a Karen guide and a cook, and began the overland ascent through the eastern hill country of Burma. Once he crossed the Thanlyin River, his guides told him, he'd be in Siam. And in less than a week, Chiang Mai. It wasn't Bangkok—that city was forever off-limits, and the poison Halifax had put in his mind about Anya somewhat cured him of his desire to return there. But Siam was a big country, and with only a small British presence in Chiang Mai, he imagined he could live a simple life unmolested, unrecognized. Perhaps he could open a bar and drink and fuck his way to a gentle oblivion. He would do so under a name not yet ruined. Sebastian Flint had been expelled from Thailand. Simon Faulk had been banned from the United States. And Simon Alessandro Epifanio Ferguson had just deserted from his latest posting to the Burmese imperial police in Mandalay. It had been the best Uncle Paul could do, given the circumstances. The Service had finally washed their hands of him. But there was no way in hell he was going to be a bloody policeman.

Three days into their ascent, his guides spotted a tiger. The damned fools had gone after it and disappeared. Whether they or the tiger were still alive, he didn't know. But in fleeing, he'd fallen and put his thigh right through a sharp piece of bamboo. Skewered, like a bit of lamb at Omar Khayyam's. The damned bugs were drawn to it like a feeding trough. He was too weak to slap them away. Too weak even to hack at the foliage. He lost the trail almost immediately and was soon just clawing his way through dense jungle, praying to run into a river. The fronds and leaves and saw grass all left their mark on his cheeks, nature's gentlemen demanding satisfaction. Each one stung no more than a leather glove, yet within hours, with the damp and the heat, he was sliced to ribbons. He dropped to his knees, bleeding, exhausted, the remains of his canteen drunk and instantly converted into sweat, listening for the sounds of the river but hearing nothing but his own labored breath.

It looked as though his destiny was to become a pile of meat here in the jungle. On the very mountains his nemesis had once "traipsed" through, supposedly becoming best mates with every hill tribesman and dacoit he came across while collecting raw material for his next breezy book of lies. He even claimed they had named their children after him. The truth was, Halifax had probably never even set foot here, the lying bastard.

As the fire ants crawled across his face, it occurred to him that he'd never had much luck. Plenty of privilege, sure, but that's not quite enough to make a life hold together. Even with everything given to him, he seemed always to untie the strings of his own hammock. Undone by his own ambition. Recipe for misery, that. Best to rid yourself of it.

That's what Siam meant to him. The end of ambition. A place simply to be. Where a man could properly go to seed, content to do nothing more than follow the meandering lines on Corvo's endless patterns. And yet it seemed his lines would converge not in Siam but here in this muddy grave some miles beyond the border. That was the last thing he remembered before the tribunal had materialized and demanded his testimony.

The next time he awakes, he feels a persistent pressure in the area of his wounded leg, as though something were gnawing him. He looks down, half-expecting to see a tiger, or a python coiling round his thigh. But instead he sees a boy.

A hilltribesman, but he can't be more than ten or eleven years old. He is squatting over him, applying some kind of poultice to his festering wound. Their eyes meet and the boy smiles, showing a mouth dark with betel nut.

He notices that his own pistol, tobacco pouch, and billfold are tucked into the boy's sash. He's hardly in a position to demand them back. Instead, he touches his chest and says, "I go Thailand. *Pom bai Mueang Thai. Chuay pom duay, khrap?* Can you help me?"

The child, not seeming to understand either English or Thai, touches his chest and flashes his black-toothed grin. "My name Di-kee. Di-kee Hafash."

A scream echoes through the forest, then fades into oblivion.

Historical Note and Acknowledgments

THROUGHOUT THE interwar period Richard Halliburton made a name for himself as a writer-adventurer, traversing the globe and distilling his wanderlust and buffoonery into popular travelogues. Ernest Hemingway felt sufficiently contemptuous of his renown to refer to him as the *"Ladies Home Journal* adventurer." In 1939, with a war on in Asia, Halliburton attempted to defy danger and stay in the limelight by sailing a custom-built Chinese junk from Hong Kong to San Francisco in conjunction with the World's Fair on Treasure Island. He disappeared in the middle of the Pacific and was never heard from again.

When I read that Halliburton raised funds for his expedition through a subscription service for young readers who would receive mimeographed letters written from aboard his *Sea Dragon*, I knew Richard Halliburton had to return from the dead—this time as Richard Halifax and through the funhouse mirror of fiction.

I have taken a number of liberties to make Dicky Halifax—many of them drawn from the precise details of Halliburton's life, some borrowed from figures as diverse as Edmund Backhouse and Errol Flynn, others simply invented. The same historical pastiche and reimagining goes for several other characters in the novel. Those familiar with twentieth-century German literature will recognize the palimpsest of Thomas Mann and his family in the figure of Theodor Rauch and his children, Hildegard and Hank, who are modeled loosely (and at times very closely) on siblings Erika and Klaus Mann. Thomas Mann, while escaping from Hitler's Germany, even temporarily lost a diary that contained rather shocking, and potentially damning, expressions of desire.

While Simon Faulk has no direct historical inspiration, he is pieced together from the annals of espionage and a dash of Evelyn Waugh. But Fritz Wiedemann really was Hitler's former commanding officer and Nazi aide-de-camp, who, in 1939, was suddenly dispatched to the position of German consul in San Francisco, where he allegedly operated a vast Pacific spy network and tried on multiple occasions to offer himself as a defector to the Allies—to no avail. Karl Dieter the Coconut King, in exile on Saipan, could have indeed been a real follower of the Order of the Sun, a group of racially minded German health nuts dedicated to living exclusively off a diet of coconuts in Imperial New Guinea. Salka Viertel really was the social glue of émigré Los Angeles, aka Weimar on the Pacific. The German-American Bund was indeed active at the start of the war, dreaming up domestic terror plots while officially promoting peace in the interests of Hitler's conquest of Europe. And the preponderance of Nazi spies on American soil was only just beginning to get the attention of the FBI, who soon entered into secret cooperation with British intelligence. The Comintern had also penetrated the American cultural landscape under the guise of the Popular Front, and after the Nazi-Soviet Pact of 1939, many on the American left made some truly head-spinning moral contortions in the name of so-called peace. Others were understandably revolted. And of all the fair attractions on the Treasure Island "Gayway," the most popular by far was Sally Rand's (not Bent's) Nude Ranch.

All this is to say that the world of *World Pacific* is steeped in historical fact. Though I'll admit that, in the Halifaxian spirit of storytelling, I've made a few sartorial nips and tucks to narrow the waist and fill out the crotch.

* * *

I'd like to thank my agent Susan Golomb of Writers House, my editor Noah Eaker, and the entire team at Harper. In particular: Edie Astley, Milan Bošić, Jonathan Burnham, Elina Cohen, Heather Drucker, Emi Battaglia, and Frieda Duggan. Thanks to Noah for seeing the spark in this project before it was fully fledged and for seeing it through to the best version of itself. Thanks to Milan for allowing me to suggest Benedetta Cappa's 1923 painting *Speeding Motorboat* and for turning it into a gorgeous, world-conquering cover. Thanks to Elina for the elegant interior design and for letting me add a homespun Junior Adventurers seal to Dicky's letters. And thanks to Kathy Lord, copy editor of my dreams, for keeping me honest and fit for the public. Any anachronisms are of my own doing. Thanks also to audio producer Alison Elliott-Yarden and to voice actors Josh Innerst, Kathrin Kana, and James Meunier for bringing the novel brilliantly to life as an audiobook.

I owe a marlin-sized hunk of gratitude to the Writer-in-Residence program at the Hemingway House in Ketchum, Idaho, for inviting me to live in Ernest's garage during a crucial period in the writing of this book. Thanks to Jenny Emery Davidson, Martha Williams, and Carter Hedberg of the Community Library (and to Katrina Jankowski for putting me on its radar)—my residency in the mountains was a magical, snowcapped experience. Thanks also to Rick and Megan Prelinger of the one-of-a-kind Prelinger Library in San Francisco for letting me come sift through their stellar collection of materials from the Treasure Island World's Fair. I am appreciative of San Francisco's many other independent institutions of historical memory and research, including FoundSF, the Open SF History program of the Western Neighborhoods Project, and the Mechanics' Institute and Library. They run important operations against the forces of oblivion, and our city is lucky to have them.

I am grateful for early reads from Marissa Kunz, Colin MacNaughton, Ben Mann, Elaine Mann, Matt McLean, Josh Sommovilla, and Jeremy Sabol. Thanks to Raffi Vesco for supplying me with some colorful Venetian; to Ian Morgan for an eleventh-hour German query; to John Scheib for checking the nautical charts; and to bandmates Bruce, Paul, and Derek for the Slop n' Stinker inspiration. Thanks also to all my friends and family— along with my students at Stanford over the years in the MLA, Continuing Studies, and SLE—who are a welcome counterpoint to the solitude of writing.

Finally, thanks to Marissa (aka Sami) for her wisdom and support, for letting me sound her out on sentences, for correcting my Thai, and for being my best mate aboard the ship of life— storm-tossed, leak-prone, but with you it's good.

About the Author

PETER MANN IS the author of the novel *The Torqued Man*, named one of *The New Yorker*'s Best Books of 2022 and Best Historical Fiction of the Year by CrimeReads. Originally from Kansas City, he is a longtime resident of San Francisco and teaches history and literature at Stanford. He also draws comics on his Substack newsletter, *The Quixote Syndrome*.